Starlight
At
Snow
Pine
Lodge

Starlight
At
Snow
Pine
Lodge

Rachel Barnett

embla
books

First published in Great Britain in 2023 by

Bonnier Books UK Limited
4th Floor, Victoria House, Bloomsbury Square, London, WC1B 4DA
Owned by Bonnier Books
Sveavägen 56, Stockholm, Sweden

A CIP catalogue record for this book is available from the British Library.

ISBN: 9781471415746

This book is typeset using Atomik ePublisher

Embla Books is an imprint of Bonnier Books UK
www.bonnierbooks.co.uk

For Charlotte

Chapter 1

Clara shoved her glass onto the bar, frowning at the tinsel taped to the edge of the wooden panels. Were there two strings, or just one? Too drunk to make the distinction, she pulled at it to check, the strands of frayed plastic folding in on themselves under her touch. She must have pulled too hard because the pieces of tape gave way, the tinsel slumping towards the floor. Clara let go, allowing the string – it was only one – to complete its journey, watching as it became part of the detritus being trodden underfoot.

Not for the first time, she wondered if this trip had been a good idea. Whether, in fact, she was even remotely ready for this. The bar was buzzing with adrenalin-fuelled noise, the excitement fizzing out of everyone in this packed space was palpable. Christmas week in a ski resort deep in the Alps should be a dream come true.

But Christmas week, with everything that it embodied?

Not that the alternative to being here was a realistic option either. Home alone for the first Christmas in . . . Well, in a long time. That prospect had been even worse. Which was why she had agreed to this trip in the first place.

Although, now she was here, she didn't so much remember the conversation with Tania being about agreeing to a nostalgic girly ski trip. It had focused more on Tania giving her the dates and Clara not having any reason to refuse. After all, there was nothing to keep her at home for Christmas. Nothing to keep her anywhere much. And her lack of a refusal had snowballed, with Tania sorting all the details, staying over the night before the flight and helping her to pack, making sure she had her passport, checking them in online to save time. Meeting up with Rose, and Rose's friend Madeleine at the airport. The flight out. The transfer. All of it so familiar to her, even though it had been years since their last trip. All of it happening in a bit of a blur, and now she was here. In the Alps. With her two best friends and a skinful of booze to try to dull the ache.

Downing the remnants of whatever had been in her glass, she turned to the bartender. '*Un autre, s'il vous plaît*,' she said, her French GCSE finding its relevance.

'What are you drinking?' he said, his French accent thick enough to spread on toast.

She frowned. What *was* she drinking? The last mouthful had barely been consumed and it wasn't even a ghost of a memory. Did it even matter what she drank? So long as it was something alcoholic, the rest of it was pure semantics. Attempting to answer his question, she lifted the glass to her nose and sniffed. The heavy sweet lilt of Coke clung to the walls of the glass. 'Rum and Coke?' It escaped her lips as more of a question than a statement.

He nodded and turned for a fresh glass.

Perhaps, with enough alcohol, she could completely forget Christmas. Forget everything except the here and now.

'Make it a double,' she said.

Standing at the other end of the bar with Madeleine, Rose watched Clara order yet another drink, then checked her watch. Already way past midnight. Surely it was time to head back to Snow Pine Lodge?

She craned her neck to see past a group of young guys; dressed in salopettes and ski boots and wobbling into one another, they were clearly well into a very liquid après-ski and were still having fun. Behind them she caught sight of Tania. A glance was enough to suggest to Rose that her oldest friend wasn't finished with Le Bar yet. With a Kir Royale in one hand, mobile in the other, Tania posed for another selfie. This time with the old-fashioned wooden skis and leather boots fixed against the stuccoed wall as her background. It should have been annoying, but Rose had known Tania forever and, somehow, when Tania posed her skinny white frame again and again, searching for the perfect piece of proof that she was somebody worth looking at, all Rose felt was sympathy.

Not that Tania wanted sympathy. Quite the opposite. If Rose had told her oldest friend how uncomfortable her endless posing made her feel, Tania would have been shocked. At best. Insulted, probably. At worst? Devastated.

After all, what could be more usual than posting photos of what you were doing on social media? Everybody did it.

But perhaps it was Rose who had it all wrong. Maybe it was naive to want to be judged on what kind of a person you were, rather than how you looked.

'Would it sound whiny if I said I'm knackered?' Beside her, Madeleine slid her empty glass onto the bar. 'It's just that I think I've tipped over from being a party popper, and am now sliding dangerously close to becoming a party pooper. Amazing the difference that part of a letter can make.'

'Part of a letter?' Rose took a moment to catch up with what Madeleine had said, then grinned. 'Oh, yes. I see. Very clever. I'm pretty much done, too, to be honest.'

Madeleine smiled, but the tiredness behind her expression was clear to see as she pointed to seating at the edge of the bar. 'I could always go and crash on one of those benches, I'm more than happy to be carried to the bus when you've all finished in here. But I am quite heavy. Just thought it only fair to warn you.'

Rose huffed a laugh. Madeleine's buoyant sense of humour and openness were some of the qualities Rose most liked about her, and part of the reason she'd had no qualms inviting her along on this trip, even though Madeleine had never even met Tania or Clara before. Rose had had no doubt they'd all get along, just so long as Madeleine remembered what they'd agreed before they got on the plane. Remembered not to be too open. 'No way am I going to carry you,' she said. 'We'll go. I'll just let the others know.'

Tania chose that moment to head back to them, wrapping an arm around Rose's shoulder. 'Smile,' she said.

Automatically, Rose tipped her chin and grinned for Tania's iPhone, holding still as the flash momentarily blinded her. 'Have you seen the time?'

'No. Why?'

'We're going to head back to the lodge.' Rose was looking forward to the cold wait at the '*gratuit*' bus stop, to watching her own expelled breath crystallising like a cloud of minuscule ice-flies circling in the resort's winter-season lights and the stars above. The ten-minute wheel-spinning drive back up the mountain along the slick tarmac was as integral a part of Près du Ciel as the snow itself. The road carved between the ever-expanding piles of bulldozed snow. She was looking forward to sharing it all with Madeleine for the first time.

'Oh, God. Really?' Tania draped a crestfallen expression over her features. It was an expression Rose had seen a thousand times, when her friend knew the evening was almost over, but wasn't quite ready to relinquish her hold on it. Tania had always known how to party. Hardly surprising, with an A-list actor for a father and a half-brother recognised the world over as he melted millions of hearts from the covers of fashion magazines. Tania hadn't really been given a choice in the high-octane pace she was expected to live her life, with the media hot in pursuit and desperate for any little titbit they could find on her.

'Yes. Really.'

'Blame me, if you like,' Madeleine said. 'It's been a long day. And I want to enjoy tomorrow.'

'Well, I might stay a little longer,' Tania said, a touch of irritation in her voice. Or was that Rose's imagination?

'Will you be OK with Clara, or should we take her home with us?'

'You go. I'll look after her,' Tania said.

Clara had necked glass after glass of wine in the pizzeria and was on goodness knows which number drink since they'd arrived at Le Bar. They'd noticed Clara was drinking more and more. To be honest, Rose couldn't remember the last time she'd spent a sober evening with her diminutive friend. But she couldn't really blame Clara for her slip into the abyss. Wasn't sure anybody else would have coped any better. Not after what happened.

'If you're sure?' Rose said, looping a scarf around her neck and pulling on her jacket.

'I'm sure,' Tania said. 'It's not as if it's the first time I've dealt with her in this state. We'll be fine.'

Once Rose and Madeleine had left, Tania kicked a piece of fallen tinsel out of her way and took a seat at the bar – or should that be Le Bar – toying with the bottom half of her glass of Kir Royale. A solid Harrington family tradition, to drink champagne mixed with the sweet blackcurrant syrup liqueur on the first night of a ski trip. One of the few family traditions she did still hold onto, although since her mid-teens Tania had observed the tradition in Le Bar, rather than in Snow Pine Lodge. And tonight, this glass was rapidly losing its appeal, the bubbles were all but gone and the liquid had warmed in the fug of the heaving bar.

Sighing, she pushed the glass away, scrolling through the photos she'd taken since their arrival in France. She would create a montage and post them everywhere in the morning. Maybe she would claim she had been partying too hard to have a moment to think about social media this evening. She paused. Or maybe she wouldn't.

She'd flirted with her social media audience – as well as the media in general – for as long as she could remember. There hadn't really been any way to avoid it, with her father being who he was. And she thought she'd worked out how to navigate the fine line between courting the media and being eaten alive by it. But recently she'd almost come unstuck. She'd felt the metaphorical snap of the press's teeth at her heels, had only escaped being named in the tabloids because almost everyone who played this game knew when to close ranks. When to stay quiet.

The thing was, she would have deserved a mauling. Her behaviour had left her open to accusations and criticism; there was no doubt the whole episode had shown a distinct lack of good judgement on her behalf. The situation had left her questioning whether she wanted to play the game any longer. The pressure of having to think about how everything she did looked to other people was relentless. It was exhausting.

Maybe now was as good a time as any to change direction. She wondered what it would be like to disappear, even if it were only for a little while. Scrolling through the pictures, she began to delete them, one by one. Maybe this was the week to find out.

'Can I buy you a drink?'

'No thank you,' Tania said, without looking up. How many times had she heard that? If that was the best introductory line the guy could think up, then she already knew she wasn't interested. Oliver Ordinary. Vincent Vanilla. Felix Forgettable.

'Shall we short cut straight to sex in a hot tub instead, then?'

That got her attention. She looked at him, taking in a rough approximation of his face: a heavy jawline, dark eyes set perfectly beneath a rough mop of hair, eyebrows thick and arched as if he was seriously waiting for her to reply. Her mouth had already begun to form the expletives required to tell him exactly what he could do with his proposition, but the words never got the chance to materialise. Instead, a crash on the other side of the room loud enough to eclipse the noise of the DJ's bass-heavy track took everyone's attention.

Tania swung around in time to see Clara sliding the final few inches onto the floor, an upturned table and the accompanying flotsam and jetsam of broken bottles and glasses the clear markers of her undoing.

A different range of expletives made themselves available for Tania to pick through as she pocketed her phone, pushed past Mr Explicit, and headed for her friend. In the end, the glass cut on Clara's hand aided her choice of words.

'Oh, shit,' Tania said, quietly.

Chapter 2

The next morning, Tania was at the picture window on the top level of the lodge, staring out at a view she knew well, but never tired of. She'd missed seeing the rose-coloured tips of the mountains which came with the sun rising behind them, but the sky still managed to make up for her tardiness. Without a cloud in sight, the pale blue stretched to infinity above the jagged beauty of the scenery below.

'Tom?' She glanced briefly away from the view. 'It is Tom, isn't it?'

A figure peered around the pillar separating the kitchen area from the rest of the open-plan living area. The new chef was pale-skinned, with messy dark hair and tattoos it was impossible to ignore winding their way up both arms. He wore a nervy smile. 'Yes? And yes, I'm Tom.' The touches of a Scottish accent swirled around the edges of his words.

'Could I have a coffee, when you have a moment? Black, no sugar, thank you.'

He probably thought she was a lazy privileged bitch. She expected he already had a cast-iron idea in his head of what she was like.

Well, he could think what he wanted. She could make her own coffee, but that would involve turning away from this window – which framed her favourite view in the entire world – and she didn't want to do that just yet. Anyway, she thought with a wry smile, if he thought this week was going to be bad, he had no idea what he'd signed up for. He

8

couldn't predict the perfect storm he would be facing when her stepmother, Brigitte, and her cronies turned up. Pouring a mug of coffee would be the least of his worries once they arrived. She was doing him a favour, breaking him in gently.

Tania had had to fight tooth and nail to get Christmas week, this year, a week usually favoured by Brigitte. And in usual circumstances, Tania would prefer to wait until later in the season; sometimes the snow wasn't all that great this early on. But she wanted to get Clara away from her empty cottage, take her away from the hideousness of being at home, alone, for her first Christmas since it had happened. So far, everything had fallen into place. Clara had agreed to come to France, the snow was exceptional for so early in the season, and Tania was going to spend Christmas skiing with Rose and Clara – the two people she treasured the most in the world.

A few moments later, Tom appeared at her shoulder.

'Thank you,' she said, taking the mug he offered.

'Awesome view.'

She watched from the corner of her eye as he scanned the full panorama. 'It's the best thing about the lodge,' she said. 'How are you settling in?'

'Well, thank you,' he said. 'I wanted to ask; would you like me to get a tree?'

Tania pulled in a breath. She hadn't decided yet how much they should acknowledge the fact that it was Christmas week, or whether it would be easier for Clara if they ignored it – as far as was possible to, in a resort permanently glittering with strings of winter fairy lights. 'Perhaps a small one,' she said, gesturing to the corner nearest the doors out onto the wrap-around balcony. 'It could go over there.'

It would also go some way towards hiding the new painting hanging on the wall. The painting she was doing her best to ignore.

'You're not big on Christmas?' he asked.

'Not this year,' she said, but didn't elaborate. She'd brought little presents for Clara and Rose, a token gift for Madeleine. It would be good to have somewhere to put them. 'The decorations are in a box in the storeroom.'

He nodded. 'I've seen it. I'll do that later today for you.'

'Thanks. Have you worked in Près du Ciel before?'

'Aye. I did last season for Ice and Fire in a little chalet at the base of Près Village, but I have to say the views from up here are amazing.'

'Do you ski?'

'I board, mostly. But I like skiing. It depends on the snow.'

She nodded. She'd had a go at snowboarding a few times but had concluded years ago that she preferred skis.

'Does your father still get out on the slopes?' he asked.

And there it was.

It never took too long, when people knew who she was, before talk turned to her father.

'He'd hardly bother to own a property up here if he didn't, would he?' Her tone was icy, her eyes narrowing. She was angry with herself for being upset by it. Though she'd lived her whole life under his shadow, even in direct sunlight the shadow never seemed to diminish. And the annoyance raged through her, every time.

Maybe that was what had been driving her, why she'd flirted with the media for so long. Maybe it was an underlying feeling that no one was interested in *her*, that there always had to be some reference made to her father. She sniffed. 'Is something burning?' she asked, the words stalking their way from her mouth, forcing their way out from between tight lips.

Keeping her gaze firmly on the view, she ignored him as he mumbled something about bacon and retreated to the kitchen area. She remained put when footsteps up the twisting wooden staircase announced the arrival of someone else.

'Morning.' It was Rose. 'That view is as picture perfect as ever.'

Rose was right. It didn't matter what time of day you

looked at the mountains, there was always something changing out there, and it was always beautiful: the colours, from vibrant sun-soaked morning pinks through to the grey-blues of the failing afternoon light, and every infinitesimal shade in between; the eerie sharp granite peaks, partially cloaked in white and bathed in starlight; the way the clusters of pine trees clung to impossibly rocky outcrops, smudges of green amongst the monotones.

After greeting the chef, Rose pulled one of the heavy wooden chairs out far enough to be able to slip onto it, and poured herself orange juice from a clear jug already on the table. Tania watched her in the reflection of the window as she passed her fingers over the knobbles of the plaits running down each side of her head, checking they were even. 'No one else up yet?'

Tania didn't reply, her attention back on the view.

'Just the two of you so far,' Tom said, filling the silence. 'Would you like breakfast now, or will you wait for the others?'

'Oh God, I'm not waiting for Clara. She might not make it out of bed until tomorrow, the state she was in last night. You got her back here all right?'

Finally, Tania turned away from the view and took a seat at the table. 'She fell and managed to cut her hand on some broken glass before we left the bar.' She shook her head a little but didn't say anything else, didn't want to acknowledge how bad the journey back from the bar had been.

'She's getting worse, isn't she?' Rose said.

Tania pulled in a deep breath. 'A few days of mountain air will do her good. Sort her out in no time. Put things into perspective.'

Was she trying to persuade Rose or herself? Before she could say anything more, another set of footsteps clumped up the stairs and heralded the arrival of another breakfaster. The crown of Madeleine's head appeared, a warm, open smile alighting on her face when she saw Rose at the table.

'We'll talk about it later.' Tania spoke quietly, then engaged Madeleine in trivial conversation about how well she had slept. She hoped the message was clear. Clara's private hell was to remain just that, private. Her own Pandora's box of troubles.

But Tania was beginning to wonder just how much longer it would be before the lid blew itself open, whether they liked it or not.

Madeleine had been right. She'd thought she could smell the sweet scent of frying bacon. The soft curls of that delicious smell had made it all the way down from the top floor – the living area of this upside-down lodge – so she'd known the cooking was well underway.

The unfolding knowledge that someone was cooking breakfast for you, and that bacon was involved, had to be one of life's most glorious awakenings.

Not that getting out of bed had been easy. She'd woken up with a heaviness similar to a hangover, but she'd only had a couple of glasses of wine the previous evening. No, she didn't have a hangover, instead the feeling was more one of exhaustion. The previous day had been a long one. Catching a lift with Rose to the airport had meant being ready to leave home before dawn; before the sun had even peeked out from beneath the comfort of its thirteen-tog duvet. But it wasn't only that which had Madeleine exhausted, it was the role she was trying to play. Having to watch everything she said and everything she did in front of Rose's friends.

She hadn't appreciated how tiring subterfuge was, it was proving far harder to maintain than she had expected. So, she'd made the most of the last few moments in bed this morning, stretching, then starfishing under the covers, revelling in the amount of space. The bed in her room must be king-size. Maybe even super-king. Was that as big as beds went, or was there an even bigger version? Mega-king? Galactic overlord-size?

Either way, this made her standard double at home feel a bit underwhelming in comparison. And changing the duvet cover was challenge enough with the size of bed she already had. Now was not the moment to recall the time she ended up inside the duvet cover, when she mistimed things and tripped over the edge of the bed. The fact that there was no one in the room to witness her embarrassment didn't diminish it a whole lot.

As Madeleine had crested the top of the stairs, and zeroed in on Rose who was already seated at the dining table, she realised she could smell freshly baked pastries, too. Rose had told her their stay would be fully catered, but Madeleine hadn't been entirely sure what that meant in this setting. She'd been expecting a choice between cornflakes and muesli for breakfast, to be honest. Maybe a filled and ready to boil kettle for hot drinks. There was clearly a great deal more to fully catered than that. Her reservations about going on a skiing holiday hadn't gone anywhere. After all, the closest she'd been to a pair of skis was watching *Ski Sunday* in her pyjamas with a hot chocolate in her hand. But she decided she'd worry about all of that after breakfast.

Chapter 3

'She's keen,' Madeleine said, puffing under the unfamiliar weight of her skis an hour or so later, as she watched Tania heading out onto the dazzling white of the piste. Madeleine had to stop again to readjust the damned things, one seemed determined to slide out from the other at any opportunity. She decided that on a scale of one to impossible, skis had to come close to being one of the most awkward things on the face of the planet to carry. Perhaps only topped by something like an angry porpoise, or an armful of squabbling polecats. A sea of skiers flowed around her like a river around a rock.

If the rest of the people exiting the bubble station were a river, then Tania was riding the current, her lanky frame barely visible now, even though she was wearing an electric-blue ski jacket with a matching helmet.

'Sorry I'm so slow.' Madeleine hefted the skis up again and headed for the sunlight. She was already exhausted, and she hadn't even reached the piste yet. Maybe this whole thing had been a terrible mistake.

'Don't be silly. I'm happy to show you the ropes,' Rose said, waiting as Madeleine managed to get a ski-pole wedged between the metal grille flooring and the rubber matting and almost tripped over it. 'Tania will want to see how many runs she can do before we meet up for lunch. The woman's a demon skier.'

'Perhaps you should just park me at the nearest restaurant and catch up with her,' Madeleine said, as they made it out onto the slippery stuff. 'Leave me, save yourself – that kind of thing?'

'Not going to happen,' Rose said. 'I see your plan, my friend, and you don't get a *chocolat chaud* that easily.'

'Damn it.' Grinning, Madeleine dropped her skis onto the snow, both landing upside down. 'Typical,' she said, puffing as she leaned over, trying to work out how to bend low enough to turn them right-side up while hampered by the unyielding ski boots the lower section of her legs were strait-jacketed into. The only saving grace was that Tania was already lost to her sight, having swished away moments after hitting the snow, so hadn't witnessed her ineptitude.

'You'll get used to it all,' Rose said, dropping her skis and slotting her feet into them. Madeleine wasn't so sure about that. She suddenly wished she'd offered to stay behind, to wait for Clara to surface.

But Clara was noticeable, Madeleine thought, by her absence. Tania had checked on her before they left the lodge, but she hadn't been mentioned since. Probably sleeping off the monster hangover she must be suffering. Rose had told her what Clara had been through, and it was impossible not to feel the weight of it, even for someone who had only just met the woman. Clara's sadness was palpable, and Madeleine didn't begrudge her a gentle start to the day. But she wondered for how long they should leave her alone. 'Will Clara join us for lunch, too?' Madeleine asked.

Rose sighed, pulling her goggles down to hide her eyes. 'Maybe.'

Not a particularly forthcoming answer, but perhaps now wasn't the best moment to press Rose any further. And glancing around at all the other skiers, slotting boots into skis and heading off with a nonchalance she felt sure she would never have the pleasure of experiencing, Madeleine figured she also had more immediate things to worry about. Like how to keep the ski she was attached to from sliding around while she balanced on it and tried to get the other boot to lock onto the other ski.

Eventually she had her feet in her skis, with both poles dug firmly into the snow to stop herself from slipping. Her upper arms already ached with the effort of staying motionless. 'OK,' she said. 'God help me, but I think I'm ready.'

Thank goodness she'd brought her dark glasses with her. That was Clara's overriding thought when she finally admitted to being fully awake. She slotted them over eyes that burned to the touch before dealing with the next immediacy. Water. She needed a lot of water.

With the tumbler someone had been thoughtful enough to leave beside her bed emptied and teetering on the edge of the bedside cabinet, Clara slumped back against the set of pillows and closed her eyes. Absolute dark was way better, even if the spinning sensation remained.

She shuffled herself around under the covers, without moving her head too quickly, and frowned. Why did her hand hurt?

Extracting an arm from the warmth of the bed, she unfurled her fingers to find a large Elastoplast stuck across her palm, the edges dog-eared and covered in cotton fluff from the sheets. Tentatively, she pushed the dark glasses onto the top of her head and made a closer examination, peeling back an edge until she saw the crusted slash of red and felt a sudden urge to retch. Slapping the plaster back into place, Clara repositioned the dark glasses and closed her eyes, concentrating on her breathing until the hot prickle threatening the back of her throat subsided.

What had she done last night? She realised she couldn't remember anything much after the pizza and red wine in the restaurant. The rest of the evening was nothing more than grey fog. The fizzing of an untuned television screen before the satellite connection fired up. There was a rough memory of Tania coming into her room – maybe that had been the previous night . . . no, it must have been this morning – suggesting she take it easy for a few hours and aim to meet them for lunch.

The thought of food had the prickle returning to the back of her throat, accompanied by a sudden hot sweat which silently informed her just how forcibly her body would reject any attempts at eating.

This had to stop. She knew that much. Somehow, she had to find a way to make it stop.

For now, though, staying still was all she could master. Clara waited until the nausea had subsided. Waited until the throbbing in her head was nothing more than the heavy bass drumbeat she'd become used to. Waited until the excited chatter in the boot room had been replaced by the clumping of boots and the slamming of the front door, and she was certain they'd all left. She stayed put until she was sure the chef had finished cleaning down the kitchen and was also gone.

Convinced she was alone, she pulled on some clothes and headed upstairs. Raiding the cupboards until she located a first-aid kit, Clara held her breath as she peeled back the plaster on her palm and held her hand under a running tap. With her eyes closed, she rubbed tentatively, shifting the crusty dried blood from her skin. She'd never been good with the sight of blood.

She remembered the day Poppy sliced her arm open on one of the flints which made up the cottage's garden wall. Clara had only turned her back for a moment, but a moment was all it took for Poppy to overbalance and topple against a razor-sharp knapped stone. She'd not long started walking, her balance still a little dubious. But the moment of suspension, between Poppy looking up at her with huge eyes and the realisation of what she'd done with its accompanying wail, was still crystal clear in Clara's memory. As was the expression on Mike's face when she video-called him for help. His insistence that she take Poppy to the Accident and Emergency department at their local hospital. His assurance that he would leave work immediately and meet them there. Her memory of later that evening, all three of them on the sofa; Poppy jiggling up and down to some kids' programme's theme tune with her bandaged arm held aloft, while Mike tightened his arm around Clara's shoulder and told her she was amazing, and how lucky Poppy was to have such an awesome mummy. His lips close to her ear, his breath hot against her skin. The overwhelming feeling of reassurance and security, the three of them safe and together. The storm weathered and survived.

Clara removed her hand from the water, absently wrapping it in a tea towel. Heading across to the picture window, she pulled out her phone with her good hand. She shouldn't listen to his final message again; she knew she shouldn't. It didn't help. Nothing helped.

Pressing the phone to her ear anyway, she closed her eyes on the mountain view as his words flooded her senses, all over again.

She was still stood there, phone against her ear, when the spell was broken by footsteps on the wooden stairs.

'Oh, I'm sorry.'

A male voice, with a Scottish burr edging the words. Clara swung around and pocketed her phone.

'I thought you'd all gone out for the day. I popped back to set this up and get some prep done for tonight.' The man dumped a small fir tree at the top of the stairs and turned off the tap Clara had forgotten she'd left running. He smiled at her. 'I don't think we've met. I'm Tom. I'm your chef for the week.' He glanced at the tree. 'Well, maybe chef and general festive dogsbody might be a better description.'

'Oh, right. Hello. Bit of a slow start for me this morning, I'm afraid.' Shrugging, she ignored the tree. 'I'm Clara.'

He gestured towards the towel wrapped around her hand. 'Anything I can help you with?' His gaze flicked across the first-aid kit; its contents strewn along the freshly wiped-down work surface. Next to it sat the blood-soaked, dog-eared plaster she hadn't got around to putting into the bin.

'No. Thanks. I cut my hand, that's all.'

'I've done first-aid training,' he said, then grinned. 'Makes me sound like a total Boy Scout.' He took a step in her direction. 'Seriously, though. Let me look. Let me help patch you up.'

It'll take a hell of a lot more than a plaster and a smile to patch me up, Clara thought.

When Tania reached the restaurant at which they'd agreed to meet for lunch, she could see Rose and Madeleine already seated at a table outside, discarded mugs in front of them. She slid to a stop, removed her skis and headed up the slope onto the wooden decking with a spring in her step. The snow on the highest runs had been superb, and she intended to head over to the glacier after lunch. It had been past eleven by the time they made it onto the slopes and although she had skied hard for an hour and a half it wouldn't take long for her to feel the pent-up adrenalin again, as it alternated between warming her muscles and making them feel strangely numb. It had always been the same, ever since she was a kid.

The discomfort of awkward ski boots, which made everybody else moan and complain, only served to heighten Tania's sense of excitement. Her muscle memory slotted nothing but positive emotions alongside the physical sensations. While others shifted uncomfortably under the weight and the hard lines of the skis propped against their shoulders on the first bubble lift ride of the day, it was all she could do not to yank the doors open and throw herself out, James Bond-style, to get first go at the powder between the trees below.

She glanced across at Madeleine – she had questioned the sense of inviting someone with no skiing experience on the trip. But Rose had been insistent. Madeleine was great fun, she'd said. She was willing to give skiing a go, apparently, and if it didn't work out, would be equally happy to relax in the lodge instead. However, it looked as though Madeleine had survived her first few hours on the snow after all.

'Have you eaten?' Tania asked, shoving her gloves onto the table before removing her goggles and helmet. She slid them alongside the gloves and sank into a chair, running a hand through her hair and tipping her face towards the sun as she did so. Aching legs and cold cheeks, crystals of snow filling the clear air? Her idea of heaven.

'Not yet. We thought we'd wait for you,' Rose said.

Tania was on her feet again. 'Come on then, let's get in the queue. I don't want to waste time.' She headed for the entrance to the restaurant, the building a perfectly proportioned alpine chalet, constructed from huge and darkly seasoned whole timbers which gave the place an aura of overwhelming solidity. The kind of building that gave the feeling it had been here forever and would remain forever, regardless of the harsh nature of the mountain seasons.

The Cocoon was also one of the less pretentious of the mountain pit stops. Another reason it was one of Tania's favourites. There was no doubt the restaurants positioned at the very tops of the bubble lifts and the cable car, on the crests of the mountains, commanded outrageously beautiful views. And the food served in them was delicious, often cordon bleu. But the prices they charged were also outrageous; they were the kind of places people would visit once during their ski trip, even if the bill-payer did need to suppress a sob when *l'addition* arrived.

They were also the kind of places her stepmother would insist she and her father should frequent, and that was reason enough for Tania to lose interest in going anywhere near them.

The no-nonsense, queue up with a tray, school dinner approach at the Cocoon worked just as well, in Tania's opinion. Better, probably, if you timed it right and the queue wasn't long. Quicker. More time for skiing.

She pushed through the doors, sidestepped a slippery-looking patch of melted ice on the floorboards and headed for the pile of trays. With her line of sight on the menu board, trying to decide whether to go for a croque monsieur or *tartiflette*, she didn't notice the man walking in the opposite direction. He wasn't paying attention either, preoccupied with fixing one glove to the other with a carabiner. They collided shoulder to shoulder, Tania jerking to attention with a reflexive '*pardon*' and taking a step backwards before it dawned on her that she recognised him.

It was Mr Explicit from the bar the previous evening. Mr 'Let's have sex in a hot tub'.

From the changing expression on his face, it was clear he also recognised who it was he'd collided with.

'Oh. Hello again,' he said.

Was that a hint of embarrassment she could hear in his voice? A crease formed between his dark eyes, and he ran a hand across a jawline which hadn't seen a razor this morning.

'It's "hello" for the first time, I think you'll find. I don't remember any mention of a "hello" last night,' she said, her eyebrows jacking to emphasise her point.

He cleared his throat. 'Ah. Yes. Well . . . in my defence, I did offer to buy you a drink.'

'Well done,' she said, leaning forward to reach past him for a tray.

'The offer still stands,' he said, picking up a couple of trays and handing her one of them.

'Which offer?' she asked, challenging him again.

He paused for a beat, then said, 'Both of them?' The crease between his eyes deepened for a moment before he smiled, a sudden flash of brilliant sunshine in an otherwise brooding skyline. He closed it down just as quickly and shrugged. 'Sorry. I'd had a few too many last night. The phrasing might have been off, but the sentiment wasn't.'

'Still totally inappropriate,' she said, gesturing for him to join the queue and allowing herself a final glance up at him. 'Please. Carry on. I'm waiting for my friends.'

Holding the tray against her jacket like a shield, she purposefully looked away from him towards the doorway, where Madeleine was making painstakingly slow progress in her boots, laughing about something with Rose.

The smallest of smiles mustered itself on Tania's face, alongside a feeling of confusion whose origin she couldn't place. She flicked a final look in Mr Explicit's direction, killed the smile when she realised that he was looking at her, and frowned instead.

Chapter 4

It was only a small victory, Madeleine thought, as she shuffled her way around the wet patch inside the restaurant door rather than slipping over in it and headed towards Tania. But with the way her body was aching from all the falls she'd already sustained, she'd take a victory of any proportion and hold onto it with both hands.

As it was, she still ended up grabbing hold of Rose's arm with both hands when she caught the tip of a boot against a wooden pillar. Rose called her a total clown and they both started laughing, but not before Madeleine had clocked Tania talking to a tall, dark-haired guy. A casual conversation, she assumed, until she noticed the way they both glanced at one another. And then pretended they hadn't.

Madeleine needed to ask Rose about all things love life where Tania was concerned. She was curious to know if any of the numerous rumours were true. But for now, lunch was a much more pressing issue.

'I'm totally rubbish at skiing,' she announced once they were again seated at the outside table. She mixed parmesan into her bowl of spaghetti Bolognese, sniffing at the rising spirals of glorious steam as she moved her fork around. She'd lost count of the number of times she'd ended up butt-first in the snow that morning. Not that it should come as a total surprise, she supposed, sport hadn't ever really been her thing.

'You're doing fine,' Rose said, her nose wrinkling a little. They both knew she was being generous.

'Yes, if "fine" is the definition of a skier who falls over every five minutes.'

The edges of Rose's mouth quirked up before she squashed her lips tightly together.

'Don't laugh,' Madeleine said, shuffling on the bench to move her weight away from one of the many bruises already forming. 'I told you "Never knowingly sporty" will probably appear on my headstone.'

'She fell over on the flattest bit of the green run which goes under the Près Hotel.' Rose mimed flailing arms for Tania's benefit, as if the embarrassment wasn't already sufficient.

'There was some loose snow,' Madeleine replied, her eyebrows furrowing. 'Plus, that toddler came past so fast I thought he was going to crash into me.'

Rose did little to contain a hoot of laughter.

'I'm sure you'll get the hang of it,' Tania said.

Madeleine wished she knew Tania well enough to gauge the level of conviction behind the statement.

'Anyway, I've decided I'm getting some lessons,' she said, spinning spaghetti around her fork. 'Starting tomorrow.'

'I don't think it's a bad idea,' Rose said. 'If I'm being honest.'

'Quickest way to learn,' Tania said, taking a sip from her glass of hot wine. 'No doubt.'

'Do you think?' Madeleine was keen to forge some kind of a connection with Tania. Rose had already advised her not to mention Tania's father, that any kind of fangirl comments would not go down well. She supposed she understood. It must be hard to live in the shadow of an extremely successful parent. Her own parents were totally run-of-the-mill. They'd been married for twenty-five years and lived in a nice-enough semi. Her mother worked at the local school; her father ran the logistics for the town's haulage company. Not the kind of people who went skiing in France. They were the kind of people who booked a week in a National Trust cottage in Cornwall. And they were happy being invisible. Totally opposite to the Harringtons, who lived their lives permanently in the spotlight.

Tania smiled at her. It was brief, but it was there. 'Of course. If you learn the correct technique from the beginning, it'll make it all so much easier.'

'Right, that's decided, then,' Madeleine said. She took a mouthful of Bolognese. 'Mmm. This is so good.'

'Have you spoken to Clara?' Rose asked, looking at Tania. 'She was going to meet us for lunch, wasn't she?'

'Yes. I messaged her earlier. She said she might come out this afternoon. That she was grabbing something to eat at the lodge first.'

'How is she feeling?' Madeleine asked. The look which passed between Tania and Rose made her feel as if she'd taken a seat at the wrong table without realising and tried to join in a conversation with a group of total strangers. To be fair, Tania wasn't much more than a stranger, but she'd known Rose for the last eight months.

Tania recovered her expression quickly. 'She's just hungover, that's all.'

'Yeah, she did drink enough to floor an elephant last night,' Rose said, earning herself a sharp look from Tania.

She should probably quit while she was ahead, but that had never been Madeleine's style, so she changed tack a little and ploughed on, headlong. 'Who was the guy you were talking to in the queue?' she asked Tania. 'He looked nice.'

Tania laughed. 'He might have looked nice, but I can assure you he probably isn't.'

'Why?'

Tania shook her head. 'Don't ask.' She pushed the remnants of *tartiflette* to one side of her plate and drained her glass.

'Come on,' Rose said. 'Spill. There's no way you can say that and then not expand. In what way not nice?'

Tania sighed. 'He asked me if I wanted to shag him in a hot tub, that's why.'

'Whoa. Are you telling me he asked you that just now, in the food queue?' Rose's incredulous tone echoed Madeleine's thought process.

'No – last night, in Le Bar. It was his opening gambit.'

'Seriously?' Rose said. 'That's properly shady.'

It dawned on Madeleine that her mouth was hanging open. She glanced around to catch sight of where the guy had gone, but she couldn't see him. Nobody had ever so much as asked her if she fancied sharing a packet of Smarties in a hot tub, let alone bodily fluids. Not that spending time in a hot tub was something she did on a regular basis – actually, make that ever – or that she wanted to be propositioned like that, but the point still held.

And, anyway, she thought, what happened about the next people who wanted to use the hot tub, once a couple had – you know – done it in the water? Did someone change the water out? Madeleine hoped that was the case, but she wondered how easy that was, in the sub-zero temperatures on the mountain.

She frowned. 'What happens about the water?' she asked. 'Afterwards, I mean?'

Tania looked at her for a moment, then her face creased into a smile. She chuckled. 'What happens about the water? That's funny.'

Madeleine smiled back. Then she said, 'But do they change it?' Now she'd had the thought, she really wanted to know the answer. There was a hot tub at the lodge, but she was rapidly going off the idea of getting into it.

'You said no to him, I assume?' Rose asked.

'I didn't give him any answer,' Tania said. 'I was a bit distracted by Clara falling off her chair and slicing her hand open.'

'So, do they change the water or not?' Madeleine said.

'What did he say to you just now?'

'Some nonsense about having had too much to drink last night.'

'I'm not sure I fancy the hot tub now I've got this thought running around my brain,' Madeleine said. She'd brought a swimming costume with her, on Rose's insistence, but it was looking increasingly likely that it would be staying in a drawer. 'Are there filters, like in swimming pools?'

'Did he apologise?' Rose asked.

'Not in so many words,' Tania said.

'What a dick.' Rose shook her head.

'Is the water cleaned between guests, or do they empty the tub and refill it?' Madeleine's brows furrowed together.

Rose and Tania both turned to her. 'What the hell are you wittering on about, Maddy?' Rose asked.

'Sorry, it's just . . . I was thinking about how hard it must be to maintain hygiene in something like a hot tub, bearing in mind what you're talking about and I . . .'

Tania laughed again, then ran a hand through her hair. 'Tell you what, Madeleine. If it makes you feel better, I'll make sure you're the first person to know if I decide to have sex with someone in the hot tub. Deal?'

Chapter 5

In Snow Pine Lodge, Clara watched as Tom pulled cold meats and cheeses from the fridge. 'All right then, yes,' she said. 'Some food would be really nice, thank you.'

Tom smiled. 'Take a seat. Lunch will be ready in no time.'

She settled onto one of the heavy dining chairs and watched as he sliced a baguette, then arranged it on a platter with some of the cold meats and slices of cheese. He selected a huge red apple from the fruit bowl and cut that into sections, adding them to the plate in an elegant fan. It seemed even the simplest of dishes required a flourish in its presentation. To be honest, she wasn't sure she could manage much more than a slice or two of the apple, maybe a piece of dry bread, but she appreciated how much effort he was going to on her behalf.

Gathering a smaller plate and some cutlery, Tom brought the food to the table, placing everything in front of her.

'Can I get you a drink?' he said.

She wanted to ask him to open a bottle of wine. Or pour her a gin and tonic. Or maybe get her a double vodka. That the hair of the dog might be the best way to deal with her hangover. Then she felt the sting of her hand, underneath his neat bandaging, and shook her head. 'I'll stick with water, thanks.'

'OK. Do you mind if I get on with some prep work for this evening?' he said. 'Or I can leave you alone, and come back later, if you'd prefer?'

'No. Please, carry on. But don't you want to go skiing?'

'I wasn't planning on going out today.' He glanced through the window on his way back to the kitchen area, then pulled

28

a large chicken from the fridge and found a cutting board. 'Plenty to keep me occupied here.'

'I suppose it's different when you're here for the whole season. You can pick and choose when you want to ski.'

He nodded. 'Exactly. It's not like being here for a week, grabbing every second on the snow.' A frown crossed his brow. 'Don't *you* want to go skiing today? Apparently, there might be a storm later in the week. It might be worth getting some good days in early, just in case.'

Clara chewed on a piece of apple, which gave her time to decide what to say. Was she going to get outside today, or was she going to fester in the comfort of the lodge? She had promised Tania that she would join in, that she would rediscover her ski legs and enjoy the beauty of the mountains. And so far, she had done the complete opposite.

In the end, she opted for a non-committal shrug.

'Well, if you do go out, head for the runs higher up. The lower ones get a bit busy in the afternoons and you'll waste time queuing at the lifts. Creux is nice, or if you fancy a challenge, try Becoin on your way back. I could show you, if you like, another day?'

Clara shook her head. 'No need, Tania knows this place like the back of her hand. You don't want to have to waste your time nannying me about.' She picked up one of the slices of cheese and bit a little from one end. It had a delicate flavour. 'What's this called?' She turned it over in her fingers. The cheese was pale and soft, with a grey line running through the middle.

'It's called Morbier. It's a locally produced cheese.'

'What's the grey line?'

He started to laugh.

'What's funny?'

'It's ash,' he said.

'It's what?'

'Ash. From a fire.'

She put the piece down, frowning.

'No, don't do that,' he said. 'It's supposed to be there.'

'Why?'

'Way back when, if the farmer had leftover curd from the cheese-making which wasn't enough for a whole cheese, he put it in a mould, then covered it with a layer of ash to protect it. The next day, he topped it up from the morning milking and completed the cheese. It's the way it's always been made. Ta-daa.' He took a theatrical bow.

Clara nodded. 'Impressed by your knowledge, without doubt. But why do you know that?'

'Rather than simply having a cheese board, I thought it would be more interesting to sample a different, unusual cheese each evening. There's a little story to go with each one. And now you know the Morbier story, you'll have a bit of a head start on the others tonight.'

'I feel honoured,' she said. 'Don't worry, I won't spoil the surprise.' Picking the cheese up again, she ate quietly for a while, then sat and watched as Tom deboned the chicken and rolled it with a centre filled with chopped fresh herbs and some dried fruit which he'd soaked in something. Armagnac, she thought. Very French. After a while she fetched a book and settled on one of the sofas while he set about preparing vegetables and then the dessert.

The room was completely quiet, except for the noise from the kitchen and the occasional rustle as she turned a page. Clara realised she had been avoiding quietness, that it usually brought with it a flood of memories. Reminded her too much of the quietness of that final day at home, before she found out what had happened. A quietness she'd been trying to drown out ever since, one way or another. She waited for the flood to wash her away, but it didn't come. She glanced across at Tom, who was totally absorbed in his cooking, then tried to focus on the pages of her book.

Clara couldn't remember the last time she'd felt this level of calm. And she wasn't sure what to do with it.

* * *

Tania was on top of the world. Literally. Coming off the resort's oldest bubble lift at the summit of the glacier, the graffiti-covered capsules creaking on the massive wires as they turned and headed back down the hill, Tania stopped and took a 360-degree turn. Spectacular.

She pulled her phone from a pocket and took a couple of panoramic shots, followed by a few selfies. Then she stopped, frowning at herself. It had become such an ingrained habit.

After zipping the phone away and slotting her feet into her skis, Tania took a deep breath before deciding which run to take. Red or black?

The black was narrow and icy, but it twisted around the very edge of the world. By the time she'd reached the bottom, Tania had run out of superlatives to describe the experience. She had long ago decided that skiing epitomised the whole reason for being alive.

In her opinion, it was a microcosm of everything – the beauty of the scenery lived hand in glove with the harshness of the environment should you get caught out by bad weather, or by being in the wrong place; beauty and the beast, if you like. And while the exhilaration of the physical activity made her feel as if every nerve ending fizzed with life, it was impossible to forget it was laced with the ever-present possibility for your whole world to tip literally upside down at a moment's notice.

If you made a mistake – a badly placed ski, or an ill-judged turn – the slope might choose to punish you, or it might let you get away with it. Equally, if you did everything with perfect technique, the mountain could still choose to bring you to your knees, just because it wanted to.

This run had been completed without incident, however. The gods of the mountain were smiling today, and so was she. Picking up the red run, she twisted her way back to the base of the glacier, then stood fidgeting as she queued for a bubble to take her back up to the summit, the adrenalin still coursing through her body.

Most of the skiers on the glacier were focused. Many were up here alone, GoPros attached to helmets to record every downhill moment, earbuds feeding music directly into brains. Everyone was up here for the thrill. Simple as that. Each bubble ride back to the summit laden with anticipation; silent except for a sudden ringtone, a loud, one-way conversation held in unintelligibly rapid French.

At the summit this time, Tania checked her watch. Much as she was loving every moment, she was aware she should get back to Clara. The whole point of this trip was to support their friend. To help her. And as far as Tania was concerned, nothing helped the soul like time spent on the mountain. In the fresh air. Seeing the bigger picture, if that were possible. Clara had spiralled down into such a tight rabbit hole, Tania wasn't sure anyone would be able to pull her back out again, but she was determined to try. Not that leaving her friend to fend for herself while she spent the day on the slopes had been a great start to Project Clara. Bad friend. Must do better.

She would complete this run down the glacier and head back to the lodge.

Opting for the red run this time, she set off with a series of arcing turns, concentrating on the steep upper section, tucking herself more tightly to gain some speed when the slope opened out. She grinned under her bandanna – she was flying. Halfway down, she slid to a stop at the side of the run to grab her breath. A gaggle of skiers shot past, and she waited until there was a little distance between them before turning her own skis downhill, allowing gravity to take effect, picking up speed until she was hurtling.

In no time, she'd caught up to the group. Picking her moment, as they opted to turn across the slope, she headed straight down and threaded her way between them. She kept her speed up all the way to the Saulire chairlift, sliding her way into the queue.

A large family group at the head of the queue took a chair, followed by a group of boarders, shuffling and jumping their boards to the barrier. She pulled her bandanna down and pushed her goggles onto her helmet, slotting her poles into one hand. A waft of tobacco smoke escaped the lips of one of the lift operators and passed between the moving chairs like a will-o'-the-wisp, catching on a current of air, twisting and disappearing as quickly as it had formed.

When the lifts weren't busy, it was possible to have the whole chair to yourself, but at times like this, with perfect weather and the clock ticking towards the end of the afternoon, every chair was full. Other skiers jostled for position on either side of her, lining up like racehorses in the starting gates. The barrier ticked open, the line of skiers sliding forward in unison onto the red and black striped 'magic carpet' which trundled them into position to await the next chair.

As they sat down and pulled the safety bar into position, the man occupying the seat to the far left of the chair folded his sunglasses and turned to the next group waiting for a chair.

'See you at the top, you losers,' he called at them cheerfully, slotting the black-lensed Oakleys into a soft pouch before pocketing the glasses. Glancing across, the open smile he'd been wearing for his queue-bound friends dissolved into a frown as he saw her. It was Mr Explicit. Hot tub guy.

The two teenage girls sitting between them struck up a highly animated conversation in what sounded like Italian. It gave her the chance to look away from him without having to say anything. She studied the trees passing beside the lift, wondering not for the first time how many different types of firs there were on the mountain. Lots, judging by the variety of the pinecones hanging from their branches.

'I really am sorry.'

She studied a particularly fine tree, flanked by a couple of smaller ones, wondering how long it took for a fir to mature to that size.

'Will you let me apologise properly?'

She allowed her gaze to travel across to him. He looked awkward but determined, his concentration fixed on her.

'There's no need. Forget about it,' she said.

'I realised this afternoon that I never even asked your name.'

'I know.'

'Would you have told me if I'd asked?'

'Probably not.' Disappearing for a week was hardly likely to involve telling the first stranger she met exactly who she was. And anyway, it was none of his business.

He shook his head. 'You're not making this easy.'

She laughed. 'Why should I? Listen, I get that you were hoping I was going to be easy. Really easy. Sorry to disappoint.'

'Oh, believe me, I've already worked out you're anything but easy . . .' He looked frustrated, but his gaze didn't falter, staying resolutely on her.

'Probably not worth bothering to find out my name, then.' Pulling her goggles down to hide her eyes, she shuffled in the seat in preparation for the rise at the top of the chairlift. Tugging impatiently at the safety bar, she made ready for a sharp exit.

What was it about this man which annoyed her so much? It wasn't like she hadn't been propositioned before. It wasn't even like she hadn't accepted propositions in the past, it wasn't that which was getting to her. But this man irritated her in a way she'd never felt before. She wanted to get away from him, and yet something held her in this moment, even though she didn't want to be held. Something at the base of her stomach felt out of kilter. It was almost as if she felt sick.

As soon as the chair hit the top of the lift, she pushed away from the vinyl seat and headed for the run that would take her back to Snow Pine Lodge. Without stopping to sort out her poles or her bandanna – she could do that on the move – she didn't look in his direction again, she just went.

The sooner she got away from him the better. The resort was huge, the chances of running – or skiing – into him again had to be minimal.

Even though she headed straight down, full pelt, she became aware of a figure beside her, keeping pace. It was him. Pulling to a stop again, she ripped her bandanna away from her mouth as he stopped, too. 'Are you stalking me?' The words came out hot and fast, and loud. The adrenalin was pumping, only added to in intensity by the feeling she was being chased. Perhaps he knew exactly who she was, and that was why he was following her so doggedly. 'Will you just go away?'

'Can we start again? I really would like to buy you a drink.' He was out of breath, one of the bindings on his ski boots undone and sticking up through the snow. Tugging a hand free from its glove, he raised it to shield his squinting eyes, then pulled his glasses from a pocket and slotted them on instead.

'Like I said last night, no thank you. I can buy my own drinks.'

Glancing skywards, a huge breath escaped his mouth in a plume of tiny white crystals and his shoulders slumped a little. 'OK. I give up. But whether you care or not, I am genuinely sorry about what I said.' With a final nod, he turned his skis downhill. 'Just in case you change your mind about the drink – I'll be in the Cocoon tomorrow, at one o'clock.'

And before she could tell him she'd rather drop dead than meet him at the Cocoon, he was gone.

Chapter 6

Madeleine wondered if she would ever get full use of her legs back. Having made it safely back to the lodge, it was all she could do not to whimper as Rose pulled her boots off for her.

'Is it supposed to hurt this much?' she said.

Rose laughed, slotting Madeleine's boots onto the heated rack fixed to the wall before she pulled her own feet free. 'You'll get used to it,' she said, putting her own boots beside Madeleine's. Sliding onto the bench, she wiggled her toes around. 'Hello, feet.'

'You're so cheerful about it,' Madeleine said, aware her voice was dangerously close to sounding whiny, but unable to do anything about it. She sniffed, the rise in temperature compared to outside taking effect on her nose.

'What you need is a hot shower and a cup of tea. You'll be good as new.'

'If you say so.'

'There'll be cake, too.'

That piqued her interest. 'What kind?' Say chocolate, she thought. A piece of chocolate cake would be just what the doctor ordered.

'Not sure. There's usually a different one each day.'

'Wrong answer,' she said.

'Chocolate?' Rose suggested.

'That's better,' Madeleine said. 'I was considering just getting it over and done with and dying right here before I have to attempt the stairs. But if there's chocolate cake. . .' She grinned.

'And hot tea.' Rose grinned in return.

Madeleine heaved herself up. 'Let's go. But just so you know, if the cake isn't chocolate, there might still be a problem.'

'Get up those stairs, Maddy, before I kick your backside up them.'

'You bloody would, too. Wouldn't you?'

'Well, I'm not carrying you up, that's for sure.'

Two painfully steep flights later, and Madeleine crested the top of the stairs leading to the main living area. Clara was looking revoltingly comfortable on one of the three-seater sofas, stretched out lengthways with a book in her hand.

'I thought I heard people,' Clara said. She checked her watch. 'You're back early, it's only half three.'

'Yes, well,' Madeleine said. 'Thing is, I've discovered I'm a truly shocking skier. Literally, the least proficient person ever.' Flopping onto another sofa, she pulled a fur-covered cushion from behind the small of her back and threw it onto a spare chair. 'God, that's good,' she said, sinking into the sofa's welcoming folds.

'You probably need lessons,' Clara said, folding the corner of a page and closing her paperback. 'Most people do.'

'We've booked some up, starting in the morning,' Rose said, hovering near the kettle. 'Shall I make the tea, then?'

'What flavour is the cake?' Madeleine asked.

'If I say "chocolate", will you come and help make the tea?'

'Is it?'

'Come and find out.'

Puffing out rapidly warming cheeks, she heaved herself to her feet. 'Ouch, I think my leg muscles are turning to rock,' she said, pulling a face.

'You should get in the hot tub,' Clara said. 'The hot water will ease them in no time.'

Madeleine managed little more than a glance in Rose's direction before she dissolved into giggles.

'What's so funny?' Clara said, shuffling herself up and swinging her legs onto the floor.

Rose shook her head. 'Oh, my God, Maddy. Stop it.'

'I can't help it,' Madeleine said, doing her best to snuffle back her giggles. It must be the exhaustion which made the reminder of the earlier hot tub revelation so hilarious, but whatever the reason, she couldn't seem to stop laughing. Rose's face quirked into a smile, probably more at her hysterics than anything else. Then she, too, began to laugh.

Clara looked from one to the other, a crease appearing on her forehead. 'What did I say? What's wrong with the hot tub?'

Madeleine fought to contain her giggles, and managed to say, 'You need to ask Tania,' before she completely lost control.

Clara looked from Rose to Madeleine. She hadn't realised they were so close. She knew Rose and Tania were tight. They went way back – having been at the same exclusive boarding school since they were eleven. A place that Rose's family had still struggled to finance, even though her father was the CEO of his company. In comparison, Tania's father had seemingly paid the fees from the loose change in his back pocket. He'd financed the addition of the 'Anthony Harrington' wing onto the drama block at Kittering College when Tania's younger half-brother, Lysander, had finished the sixth form. Apparently as nothing more than a gesture of goodwill.

But the realisation that Rose had grown so close to Madeleine, someone Clara had only just met, was a surprise to her. Not that she'd been paying any of her friends much attention lately, Clara supposed. She'd been conspicuous by her absence, absorbed totally by her life with Mike and Poppy, and subsequently with the void which had once been her life with Mike and Poppy. Latterly, she'd spiralled into the black hole that had taken over the space her life had once inhabited. A black hole which, at some point, seemed to have decided to inhabit her, rather than the other way around.

Watching Rose and Madeleine continue to laugh over teabags and the size of slices of cake Madeleine was cutting only served to accentuate how lonely Clara felt. The calm of earlier in the afternoon evaporated, replaced by a sense of desolation, which washed over her with the suddenness of a tsunami that no one had forecast, but which was so large it seemed impossible that no one had seen it coming.

She waited for the worst of the wave to subside, shoved her book onto the coffee table and stood. 'Never mind tea,' she said, forcing a brightness into her words. 'I'm going to have a glass of wine, I think. Anyone want to join me?'

By the time they sat down to dinner, Tania had counted Clara refilling her glass with Merlot at least three times. And according to Rose, she'd started early. Really early. As Clara reached for the bottle again, Tania put a hand on her arm.

'Why don't you have something to eat before you have another top-up?' she said, lifting the breadbasket and placing it in front of Clara.

Clara frowned at her and flopped back in her chair. 'I'm not very hungry.'

'It must be being outside in the mountain air, then,' Madeleine said, reaching a hand into the basket for another piece of baguette. 'Or maybe it's all the falling over I've done today. Either way, I'm starving.'

'After all the cake you ate at teatime?' Rose said.

'I know.' Madeleine shrugged. 'I can always diet in the new year, I suppose.' She spread some butter on a knob of bread and popped it into her mouth.

Tania had decided she quite liked Madeleine, with her unfiltered approach to life. It was a welcome change to most of the people she knew, with their guards permanently up, utterly consumed with inflating or airbrushing their lives, presenting things in the right light for mass-consumption. Not that Tania could throw stones. She'd done her fair share of airbrushing and soft-focusing things, over the years.

With the main course – a tasty chicken dish, with a centre of soaked fruits – in front of them and the tales of their varying experiences from the day relayed around the table, she was pleased to notice that Clara seemed to have slowed down on the vin rouge and was looking more relaxed, joking with the chef about something Tania didn't catch.

'That reminds me,' Clara said, focusing her attention on Tania. 'What's all this about there being a problem with the hot tub? They said I should ask you about it.'

Tania rolled her eyes, trying to ignore Madeleine's barely suppressed snort of laughter from across the table. 'There's nothing wrong with the hot tub. Can we please draw a line under the whole thing?' She shot a furious look in their direction. 'I wish I'd never said anything.'

'I suppose he might have meant *his* hot tub,' Madeleine said. 'You know, wherever he's staying might have one. Mightn't it?' She put her fork down. 'I just couldn't get the questions out of my head, once they were there. They just kept rattling around. But if he's got his own hot tub, then we don't need to worry, do we? We can feel free to use this one as and when, I suppose.'

'Jesus wept,' Tania said, with more volume than she intended. 'It doesn't matter whose sodding hot tub he was talking about; I'm still not going to fuck him in it. End of conversation. Please.' The table fell silent, and she couldn't fail to notice how the chef made himself busy, hulling some strawberries. She clocked the raise of his eyebrows, too. She should control herself better than this. Last thing she wanted was some crappy nonsense story appearing in the press, about her sleeping with a mystery man on her ski retreat. Especially so hot on the heels of her last brush with the media.

Tania suspected someone in her father's entourage would have ensured Tom had signed a privacy agreement prior to starting the job; her father would not be the only famous face to grace the rooms of Snow Pine Lodge during the season, and discretion from staff was of the utmost importance. What happened on tour always stayed on tour. At least, that was the theory. There was never a cast-iron guarantee of privacy, though, however intimidating the document might be that he'd been made to sign.

She took a sip of wine, then said, 'Just for the record, Clara, some guy propositioned me in Le Bar last night. I said no. End of story. OK?' She fixed the other two with a stare. 'OK?'

'You said you never actually told him no,' Madeleine said.

The chef's eyebrows arched again.

Tania reviewed her feelings about Madeleine's lack of filter. Perhaps the girl needed to install one, if they were going to be friends. People like Madeleine had no idea the lengths the paparazzi would go to for a sniff at gossip. How it was that anyone inside the velvet ropes was considered fair game. And how the well-publicised scandals involving phone tapping and email hacking were only the tip of a sordid iceberg.

For now, she said, 'Suffice to say, it's never going to happen. Never.' She drew the final word out, syllable by syllable, to make her point crystal clear. There was no way she was going to mention her subsequent meeting with him on the chairlift, or the fact that he chased her halfway down the mountain to apologise. Again.

Thankfully, the conversation travelled forwards, to plans for the following day. Madeleine was having a couple of hours' worth of lessons, Rose said she wanted to ski with Tania, and they successfully persuaded Clara to join them. With a plan in place, Tania began to relax. She took a spoonful from her pot of chocolate mousse, savouring the rich flavour. It was good, the texture light enough to balance the strong taste, so that it didn't cloy the inside of her mouth.

'Yum,' Madeleine said. 'Tom, this is delicious. Thank you.'

'My pleasure. Leave room for some cheese, won't you?'

The corners of Clara's mouth turned upwards at the

mention, her eyes darting across to where Tom was arranging crackers in a bowl. Tania wondered why, then decided it didn't matter. Clara hadn't refilled her wine glass for at least half an hour, and that was already a massive improvement on the previous evening.

'Do they serve chocolate mousse at the Cocoon?' Madeleine asked.

'Probably. Why?' Tania said.

'I'm already planning tomorrow's lunch,' Madeleine said, with a grin.

'I'm meeting Maddy there after her lesson,' Rose said. 'So, it makes sense if we all go there for lunch, don't you think?'

'Great idea,' Clara said. 'I love that place.'

Tania frowned. The Cocoon was the last place she wanted to be tomorrow, at lunchtime. He'd think she was there because of his invitation. He'd think she was interested in him. Well, she decided, that would be his problem. She was free to go wherever she chose, and if he misinterpreted the situation that would be his fault. Because she couldn't be less interested in him if she tried. Of that she was sure.

Distraction from her thoughts came in the form of a platter of cheese and biscuits which Tom brought across to the table. Tania didn't have a massive appetite at the best of times and had already eaten far too much. Which was annoying because the cheese looked unfamiliar and interesting. Pale and semi-soft, with a grey line running through its centre. She was determined to try it, even though her stomach was telling her that its cup was already dangerously near to runneth-ing over.

Tom stayed at the side of the table, standing close to Clara as he began to explain the history of the locally produced cheese. Madeleine piped up with a question.

'What's the grey stuff in the middle?'

Tom laughed, and to Tania's surprise, Clara joined in, her head tipped up, her gaze finding and resting lightly on the chef.

'Shall I tell them, or do you want to?' Tom said, the crinkles at the edges of his eyes deepening as he looked at Clara.

For all the world, Tania wouldn't have been surprised if Tom had placed a hand on Clara's shoulder, the scene had that kind of feel to it. Tania stilled; she must be imagining things. Although she thought it could only be a good thing if Clara managed to move forwards, in whatever way that might be, she couldn't see her engaging in a holiday romance, not so soon after losing Mike and Poppy. They'd been at a loss as to how to help her, and Tania had floundered about for ages wondering if organising this trip would be of any positive benefit. After all, what could you say or do to help someone whose husband and infant daughter had both been killed in a car accident? But a new relationship, so soon? No, that didn't seem right. That wasn't Clara.

'It's ash,' Clara said. 'Tell them the rest, Tom.' She looked around the table, eyes brighter than Tania had seen them in a long time. 'He'll explain it properly.'

Tania didn't listen to the explanation about the grey line properly. She tasted the cheese and listened politely, but her thoughts were elsewhere. She was watching Clara watching Tom. Blowing out her cheeks, she tried, unsuccessfully, to catch Rose's eye. The whole idea of this holiday was to try to make a dent in the grip the black dog seemed to have on their friend. Was a stranger going to be able to help with that? Only time would tell, she supposed.

Tom was taking coffee orders when they heard the main door opening. Tania frowned and climbed to her feet.

'Are we expecting anyone?' she said.

Sometimes the ski-hire firms sent people around to check clients were happy with their equipment, but Madeleine was the only other person who'd hired skis and boots for this week, and she shook her head.

'Do you want me to see who it is?' Tom said.

The outside door was opened by code, so whoever was

downstairs had to know it. It was unlikely to be an intruder, and yet they all looked at one another in confusion.

'Hello?' A voice shouted from below, footsteps sounding on the wooden staircase. 'Anyone home?'

'Oh, for Christ's sake,' Tania said, feeling her shoulders tighten. 'What's he doing here?'

The voice was unmistakeable. It was Lysander. Tania's brother.

Chapter 7

Madeleine had never met Tania's brother, never even seen him in person; she'd only ever seen photos of him advertising products in magazines. It was fair to say that the tousled poses they had him adopting, with an arm draped around a wisp of a female model after a supposedly amazing night out, a hand running casually through his messy blond hair while his clothing looked suitably dishevelled but devilishly desirable, had him looking drop dead gorgeous. But none of those photos did justice to seeing him in the flesh.

Looking at him, standing at the top of the staircase with a duffel bag slung over one shoulder and a lazy smile accentuating his features, Madeleine could only think of one description which did Lysander Harrington justice.

Gods of Olympus made mortal.

If someone had carved the perfect man from a block of marble, they couldn't have done a better job.

Aware her mouth was hanging open for the second time that day, her gaze alternated between the chiselled perfection of Lysander's face, and Tania, who did not seem at all pleased to see him.

'What the hell are you doing here, Donkey?' Tania said, her voice as pinched as her features. 'This is my week. And it's Christmas, for the love of God. I thought you were spending it in LA.'

'I know, I know. I should have been at a house party in the Hills, with Justin and Kenny. In living legend Cindy Crawford's guest house, to be precise. They promised me dinner at Mr Chow's – chicken satay and lemon drops – you must remember those cocktails? Brigitte would have turned green, if she wasn't already busy entertaining Ron Howard for the holidays. She's determined to get the old man cast in a film with Hanks. But instead, I took a last-minute job shooting here in the mountains. And I decided I couldn't think of anything nicer than spending Christmas with my loving sister.'

'Sarcastic sod. Well, anyway it's tough luck. All the rooms are full. You'll have to find somewhere else to sleep.' She raised an eyebrow. 'Shouldn't be a problem.'

'Oh, come on, Tits. Remember we talked about how you need to work on your anger-management skills. Chill out a little.'

Amidst trying to keep up with the name-dropping – which didn't seem so much like dropping, more like napalm bombing – Madeleine had so many questions. Donkey? Tits? The accompanying sub-questions were backing up behind the main ones. She turned to Rose, her lips already forming the first one. The one burning a hole in Madeleine's brain. Why did Tania call him Donkey? The ramifications were endless. . . But Rose's expression made her pause and close her mouth. Then frown. Rose was staring openly at Lysander, but she looked about as pleased to see him as Tania did. Her nose wrinkled in distaste, as though Lysander had brought with him some rotting carcass or weeks-old milk.

'The couch will do fine,' Lysander said, advancing into the space. Dropping his bag at the end of a sofa, he warmed his hands in the heat radiating from the hexagonal glass wood burner in the centre of the living space. Greeting Clara with a comment on her radiant beauty and a kiss on each cheek, he rounded the end of the table and stopped in front of Rose. He drew in a lengthy breath as he looked at her. 'It's been a while,' he said. 'How are you?'

'Very well. How are you?' Rose said, starchy and unusually formal.

'Good. You didn't reply to my messages.'

'No. I didn't.' Rose crossed her arms.

Even though she sounded calm, there was something behind the words that sounded anything but, in Madeleine's opinion. Her frown deepened and settled into place, even though she did her best to hide it when Lysander sighed, then shifted his gaze onto her.

'I don't think we've met,' he said.

'No, I'm Madeleine.'

'Hi, Madeleine. I'm Lysander, the Ice Queen's brother.'

'I know,' she said, failing to stop herself from sounding gushy. 'I mean, I know who you are. I've seen you in magazines.' She bit her lip as Tania snorted in what Madeleine could only assume was disgust.

Turning away, he acknowledged Tom for the first time. 'Any chance of something to eat?' he said.

'No, there isn't,' Tania said, before Tom had a chance to reply. 'You're far too late for dinner. Maybe you should go into Près du Ciel centre and find something there?'

'It's not a problem,' Tom said, lining up coffee cups onto a tray. 'I can make something.'

'Yes. It is a problem,' Tania said, her frown gaining traction. 'You've finished cooking for the evening.' She huffed. 'He can have what's left of the cheese and biscuits.'

'Whatever,' Lysander said, a lazy tone joining the lazy smile which had reasserted itself. 'Is there a glass of plonk to go with it?' He pulled the cheeseboard across and sat down.

Rose got abruptly to her feet. 'Think I'm going to turn in,' she said.

'I might come down with you,' Madeleine said. Combined with the tone of her voice, the way Rose was heading for the stairs like a cat with its tail on fire had her wanting to make sure she was OK.

''Night, then,' Lysander said, a definite prickle behind the seemingly innocuous words.

Rose's shoulders stiffened, but she kept moving and headed out of sight. On the top flight of the steps, Madeleine heard

Tania telling Lysander under her breath not to be such a bastard, to leave Rose alone.

At the doorway to Rose's bedroom, Madeleine asked again if she was all right.

'I'm fine,' Rose said, but Madeleine remained unconvinced.

'I don't mean to pry,' she said. Rose huffed a laugh. 'No, really, I don't. You guys clearly have history. You don't want to talk about it. That's fine. I just want you to know I'm here for you.'

Rose sighed, then nodded. 'I know you are. And thank you. I mean it.'

'Thing is, I have so many questions,' Madeleine said, unable to stop herself. 'Why does he call her "Tits", for example?' She shook her head at herself. 'But now is clearly not the time.'

The earnest expression on her face made Rose laugh.

'That's better,' she said. 'I can always stay if you want?'

Madeleine knew it wasn't what they'd agreed, it wasn't how this week was supposed to go, but equally she didn't want to leave Rose alone – not when Lysander's arrival had had such a profound effect on her. But Rose shook her head.

Madeleine sighed. 'OK. But listen, feel free to text me in the night if you need anything. Or you could go old style and knock on my actual door. You know, like they did back in the nineties.'

'I know. Thank you.' Rose smiled. 'I'm so lucky to have you, Maddy. You know that don't you?'

Madeleine headed for her room. 'I'll see you in the morning.'

Rose nodded.

'It'll all work itself out, I promise,' Madeleine said.

'Yeah. 'Night, Maddy.'

Chapter 8

Madeleine checked her watch. It was still dark outside and early enough to be pre-arrival of the daily delivery of fresh baguettes, lodged on the windowsill outside her room with such forceful scrunching of the large brown paper sack the previous morning that she'd thought someone was coming in through the window.

Was it too early to go and make tea? Trouble was, if she left it too long, Tom would begin his breakfast preparations and then the opportunity would be lost. She grinned in the dark. She was being so immature. But the thought of catching a glimpse of a world-famous male model asleep on one of the sofas upstairs had been chewing away at her since she'd woken.

It wasn't that she was attracted to him. Not that it would matter if she were, he wouldn't give a plain Jane like her a second glance.

But these kinds of situations didn't happen to Madeleine. At this moment in time, she was about as far away from her real life as she could imagine being. She could see herself, when she got home, sitting at her mum's kitchen table explaining how it was that the bloke from the magazine adverts had slept on one of the sofas. 'You know,' she imagined herself saying, 'Anthony Harrington's son.'

She felt sure her dad would adopt a dramatic tone and then utter the immortal words 'travelling through the wormhole was just the beginning'; he might even make the signal with his fingers and they would try to remember how many films were in the First Galaxy franchise, and whether to include the spin-offs or not. Then her dad would ask, not for the first time, how much they reckoned Anthony Harrington got paid to star as Galactic Commander Robson in those blockbuster movies.

To be able to take home a tiny piece of this world, she needed just a little bit of insider knowledge that hardly anyone else had – like, did Lysander Harrington sleep with his mouth open? Did he snore? Well, that would be golden.

It would also go some way towards making up for missing Christmas with her parents – for the first time ever. It would be great to take back a treasure trove of stories about how the other half live. Something to make up for the lack of traditional family time she'd never wanted to miss until she'd heard her brother and his family would be descending for the first time since he stopped talking to her. Awkward didn't quite cover how that situation would have played out, and she hadn't wanted to make Christmas an ordeal for her parents – it had seemed far simpler to accept Rose's invite instead.

Madeleine threw the covers back, shoved her feet into her slippers and wrapped her dressing gown firmly around herself. She heard the bag of bread being shoved against her window as she left her room and headed as quietly as she could up the dimly illuminated staircases.

At the top of the second flight, Madeleine paused and peered through the gloom, wondering which of the sofas Lysander had settled on for the night. All seemed quiet, so she padded towards the kitchen area.

'No need to tiptoe around on my account.'

Damn. Rumbled. She flicked on the small light over the counter and peered over at him. 'I'm sorry. Did I wake you?'

Lysander clicked on the standard lamp beside his sofa and Madeleine had to pretend not to stare at the nakedness of his perfectly smooth torso, even if it was almost impossible to look anywhere else.

'Nah. This couch is bloody purgatory; I don't think I got more than a couple of hours.'

She flicked the kettle on. 'Can I make you some tea?'

'I'll take a coffee. Black.' As he swung his legs out from under the fur throw, he stretched his arms up above his head.

Madeleine held her breath as he stood. For a split second she thought he might be completely naked, but there was underwear concealing everything relevant. Lysander rummaged beside the sofa and pulled on the pair of jeans he had been wearing the night before, then flopped back onto the seating, yawning as he reached for his mobile.

With two mugs of tea and a black coffee made, she lifted all three and headed for Lysander, placing the coffee in front of him.

'Thanks, sweetheart,' he said, his gaze on the remaining two mugs she held. 'Is one of those for Rose?'

'Yes.'

'You two close?'

Madeleine frowned, unsure of what to say. She settled for a non-committal response. 'Yes, she's great fun.' She nearly added, 'Don't you think?' and then thought better of it. Without knowing the depths of Rose and Lysander's relationship, or the reason for Rose's reaction to his arrival the previous evening, she decided it would be better to skate along the surface. She should keep her nose out, wait for Rose to fill in the blanks.

His nod was dismissive as he picked up his mug.

Rose stiffened as she heard the knock on her door. 'Who is it?' she said.

'It's me. I brought tea.'

Rose smiled, slipped from the bed, and unlocked the door. With Madeleine inside the room, she relocked the door and retreated into the warmth of her duvet. Madeleine concentrated on setting the mugs on one of the bedside cabinets. A beat of time passed – it was as if Madeleine were waiting for permission – before she shed her slippers and dressing gown and slid beneath the covers to join her.

'I've missed this,' she said.

'It's only been a few days.' In truth, Rose had missed it, too. She reached out, brushing a wayward strand of Madeleine's hair away from her face.

'Yeah, well, I'm not very good at being patient.' Madeleine caught hold of her hand and threaded their fingers together. She leaned over and kissed her, the feather soft warmth of their lips brushing together gone almost before Rose was able to process it, and way too quickly. 'Have I ever told you how amazing you look first thing in the morning?'

Rose drew back and deliberately changed tack. 'Thanks for the tea,' she said.

'I had an ulterior motive,' Madeleine said, passing her one of the mugs. 'It's not everyone who gets the chance to see what the face of Ralph Lauren looks like first thing in the morning.' Glancing across, a frown flitted between her eyes as the grin slid from her face. 'Oh, God. Have I put my foot in it?'

Rose studied her for sarcasm, but that wasn't Madeleine's style. She sighed. 'Was it that obvious?'

'No.' Madeleine drew the word out as if she wasn't totally convinced by it. 'You were upset by his arrival. Obviously. But that could be for loads of reasons.' She took a sip from her mug. 'I'm not going to ask. I know I ask questions about everything. All the time.' Rose grinned. 'But I'm not going to ask about that. The past is the past. Tell me if you want to, but otherwise I promise I won't pry.'

As her shoulders dropped, Rose realised how much she wanted to hear Madeleine say that. Lysander shouldn't have the ability to make her feel like this, not after all this time. They were kids when it started, stupid young kids. Initially, she'd been flattered by his attention. Even back then, when all the other boys were gawky and awkward, he'd been poised and good-looking. No, not just good-looking, he'd been ridiculously handsome. Everyone said so. On top of which there was something else. An aura? His self-confidence? She'd never been able to put her finger on it, but it had propelled him into the spotlight, secured him an exclusive modelling deal with one of the world's most renowned male outfitters, at the tender age of nineteen.

Perhaps it wasn't surprising, Rose thought, being the son of one of the most iconic film stars of the last thirty years and his supermodel wife. Second wife. Rose made the clarification. Tania's mother unceremoniously dumped in favour of Brigitte. Both women pregnant at the same time, Tania just a tiny baby and Lysander no more than a discreet bump when their father dropped the bombshell that he was permanently swapping beds.

When Rose began dating him, in the sixth form, everyone around her was in awe of Lysander – and his family. Rose would still challenge anyone in her situation not to have been swept along by the tide. Even the people in authority at the school, with its supposedly strict rules against students engaging in relationships, seemed to turn a blind eye where Lysander Harrington was concerned.

To this day Rose wasn't sure why Lysander had singled her out. They knew one another outside school, had been on ski trips together to the lodge a few times, fair enough. But so what? The majority of the girls – and a decent percentage of the boys – at Kittering College would have leaped at the chance to get the kind of attention she'd received from him. So why had he zeroed in on her as if she were a rabbit and he was a hawk? He'd hunted her down. There was no other way to describe it.

She had wondered if it was purely because she was best friends with Tania. Wondered if that made her a perversely attractive proposition. Lysander had always enjoyed taking Tania's toys, after all. Or maybe it had more to do with his – even then – desire to be seen ticking all the right boxes in the eyes of the fickle world of celebrity. Mixed-race girlfriend. Tick.

Either way, as far as Lysander Harrington had been concerned, it had ended up being nothing more than an early notch in a long line of conquests on his bedpost. Just a stupid teenage fling with a girl who he'd decided didn't like sex very much. And she'd never verbalised this deepest issue, at that point in her life she didn't have the confidence to do so – she didn't have the right words, didn't have the understanding. Didn't connect the dots as to why his seduction of her had only ever felt like pressure, something she came to dread, rather than dream about. With hindsight, Rose knew she'd withdrawn further and further into herself, battened down the hatches while she waited for the storm to pass.

It had taken her a long time to move forwards. Longer than she'd wanted to allow herself – probably because her path continued to criss-cross that of Lysander's. And he had a way of turning on the charm, wheedling his way back into favour. Rose found him difficult to gauge, had decided it was almost impossible to be sure whether he meant anything in a genuine way.

And then there had been the debacle with the dress. Eighteen months previously, Tania had determined to wear a dress designed by one of her art school friends to a First Galaxy premiere – the last Harrington three-line whip she'd been subjected to. The dress was supposed to be a secret – a flourish for the press, followed by a spotlight of publicity for the friend and her fledgling designer business. Somehow the details had been leaked, and by the time Tania was on the red carpet, nobody cared a toss about the dress. Instead, the focus was on Lysander and some outrageous suit he'd chosen for the occasion.

Lysander had asked Rose what Tania was going to wear to that premiere. He'd said he didn't want to clash with his sister, had made it sound a genuine request, and so Rose had told him. It had ruined the moment for Tania's designer friend, and Rose had never managed to shake the feeling it had all been her fault. From that day, she'd resolved to keep her mouth shut whenever Lysander was around.

And now, finally, when she felt as though her life was truly beginning to move forwards with Madeleine, here he was again. Dragging her back to a place of insecurity and indecision.

'However, while I promise not to pry. . .' Madeleine's voice jolted Rose out of her thoughts and she refocused as Madeleine prodded at the side of her head. 'Holes are being burned up here, so I am going to have to ask a few things.'

'OK. Go for it.' Rose grasped her mug, welcoming its warmth against her fingers.

'Number one is about the Donkey thing.' Madeleine frowned. 'Let's dodge that one for a moment, on account of me not prying. But hot on its heels is the next one. Why the hell does he call her Tits? It's not even like she's particularly well endowed in that department. Or have I got the wrong end of the stick?'

Rose nodded, and smiled at Madeleine's observation, all at the same time. 'Totally the wrong end. Thing is, she's really called Titania. Unsurprisingly, she'd already dumped that in favour of Tania by the time I met her. But Lysander insists on reminding her, in his own particular way.'

'By calling her Tits? Doesn't he ever call her Tania?'

'In front of their father, yes. Apart from that, not really.'

'Nice. And that's why she wasn't impressed to see him?'

'I think so.' It was a little more complicated than that, but Rose left it there, for now at least. Explaining the complexity of rivalry and the tug of emotions between Tania and Lysander would take more than a sentence or two. Or the fact that she found herself caught up in that complexity. Sometimes Lysander rallied to Tania's defence, forming the Harrington line. But then, at other times he did the complete opposite and threw her to the wolves.

Madeleine lapsed into silence, frowning as she downed a couple of swigs of tea. 'Why did they call her Titania? In the first place, I mean.' She set her mug down. 'Seems rather cruel to land her with such a God-awful name.'

Rose laughed. 'Yes, I suppose it is. I've only ever thought of her as Tania. She told me it's because her father had his big break in a Shakespeare play which they made into a film – *A Midsummer Night's Dream.* Apparently it led to his first role as Commander Robson.'

'Oh.'

'Yes, and he decided he owed that film so much that he'd name his children after characters from it.'

'Oh. Lucky children.'

'Mmm. It's where Donkey comes from, too. Before you get too carried away with any other lines of thought. Tania decided to get her own back on Lysander by referring to him as one of the characters that Bottom plays.'

'Oh. Who's Bottom?'

'One of the characters Shakespeare included to bring comedy into the play.'

'You know a lot about it.'

'We studied it at school.'

'I'll bet Tania loved that.'

'Not really.' Rose grinned at the memory. 'She was convinced the English teacher was getting at her by choosing it.' She took a sip of tea. With hindsight, she thought Tania had probably been right. Some of the staff went out of their way to fawn over the Harringtons, but others had gone the other way and treated Tania unnecessarily harshly.

'That must backfire though. I can't be the only person who thinks "Donkey" might refer to something else about him.' The frown was back. 'Sorry. Trying not to pry. Failing.'

Rose smiled, rather thinly. 'I don't suppose she thinks of him in that way. And I'm not about to point it out to her.'

'No. Fair enough.'

They lapsed into a companionable silence. Eventually, Madeleine said, 'Do you think I should offer him my bed?'

Rose almost let her mug slip from between her fingers. 'What?'

The tone of her voice must have belied her confusion, or concern. She wasn't sure which one had the upper hand at the thought of Madeleine and Lysander together.

'Obviously not like that . . . Idiot.' Madeleine grinned. 'I meant I wondered if I should offer him my room and share with you instead.'

'But we agreed—'

Lines formed between Madeleine's eyes. 'Yes. I know. We did. I'm not suggesting anything changes in that respect. That ball is completely in your court. But this is a big room. And there is a spare bed in it, so no one would be any the wiser.' She gestured towards the single bed set in the far corner of the room. 'He said he didn't get much sleep on the sofa upstairs, that's all.' She shook her head. 'It's just an idle thought.'

'But it's a lot of hassle for you, moving all your stuff.'

'Like that matters.' She shifted to face Rose. 'It doesn't have to be a big deal, I just thought it made sense.'

When Rose failed to reply, Madeleine lifted the mug from her hand and set it alongside her own, then kissed her again. This time her lips lingered. Rose breathed in Madeleine's scent, the freshness of the lemon soap she favoured mixing with the softer notes from the face cream she pretended she didn't use. Unable to resist, she pulled her close, the pair of them sliding into the welcoming softness of the goose-down pillows. She might have wanted an uncomplicated week, but the effect of Madeleine's soft curves against her own body banished her logical wants, replacing them with a much deeper one. A want that mixed with need and heat and sensations which Rose hadn't even known existed before she met Madeleine.

Lysander was an unsettling presence, and not just as far as

Rose was concerned. But with Madeleine at her side, Rose felt more capable of dealing with any curveballs aimed in her direction than ever before.

Chapter 9

By mid-morning, Clara had to admit it was good to finally be out on the snow. With Madeleine dispatched for her lesson, Tania, Rose and she had managed to cover a lot of the resort's kinder slopes already.

'Shall we head up on the bubble again?' Tania asked, when the three of them paused at the top of one of the undulations leading back into the centre of the Près du Ciel resort. 'Or take the Becoin chair this time?'

Rose fumbled with her sleeve and checked her watch. 'I don't want to be late for Maddy.'

'We won't be, I promise,' Tania said.

'I think we should do the chair,' Clara said. 'I love the slopes over on that side.'

'OK, Becoin it is. Last one to the chairlift is buying the *vin chaud* at lunchtime,' Tania said, pushing off with her poles.

Clara grinned as she tucked her body in and allowed gravity to take effect, listening to Rose squealing as she too pushed off and hustled to overtake Tania. As the massive spiral wire pulled the chairlift up the mountain, Clara allowed herself to take in the view, admiring the sheer expanse of cloudless blue sky. She craned her neck to look back at Près du Ciel centre as it shrunk into miniature with their increasing height and distance, then watched the puffs of snow kicked up by the skiers each time they turned across the slope far below. It was good to sit quietly and take it all in.

She'd never managed to persuade Mike to take a ski holiday. He had been more of a camping and hiking kind of guy. And Clara had discovered she was happy to become a camping and hiking kind of girl if it meant she got to spend uninterrupted time with him. She didn't even mind when he revealed he was a closet fisherman, because while he was focused on his bait and his line and the run of the water at his favourite spot beside a local river, she got to relax on a picnic rug beside him, sketchbook in hand, with a backdrop of the sound of the water and birdsong as she doodled. Plus, in return for aiding and abetting his leisure pursuits, he didn't question her girly trips with Tania to get her winter fix of snow, and she'd loved him even more for that.

She hadn't been to Près du Ciel for over three years, she realised. When Poppy came along all that kind of stuff went out of the window and life took her on a different road. In time she'd planned to bring Poppy, though. When her baby girl got big enough to cope with learning to ski, Clara had intended to persuade Mike to put his reservations aside and take the trip as a family. Her husband and her daughter could learn to ski at the same time, she'd thought. All sorts of amusing images had floated through her mind, including one of Poppy calling Mike a 'Silly Billy' whenever he fell over, just as he had done to her when she was learning to walk.

It would have been perfect. It should have been perfect. Except it wasn't, and it never would be, now. Because they were gone. It was all gone.

And it was all her fault.

By the time they disembarked at the top of the lift, Clara couldn't see where she was going. The tears she had been supressing for longer than she could remember refused to stop flowing and her goggles had clouded up.

'Hang on a minute,' she said, her voice strangled with the effort of sounding normal. 'My goggles are fogged up.'

Rose rounded her on one side and Tania appeared on the other. Pulling the goggles from her helmet, she sniffed as she dried them.

'Are you OK?' Rose said.

'Yes. 'Course I am.' She nodded and attempted a smile. Then she shook her head, unable to suppress another wave of tears. Her face creased up as the force of her sense of loss took control of her. Again. Like some sort of infection, resistant to every kind of medication, ebbing and flowing, but inexorably gaining a firmer hold on its victim, eating her up until she feared eventually there was going to be nothing left.

Tania slid closer, dug her poles into the snow and wrapped her arms around her with a forcefulness Clara hadn't felt since the funeral. Rose did the same and they stood there, at the top of the Becoin run, for what felt like an eternity.

Eventually, Rose pulled back and stared out across the view. Clara heard Tania let out a sigh and she, too, slid back a few inches.

Nobody moved, no one spoke. With her friends flanking her like sentinels, they looked out over one of the most exhilarating views on Earth while Clara did her best to push away enough of the blackness to see it.

An hour or so later, Tania slid to a stop outside the Cocoon. Clara had already dumped her skis and was heading up the slope towards Madeleine. Rose came to a stop beside her.

'I don't think I've seen Clara cry before. About Mike and Poppy, I mean,' Rose said.

'I've seen her in denial. Pretending she's all right. Or blind drunk – I've seen that a lot. But you're right,' Tania said, 'I haven't seen her cry either. Not even at the funeral.'

'Do you think it's a good sign?'

Tania puffed out her cheeks. 'I don't know. I hope so.'

'Yeah. Me too.' Rose stood her skis together and sunk them into a pile of snow, then headed up the slope after Clara.

Tania scanned the Cocoon as she followed Rose, then checked her watch. One o'clock. Exactly the time she didn't want to be here, in case hot tub guy, the man she'd come to think of as Mr Explicit, should appear and get the wrong idea. It was hard to see inside, and difficult to identify the people wearing helmets or with woollen hats pulled down over ears to keep heads warm, but she couldn't see anyone who resembled Mr Explicit. Perhaps he'd changed his plans and decided to stop somewhere else for something to eat. Relaxing a little, she took a seat at the table with the others.

'Shall I get us some drinks?' Madeleine said.

'That would be lovely,' Tania said.

'No, hang on a minute,' Rose said. 'You said last one to the Becoin chairlift was buying the drinks.' She raised her eyebrows. 'And I think you'll find that was you.'

'Oh, yes. I'd forgotten that.' Unusually, she'd caught an edge on the very last descent to the chairlift and almost ended up on the ground, allowing the other two to leave her in their wake. It seemed like a long time ago. 'Well, if you're determined to hold me to it, I suppose I can go.'

'Oh, we'll hold you to it,' Clara said. 'That's not a problem.'

With everyone's drink order memorised, she went inside, unzipping her jacket as the warmth hit her from the roaring log burner on one side of the restaurant. The drinks queue was minimal, the server efficient and so she was heading back outside with a tray in next to no time. She threaded her way back across the decking, then lodged the tray on one end of the table.

'OK,' she said. 'Black Americano for Clara . . . *Vin chaud* for Rose . . .' She glanced across at the group taking command of a nearby table. Mostly men, a couple of women in the mix. Unclasping helmets and peeling off gloves. 'Oh, shit . . .'

'Nope,' Madeleine piped up. 'Pretty sure none of us ordered that.'

Pulling off his helmet and taking a seat at the furthest end of the table was hot tub guy. Mr Explicit. Tania slid into a chair. If she positioned herself behind Clara, he might not see her.

'What are you doing?' Clara said, looking sideways at her before taking a sachet of sugar and ripping it open.

Clara was right, trying to hide was ridiculous. She would

just ignore him. He would get the message about her lack of interest, one way or another. Sliding a hot chocolate over towards Madeleine, she took a mouthful from her own.

'Thanks. Is it a bit piggy to have a hot chocolate as well as mousse for pudding?' Madeleine said, her eyes scanning the arrivals on the neighbouring table. 'It is only lunchtime, after all . . . Oh, blimey.' She swung back towards Tania, eyes ablaze. 'You'll never guess who's on the next table.'

Tania nodded. 'I know. I've seen him.'

'Him who?' Clara said.

'Hot tub man,' Madeleine said.

'Really? Which one?' Clara asked.

Once Madeleine had pointed him out, none too subtly in Tania's opinion, Clara leaned across the table.

'What's happening with Rory?' she asked.

Tania shook her head. 'It's done. Finished.'

'You've said that before.'

She had said it before. She'd thought she'd meant it before. But this time there was no shadow of a doubt. Her on-off relationship with one of her father's co-stars in the latest of the First Galaxy spin-offs had started as nothing more than a way to get at Daddy Dearest. Rory was married, she'd known that all along, and the whole thing was supposed to be under the radar. Just her way to remind her father what happened to her mother, all those years ago – a beguiling young woman cutting in on another woman's husband, in secret? The irony seemed too delightful to pass up. Having sex in Rory's trailer, with her father in the adjoining one? It might have been a low blow, but Tania enjoyed the tortured expression on her father's face a little too much. The fact that he knew precisely what was going on but was unable to do anything about it had given her an unexpected level of satisfaction.

But then Tania had found out that Rory's wife was pregnant. And in that moment, everything had changed. She hadn't ever intended for it to get serious; on her part it had been nothing more than a way to embarrass her father, a silly fling which should have stayed on set. But once she heard that Rory's wife was expecting a baby, she realised she had been playing with fire. It hadn't been about her getting at her father, as she had thought. There were other people involved. Other people's lives. A child's future.

And then the press found out.

Rory had denied the whole thing, had absolutely refuted the suggestion that a man lucky enough to have as beautiful a wife as his would be foolish enough to enter into an extra-marital affair, especially when he had a baby on the way. And Tania had felt sick listening to every word, knowing the press would still run with the story, regardless of what anyone said. A bubble of nausea still lodged in her belly at the thought of a connection being established between herself and Rory, one strong enough for her to potentially be named. The knowledge that reporters would be scrabbling around to find someone willing to squeal, anyone with pertinent details and the need for some easy money.

She'd spoken to Rory one final time, shortly before she left for France. He had been cordial, as always. A little surprised, she thought, to have had his fun taken away. She had no doubt he would find himself someone else to share his trailer with, if he felt so inclined. But Tania knew, without question, that whoever it was it wouldn't be her.

'He's looking at you,' Rose said.

Tania frowned, and looked up. Hot tub guy was staring at her, his expression hard to read, but with surprise in the arch of his eyebrows.

'He looks like he's just won the lottery,' Madeleine said. Rose told her to shush, and Madeleine asked why she should be quiet, and Clara began to laugh. Tania held his gaze. If she was going to get through to this man that she wasn't interested, that he would be better off running a mile in the opposite direction, that he had no idea of the baggage she came with, then there was no point in hiding from him.

'He's coming over,' Madeleine said, in a stage whisper.

'Shut up, you muppet,' Rose said.

Tania stood and met him halfway.

'Hello again,' he said.

'I'll give you that one,' she said.

'Wow, thanks.' He smiled. 'I was waiting for the cutting remark, if I'm honest.'

She wasn't sure if she'd noticed the crow's feet at the edges of his eyes the previous day, made more prominent when he smiled. Or the wild curls of his brown hair mirrored by his no-nonsense attitude to male grooming. He'd shaved today, but that was about it.

'In fact,' he said. 'I wasn't expecting to see you at all.'

He was warming to the conversation. Time to shut him down. She frowned. 'I'm not here because you are.'

'Oh?'

'My friends arranged to meet here. I didn't want to make a fuss, so I went along with the arrangement. I want to make that clear.'

'Right.'

'I just want to say, I accept your apology, and I don't want you to give it another thought.'

He smiled again. 'That's a relief.'

'No, you misunderstand. I don't want you to give it, or me, another thought. I want you to draw a line underneath whatever you think this is and leave me alone.'

'Right.' He furrowed his brows together, which wasn't difficult. They'd clearly never seen any kind of grooming tool. She kind of liked their wild wilfulness. They balanced out the incredibly long eyelashes which framed his dark eyes. 'I'm Gull, by the way.' He held out a hand. She ignored it, wondering if he was always this persistent.

'Gull?'

'I know.' He shook his head. 'My parents totally stiffed me with that. Short for Gulliver. Can you believe it?'

Against her better judgement, she felt herself smile. 'I can,' she said, shaking his hand.

'Ah,' he said, grasping her fingers with an exceptionally firm grip. 'First-hand experience?'

Tania laughed. 'You could say that.'

'But you're not going to elaborate?'

'Nope.'

'Why am I not surprised.'

'Can't imagine. Everyone calls me Tania, let's leave it at that.'

'Tania.' He sounded as if he was trying the word out.

'This is where I say, "It was nice to meet you, Gull. Goodbye",' she said. *Gull.* The word sat more comfortably on her lips than she thought it would. She frowned again, but the frustration wasn't to do with him, this time, it was to do with her. She felt it again, an invisible string binding her to this square foot of space outside the Cocoon, with servers pushing past them to clear tables, customers arriving and leaving, the sound of ski boots clumping on the wooden decking.

'Why?' he said.

'Why what?'

'Why do you need to say goodbye?'

She studied his face for a moment, her frown deepening as she realised that she didn't have an answer.

Chapter 10

Tania glanced towards her friends as Gull held his ground and asked if he could buy her some lunch.

'I should get back to the others,' she said. The words sounded weak, and he still had hold of her hand. She shook herself free from his fingers and gestured towards the group Gull had arrived with. 'And aren't you with those people? They'll be wondering what you're doing, won't they?'

He shrugged. 'I think it's fairly obvious what I'm doing. Isn't it?' His eyebrows arched again, his face breaking into a broad grin. Then he buried it under a frown. 'You didn't answer my question.'

'No,' she said. 'I didn't.'

'Shall I rephrase it? Do you want to sit at the same table as me while we eat some lunch purchased by an, as yet, unspecified individual or individuals?'

'Are you this persistent in everything you do?' she asked, trying not to notice Madeleine grinning at her, while Clara and Rose seemed to be craning their necks to hear the conversation.

'No.'

She raised her eyebrows.

'Maybe I should clarify,' he said. 'If you asked David that question – he's the one over there in the green jacket – he'd probably tell you I'm about as gentle in my approach as a sledgehammer. But I've never agreed with that. I think I'm really relaxed. Unless it's something I consider to be important.'

'Who is David?' she asked.

'He's my brother.'

She glanced across, noting the physical similarities. 'He should know, then.'

'Maybe,' Gull said. 'Do you have siblings?'

'A half-brother. But I wouldn't trust him to have any reliable opinions about *my* personality.'

'You don't get on?'

She laughed. 'He's . . . Well, let's just say it's complicated.'

'You have an amazing smile, by the way.'

Tania frowned and looked away.

'Maybe I am being a bit of a sledgehammer,' he said and took a step back. 'Sorry.'

'No, it's not you . . .'

'Oh, Christ. We've got to the "it's not you, it's me" line already. And our relationship is only five minutes old.' He mimed a stab to the heart. 'Listen, before we split our assets and decide who gets the dog, why don't we have something to eat?'

Tania couldn't stop herself from smiling and nodding. 'All right,' she said. 'But I'm keeping the dog.'

'I don't think Tania's having lunch with us any longer,' Rose said, as they watched her disappear into the restaurant with the hot tub guy.

'I wonder what he said to win her round?' Clara said.

'Does anyone else want her hot chocolate?' Madeleine asked. 'If it's going to go to waste, I'll have it and forgo the pudding I had planned.'

'Did you know about Rory Flannagan?' Clara asked. The question was aimed in her direction, but Rose hesitated. She knew all about Rory Flannagan.

Madeleine licked chocolatey foam from her spoon. 'The First Galaxy actor?'

'Yes,' Clara said, frowning.

'He's married, isn't he?' Madeleine said. 'I read something about him recently, and some affair he was supposed to be having—' She paused, glancing across to where Tania had been standing. 'Oh . . . Was it . . . ?'

Rose huffed a breath. 'Don't say anything.'

'She told me it's over. That she ended it,' Clara said.

Rose nodded. 'Yes. But I've never understood why she does that. Why she always goes for men who are ultimately unavailable, in some way. Or she dates them for two minutes and then dumps them. There's always something that means it's only ever destined for failure. Like that guy who was in training for the British Olympic ski team? Do you remember him?'

'The fitness freak? Egg-white omelette man?'

Rose grinned. 'Yes. Mr Navel Gazer. Told her he couldn't have a proper relationship because it didn't fit in with his training schedule. My point is, it's always been the same. It's as if she chooses the wrong men on purpose. Or chooses the right men but dumps them before she finds out if they have the potential to be long term. Perhaps she just prefers short term. She keeps saying she's never going to fall in love.'

Clara drained her mug. 'Do you think that's why she's talking to this guy? Because she's ultimately not that interested in him?'

Rose shrugged. 'Why change the habit of a lifetime?'

'What will it take for you to allow me to buy you a drink this evening?' Gull said.

'I already told you, I can buy my own drinks,' Tania replied. She'd bought her own lunch, all but ignoring him in the Cocoon queue, holding an internal argument with herself about the point of sitting at a table with him while they ate.

'And I already heard you. I get it. You're single and independent and capable and you don't need anyone to buy you anything.' He pushed his empty plate away, folding his arms and resting them on the table. 'But it's just a drink. It's not as if I'm asking if I can buy *you*.'

'See, that's where you're wrong. That's exactly what you're asking. You just don't realise it.'

He blew out his cheeks. 'I feel like I'm on a tightrope.'

'How good is your balance?' she asked, watching as the edges of his lips curled into a smile. He wasn't backing down, and he didn't seem to mind that she wasn't, either.

The interesting thing was, Tania thought, that she was still seated at a table, with him, even though they'd both finished eating. It would have been easy to get up and leave. Why hadn't she done exactly that? Never mind the tightrope he felt she was making him walk; she was negotiating her own invisible strings, which seemed determined to keep her exactly where she was. But if the irritation she'd felt about him was turning into a twisted sense of attraction, she was determined she was going to make him work for it.

'OK,' he said. 'How about this? You choose a run for us to ski this afternoon, and whoever gets to the bottom first allows the other to buy them a drink.' He ran a hand through his hair. 'Surely that idea balances?'

'Not really,' she said. 'Because I'm probably going to win.'

'Ah. Cocky. As well as feisty and independent and capable. The list grows. OK. First one to the bottom buys the drinks. Happy now?'

'You want to feel bought?' she said, but there was a smile teasing at the edge of her lips, now, too.

'At this point I'll take anything that's on offer, yes.'

'Anything?'

'Am I back on the tightrope with this answer?' he asked. 'I wasn't aware you'd left it.'

'Then I'll take whatever is on offer.' His eyebrows furrowed together suddenly as he reached out with one hand and placed it on hers, squeezing hard before he let go. 'You're driving me mad, Tania.'

'Already?' She stood. 'That's probably a record. Shall we go?'

* * *

Tania already knew Gull was competent on skis. The way he'd chased her down the run the previous afternoon told her that. But she decided not to test the man to destruction. Not yet, anyway.

She chose a wide red run, one which swept its way down the side of the mountain currently bathed in the afternoon sun. Once they'd exited the bubble, she clicked her boots into her skis and settled her goggles onto her face. 'Are you ready?'

'Where's the finish line?' he asked.

'How about the ski stand outside Le Bar?' She pulled her bandanna up over her mouth and slotted her poles into her hands.

He nodded, slid his sunglasses into place and grabbed his poles. 'OK. See you there,' he said. With a kick of a ski, he tipped himself downhill and shot away. Tania grinned underneath her bandanna, wondering if she should give him a bit of a head start. But Gull wasn't taking any prisoners. He disappeared over the first major undulation and Tania pushed off to follow him.

She kept him in sight down the first half of the run, letting him settle into the lead. It gave her the opportunity to watch him, to see his skiing style. It was neat and no-nonsense, and he took advantage of the natural terrain, picking up speed in all the places she did. After a while, she tightened her lines, and began to gain on him.

He headed over a deceptively sharp lip and she saw his skis momentarily leave the ground. Ready to absorb the change in gradient with her knees, Tania shot over the lip. She landed in time to see Gull losing control as he battled to avoid a fallen skier. She changed direction neatly to avoid the prone figure, taking a wide semicircle back to where one of Gull's skis had ended up. She scooped it up and walked her skis back to where Gull lay, breathing hard.

'Are you OK?' she said, pulling her bandanna from her mouth as she waited for him to reply.

'Christ,' he said. 'I almost went straight over him.' Sitting up, he took Tania's hand and she pulled him to his feet. 'Is he all right?' He looked past her at the fallen skier, now also standing and facing their direction, a hand raised in apology. Gull held his hand up, in acknowledgement, then turned back to her. He lined his skis up and slotted his feet back into them, his face creasing as he did so.

'Are you OK?' she repeated.

He clearly wasn't. As he rubbed at his left knee, his expression became taut with pain. 'Twisted my damn knee,' he said through gritted teeth.

'Can you ski, or do we need to get the blood wagon out for you?' she said.

He managed a laugh at the reference to one of the mountain's emergency services, which traditionally involved a paramedic skier pulling a gurney on a sledge behind him, or sometimes – depending on ease of access – riding a snowmobile. Putting more weight on the knee, he sucked in a tight breath, but kept the weight even on both legs. 'No,' he said. 'I'm OK.' He attempted to smile at her. 'Might have to forfeit the race, though.'

'Told you I'd win,' she said.

'That's hardly a victory to write home about.' He winced again.

They weren't far from the top of the Près du Ciel village, only a few hundred metres from Snow Pine Lodge, which nestled amongst the trees demarcating the highest end of the resort. She knew she should suggest they take the Rhodos run and ski back to her place, and then he could arrange a taxi back to wherever he was staying. It was the logical and sensible thing to do. She wasn't sure why she hesitated to suggest it, except that Lysander might be at the lodge. Gull might recognise him. He might put two and two together and realise she was part of the Harrington family, and then talk would turn, as it invariably did, to her father and his career.

Tania wondered why it felt as if that would matter.

Twenty-four hours ago, she'd decided she felt nothing more than irritation about this man, that she wanted nothing to do with him. So, why would it matter if Lysander were there? Why would it matter if Gull pieced together who she was?

She handed Gull his poles. The fact was that she was enjoying the company of someone who had no idea of her identity, past the fact that her name was Tania. Someone who didn't have a preconceived idea of what she would be like. Someone with whom she could be whoever she wanted to be, even if it was just for a while.

And she realised she didn't want to bring the rest of the world into whatever was happening between them. This was a little piece of life that was happening to her. It had nothing to do with who she was, or who her father was, or the fact that she was Donkey's sister, and Tania wanted to keep it that way.

It wasn't as if this thing was going to go anywhere, anyway. It was simply a bit of fun, a chance to flirt with a stranger for a week – if she decided she wanted to. He'd already made it clear what his primary interest in her was, even if he had claimed to be drunk at the time. And he hadn't backed down from that assertion. He'd apologised for his lack of subtlety, but he hadn't apologised for the feelings behind the inappropriateness of his words. She liked that. He seemed refreshingly straightforward.

After a couple more turns down the run, it became clear Gull's knee was causing him more pain than he was willing to admit. When he stopped at the side of the piste, bending his weight over his poles to relieve the pressure on his knee, she came up alongside him.

'My place isn't far from here,' she said. Practicalities were outweighing her sensibilities. There was only one real choice to be made. 'Why don't we get you there and then reassess how your knee feels?'

He nodded. 'Have you got a hot tub?' he said, his gritted teeth breaking into a smile.

'Will you stop with the hot tub thing.'

'Sorry. Bad joke. My forte, I'm afraid,' he said, his brows knitting together again.

'Anyway, you'll probably be better off with ice on your knee, not heat.'

'Spoil-sport.' He straightened, allowing her to lead the way.

Tania's father had bought Snow Pine Lodge when the First Galaxy movies began breaking box-office records. With its stunning views and accessibility directly onto the piste, the lodge hadn't been cheap. But with the money Anthony Harrington was earning for his lead role in the films, cheap hadn't been a requirement. Secluded had been on the list. As well as spacious. Family-orientated, too, had been high up the list at the time of its purchase. Tania, aged about seven, and Lysander no more than six when they embarked on their first trip to the Alps.

The family dynamics were, to say the least, strained – and with hindsight also rather weird – with Tania and her mother accompanying her father, his second wife Brigitte and golden boy Lysander. Tania still remembered his name for her and her mother. His 'extended family'. As if she wasn't actually his child but had been included in some sort of a benevolent umbrella 'catch-all' arrangement.

She remembered a time when she wondered if being a boy would have made a difference, if it was the fact she was born a girl that had driven her father away. After all, Lysander could do no wrong. And, it seemed, Tania didn't manage to get a whole lot right. Even her art – the one thing she loved – had so little impact on her father that he had never been to her studio, let alone allowed examples of her work to grace any of his homes. And yet, being Anthony Harrington's daughter was a label she'd never managed to shake off, like flypaper. The more she tried to get away, the more she seemed to become stuck.

And all the while, Lysander – the boy with golden hair and, it seemed, a golden halo to match – remained determined to score points off her. Tania had never fully understood why. After all, Lysander was the one with the fame, the existence littered with celebrities and parties. He was the one gracing every red carpet he could get his size nines onto. Living the dream – or so he kept telling her. While all she had to show for herself was a stack of canvases in her studio, a couple of moderately successful exhibitions and a determination not to use her name to promote her work.

She skied gently, marginally in the lead to show Gull the way, keeping her pace right down. He'd lost the confident fluidity to his style, his turns blocky and laboured when the bad knee had to take more weight.

When they reached the tree-line, she signalled to him that they would be peeling off to the right, then kept an eye out for the wooden post, set at a discreet distance behind the piste markers, which indicated the little cut-through track which would take them to Snow Pine Lodge.

Chapter 11

Tania punched the door code, pushing the lodge door until it caught open.

'Where shall I leave my skis?' Gull asked. He glanced around outside, looking for the ski locker.

'Bring them inside, it's easier than faffing around out there.'

Following her inside the building, he leaned his skis alongside hers, in a corner. 'Won't the lodge people moan about all the water?' A little puddle was already forming at the base of Tania's skis, where the ice had begun to melt.

'This is an emergency,' she said, then grinned at him. 'You're injured.' She wasn't about to tell him that it was her family's property, and she could put her skis wherever she liked. After all, it made sense to keep the skis outside, there was a perfectly good locker to put them in, but Gull's face had been so pale by the time they'd reached the lodge that Tania wanted to get him off his knee as quickly as possible.

'It's two flights up to the living area, will you be all right with that?' It dawned on her she hadn't considered the stairs.

Perching on a bench, he eased his feet from his boots. 'It's fine. I'll get some ice on it and give our chalet manager a call. I'm sure I won't be in your way for long.'

Tania considered running upstairs, to check whether anyone else was in the lodge – primarily Lysander – then decided it was too late to worry about that. Instead, she shoved her own boots out of the way, discarded her jacket and helmet and waited for him to stand.

'Lead the way,' he said, leaving his helmet and gloves on the bench.

He'd lost some of his bluster, Tania thought, wondering just how badly he'd twisted his knee. Once they'd scaled the stairs, she headed for the freezer to find ice. 'Take a seat.' She waved her hand in the general direction of the living area, but he didn't. Instead, he hobbled to the picture window.

'Wow.' Peeling off his jacket, he stood and admired the view. 'This is sensational.'

Tania smiled as she wrapped ice in a tea-towel and headed back to him. 'Isn't it?'

'I'm not even going to ask how much this place is for a week. Our chalet hasn't got anything like this setting and that cost the best part of a second-hand hatchback for our stay. Luckily, there are loads of us to split the cost. And I suppose it is Christmas week. Fish in a barrel, and all that.'

'Yes. Here you go.' Keen to move the conversation on, she held out the cold compress. He took a seat at the end of a sofa and tugged at the bottom of his ski trouser leg, pulling it up as far as he could. There was no way it was going up past his knee.

Glancing at her, he pulled a face. 'Houston, we have a problem.'

'Take them off . . . If it's easier.'

'Thought you'd never suggest it.' He offered her a lopsided smile.

Trying to ignore the way his eyes sparkled as he smiled, she rolled her eyes to deny it. 'I promise I won't look.'

'Shame.'

She did look, though. He stood and turned away from her, unfastening and dropping the insulated trousers to the ground before he sat again and applied the ice. Tania headed for the kitchen area, but not before she'd taken in the black compression shorts, tightly fitted against the substantial muscles of his thighs, an unashamed forest of dark hairs covering his newly exposed calves.

'I might have a mint tea. Do you want anything?' she said.

He shook his head. 'No thanks. I'm OK.'

'Painkillers?'

Another shake of his head as he leaned forward to rifle through his trousers. He held up his phone. 'I'll find the appropriate number and get someone to fetch me. We're in Snow Pine Lodge, that's right, isn't it?'

Tania nodded. It hadn't always been called Snow Pine Lodge. When her father had bought the building, it had been called Chalet Génépi. She'd rather liked it, liked the fact the place had been given the same name as a mountain liqueur, but her stepmother had taken an instant dislike to it. Or perhaps she just wanted to make the building her own. Either way, Brigitte insisted the change be made.

Busying herself filling the kettle, Tania found a mug and a herbal teabag while Gull made his call. She glanced across again, her gaze settling on him as he leaned back against the cushions of the sofa, eyes closed, traces of pain still embedded between them.

The kettle clicked off. He opened his eyes and looked in her direction before she could pretend she'd been doing anything else in the time it took the water to boil other than stare at him. The heat notched up in her cheeks when he didn't change his expression, he just held her gaze.

She swallowed and poured water into her mug, then took hold of the paper tab at the end of the teabag's string. The distraction was welcome, as she concentrated on jiggling the bag around in the water. She glanced at him again. This time he was staring through the window, and she stole a few moments to take in the profile of his face. He wasn't classically handsome; probably wouldn't score on any Hollywood scale. He wasn't in the least bit chiselled. There was nothing refined about him, nothing particularly photogenic. There was a definite roughness to his edges. She would term him as rugged if that didn't conjure up so many clichés. If her father's stylist was given Gull as a project, he'd probably have a nervous breakdown trying to work out where to start. And yet, Tania couldn't seem to drag her eyes away from him.

'Are you here with family, or friends?' Gull swung around to look at her.

'Girlfriends,' she replied, wondering why she'd felt the need to include their gender. Heat notched again in her cheeks. 'You?'

'My brother and his almost fiancée. Some other friends.' He paused, a frown pressing itself into his forehead. 'My sister was supposed to be here too, a big sibling get-together but . . . Well, she's seven months pregnant . . .'

'Didn't she want to fly?'

The frown on his face didn't let up. 'No, it wasn't the flying – she'd have been fine to fly. It was that bloody husband of hers. They were both supposed to be here, that is until Ellie discovered he was having an affair.' His face clouded further. 'She's devastated, obviously. Couldn't face the trip out. So she stayed at home with our parents.'

'Oh, Gull. I'm so sorry.'

He pulled in a breath, his expression intense. 'How does somebody do that to someone they supposedly love? And what woman does that to another?'

'I don't know.' It had happened with alarming regularity in her own family, not that there was a great deal of similarity between her family and any family which operated in even a remotely functional manner. Her experiences felt like they had little relevance in the face of the level of emotion Gull was displaying.

His voice softened. 'Ignore me. You don't want to hear about my family dramas. She'll work it out. She'll have to.'

'But she's got you to turn to for support?' Tania asked. He nodded. 'Then she's luckier than some.'

'I suppose. She can always rely on me, and David. We've told her we'll happily go round and break Harry's legs if it'll help.'

'And you're joking, now, I presume?' Tania said.

79

The frown gave way to a grin. 'It's almost completely a joke. Ninety-nine per cent, anyway.'

Tania sipped her tea, allowing the last of his tension to ease, then said, 'I take it you've been skiing for a while?'

'Fifteen years or so now, I suppose. It fits in well with work, and the mountains are always stunning. You?'

'Forever. I love it.' She smiled, considering whether she might move closer to him, maybe take a seat on the other sofa while they waited.

A hammering on the lodge door interrupted her plans.

Gull sighed and shifted to the edge of the sofa. 'That'll be my transport. He said he wouldn't be long.'

'I'll go down and open the door.' Tania headed for the stairs. Having him here had been a mistake. It was stirring too many feelings inside her.

'Wait.' Gull climbed to his feet, testing his leg with a frown. He reached down and pulled up his ski trousers. 'I don't want this to be it.' He looked as if his words made him feel more uncomfortable than his injured knee.

Tania hesitated at the top of the steps; she had to admit she didn't either. 'Well, as we had to forgo our race, how about we find some other way to decide who should buy the drinks?'

He frowned. 'What did you have in mind?'

Pulling a euro from her pocket, she said, 'Winner buys. Heads or tails?'

'OK. Tails.'

Flipping the coin, she caught it and slapped her free hand over it before he could look. 'Heads,' she said, pocketing the coin.

'Hang on, that's not fair. I didn't see it.'

'Are you questioning my integrity?'

He huffed a laugh. 'No, I'm questioning your overwhelming desire to win.'

'Do you want to see me again, or not?' She folded her arms in mock defiance.

'Does this mean you're going to be buying the drinks?'
He hobbled closer.

'Are you trying to pull the "poor injured skier" card?'
Tilting her head, she glanced at his knee.

'No, Tania.' The intensity of his expression was inescapable.
'I'm trying to pull you.'

'I know you are.' She left the words hanging and headed
down the stairs.

Clara was surprised to find Tania's skiing equipment already
at the lodge when she returned. Rose and Madeleine had
opted to stay in Près du Ciel centre for a drink at one of the
many restaurants before heading back, while Clara decided
she would take the bubble and ski back to the lodge on her
own.

Still flushed from the final run back, she left all her gear
in the boot room, wondering idly why there was so much
water on the floor, before climbing the stairs to the living area.

Tom was busy topping and tailing green beans when she
headed for the kettle.

'Can I make you something?' he said.

'I can do it,' she said. 'I'm just going to have some tea.'

'Go and sit down,' he said. 'Let me do it.'

'What are we having for supper tonight?' she asked.

'You're starting with a fresh tomato soup, then the main
is grilled hake with dauphinoise potatoes. Then lemon tart
for dessert.'

'Sounds fantastic. And do we get a mystery cheese today,
too?'

Grinning, he knocked the side of his nose with a finger.
'That would be telling, now wouldn't it? A man's got to
preserve a little of his mystique, hasn't he?' He looked at
her for a moment, a frown momentarily crossing his face
as if he were making a decision. Then he headed across the
kitchen and returned with a sliver of cheese. He held it out
for her to take.

She sampled it. 'Mmm, that's nice. What is it?'

'It's called Comte.'

'That will be perfect for our cheese adventure,' she said.

'Cheese adventure. I like that.'

'Well don't tell me anything else about it,' she said. 'I want it to be a surprise.'

'No problem,' he said.

'Is Tania around?'

'I'm not sure,' he said. 'I haven't seen her.'

Clara frowned. Tania's skis and helmet were here, so she must have returned at some point. Perhaps she was just resting in her room. Perhaps she was in her room, but wasn't resting . . . But there had been no sign of any strange skis in the locker, or boots in the boot room, no sign that anyone else was here. No sign that hot tub guy was here. Clara knew Tania was no angel, that a casual fling with a stranger wasn't outside the realms of possibility, but she also knew that the whole experience with Rory Flannagan had caught her friend up short.

Clara hoped that particular lesson would be well learned. She wanted Tania to find someone special. Someone who deserved her. Someone who would love her bright, vivacious, kind friend for those qualities alone. Someone who would be strong enough to navigate Tania's family without being swallowed up by their hype. Not just some silly Christmas fling with someone who would fill her brain and her bed for a few days but would ultimately use her identity for his own benefit.

Clara wanted her to find someone who meant as much to Tania as Mike meant to her.

The day she'd met Mike, Clara was in the supermarket. The confectionary aisle, to be precise. In a world of her own, she was searching the lines of sweets for a packet of jelly babies. Her hand closed around the final packet on the shelf and she straightened up to come face to face with a blond man, whose gaze was fixed on her packet of sweets.

Turned out his mother also loved them, and that he was on his way to visit her as she recovered from an operation in the local hospital.

It spiked at her that he still had his mother, his obvious love mixed with concern for her clear in his eyes. She'd lost her own a number of years before and was in the process of losing her father to Alzheimer's. Clara ended up letting him have the packet, and shortly afterwards, when he surprised her with a bag containing nothing but her favourite orange babies as a thank you, she let him have her heart, too.

To say that everything had been perfect from that day forwards wouldn't be strictly true, like all relationships there had been challenges. But nothing had overwhelmed them or ripped them apart and with Poppy they'd completed their family. Noisy and laughing and messy and fun, the three of them a strong, impenetrable bubble that had given Clara a taste of how she'd always wanted her life to be. Vibrant and alive and very different to the quiet solitude and dusty hallways of her own childhood, with her invalid mother (now long gone) and aged father (who no longer recognised her when she visited him in the residential home) and their constant requests for her to be seen and not heard.

She knew she would never stop loving Mike even though he was gone. She didn't think she ever could. And she wanted that feeling for Tania – without Tania ever having to experience the crushing sense of desolation which had accompanied Clara's loss.

She sighed; she could feel that the spiralling blackness was back, creeping with long, gnarled fingers into the forefront of her brain. Squeezing tighter and tighter until she could think of nothing else but that void. Tom was looking at her strangely, it took her a moment to realise that what she'd thought was a sigh had in reality been a groan.

'Are you OK?' he said.

She sucked in a big breath. 'I'm fine. Listen, forget the tea, I think I might open a bottle of something. What's in the fridge?'

Chapter 12

Rose would happily have stayed in Près du Ciel centre all evening. Mostly because she was enjoying a bit of relaxed time with Madeleine, and because the atmosphere outside the little café/bar they'd settled at was fun. Part of her, though, also wanted to be where Lysander wasn't, and chances were he'd be back at Snow Pine Lodge by now.

But it was clear Madeleine was ready to head back. The exertions of the past couple of days on the snow had taken their toll. She yawned, tried to hide it with the back of her hand and then apologised.

'Poke me with a fork,' Madeleine said. 'Because I'm done.'

Rose grinned. 'We can take the bus and walk the last bit back if you like,' she said. 'Or we can take the bubble to the first station and ski back.' She checked her watch. 'It'll take about twenty minutes either way.'

Madeleine weighed up her options. 'More skiing versus carrying skis. Hmmm.'

'If we take the bubble, there's a lovely blue run which twists gently back to the lodge. It's really easy.'

'At this stage in the game,' Madeleine said, 'easy is the only option I'm prepared to consider. Can we do that?'

Twenty minutes later, Rose sighted the post to indicate the cut-through to Snow Pine Lodge and pointed it out. Madeleine snowploughed to get her skis under control and followed. They slid as far along the track as their momentum allowed, then walked their skis the rest of the way.

'My thighs are literally on fire,' Madeleine said, unclipping her boots. 'I'm so glad we're back.'

Rose frowned but said nothing, hoping beyond hope Lysander wasn't there. She didn't want to have to deal with him, didn't have the first clue what to say. Having run away from the situation last night, the relief had been palpable when she realised he'd already gone by the time she emerged from her room this morning. But it was unlikely she could avoid him completely.

Not for the first time, Rose found herself wishing she were braver. Wishing she could approach her life like Madeleine did, with a casual openness that belied her determination to remain true to herself and her feelings. It occurred to Rose that her own timidity, her desire to fit in, to not make waves, had caused her to waste so much time.

Her relationship with Lysander all those years ago had simply been the starting place for her own crippling self-doubts. And their continued sporadic contact, his occasional messages and sometimes downright nosiness about what Tania was up to; her inability to truly leave him behind and still be friends with Tania – just seemed to magnify her insecurities. But recognising shortcomings was one thing; doing something about them was quite another.

She could imagine Madeleine fronting up to an adversary without too much trouble, and Tania never took any nonsense from anybody. Even Clara – quiet and thoughtful Clara – was nobody's fool. Rose wished she had their confidence.

But Rose had never managed to find the courage to properly confront Lysander about anything, let alone something as delicate as his relationship with his sister. Part of her remained keen to hide away from it. After all, it wasn't really any of her business. Tania had always managed to take care of herself. Had a lifetime of dealing with the backstabbing nature of her family. She didn't need any help from Rose. And for her part, Rose had become increasingly careful around Lysander. It was part of the reason why she hadn't replied to his latest message – in case she unwittingly told him something she shouldn't.

And this week certainly wasn't the right time for any kind of major revelation, for Clara's sake if nobody else's. They were here to support and spend uncomplicated time with Clara, not untangle years of sibling rivalry. Nor were they here to broach the subject of Rose and Madeleine's relationship status, however happy Madeleine might be to take that step.

Although Madeleine hadn't seemed to mind when Rose requested an under-the-radar approach to their relationship for this holiday, it didn't seem fair to her. It wasn't as if they had been together for long, and – unlike Lysander – Madeleine never demanded anything that Rose wasn't willing to give. Nevertheless, Rose had decided it would be easier all round to keep the status quo. Before they'd left the UK, she had told Madeleine she was doing it for Clara's sake. That after what had happened, the last thing Clara needed was a new couple shoving their happiness in her face.

Rose's frown deepened. Was it really for Clara's benefit? Or was it more deeply embedded in the response she might receive from her oldest friends. It was strange, because none of them had ever expressed homophobic attitudes. But even though Rose knew this, the void between that knowledge and actually telling them remained crevasse-deep, and impossibly wide. It made no sense, but it was Rose's reality. It was how she felt.

It was beginning to dawn on Rose that it might have been better to have found a way to get it into the light right at the start, when she first started seeing Madeleine. Or to have been open about things before this trip, or as soon as they arrived. Either way, now Lysander had added himself to the mix, things had become way too complicated for Rose's tastes. The crevasse creaked and became ever wider, and even deeper.

'If your thighs are on fire,' Rose said, tuning out her thoughts and focusing on Madeleine, 'then it's definitely time to try the hot tub.'

Madeleine pulled a face.

'No, seriously, you'll love it. There's nothing like it to ease sore muscles.'

'Talking of hot tubs,' Madeleine said, gesturing towards a figure approaching the lodge in the opposite direction. It was Tania, still in her ski trousers and jacket, but with snow boots and a woolly hat instead of ski gear. With her hands pushed way down in her pockets, she looked deep in thought, though her expression brightened when she saw them.

'Did you have a good afternoon?' she asked.

'Yes, thanks. What happened to you?' Rose said. 'How come you're not still out skiing?'

'Gull took a bit of a fall, so it rather cut the afternoon short.'

'Gull?'

Madeleine poked her with an elbow. 'Hot tub guy.' She looked at Tania. 'At least, I presume that's who you mean?'

Tania nodded. So much had happened in the last few hours that she'd forgotten the others didn't even know his name. She bit her lip; she hadn't even texted them to let them know she was back at Snow Pine Lodge.

'Is he badly hurt?' Madeleine asked.

'Twisted his knee, but he'll be fine.' Tania noticed the frown creasing Rose's forehead. 'I know, I'm sorry. I should have let you know what was going on. It's just that . . .'

Tania wasn't sure how to complete the sentence. It was the reason she'd taken herself off for a walk. To give herself a chance to think about the fact that she'd arranged to meet Gull in Près du Ciel centre, that they'd settled on meeting for lunch, the following day, after she'd told him she wasn't interested in another evening encounter ending in a clumsy proposition. They just about managed to agree on where to meet, but the verbal sparring had continued right up until the driver slid the minivan door closed on Gull and they drove away. It wasn't until the van crunched over the icy kerb and disappeared around a corner, and she'd thought of the perfect comeback to his parting comment but was too late to say it, that she felt it. Again. That invisible pull in the direction the van had taken. In his direction.

She'd dated plenty of men, but Tania had always promised herself she would never fall in love. She was determined to remain in control of her emotions, in control of how she allowed other people to treat her, how she allowed them to make her feel. She had her reasons.

Her mother had fallen in love – in fact, her mother was still in love – with her father, and Tania's whole life was testament to how that had turned out. Even though she had been thrown over for another woman, Tania's mother remained loyal to her ex-husband. Strange and skewed family dynamics were the norm in Tania's formative years, with her mother taking any crumb Anthony was willing to drop from his table. Being trotted out alongside Lysander, like a show pony, whenever the red-carpet event required a family bias, she learned early what 'smile for the cameras' really meant as Lysander secretly pinched and twisted at her skin with hard fingers if she dared stand in front of him. Second wife Brigitte turned a pitying, but essentially blind eye to what was going on, choosing to play the role of the perfect Hollywood wife.

Too much of Tania's childhood had been spent listening to her mother cry, when she thought nobody was around, or enduring her mother's list of excuses for her father's behaviour. So, Tania had determined she would never allow herself to love someone deeply enough for them to make her feel the way her mother did about her father. No way was she going to end up like her. Desperately clinging to what had been, but which never would be again.

And so far, she never had. Tania had learned to enjoy men, to enjoy their company, but she'd never taken the next step. She'd never allowed any of them to get under her skin, not properly.

She wasn't about to change her ways now, either. All she needed to do was decide how far she was going to let this thing with Gull go. On a physical level, at least. There was no point denying that the irritation she'd felt initially had given way to a certain level of attraction. He had managed to pique her interest, even though she knew next to nothing about him, and that was interesting in itself. She would just have to ignore the unfamiliar and rather unsettling way the base of her stomach drew attention to itself whenever he was around and enjoy the next few days.

The feeling was probably nothing more than something to do with the lodge chef's cooking anyway, she thought.

'It's just that . . . what?' Rose said.

Tania considered what to say, then settled on, 'It's just that I lost track of time. I'm sorry.' She looked around. 'Where's Clara?'

'She headed back a while ago,' Rose said. 'Haven't you seen her?'

Shaking her head, Tania turned towards the lodge.

'Is he here?' Rose asked.

For a moment Tania thought she was talking about Gull, but the tautness around her lips and the fidgeting of her fingers made it clear that Rose was referring to Lysander. He might only be Tania's half-brother, but he'd always taken a whole and complete delight in treading on the metaphorical backs of Tania's shoes, tripping her up in so many ways through the years. He loved to stir up a bit of drama. And there was no doubt it was a classic Lysander move for him to turn up at the lodge, knowing full well who would be there. Knowing that Rose would be there, and he could pick at that scab all over again.

'He wasn't when I got back this afternoon,' she said. 'A car came for him early this morning and he muttered something about the torture of wardrobe choices for whatever shoot he's doing. I wasn't really listening, but I got the impression that he was going to be gone a while.'

Rose nodded. She said nothing more, but she didn't really need to. Her whole demeanour shouted her feelings loudly enough to negate the need for any words.

Tania could feel Rose's discomfort, but she said nothing and began to trudge towards the lodge. She couldn't control what Lysander did any more than she could control the weather, all she could do was try to mitigate the situation until he got bored and moved on. She'd learned a long time ago that she had little – actually, make that no – control over her brother's behaviour.

There was music playing in the living area, the bass notes audible from the boot room, the rest of it undiscernible until they'd climbed the sets of stairs. Tom stood in the kitchen, mixing something in a bowl. He looked up and nodded in greeting.

Coldplay. That was the music playing from the speakers embedded in the wooden walls. Tania looked around, her mouth going dry. 'Where's Clara?' she said, swinging back towards Tom.

He gestured towards a barrel chair, turned towards the window. 'She's over there.'

Coldplay had been Mike's favourite band.

Tania headed for the chair, finding Clara wrapped in one of the fur throws, her fingers tight and white around an empty glass, her expression blank, eyes open but blind to the view they were fixed on.

'Tom?' Tania said. 'Will you change the music, please.'

'Certainly. What to?'

'Anything. Anything else.'

'No,' Clara said, her voice brittle as dry twigs. 'I want this.'

Rose appeared the other side of the chair, her face creasing into a frown. 'Maddy's making some tea, Clara. Do you want a cup? Something to eat?' She reached for the glass, but Clara clung on to it.

Tania looked across to where Tom and Madeleine stood on

opposite sides of the kitchen counter, both wearing confused expressions. 'Tom. Change the music. Now.'

'Stop treating me like I'm a child.' Standing abruptly, Clara hurled the glass against the wall, letting out a sound that was part scream, part wail. The shattered pieces glittered momentarily in the lights from the little Christmas tree before they cascaded onto the floor. She hitched another breath then turned and headed downstairs, her bedroom door slamming moments later.

Tania looked at Rose. Perhaps she had been naive to believe that she could help Clara, that something as simple as bringing her to the mountains would provide anything more than a momentary distraction from her grief. Perhaps Tania had bitten off more than she could chew this time.

Chapter 13

Clara slammed the door as hard as she could. Then she slammed her fists into the wood, squealing in pain as the cut on her hand reopened under the bandage.

They didn't understand. Nobody understood. People told her she would get over it, that she would move forwards, that the pain would go away. That with time, her grief would lessen, and she would be able to pick up her life again.

The logical part of her brain told her that her friends were only trying to help her. People survived losing loved ones every day, and life appeared to be carrying on, regardless of whether or not she wanted it to.

But she was firm in certain respects. In ways that they didn't seem able to understand.

She didn't *want* to get over the loss, she didn't want Mike and Poppy to fade into the background, or to avoid Mike's favourite music. She didn't want the pain to go away. She didn't even deserve for that to happen. And Tania and Rose would agree with her if they knew all of it.

Somehow it made their sympathy and their concern even harder to accept. She'd never found a way to tell them the complete truth about the day of the accident. And as the months had passed, it had only become harder.

The last thing she wanted to do was to move forwards if that meant leaving Mike and Poppy behind. She wanted them to remain front and centre in her brain, for the rest of her life. She couldn't bear the thought that they would become nothing more than shadows, names that people mentioned every now and again and then felt guilty about having done so.

Clara settled on the edge of her bed, then curled up against the pillow and pressed her mobile against her ear. Maybe she would listen to his message. Just once. She slid her damaged hand beneath the pillow and closed her eyes as she listened to his voice.

It didn't take Madeleine long to pack up her clothes. She wasn't quite sure what to do when Clara stormed off. Tania and Rose both looked a bit shell-shocked and Tom turned the music off completely which only added to the awkwardness of the atmosphere.

When she suggested it might be a good time to shift her stuff, Rose had agreed, albeit with a distracted smile.

A few minutes to herself wouldn't hurt, she thought as she shoved her things into her suitcase and then stood deciding where to put her toothbrush in Rose's little bathroom. She'd imagined the drama for the week was going to consist of struggling to make herself understood in her pidgin French, or spending more time sliding down the slopes on her rear end than on skis. She'd done her best to bury the niggling concern she'd felt when Rose's features had closed down and she'd suggested they might not tell the others about the extent of their relationship. Told herself the holiday would be the perfect way to find out more about Rose and being a part of her life without any of the accompanying scrutiny the full disclosure of their relationship would bring.

Although Rose had outlined what had happened to Clara's family and Madeleine had been shocked by the tragedy of it, she hadn't been prepared for the force of Clara's outburst, the sheer intensity of the emotion she'd just witnessed. She hadn't been sure what to expect, truth be told. But Clara was clearly existing on a knife-edge.

Madeleine puffed out her cheeks. Her aching muscles and franglais seemed rather insignificant against the backdrop of the environment she found herself inhabiting.

Her frame of reference for the death of loved ones was a

little sketchy, if she were being honest. Grandpa Murray and Granny Helen had both passed away before Madeleine had reached double digits in age; she remembered their names and that Granny Helen had been keen on knitting – and gin – but that was as far as her memories stretched. Her mother's father, 'Grumpy Ken', had died a couple of years previously, after a long fight with prostate cancer. Madeleine remembered how sad she had felt, how difficult the last few visits to the hospice had been and how little she'd wanted to be in the crematorium for the service. But Grumpy Ken had been well over eighty. He'd lived a full life, he'd seen his children grow up and produce grandchildren, he'd been a lifelong supporter of the Reds. A devoted darts player in his local pub, at least while he could still see the board well enough to aim.

People were sad at his funeral, of course they were. But the sadness was tinged with the feeling that this was the natural order, that it would have been nice for him to have eked out a few more years but that his death was ultimately acceptable.

It was difficult to even imagine what it must be like to have lost someone in the prime of their life, like Mike. Someone you'd given your heart to. And she was in no doubt that she didn't have the faintest clue what it would feel like to ride the express train of grief which must accompany the loss of a child.

Rose had told her how Mike and Poppy had been caught in a massive pile-up on a dual carriageway when an articulated lorry hammering along the fast lane had suffered a tyre blow-out. How Clara had been waiting for them at home. How she waited for them to return, completely oblivious to the fact that they never would until the police came to her door.

It was unthinkable.

And the noise Clara had made when she threw the glass? There weren't words to describe it. Like the screaming of a wounded animal, trapped and beginning to understand that it wouldn't ever get free, that things would never be right again. Madeleine felt her eyes fill with tears. She barely knew Clara, only knew as much about her situation as Rose had told her, but it was impossible to remain immune to her pain when it was laid so bare. She gripped the edge of the sink and hung on to it for a while, closing her eyes as tears dripped into the ceramic bowl.

After a while, she wiped her eyes, shoving her toothbrush into the spare glass beside the sink. She would unpack later. Her bag could stay down beside the spare bed for now.

Checking her reflection in the bathroom mirror, she headed back along the corridor. Clara's door was firmly closed and she lingered outside, unsure why – she didn't intend to knock on the door, or intrude. She had no idea what she would say, anyway.

Upstairs, Rose was sitting at the dining table, resting her chin on her hand. Tania stared through the picture window. With her hands on her hips, she appeared to be taking in the view, but her shoulders were jacked up tight.

'I don't know how to help her,' she said.

'You can't magic it better, Tania,' Rose said, smiling thinly at Madeleine as she took a seat at the table.

'She doesn't deserve to have to go through this, though. Does she?' Tania swung round and looked at Rose, her face tight with concern.

'No. She doesn't.'

'So, what do we do?'

'Be here for her. That's all we can do.'

Tania pulled in a breath. 'But what if that isn't enough?'

Tania wished she'd taken Gull's mobile number. She was beginning to think they should hunker down in the lodge with Clara for the remainder of the week. There was no way Clara was going to cope with Christmas Day at this rate. Tania's grand plans of skiing with her friends in the morning, then enjoying a lazy afternoon eating seasonal food and opening a few gifts were spiralling into nothing more than working out how to survive the day.

There was no way she could meet Gull for lunch the following day. She should have taken his number, so she could phone and cancel, but she hadn't. Part of her obstinance, her insistence that her attraction to him was nothing more than a passing infatuation, that there would be no reason to want his number. That there was only one thing they wanted from one another.

It didn't matter. Her priority was Clara, it had to be. Especially after this afternoon. Wrapping her hands around herself, she stared out of the window again. She'd thought Clara was doing OK, had hoped that bringing her back to the mountains would begin to show Clara that the world was still turning, that it was ready for her – whenever she felt ready for it. She'd been so conceited about her plan that she'd persuaded herself that the mountain had worked a little of its magic. She'd taken her eye off the ball, become distracted by Gull, and that wouldn't do.

'I'm not sure what you want to do,' Tom said, his voice quiet. 'I can hold dinner if you'd prefer?'

While Tania had been studying the view, Tom must have cleared the tea things and laid the table for supper. She hadn't even noticed how much time had passed.

'I didn't realise,' he said. 'She just asked me to put the music on. I didn't realise . . .'

Rose looked at Tania, the pinch between her eyes telegraphing that it was time to let Tom have a little more information. She was right, it wasn't as if it was a secret.

'It's not your fault,' she said to him. 'The thing is, Clara recently lost some people who were close to her. Very close.'

'Her husband,' Rose said. 'Her daughter.' The last word caught in Rose's throat as she said it, forcing Tania to turn towards the window again to get control of herself.

'Oh, my God,' Tom said. 'I had no idea.'

'Car crash,' Rose said.

'Oh, my God,' he repeated. 'How old was her daughter?'

'Two.' Tania allowed the word out, then clamped her mouth closed again. Why had she thought coming skiing would be a suitable distraction for a grieving mother? She was an imbecile.

'Jesus Christ,' Tom said.

Tania shook her head. She couldn't say anything else without crying. The lodge door opened, then slammed shut. Heavy footsteps on the stairs became an unkempt blond head of hair which then turned into Donkey. He looked around the room, his perfect features taking in their expressions.

'Did somebody die?' he said.

Chapter 14

Having outlined what had just happened with Clara and the glass, Tania was incensed by her brother's flippant reply. She couldn't believe her ears. 'I dare you to say that again,' she said, through clenched teeth.

'What?' Lysander stood his ground at the top of the stairs. He looked genuinely mystified. 'He died months ago. Awful, I get that. I just said that she's a beautiful woman, she'll find someone else, no problem.' He barrelled on. 'It's terribly sad about the little girl. No question. Of course.'

It was all Tania could do not to run across and shove him down the stairs. 'You need to shut the fuck up, Lysander. I can't believe what I'm hearing.'

'What?' he repeated. 'You wanted me to say it again.'

'I've always known you're terminally shallow, but this . . . Even for you this is shitty beyond belief.'

'I didn't mean . . . Maybe it didn't come out right. I just meant that she's young enough to find someone new, in time. When she's ready. It's not like she's some plump middle-aged matron. She's got everything to look forward for.'

'Not quite everything,' Rose said quietly, her brows furrowed together.

Lysander looked around, maybe absorbing the horrified expressions properly for the first time. His lips lost a little of the upwards inclination which formed the trademark Lysander smile. An expression which Tania had come to accept as summing him up. Only ever the creeping edge of a smile, as if he couldn't even be bothered to put much effort into something as simple as expressing happiness. As if it was too much trouble for him to show others how he felt, as if it were possibly someone else's job and he was waiting for that someone to appear and airbrush his feelings in. The Donkey's smile, a smile which seemed to have completely overwhelmed his true smile – or any real display of emotion – something Tania hadn't seen more than a handful of times in years.

He studied Rose's face, the smile fading further as his shoulders dropped. 'No. I suppose not. OK. I get it.'

Tania snorted in disgust, turning back to the view.

'I'm not sure you do, Lysander.' It was Rose's voice, clear and firm. 'I'm not sure any of us can, not properly.'

He sighed. Tania could hear it from her position near the window, and she watched his reflection as he crossed the room and took a seat alongside Madeleine, opposite Rose.

'Believe it or not,' he said, 'I was trying to be positive. About Clara, I mean.'

'Yes, well, that kind of positive we can do without,' Tania said, keeping her eyes on the view. The last of the sun's rays had long since dipped behind the mountains, the remnants of the light a thin navy-blue mountain outline gently turning black. She watched as the lights of some piste bashers came into view crawling up the slopes, the massive machines beginning the night's work of grooming the snow in preparation for the following day. 'Might I suggest you try applying a filter before you next open your mouth?'

'Sorry to interrupt, but shall I serve the canapés?' Tom asked a while later, breaking the awkward silence which had enveloped the room.

Tania turned. Tom stood with a tea towel twisted in his hand, looking at her for guidance.

'Or would you rather not—'

He didn't get to finish his sentence, the sound of more footsteps on the stairs had them all looking in that direction.

'Canapés definitely get my vote.' Clara followed her words into the room, a smile edged with her favourite plum lipstick danced across her face. She looked at them all, in turn. 'I apologise for earlier,' she said. The smile slipped a little, a crease appearing between her eyes. 'This whole thing is . . . complex. I can't seem to get a grip on the way I feel. I'm so sorry.' Then she looked at Tom, her expression brightening a little. 'Something smells delicious.'

Tania wanted to wrap her up in a hug and tell her it was fine for her to scream and shout and throw things all she liked, just so long as it meant she was somehow coming to terms with losing Mike and Poppy. She didn't. Instead, she smiled and joined the others at the table.

By the time they reached dessert – a lemon tart with enough of a citrus tang to ensure most of their plates had been scraped clean within minutes – it felt to Madeleine as if everyone had managed to relax into the evening. It was as if Clara had flicked a switch. Her anguish from earlier seemed to be shut away in a box, for a while at least.

If anyone was having trouble relaxing, it was Madeleine herself. Being sat thigh to thigh with a world-renowned model whose cheekbones and jawline looked even better from her side-on view was making it a little difficult to relax. The others might think he was a bit of a prat, but he was still a famous prat who was monumentally easy to look at. And he smelled really good, too. Like fresh wood shavings mixed with orange peel.

'Do you enjoy skiing?' she asked him.

'Sure,' he said, looking at her from the corner of an eye. 'But the agency won't let me, not when I'm under contract. Plaster casts don't look particularly good on camera.' He grinned.

'Why are they doing a shoot so close to Christmas?' Tania said.

'Don't ask me. Bloody ridiculous. But they didn't bat an eyelid when I said I'd only do it if they chartered a flight. Plus, I said I wanted to visit the lodge, so they sorted the transport to get me here and back.' Lifting his glass, he glanced at Madeleine again. 'I haven't been here for a couple of years, you see. I've missed the old heap.'

Tania snorted a laugh. 'Yeah, right.'

Lysander frowned. 'No, really. I have missed this place. You're always so negative, Tits. Especially about me.'

His eyebrows knitted together. Or at least they would have done, Madeleine thought, if they weren't shaped to perfection. And maybe he had a point. He'd gone out of his way, throughout the meal, to chat to Clara and although he hadn't directly talked about her situation, Madeleine felt that there was a subtle positivity to his conversation that Clara seemed to appreciate. He certainly hadn't been the self-absorbed, self-obsessed 'look-at-me' she'd been bracing herself for.

'Anyway,' he said, 'I'm out of here tomorrow for a couple of nights. Then you can bitch about me all you like.'

'Oh,' Madeleine said. 'Are you only staying one more night?'

'That's right. I'll be back Christmas Eve.'

'It's just that I moved my stuff out of the ground-floor bedroom,' she said. 'So that you could have it if you wanted? After you said this morning that you didn't sleep very well on the sofa, I thought . . .'

He turned towards her, bodily shifted in his seat until he faced her, the frown replaced by a smile different to any she'd seen in the magazine photos of him. A smile that went all the way up to his eyes. 'You did that for me?' He seemed genuinely surprised.

'Yes.' She flicked a glance at Rose, who was watching her carefully, then turned back to Lysander. 'It's no problem.'

'See,' he said to Tania. 'Not everyone is as selfish as you are.'

'Yeah, well, she doesn't know you like I do, Donkey.'

He switched his attention back to Madeleine. 'You are an angel, thank you.' He grinned at her. 'I owe you one.' Then the grin slid from his face. 'So, where are you going to sleep?'

'I'm going to share with Rose. There's a spare bed in her room.' Although she wasn't particularly adept at subterfuge, she felt she did a good job of keeping her voice level. It must have worked, because when she shot a look at Rose, she was rewarded with a grateful smile.

His brows furrowed together again. 'Oh. Right.' Standing abruptly, he grabbed his glass, and took himself across to the window. 'Yes.'

Tom cleared the plates and slid a cheeseboard onto the table, taking orders for coffee, but Madeleine paid no attention. The window acted like a monochrome mirror, with the darkness outside and the brightness of the lights inside the room. She watched as Lysander's expression flexed and changed, he finished his drink and put down the glass, he stood with his hands on his hips, then folded them across his chest, before he settled for one hand in the other, a thumb working on the opposite palm.

He turned back towards the table as abruptly as he'd left it, his gaze on Rose. But before he could speak, she was on her feet, heading for the staircase.

'I'm going to get a bit of fresh air,' she said, as she disappeared from view. 'Have a wander outside on my own. See you all later.'

Chapter 15

Rose frowned at the length of time it took her to lace up her snow boots. She zipped up her coat and pulled on her gloves. Almost sprinting from the building, she was out of the pool of light spooling from the security light and crunching her way down the icy drive like there was a wolf on her tail.

Behind her, she heard the slam of the lodge's door. Expecting it to be Madeleine, she sighed in frustration when Lysander's long stride brought him into view. Exactly who she didn't want to be alone with.

She might have wanted an opportunity to talk to him at some point, but not now. Not like this. She wasn't prepared, hadn't worked out what to say.

'Rose. Wait up.'

She slowed, watching the ice crystals from her breath spiral away from her.

'Have I done something to upset you?'

However much Rose wanted to tell him that in order for someone to upset you, you first had to care about them, she knew she wouldn't get the words out straight. 'No. Not recently, Lysander. Why?'

'Why didn't you reply to my text?'

'I've been busy. I do have a life, you know.' And the casual question he'd texted about Tania's relationship status, coupled with what Rose knew about Rory Flannagan, had ensured her lack of response.

'Yeah. Sure you do.' He strode on down the drive. Did he expect her to follow, to comply with his wishes without any discussion? Rose thought she'd left all that behind.

'All right, I'm just going to come right out and ask. Is she involved in that mess with Rory Flannagan?'

'Why would you say that?' Rose could feel her cheeks colouring, hoping he couldn't see the burn in them.

'I know something's going on. The old man was all sorts of awkward when I asked him how the latest movie was shaping up. He positively squirmed when I asked if he'd seen Tits lately, if she'd watched any of the filming seeing as they were on location in London.'

Rose shrugged. 'I haven't heard anything.'

'You really are a terrible liar.' He shook his head and walked on. 'I know Tits gets through men fast, but I would have credited her with more taste. Rory Flannagan's ears stick out at least an inch on either side of his head, it's why he wears his hair so long. And he wears blocks in his shoes.' He turned, standing in Rose's path. She was expecting to see his trademark latent smile, the non-confrontational expression he wore to ease himself through life, but instead he looked genuinely concerned. It took Rose by surprise.

'Fill me in, Rose. Tell me what she thinks. Does she think it was me?'

'Lysander, I don't know what you're asking. Does Tania think you've done what, exactly?'

'Tipped the paps off about Galactic Commander Robson's sidekick and his secret lover.'

Snow Pine Lodge enjoyed a secluded location, right at the top of the resort. Even though it was situated close to the pistes, which ran either side of the lodge, the everyday skier would have no idea that a building nestled within the trees which surrounded it. Termed 'ski-in, ski-out', which essentially meant you could put your skis on at the door and never need to take them off until you returned, it enjoyed the best of all worlds. The whole of Près du Ciel opened out below it.

Lysander was framed by a backdrop of snow-capped lodges and chalets which littered the hillside, icicles catching in the winter-season twinkling lights strung around many of them. Below that sat the sprawling subterranean complex of Près du Ciel centre, marked above ground by hotels, apartment blocks and eateries and hosting the base stations of many of the resort's bubble lifts. Even with an increasingly unsettled expression creasing his face and a woolly hat pulled haphazardly onto his head, Lysander still looked as though he'd just climbed from a stylist's chair. It was amazing what could be hidden behind a pretty exterior.

'Why do you care all of a sudden?' Rose said. She took a deep breath. 'It's not like it's the first time you've done something like that, is it?'

His expression darkened, his attempts at keeping the conversation light fell away as he grabbed at her arm and shook her. 'Just answer the fucking question for once, Rose. Does she think it was me?'

Stumbling back, Rose yanked her arm from his grasp. 'I don't know, OK? She hasn't said anything.'

'Because it wasn't. I need her to know it wasn't me. It's *important*, Rose.'

'I genuinely don't know. We're here for Clara. We were doing our best to leave all that crap behind for a week. Why don't you ask her yourself?'

'I see you're still the loyal little lapdog. She doesn't appreciate you, you know. She never has. But my sister knows an easy conquest when she sees one. You always were ridiculously grateful for the scraps she throws you.'

Lysander brushed past her, spinning her around before he strode away, heading back towards the lodge. Rose stayed still until the pool of security light illuminated the doorway. Once the building had swallowed Lysander and the door had slammed closed, Rose let out a tight breath and headed away, tucking trembling hands deep into pockets as she fled.

By the time Rose returned, most of the lights were off. Snow Pine Lodge looked peaceful. And Rose felt quieter, too. She'd walked and walked until her hands stopped shaking and she'd managed to shed the feeling of Lysander's hand grasping at her arm.

She punched in the door code and slipped inside, unlacing her boots and setting them quietly in the rack before she hung up her coat. Tiptoeing up the first flight of stairs, she wondered if Madeleine would already have fallen asleep. Unlikely, she thought. Although Madeleine hadn't followed her outside, she was probably reading, waiting for her return. Her fingers curled around the handle of her bedroom door, and she was about to turn it when she heard muffled voices coming from the upstairs living area. Whispers with harsh edges, barely contained and urgent, rising every now and again to an emphasised word. It was Tania and Lysander.

Frowning, Rose pushed at the bedroom door handle, then paused as she heard her name. She slid her fingers from the handle and slipped up the first few steps of the second staircase, then settled on a step where she could see the outlines of Tania and Lysander against the dying light of the wood burning stove, but she remained hidden in deep shadow.

'All I did was follow her outside, I had some questions for her.' Lysander's voice.

'Questions about what? She's been gone for ages. What exactly did you say to her?' Tania sounded exasperated.

'None of your business.'

'God, Lysander. You're such a dick. You need to stop upsetting my friends. They aren't here for your entertainment, whatever you may think.'

'Believe me, there's nothing entertaining about Rose.'

On the stairs, Rose tightened her arms around her knees, feeling a muscle tic in her cheek.

'So why can't you leave her alone? What did you want to find out this time?'

'What do you mean, "this time"?'

'Lysander, I'm not an idiot and nor are you. I know you try and wheedle information out of my friends. So, stop acting like you don't know what I'm talking about. Were you trying to get the latest details out of Rose? So you could tell your tame "staff writer" on whichever publication you've got in your pocket.' The exasperation was clear in Tania's voice.

'Latest details about what?'

'You tell me.'

Lysander huffed a sigh. 'If you must know, I wanted to know if you thought I'd given them the story on Rory Flannagan.'

'Did you?'

'No! That was the whole point of me asking her. It's important that you believe me.'

Tania didn't speak, instead she folded defensive arms across her body as Lysander fidgeted.

'You need to believe me,' he repeated.

'Do you understand how important this is?' she said.

'Of course I do, that's why I'm asking.'

'No. I don't mean whether or not I believe *you*, you donkey. This time it really matters. It's not just about you and me, and your ridiculous point scoring. This time the stakes are much higher for Rory and his wife. Lysander, there's a baby . . .'

There was a pause, time in which Rose became aware of her own breath, how loud it seemed as she watched the two siblings absorb what Tania had just said.

Eventually, he shook his head. 'It wasn't me. Genuinely wasn't. I swear.'

Another pause, punctuated by Tania drawing in a deep breath. She gave a single nod. 'So why *are* you here?' Her voice had softened, even if by only a fraction.

'I got offered a job. The pay is ridiculously good – good enough for me not to turn it down.'

'You said all that, but I don't buy it, Donkey. I know you, and I also know your work ethic. Or rather your lack of one. Why aren't you partying in LA, or even spending the holidays with Father and Brigitte? You never work if there's something more fun to do.'

Rose strained to hear, but Lysander didn't reply. The pause in the conversation was punctuated by a log popping and clunking in the burner, making Rose startle.

'I need the money.' Barely more than a whisper.

'You . . . you what?' Tania sounded incredulous. 'You were one of the highest grossing models in the world last year. What are you talking about?'

Another pause. 'I have some expensive habits.'

'Is it *that* out of control?' For the first time in the conversation, there was a hint of concern in Tania's voice.

Lysander cleared his throat. 'It does appear to be a rather slippery slope.'

Rose sighed, leaning against the banister. Lysander had started dabbling in drugs while they were all still at school. She remembered him being hysterically amused by the shape of a carved newel post at the base of a staircase after someone had smuggled in some dodgy mushrooms. He'd rolled his own spliffs, taken pills. Just experimenting, he said. Nothing heavy, nothing hard. He had it all under control, he'd said. Until he didn't, and he was pretending he could stop taking the cocaine whenever he wanted to.

'I've tried to cut down, but things are spiralling. And it's not just that. Money seems to have a way of doing a disappearing act on me.'

'What have you done with it all?' Tania's voice remained soft, and in the subdued light, Rose could see her reach out a hand, squeezing Lysander's arm.

'Oh, I don't know. Renting a penthouse suite in LA doesn't come cheap, nor do charter jets. Hiring restaurants for an evening out with friends is surprisingly costly. And the parties are expensive. Legendary though, I'll have you know . . .'

'I wouldn't know, Sander. You've never invited me.'

'Haven't I?' Lysander sounded unsure. 'I thought I had. Thought you'd just not bothered to reply. Anyway, it's all getting too much, it's getting away from me. Add to that the pressures I face . . . You have no idea.'

Tania pulled in a breath, the softness from a moment ago gone as she said, 'Can't Daddy Dearest bail you out?'

'The old man appears to have pulled up the drawbridge in that respect. Although I'm not sure it's all his doing. I think Mother might have finally had enough. I did call her a freeze-dried Barbie last time I saw her.'

'Freeze-dried Barbie?' Tania laughed. 'I like that.'

Lysander chuckled too, then said, 'Do you remember that year we were here, and she had that horrific pink shiny foil ski suit? The one with real fur at the collar and cuffs. Matching gloves?'

'Hard to forget.'

'Right. And she even wore a pink, furry hat made from the same material.'

'And you told her she looked like a dick.'

'I think my exact phrase was "an enormous penis".' Lysander grinned. 'I was thirteen, what did she expect?'

'It was a particularly awful outfit, but you were a particularly awful son back then.'

'And an awful brother, too?'

Tania shrugged. 'It wasn't great.'

'For what it's worth, I told the old man he should get one of your paintings for in here. Not that thing.' He waved a hand at the wall holding the picture window, and the new canvas. 'But apparently Mother had already chosen the artist she wanted to support.'

'Yeah. Why doesn't that surprise me?' Tania said. 'Brigitte's never been my biggest fan.'

'Do you know what *your* mother used to call me?' From the stairs, Rose saw Tania shake her head. Lysander continued, 'When nobody was around, she used to tell me I was nothing more than the product of a split condom. That I shouldn't even exist, and my father only pretended to love me because he was so far under the witch's control.'

'I didn't know that.'

'No. Well. If you ever wonder where you get your cold streak from . . .'

Tania sighed. 'So, what are you going to do?'

'I don't know.'

'You need to get some help.'

'You think?' Lysander's sarcasm was clear, even in his hushed tones. 'That's easier said than done, too.'

'Why? You find a rehab unit and book yourself in.'

'Yeah, and then I'll lose my contract. You know the company's attitude. It's one thing to use in private, nobody gives a shit about that, but it's quite another to sully the brand in the public arena. And I'm not as young as I used to be, plenty of younger models snapping at my heels. Plenty of people to replace me.' He took a step closer to Tania, pointing to the corner of an eye. 'I mean, just look at these lines.'

'Oh dear God, Donkey. There's nothing there.'

'You wouldn't understand. You can let yourself go as much as you like, your paintbrushes don't care.'

'Wow. Thanks.' The acid was back in Tania's voice. 'You could always go into acting.'

Rose felt her shoulders jack. Tania certainly knew which buttons to push to get a rise from her brother. Acting would be a natural progression for Lysander, especially with his family connections – except for one slight problem. He'd tested a few times for various roles and had never secured anything, had told her in an unguarded moment – when he was as high as a kite – that he was chronically under-gifted in the acting department. He'd laughed, told her how ironic he thought that was. But he wasn't laughing now.

'You always were a bitch. I don't know why I thought coming here was a good idea.' Lysander headed for the stairs, and Rose scuttled down the few steps she'd climbed and shot into her bedroom before he caught sight of her.

Madeleine was curled up under the thick duvet, a paperback in one hand, which she flapped down at Rose's abrupt arrival.

'You OK? You've been ages.'

'I'm fine. Sorry I've been so long.'

'Everything all right?'

'Everything's fine.' Rose wondered if her words sounded more convincing to Madeleine than they did to herself. 'How's the book?'

'Great plot, and the lead character has just worked out that her sister's husband's friend was in the right place at the right time to have been able to murder the vicar. So that's another suspect to add to the list.' She grinned as Rose raised her eyebrows. 'Yes, I know. It's ridiculously brilliant.'

Rose felt herself begin to relax, as she changed and slid under the covers. Everything was so straightforward when she was alone with Madeleine.

'Are you sure you're OK?' Madeleine said, setting the book aside. When Rose paused before she nodded, Madeleine slid across and hugged her. 'Tell me if you like?'

'Not tonight. Do you mind if we just go to sleep?'

In answer, Madeleine reached for the light switch and plunged the room into darkness.

Chapter 16

'Would it be outrageously childish to say I want to build a snowman?' Madeleine twisted under the covers until she could see Rose, pulling her duvet up until it wrapped everything up to her ears in the comfort of her own night-time warmth.

'What, right now?' Rose said, with a mouthful of foaming toothpaste. Checking her watch, she pulled the brush from her mouth, and disappeared momentarily to spit into the sink. 'It's seven in the morning, Maddy. Plus, it's still dark.'

Madeleine huffed, extracting her arms from the warm folds of bedding and squashing the covers either side of her body. 'Not right now. Obviously. I've got my lesson later, anyway. Need to conserve as much energy as possible for that.' She stretched her legs, then decided that wasn't such a good idea when her thighs executed the movement grudgingly and with the express desire to cause their owner the greatest of discomfort. She groaned. 'Someone sneaked in during the night and took my legs. They've left me with a couple of iron bars instead. Iron bars wrapped in barbed wire.' She retreated into a ball.

'You should have got into the hot tub last night,' Rose said. 'I told you it would help.'

'Well, the ideal opportunity didn't exactly present itself, did it?'

'No, I suppose not. See you in a minute,' Rose said, closing the bathroom door.

Madeleine was aware she was keeping the conversation fluffy, doing her best to float along the surface of whatever Lysander had said to Rose the previous evening. Rose had been tight-lipped when she finally came to bed and Madeleine hadn't pressed for details. Perhaps she was finally getting a handle on her nosey nature. Or perhaps it was more that she sensed that whatever their conversation had been about, it might take more than a five-minute pre-sleep chat to unpick. And that she needed to wait for Rose to initiate any discussion about it.

Right now, if she could wish for something for the day ahead, she decided it would be that nothing much happened. Nothing except for what she'd imagined was supposed to happen on a skiing holiday. Some skiing, if she must. Lots of admiring of wonderful views, preferably from one of the deckchairs she'd seen at the front of some of the mountain bars and restaurants, with a hot chocolate in one hand and a cinnamon swirl or similar in the other. The construction of a snow figure, complete with scarf and twigs of fir tree for arms.

What was the Chinese expression? *May you live in interesting times* – more of a curse, if you asked her. Living in uninteresting times had been challenging enough so far, she wasn't sure she wanted to step out fully into the blinding sunshine of this week's drama. Which was rather why she planned to make a snowman. There couldn't be any drama involved in doing that, surely?

Forcing her legs to cooperate with the challenging activity of getting out of bed, she rifled through her suitcase until she found the spare scarf she'd brought for this precise reason. Knitted for her a million years ago by her gran, it was a hotchpotch of different coloured squares and different stitches held together by a series of contrasting woollen threads winding through the edges of each of the squares. Folksy was a kind description of its rough and ready qualities. Made under the influence of a gin, or two, knowing Granny Helen.

But it had been made with love, and Madeleine had kept it in the same spirit.

She took it with her when they headed upstairs for breakfast. Was it only two days ago that Madeleine had revelled in the waft of cooking bacon which had filled the building? It seemed to be an everyday occurrence in this parallel universe. Maybe she'd slipped through a wormhole without noticing, like Commander Robson had done. Maybe she had discovered a whole new solar system, at the centre of which spun a sun made entirely of cooked bacon.

Shoving the scarf onto the edge of the table, she slid into her seat. It was strange how, even in a completely unfamiliar setting, she'd settled into taking the same chair at the table for every mealtime. Or perhaps it was more to do with the others already having occupied their favoured positions.

Tania looked at the scarf, bundled up at the far end of the table. 'What's that?'

'I thought I might make a snowman later today, it's an old scarf, for round its neck.'

Tania laughed. 'I don't think I've made a snowman in about fifteen years.'

Lysander sniffed. 'No. And if I remember correctly, you trashed the last one I made here. Kicked its head off and stamped on it.'

It didn't take Tania long to recall events, so Madeleine assumed it had been a memorable execution. 'Oh, yes. I remember,' Tania said, a smile creeping onto her face. 'Well, you were being a total dick, as usual.'

'Anyway—' Madeleine eyed the plate of perfectly crisped pieces of bacon as Tom slid it onto the table '—I thought I might have a go this afternoon, always presuming I survive my lesson.'

'Go for your life,' Lysander said. 'But make sure you don't liken it to the Ice Queen here.' He waved a hand at Tania. 'She didn't seem to appreciate my comparison.'

A knock at the lodge door had Lysander climbing to his

feet, grabbing a piece of bacon as he stood. 'Well, it's been an absolute blast,' he said, looking around the table. It was hard to tell if he was being sarcastic. But his gaze lingered on Tania, then Rose, his expression a fraction too serious. 'I'm out of here.' He reinstated the lazy half-smile Madeleine recognised as his trademark and bit the end from the bacon. Holding a hand up in farewell, he took the stairs two at a time, the blond tendrils of his hair bouncing as he disappeared.

Nobody said anything as doors banged and voices sounded, and an engine revved a little as Lysander's transport turned in the driveway and headed away.

'You OK?' Tania said, her eyes on Rose.

Rose nodded. 'You?'

Tania looked surprised by Rose's query, as if there could be no question of her being anything other than OK. 'Of course.'

Madeleine wasn't overly convinced by either of them, especially when Rose visibly took a deep breath, then forked a couple of rashers onto her plate. Something had been out of kilter the whole time Lysander had been at Snow Pine Lodge, but Madeleine had no idea why. Or why Rose had chosen not to include her in the loop.

It made her feel uncomfortable, worried her enough for a thought to pop into her brain. That perhaps the fine line between doing her best not to pry into Rose's past and being taken for a total patsy might lie closer than she had thought.

Rose took a slice of what Tom had called 'French toast', but which Madeleine had always thought of as eggy bread, then cut it into neat squares. She'd noticed how precise Rose was with her food. It was the same in her wardrobe, all her clothes folded neatly, her washbag orderly, her bed made with fierce precision. Everything folded away, hidden from view. Madeleine felt her eyebrows edge closer together. She knew Rose valued her privacy. That was fine. She was a naturally discreet person. But there was a difference between discretion and keeping secrets.

The atmosphere settled heavy over the breakfast table, like a dark cloud over a picnic, so Madeleine decided to go for her default setting. Flippancy. 'I suppose I could move back into the ground-floor bedroom again,' she said.

Rose looked across, confused. 'Really?'

'Mmm. I mean, that way I'll get to sleep in the same bed as the face of Ralph Lauren, won't I?' Madeleine waited to see Rose's expression change. Perhaps she was being unnecessarily insensitive, but she wanted to shake Rose up. 'I mean, clearly not at the same time as him, but I can just imagine people's faces when I tell them. All the straight women will be beside themselves with jealousy.'

'Not all of them,' Clara said, missing the emphasis contained within Madeleine's words. 'No offence, Tania, but your airbrushed little brother isn't everyone's cup of tea.'

Madeleine didn't listen to the rest of the conversation, instead she held Rose's eye with a fierceness she wanted Rose to feel.

A few hours later, Tania checked her watch and her mouth went dry. She should have met Gull fifteen minutes ago. They'd agreed to lunch at the pizzeria in the centre of Près du Ciel's concrete heartlands. Not the most exciting place in the resort but chosen in case Gull's knee injury proved to be worse than anticipated.

Currently, though, Tania was heading past the fun park. She pulled to a stop at the exit, to wait for Rose who was collecting Madeleine from her lesson. Clara slid to a stop beside her. They didn't say anything, but the smile on Clara's face was enough to let Tania know she'd made the right call. The thought that she had considered abandoning her friend in order to do something as inconsequential as to flirt with a stranger made her resolve even stronger.

The point of this week was to remind Clara that, even though she'd lost the two things most important in her life, she was still alive. She could still go forwards, she had to, and her friends were resolved to be with her every step of the way. Starting with sticking together to collect Madeleine from her lesson before having lunch as a group, as they'd arranged.

In comparison, meeting a man she barely knew to find out if she wanted to allow him to seduce her? She huffed a laugh. In her head it sounded even more pathetic than she'd thought it would. There was no doubt she liked Gull, he interested her. And the fact that she couldn't work out *why* he interested her made her even more curious.

Physically, he ticked boxes – he was big and solid and fit, fair enough. But in a line-up of the kind of men she usually went for, he wouldn't even figure in terms of looks. And yet, she wanted to look at him. She wanted to challenge him and butt heads with him and – actually – she wanted to find out what it would be like to argue with him. Properly argue, not the verbal sparring they'd tinkered with so far. She wondered what it would be like to completely lose her temper with him, to scream and shout and watch what his face did. Find out how he reacted. So much of Tania's life was spent buttoned up, making sure everything looked good. It had occurred to her that she wanted to know what it would be like to completely let loose, to express emotions at their most raw to someone like Gull and find out how they would react.

It was just a shame the timing was so wrong, because she needed to be present for Clara. As Rose and Madeleine came into view, she watched Clara giggle as Madeleine snow-ploughed and jinked and almost fell before she recovered her balance and slid to a stop in front of them. She watched the sense of achievement on Madeleine's face, and the grin on Rose's face as she watched Madeleine.

No, this was way more important. Her friends were more important than a random man. Her friends would be with her for the rest of her life, while a man? He would be a constant for a few days, months, years at best. And then he would be gone, in pursuit of someone younger, prettier, sexier.

It was a shame that she hadn't got to know Gull better, the pit in her stomach told her that much. But in the big scheme of things, it didn't really matter. How could it?

Chapter 17

'Maddy, if you don't get in the hot tub in the next five minutes,' Rose said, slipping her dressing gown over her swimming costume, 'then you are absolutely not allowed to complain about sore legs in the morning.'

Today had been Madeleine's biggest tally of hours on the snow by a long way. Plus, she'd spent most of them upright. In Rose's opinion she was doing exceptionally well, especially for a girl who said she could lay claim to being the least sporty individual ever, on a global platform.

Skiing took a lot longer than a few days for anyone to master.

Rose had started the sport shortly after becoming Tania's best friend. Being invited to the Harrington ski lodge as an impressionable twelve-year-old had been a daunting experience. She'd learned fast. And not just how to ski. She'd experienced Tania's family at close quarters. Tania's ethereal stepmother seemed oblivious to her stepdaughter, and by extension, also to Rose. She focused and lavished her attention on Lysander and demanded the same from her husband.

Rose remembered how she and Tania spent a lot of time at the extremities of the woodland which surrounded the property, perching on the edge of the world and looking at the view, rather than inhabiting the same space as Tania's stepfamily. Rose remembered how cold she had got, and how resolute Tania had been about staying outside for as long as possible. How Tania didn't seem to register the temperature, instead revelling in the freedom and the starlight, chatting endlessly about her hopes and dreams for the future. Her desire to paint, maybe even exhibit. Rose also remembered the way Tania clammed up the moment Lysander came within earshot.

The trouble with Lysander and Tania was that nothing was ever completely clear-cut. As teenagers they'd fought like rabid dogs about almost everything. Lysander's mother had done her best to catapult him ahead of Tania in everything they did. And yet, even though Rose remembered those family ski trips as emotionally taut, like a rubber band stretched so hard you didn't dare let go, and even though situations were manufactured in order for Lysander to continually gain the upper hand, somehow he still craved his sister's attention, her approval. Even though, when he got it, he treated it with disdain, treated her like a fool.

Once they were old enough, Tania started to visit Snow Pine Lodge with friends, rather than family. Rose was always invited, much to the delight of her father who seemed happy to live in the Harringtons' glow, if only by proxy. And Clara had joined the mix when she and Tania met at art school. The post-Harrington-family trips, as Rose dubbed them, were accompanied by an infinitely more relaxed Tania who was driven overwhelmingly by her love of careering as quickly as possible down mountains, and less by her confusion on how to maintain a foothold on the slippery slopes of her family dynamics.

Across the room, Madeleine huffed, then extracted a navy-blue ruched costume from her suitcase. She eyed the costume, then pulled a face at Rose. 'All right,' she said. 'I'll be out in a few minutes.'

'You better had,' Rose said, heading for the door.

Tania and Clara were already in the tub by the time she pulled open the balcony door and walked along the wrap-around porch onto the decking. The lodge was built into the ever-ascending hillside, with its ground level burrowed into the rock itself, windows only on the frontage of the building, alongside the front door.

The decking area stretched out from the second level of the building, surrounded by sloping ground behind and to one side, ensuring privacy, but maintaining an unparalleled view across the rooftops of Près du Ciel. The hot tub was positioned in order to maximise the privacy, and the view.

Well, Rose revised that slightly as she slid into the heat of the bubbling water. She could see most of the view, apart from the bit obscured by the snowman. She grinned as Tania handed her a glass.

'Is Madeleine joining us?' Tania asked.

Rose nodded. 'Any minute now.'

Madeleine hadn't appreciated just how hot a hot tub would be. Plus, by the time she had shed her dressing gown onto a peg on the wall and made her way across the icy lumps on the decking, she was freezing, making the difference in temperature even more extreme.

'Holy Mother of God,' she squeaked as she lowered herself into the water. 'Is it supposed to be this hot?'

Tania laughed and poured her a glass of something bubbly from a bottle chilling in a pile of snow. Madeleine couldn't help but notice the tiny bikini Tania wore. The kind of garment which shouldn't even claim that description. It was no more than a few scraps of material joined by what looked, to Madeleine, like dental floss. It instantly made her feel frumpy in her carefully shaped, but ultimately flesh-covering blue swimsuit.

Sweat prickled on her top lip. How was it possible to be so hot after having been so cold? She wondered if this came close to what a Roman caldarium would have been like. Although she assumed those existed without the jets of bubbly water which currently pummelled her shoulders and thighs, or the underwater lights set to a rotating disco of changing colours.

This was – truly – how the other half lived, she thought, as she sipped her Prosecco.

And then it began to snow.

Madeleine felt like a volcano, with her head in the feather-light falling snow and her feet in molten magma. She settled back into the jets of water and closed her eyes. 'This is fantastic,' she said.

Nobody moved, or said anything, for a while. Not even when someone hammered on the main door.

'Tom will get it,' Tania said, without even opening her eyes.

The hot tub worked through its cycles of lights and jets, systematically pummelling most of Madeleine's tight muscles. She shifted herself a few times, beginning to understand why Rose had been so keen for her to try this, then took the opportunity to study her from beneath lazy, half-open eyelids. Rose had released her hair from its complex braids so the natural spring was back in her midnight curls. With a soft gathering of snowflakes on the uppermost strands, and the steam from the tub softening the vibrancy of the red of her costume against the richness of the curves and colour of her skin, Madeleine wasn't sure that she'd ever seen Rose look more amazing. Which was saying something.

In this company, Madeleine definitely felt like the odd one out. Rose was a knock-out. Obviously. Eyes capable of melting the flintiest heart at a hundred paces, and a smile that made the recipient feel like she was the only person in the world – one look at Rose and Madeleine challenged anyone not to be captivated. And Tania was one of those women to whom fate had dealt the finest cheekbones and a body seventy-five per cent of straight men would like to get their hands on. No, make that eighty per cent. As for Clara? She was tiny in stature, and fiercely pretty with infinity-pool eyes shaded by a feathering of pale hair. Elfin. There was no other word for it. Even amidst the grief she was enduring, she still drew the eye.

Madeleine snorted a quiet laugh into her glass at the thought of how she could describe herself. Mid-brown, mid-length straight hair. Bog-standard brown eyes which were, in her opinion, undersized and placed too close to the bridge of a nose nobody would put on their Christmas list. Pale skin with a tendency towards insipidity. Chunky frame. Nothing, absolutely nothing, special about her in comparison to these other women.

The sneaking feeling of self-doubt was back. How had she managed to have Rose fall for her? Was what they had real, or was it nothing more than a massive stroke of luck? A dream she'd wake from at any moment?

She sighed and closed her eyes again.

After a while, she wiped the sweat from her forehead and finished her Prosecco. Time to mix things up. She glanced at Tania, then said, 'There is one thing I've been wondering about.' She studied the dimensions of the tub again, the hub of the jets rising into the centre of the pool, their legs slotted either side.

'Oh, yes?'

'If you have sex in a hot tub, who goes where?' she asked. 'I mean, there are only a limited number of options, aren't there? Position-wise?'

Tania rose up from the water like Halle Berry coming out of the sea, minus the big boobs. 'Do you want me to show you?' she said, advancing towards her. Then she laughed. 'You crack me up, Madeleine. But I'm getting out, I'm done. You girls stay in as long as you want.'

By the time Tania headed up to the living area, dinner was almost ready. Tom was topping tiny crostini with teaspoons full of salsa, while Clara leaned against the kitchen counter and chatted to him. There was no sign of Rose or Madeleine, but they were sharing a bathroom, so she supposed it would take them longer. Ridiculous, really, the whole moving rooms in order to accommodate the Donkey. But that was the kind of over-the-top adoration her little brother always seemed to muster from people, even complete strangers. Especially complete strangers.

'Oh, Tania?' Tom gestured towards a bottle on the edge of the kitchen work surface nearest the dining room table. 'Someone dropped that off for you earlier.'

'Who was it?'

'He didn't say. Tall, dark-haired guy; sounded English. Late twenties, maybe early thirties? There's a note with it.'

Tania felt her stomach lurch at the description. She ran a hand through her hair, still damp from the shower, and picked up the bottle. Tall and narrow, with a red wax seal and a twig of a dried flower floating within the pale golden liquid, Tania knew exactly what it was. Génépi. A liqueur flavoured with the alpine flower from which it took its name. She frowned. An envelope was taped to it, her name scrawled on it.

Nobody was paying any attention – Clara was in the kitchen, focused on helping Tom with the canapés. Her friend had more life in her face than Tania had seen for such a long time. Colour and animation and even a flicker of happiness in her bright blue eyes. The decision to spend the day – the plan to spend the rest of the week – cultivating Clara's sense of well-being was definitely the right one.

Turning the envelope over, she pulled at the flap. It wouldn't hurt to take a look. The note was short and to the point.

*I can take a hint. Probably just as well we didn't
get a dog. But you can't blame a guy for trying.
Gull.*

Chapter 18

Tania wondered how long Gull had waited at the pizzeria before he'd given up on her. Also, why had he bothered to come all the way up to the lodge, just to leave her the bottle? After making the effort to come all the way up here, why hadn't he asked to see her?

The tone of the note held the answer to her questions, though, didn't it? She wondered if he'd bought the génépi before or after her no-show at the pizza place. She'd put money on before. And then, when she didn't show, he must have decided to deliver it anyway.

She slipped the piece of paper back into the flap of the envelope and set it gently alongside the bottle on the table. Squeezing her eyes shut, she ran a hand across her forehead, her brows furrowing as she did so.

Then she shook her head and took a deep breath. He was just a man. Nothing special. She needed to remember that. All they'd done was spend a few hours in one another's company. And after the way she'd treated him, he would be mad not to forget all about her and enjoy the rest of his ski trip. All she had to do was the same. No drama. Easy-peasy.

Her stomach didn't seem to agree with her, though. It lurched as she climbed to her feet and went to join Clara. But the brightness to Clara's expression strengthened Tania's resolve to ignore her internal organs and concentrate on making this week as positive for her friend as possible.

'Those look delicious, Tom,' she said, fixing a smile on her face and ignoring the bottomless feeling her stomach was giving her.

'Crostini and homemade salsa,' he said, pointing to the left-hand side of the large piece of grey slate which had been crafted into a tray. 'And this is a smoked salmon mousse.' A small pot stood surrounded by regiments of vegetable sticks.

Tania took a stick of carrot and dipped. She tasted and nodded. 'Very good.' It was. Everything Tom had cooked so far had been very good. She hadn't been serious when she thought to blame his cooking for the way her stomach felt. However, she didn't like to tell him not to hold his breath if he was after compliments from the rest of her family. He should probably make the most of this week. He seemed to be enjoying chatting with Clara, and they were all enjoying his food. Tania felt sure whatever menus he had planned for the rest of the week, especially Christmas Day, would be excellent. But however hard he tried, the rest of her family were unlikely to offer him anything more positive than a passive-aggressive silence. Smoked salmon mousse? Her stepmother would express her feelings on that one with a single eyebrow.

At least he only had to tolerate it for a few months. Silver linings, and all that.

'Ooh, génépi. I love that stuff,' Rose said, plucking the bottle from the table. She didn't notice the piece of paper and envelope that slid to the floor as she examined the label on the bottle.

'What on earth is that?' Madeleine said, reaching down for the folded square of cream paper lying beside the wooden bun foot of one of the sofas. 'I've never heard of it.'

'It's a liqueur,' Rose said. 'Bloody strong but a really traditional way to finish a meal in the mountains. Good for the digestion. According to the French, anyway.'

'The French use any excuse to neck down booze, if you ask me,' she said.

Rose laughed. 'It's a flower, too, which is what they use to flavour it. Where did this come from?' she said, turning to Tania and Clara, waving the bottle in one hand. 'And can we open it tonight?'

Madeleine retrieved the envelope, noting the tape still sticky on the upper edge. Turning it front-side up, she saw Tania's name scrawled on it. She knew she shouldn't look at the contents of the folded piece of paper, it was clearly from the envelope addressed to Tania. Madeleine flicked a look at the others, Rose was asking where the bottle had appeared from and Tania was skirting the question, which piqued her interest further.

It couldn't hurt to look, could it? And then she would tuck it back into the envelope and nobody would be any the wiser.

Tilting away from the others, she unfurled the paper.

*I can take a hint. Probably just as well we didn't get a dog. But you can't blame a guy for trying.
Gull.*

The words were large and uninhibited, the letters bold and intertwined, as if it had been written on impulse. But the sentiment behind the words was clear-cut, she thought. Madeleine wondered when Tania had given Gull the brush-off. She hadn't given any indication of having done so the previous afternoon, although Madeleine supposed she could have done. Today, she'd spent the whole day with them and hadn't used her mobile at all. She wasn't sure when Tania would have had the opportunity to contact him.

Madeleine refolded the paper and slid it back into the envelope. Maybe that was exactly what had happened. Maybe the fact that she hadn't been in contact was the point.

She thought back through the day, to the times when she'd been able to concentrate on anything other than staying upright, that was. They'd stopped for lunch at a different restaurant, this one called L'Avalanche. She'd had *tartiflette* today, a dish Madeleine thought she'd never tried before – although in essence it was like something her Auntie Katie made, layers of cheesy potatoes with bacon bits. The cheese in the *tartiflette* she'd had today was definitely not Cheddar, like in Auntie Katie's version, it was something stringier. Yummy, but stringier.

Focus, Madeleine. Actually, if she thought about it, Tania had seemed very distracted at lunchtime, repeatedly checking her watch. She'd done it enough for Madeleine to notice, even though she hadn't asked the questions that were bubbling around in her head, about whether they were boring her – too aggressive – or, should she be somewhere else? Were they keeping her from being somewhere more important? In the end, she'd decided she didn't know Tania well enough to ask any of them, so she hadn't.

Should Tania have been somewhere else? That had to be it. She should have been meeting Gull.

Madeleine turned back to the others. Rose and Clara were chatting, but Tania was looking straight at her, at the envelope still in her fingers. Madeleine bent and set the envelope gently on the table. If only she could learn to mind her own business. Keep. Nose. Out.

Sorry, she mouthed, feeling the heat rise in her cheeks as the blatancy of her own curiosity sank in.

Tania's face took a downwards turn, a frown settling between her eyes. She strode over to the table and took the envelope, checking the note was inside.

'I'm sorry, I didn't mean to pry.' Even as she said it, Madeleine heard how weak it sounded. She waited for Tania's reaction, but she didn't say anything, just shook her head. She headed for the kitchen, hovered the envelope over the top of the bin and then shook her head again and pocketed the envelope instead.

It wasn't until the end of the meal that Madeleine plucked up enough courage to ask about Gull. Tania wouldn't allow Rose to open the génépi he'd delivered, instead she scratched around in a drinks cabinet until she found a half-empty bottle. Tania brought that, plus a pile of tiny shot glasses, to the table.

'Here, use this,' Tania said, shoving everything in front of Rose and retaking her seat.

'Are you going to see him again?' Madeleine asked quietly, while Rose was preoccupied pouring the génépi.

Tania shook her head. 'Doesn't look like it.'

'Do you mind?'

She shrugged. 'It's too late, either way. I have no way to contact him, even if I wanted to.'

As she said the words, Tania couldn't help but slide her fingers to the back pocket of her jeans. Gull's note was still in there, the edge of the envelope standing proud of the seam. She shoved it down, hiding it from sight.

Madeleine was watching her. Tania was beginning to get the feeling that Madeleine was one of those people who appeared easy-going and unobservant but was the complete opposite.

'If you could, though, would you want to?' Madeleine asked.

She crushed the smile that tried to curl her lips upwards, the tell-tale reaction to the fact that her stomach had a strong answer to that question, turning itself into a washing machine at the thought. She pushed the little glass of génépi to one side, not at all sure adding a strong liqueur to the mix would be a great idea.

Until she'd seen the note, Tania had convinced herself she'd made the right decision. She *had* made the right decision, there was no way she could make a stranger more important than her friend. However, the interesting – and frankly new to her – reaction her body was having every time she thought about Gull was a surprise. She tried to recall another time when someone she hadn't even touched had elicited a similar response. She couldn't. There wasn't anyone.

She looked at Madeleine, her generous almond eyes still trained in her direction. 'It doesn't matter, does it? I don't have any way of finding him again.' She pressed her lips together, hoping Madeleine would leave it alone.

Instead, Madeleine turned to the others, her expression brightening. 'I've had an idea.'

'Oh, yes?' Rose said.

'As you've all been so good at putting up with my appalling attempts to learn to ski, why don't I treat us all to lunch, tomorrow?'

'That sounds like a lovely idea,' Clara said.

'Well,' Madeleine said, 'the offer comes with a couple of caveats.'

Rose snorted a laugh. 'Why doesn't that surprise me.'

'Number one. You'll have to put up with me for the whole day, tomorrow. Today's lesson was my last one.'

'How come?' Clara asked.

'The instructor realised she's never going to improve and they're cutting and running while they still can,' Rose said, with a grin.

'Cow,' Madeleine said, with affection. 'No. I can't really afford any more, so I'm afraid I'm at your mercy from here on in. But I want to say thank you, to Tania primarily but to all of you for being so welcoming.' Madeleine looked around the room, then her gaze settled onto Tania. 'Snow Pine Lodge, this resort, this whole experience is, quite frankly, rather surreal for a dental nurse from Brockborough to take in. Surreal, but in a good way.'

'It's been my pleasure,' Tania said. She hadn't thought it would be, she'd thought Madeleine would end up being a spare wheel, a cog which didn't fit anywhere. She'd been wrong.

'What's the other caveat?' Rose asked.

'Our lunchtime destination tomorrow. I want to go to the Cocoon.'

'Fine by me,' Rose said. She lifted her glass of génépi into the air. 'Cheers.'

'Bottoms up,' Madeleine said, swigging at her liqueur

and then coughing a little. She recovered herself and swung around to face Tania. 'Plus,' she said quietly, 'what better place to go to start the search for the man who may buy you a dog one day?'

Chapter 19

Clara woke early the following morning. She always woke early, these days, unless she'd had a skinful the night before. Then she woke later, which was a good thing in some ways, except that she had to deal with the fallout of a hangover instead of the empty hours.

For a while, after Mike and Poppy died, drinking until she passed out had been one of the only ways to go to sleep at all. She still did that, more often than she should. But the thing with going to sleep was not so much the sleeping part, it was more the waking up bit. And that happened either way.

It had been particularly challenging this morning. The upward spiral into consciousness was always accompanied by those few seconds of freefall when she had to remember, all over again, why Mike wasn't beside her. Why Poppy wasn't stood at her bedside, tapping at the side of her face to wake her up. That momentary suspension in reality took longer to negotiate today, before it all crashed back in on her, like the seventh wave in a winter storm.

The crash had been particularly vicious this morning. Maybe it was because she'd enjoyed herself yesterday. For the first time in such a long time she'd enjoyed being alive. This must be the punishment, she supposed.

Perhaps she should have asked to share a room with someone. Would that have made the yawning chasm of the morning's realisation that her family were gone easier to bear? Or would that have achieved nothing more than filling

133

the silence with white noise? They were still gone, noise or no noise.

She stayed put for as long as she could bear to. Then Clara slipped from the bed and got on with the mechanics of preparing for another day.

Upstairs, Tom was slicing a fresh baguette and arranging the pieces into a wicker basket. She could smell croissants in the oven.

'Good morning,' he said cheerfully. 'Did you sleep well?'

A standard question, one which would be asked countless times every day, in countless buildings, in countless resorts throughout the mountains. Part of the ritual. Nothing more. The expression on Clara's face must have been the out-of-the-ordinary bit. Tom looked at her, his own expression taking on an edge of discomfort before it folded into a full-on frown.

'Sorry. Stupid of me. I didn't think . . .' He set the basket on the dining table. 'Your friends told me about . . .' He swallowed the rest of the sentence.

'Oh, right. I see. Yes, I slept fine, thank you. It's the waking up that's the hard bit.'

Nodding, he brushed her arm with his fingers. 'I can imagine.' He glanced at her hand, still bandaged. 'How's it doing?'

'I haven't looked,' she said. 'I've done my best to keep it dry, but that's harder than it seems. I remember when Poppy had to have stitches once, it was a nightmare trying to keep her arm dry.' The words were out before she realised she was saying them, the memory of Poppy strong and bright, with foam piled on top of her blonde curls, splashing around in the water with a plastic figure she called Captain Barnclues instead of Barnacles. Clara desperately trying to keep the arm encased in a plastic bag away from the water. She caught her breath in her throat, then clamped her mouth closed.

Tom's hand closed around her bandage. 'Let's take a look, shall we? It could do with a fresh dressing anyway.'

He led her to a chair, then busied himself with her hand. She heard him saying how it was looking better, but it still wasn't healed; how he would rebandage it, unless she wanted to go to the resort doctor, to get it checked out by a professional. She shook her head. A new bandage would do fine. He sat across from her as he cut a new piece of dressing and fixed it in place, the crown of his head in her line of vision as he worked. Then he wound a new bandage around her hand, his touch firm and confident as he taped the whole thing into place. His fingers rested for a moment on the soft skin of her inner wrist.

'If you ever want to talk,' he said, 'I'm also a really good listener.' Tipping his face to look at her, his eyes crinkled into a smile. 'It's another of my Boy Scout skills.'

Once he'd tidied up the first-aid equipment, he set about preparing the rest of breakfast while she stayed seated at the table. Clara wondered if she might take him up on the offer, if it might be worth finding out what it would be like to share a little of the burden with someone else, someone outside her circle of friends, someone whom she'd never see again. Someone with whom she could get everything off her chest, without having to spend the rest of her life watching them look at her out of the corner of their eye.

Madeleine was more than relieved when they slid to a stop outside the Cocoon at lunchtime. She appreciated that the other three had skied very carefully all morning to accommodate her fledgling abilities. Or her crappy style, whichever description they felt fitted best. She also appreciated just how skilful the instructor had been. He'd managed to challenge her to make dramatic improvements, without over-facing or completely exhausting her.

The morning had been spent on blue runs, not as 'easy' as green runs, but in general a lot less challenging than the red runs or the fabled blacks. Even on the blues there had been a few icy, steep places where Madeleine had worried she might completely lose control of her legs and break something, or at best completely lose control of a different part of her body and change the colour of her ski trousers.

However, she had survived. More than that, she'd enjoyed herself. Well, she'd enjoyed most of it. But she had already decided to head back to Snow Pine Lodge after lunch, to give herself a restful afternoon. After all, this was supposed to be a holiday, not a week of self-flagellation. Plus, it would give the others a chance to cut loose and enjoy their skiing without having to nanny her around.

But first, the Cocoon beckoned.

Slotting her skis against one of the wooden racks, she glanced around the outdoor seating area. Far too much to hope to see Gull sitting at one of the tables, she supposed, but it didn't stop her from looking.

Rose went with her into the restaurant, and armed with a tray each, they collected lunch and headed back to the table Madeleine had chosen. She'd chosen it partly because it was close to the restaurant door, and therefore was less distance for her to have to negotiate in her ski boots with a tray full of food; partly because it gave an excellent view of everyone who came and went to the restaurant. The chance of Gull actually being here at the same time as them was minimal, logic told her as much. However, it would be crazy to have come this far with the whole thing just to miss seeing him because she was too preoccupied with her hot chocolate.

Tania had insisted on buying the drinks, and the three of them converged back at the table which Clara held for them. She looked so small, with her short blonde hair tucked neatly behind her ears, surrounded by the pile of gloves, helmets and goggles they had abandoned on arrival. Madeleine wondered what Mike had been like. It was pure speculation, on her part, but in her mind's eye she imagined him to have been the kind of man who was quick to put an arm around Clara, quick to check how she was feeling, quick to smile. She imagined he'd been easy to fall deeply in love with, because he had clearly been difficult to lose.

Clara wore a slightly distracted expression most of the time, and it was pronounced as they walked back to the table. A momentary frown and then Clara was back in the moment, back from wherever she had been in her mind, an overly bright smile pasted onto her face as she shifted gloves to make enough space for the trays.

Madeleine was still scanning arrivals and departures at the Cocoon when their empty plates, stacked onto the trays in school canteen fashion, were whisked away by one of the ever-moving restaurant staff. Straight-faced, dark-haired, quick and efficient, jeans and trekking boots worn with a thick padded gilet emblazoned with the Cocoon logo, he flashed their group a fleeting pressured smile and was away from the table with his '*Merci, mesdames*' swirling in the cold air.

And still there was no sign of Gull. Madeleine stole a glance at Tania. She supposed it would have been too much of a fairy tale for Gull to have skied in for lunch. A fluffy image formed in her imagination, in which Gull appeared at the Cocoon. In all his tall, broad, unshaven maleness, he swept Tania up from the bench on which she sat and kissed her until the credits rolled and everyone climbed to their feet and left the cinema.

It had been worth a shot. 'Anyone want coffee?' she said, in a desperate effort to keep the group at the restaurant for a little bit longer.

'I think we should probably roll,' Rose said. 'Especially if we're going to head to the glacier this afternoon, Tania?'

Tania nodded. 'Yes. Let's head off.' She sorted through the pile of gloves until she found hers, then looked at Madeleine. 'Thanks for trying,' she said, quietly.

'Will you be OK finding your way back by yourself?' Clara asked.

'I think so,' Madeleine said. 'Worst-case scenario, I'll ski down into Près du Ciel centre and get the bus back up the hill. Don't worry about me, you've done that all morning. Go and enjoy yourselves.'

They gathered up belongings, clipping helmets on and slotting hands into gloves. Rose squeezed Madeleine's shoulder. 'See you later.'

'Have fun.' She watched them go, wondering whether she might rest at the restaurant for a few more minutes, or whether her thighs would use the opportunity to seize up even further. Maybe it would be better to get the pain over and done with and get back to the lodge. Then she could relax properly, soak up the alpine atmosphere in more comfortable footwear.

After a final sweep of the customers, she climbed to her feet, shuffled her way out from the bench, and headed across the decking towards the slope down to the wooden frames against which people lodged their skis.

She didn't notice the lump of ice until she'd caught it with the edge of a boot, that foot sliding uncontrollably until gravity demanded further action and she ended up in a painful heap, half on the decking, half in the snow.

Unbelievable. She'd made it through the entire morning on a set of long, thin, slippery-arsed pieces of wood and had managed to stay upright. The simple manoeuvre of walking, though, was proving to be beyond her. She shook her head and turned over onto her knees.

'Let me help you.'

Twizzling her head as far as she could, she caught sight of legs encased in black ski trousers. A green jacket, a gloved hand outstretched towards her, a smile behind that. She held up her own hand and gravity was no match for the strength with which he pulled her to her feet.

'Thank you.' She brushed the worst of the snow from herself. 'Hugely embarrassing,' she muttered, glancing at the smiley woman who stood beside him.

The man laughed, told her not to worry about it and continued onto the decking, taking the woman's hand as he walked. It took her a second or two to decide that there was something familiar about him. Something familiar in the lines of his face, and that distinctive green jacket. It took Madeleine a couple more seconds to work out why.

'Excuse me,' she called after him. 'This is a bit random, but do you know someone called Gull?'

Lines formed between his eyes, he nodded slowly. 'My brother's called Gull. Why?'

Madeleine's heart began to thud against her chest. Yes, she could see the resemblance properly now. Should she do this, or should she just let sleeping dogs lie? His expectant expression left her no room for manoeuvre. Too late to worry about the dog's nap now, she decided, as she asked Gull's brother if he could pass on a message.

'What's it about?' he said.

'It's about my friend. She's called Tania.'

Chapter 20

'You did *what?*' Rose said, her voice escalating high enough to pique the interest of the local huskies, as she looked at Madeleine in disbelief, the soft pale-blue jersey zip-through she'd been about to pull on dangling forgotten from her hand.

Madeleine set down her mug of tea, shifting on the sofa she had inhabited almost non-stop since she'd arrived back at the lodge a few hours ago.

'Keep your hair on,' she said, swinging her feet to the floor and sitting up.

The others had been back for little more than half an hour. Tania and Clara had headed for the hot tub; Rose had opted for a shower. Now she stood in front of the sofa, the curls of her dark hair still damp as they framed her face, her incredulous expression making Madeleine smile. She reiterated what she'd already said. 'Just after you left the Cocoon, I ran into Gull's brother, so I asked him to tell Gull that it wasn't Tania's fault she didn't catch up with him yesterday, and that she was sorry to miss him. I suggested he might want to take a walk back to the lodge this evening to see her.' She looked at Rose in mock innocence. 'What's wrong with that?'

'You and your inability to keep your nose out.' Rose shook her head.

'I checked with Tom, we're having beef and red wine casserole for supper, so there will be plenty to go around, if he does turn up.' She grinned.

'I'm not sure about this.' Rose crossed her arms, the jersey still dangling from one of her hands. 'I'm not sure Tania's

140

going to appreciate you meddling in her life. And it's not like she's serious about this bloke. She's never serious about them. She could have met him yesterday if she wanted to. She chose not to.'

'I know, but I think she regrets the decision.'

Rose shook her head. 'Men are like takeaway coffee as far as Tania is concerned. Always available, but completely disposable.'

Madeleine frowned. 'Really?'

'Really.'

'Why?'

'She's always said she isn't going to fall in love. It's just not for her.'

Madeleine shook her head. 'That's crazy.'

'You wouldn't say that if you'd grown up in her family.'

'Oh.' She hadn't thought about that. Like most people, she'd read the kiss-me-quick magazines which promised celebrity gossip you couldn't get anywhere else, and then fed you the celebrity gossip you'd already read somewhere else – usually on Twitter – and Tania's family had featured in those cringe-binge fests on more than one occasion. But that still didn't quite match with the expression on Tania's face when she pushed Gull's note further into her pocket, nor her reaction to Madeleine's crazy lunch scheme.

Which, by the way, had worked. Sort of.

'You should be patting me on the back,' she said. 'Not berating me for trying to help.'

Rose relaxed her frame a little, noticing her jersey as if for the first time and pulling it on. 'Listen, Maddy, I know you mean well. I know you want to fix everything for everyone. And I love that about you. But I think this might be a step too far. Even if he does come back, even if they are attracted to one another . . .' Rose shook her head. 'She'll eat him for breakfast.'

Madeleine didn't agree. She didn't know Tania as well as Rose, fair enough, but sometimes a fresh pair of eyes on a situation noticed different things. And Tania didn't look as if she wanted to eat Gull alive. Quite the opposite. She looked upset that he'd come to the lodge and she hadn't seen him. She looked as if she cared a great deal about that.

'Oh well,' she said, a grin forming on her face. 'If she does eat him for breakfast, I bet he'll enjoy it.'

Rose rolled her eyes, but she did huff a laugh. 'OK. I suppose. They're both adults, they can decide what they want as their happy-ever-after.'

Yes, they could, Madeleine thought. And if it took a little shove in the right direction to spin them together? Well, there was nothing wrong with that. Madeleine just wished she had someone watching out for her in the same way.

Tom served the canapés, thin rings of cucumber set on tiny pancakes with a little blob of caviar where the cucumber seeds should have been, and by the time Madeleine had tried one and decided one was enough – the caviar was a bit too salty and slimy for her taste – she'd lost track of how many times she'd looked at her watch.

Perhaps Gull wouldn't come at all. It was entirely possible that the brother might not have passed on the message. He might have forgotten. Or, he might have thought better of it and said nothing. And even if he had passed on the message, there was nothing to suggest that Gull would feel compelled to visit Snow Pine Lodge again. Except that Madeleine's gut kept pushing all those thoughts aside. He would come. She had faith in him.

Pushing the sleeve of her jumper up, she checked the time again. Rose caught her eye and shook her head. Her expression said it all. *Leave it alone. Keep your nose out. Stop meddling.*

A firm knock on the lodge door had Rose glancing at her again. Madeleine grinned. Too late to leave it alone. Or to keep her nose out. Or to stop meddling. 'I'll get it,' she said, and headed downstairs before anyone could stop her.

* * *

Two sets of footsteps ascended the stairs a few minutes later. Tania watched the crown of Madeleine's head appear, the broad grin on her face speaking volumes as she came into the room.

'You'll never guess who was at the door,' she said, widening her eyes purposefully in Tania's direction.

And then the second person reached the top of the stairs. It was Gull. One hand on the smooth wood of the curving banister, his eyebrows furrowed together in an expression that Tania didn't want to admit she'd missed.

'Hi,' he said, glancing around. 'I'm sorry to intrude.'

'I said he should come straight on up.' Madeleine grinned at her with even more fervour.

Tania knew she should greet him, invite him into the room, rather than leaving him standing awkwardly at the top of the stairs. He was clearly waiting for some indication from her, but she couldn't make her face change its expression. She was frozen in position, staring at him. Once she forced her legs into action, she headed for him, asking Tom if he could hold dinner for a little while as she swept past the kitchen area.

'Come with me,' she said, taking the stairs down two at a time. She didn't look back, heard him descending the first staircase and then the second one behind her. Down in the boot room, she slotted her feet into her snow boots and laced them up.

He pulled his boots back on and mirrored her as she zipped herself into her jacket. His expression had morphed into confusion, as she held the door open and gestured him outside.

'Where are we going?' he said.

'I can't do this with an audience,' she said. 'Let's walk.' Rather too late, she paused, glancing at his leg. 'If your knee is up to it?'

He nodded, his expression losing some of its stiffness. 'It's fine. All strapped up and ready to go.'

The door closed with a decisive click behind her. 'I'm glad. I didn't want to be responsible for ruining the rest of your week.'

He laughed. Did that mean he thought she'd already ruined the rest of his week? She had messed him around, there was no getting away from that. But she hadn't asked for his attention, hadn't wanted him to chase her halfway down a mountain or make inappropriate suggestions about hot tubs. He'd started it.

Choosing to ignore the laugh, she headed across the driveway, the tarmac scraped clean of snow, with fresh pockets of ice glistening like stars in the pale moonlight. He caught her up and together they climbed over the remnants of the shovelled snow and took the track that wound its way around the lodge, their footsteps silent on the powder snow, which lay undisturbed between the trees surrounding the building. Enough moonlight penetrated the firs to light their way.

'Thank you for the bottle,' she said. 'Why didn't you ask to see me?'

He shrugged. 'Why didn't you meet me at the pizza place?'

Fair enough, she thought. She kept moving, curving her way up through the trees. 'Be careful,' she said. 'Don't slip.'

'Where are we going?' He puffed a little as he followed.

'You'll see soon enough.' They didn't speak again. Tania headed over the wooden bridge – little wider than a couple of planks of wood – spanning an alpine stream, narrow but fast-flowing and set deceptively deeply into the mountain bedrock, then followed a trail up through the trees. Eventually, she reached the edge of the piste that ran down the left-hand side of the property. Set between the edge of the ski run and the trees was the first of a series of cowsheds. They stood abandoned through the winter but were needed during the summer months when these highest slopes were grazed by tough little cattle, animals whose milk was used to create some of the cheeses they'd been eating, courtesy of Tom.

The design of the buildings meant these, too, nestled against the mountain, with the roofs on the exposed edges almost reaching the ground. As a child, Tania had spent plenty of time up here. Once the ski lifts had closed for the afternoon, she would head up here, away from the toxic atmosphere of the lodge. She'd spent countless hours hugging her knees to her chest as she balanced on the slope of the roof, shivering with cold as she watched the moon rise and mingle with the stars to frame the view over the other peaks of the range of mountains.

She brushed away the lip of snow and leaned against the building, waiting for Gull to settle against the roof tiles beside her.

'Great view,' he said.

'Yes. I love it up here.'

'Mind you, in these mountains all you have to do is keep your eyes open and you're looking at a great view.'

'True.'

'Have you visited this place before?' he asked.

She glanced at him. 'A few times. Why?'

'To know that this is up here, I mean. It must have taken a bit of exploring to find.'

Damn. She hadn't thought about that. 'Yes, I suppose so. I like exploring.' She shrugged her shoulders to emphasise the supposed randomness of finding of this spot.

'Me too.' Shuffling a gloved hand through some of the snow resting on the sloping roof, he sent a pile cascading onto the ground. 'Are we agreeing about something?' he said, his gaze on the view.

'Must be a first,' she said. 'Don't let it go to your head.'

'Good point,' he replied. 'A sudden rush of blood to the brain like that could send me off balance. And then I'd have no chance of staying on your tightrope.'

'I thought you'd have forgotten all about that,' she said. 'Listen, I apologise for standing you up yesterday. It was immature of me, but . . .'

She huffed a breath, unsure how to phrase her explanation. How to sum up, in a few words, the complex emotions she felt and the simplistic solutions she applied to survive her relationships with the opposite sex. Or rather, her lack of relationships. Her emotionally stifled, arm's-length, taking-what-was-gratifying-without-giving-what-was-precious liaisons.

Nor did she know how to explain that the needs of her friend had crashed this particular party and had outweighed what she had presumed would be nothing more than another non-relationship anyway, with him.

On top of which, she had no idea how to express her feelings about the ramifications of that decision not to meet him. The churning of her stomach while she'd lain awake all night, with his note on the bedside table. Eyes wide open in the dark, wondering if she might just have made a huge mistake, even though she had no idea why she felt that way.

The air swirled away from her lips, giving her a momentary distraction. In the end, she decided not to explain. Never explain, never complain – wasn't that the way it was supposed to be? Certainly, it was the mantra she had adopted over the years to deal with the intrusive nature of the world. Always a smiling face for the cameras, even if you were dying inside, right?

'The thing is, after yesterday, I can't imagine why you'd care what I think of you,' she said.

He brushed more snow from the slope of the roof, watching it trickle over the edge like white sand, building up into little piles on the ground beneath.

'And I can't imagine why you'd think I didn't,' he said. He patted his gloves across one another, decisively ridding them of snow before he looked at her. 'I know I went about this whole thing wrong, in that bar.' He shook his head. 'You can't imagine the words I've been having with myself since then. But when I realised you weren't coming to the pizzeria, it crystallised for me. I'd been kidding myself that

146

you were interested, trying to force something into life from what was clearly nothing more than a self-assured, confident woman trying to politely tell a man to go and jump off a . . . well, it might as well be a mountain. For convenience's sake.'

She huffed a laugh. 'Politeness? Not one of my better-recognised qualities.'

He didn't rise to the bait, remaining focused on finishing what he wanted to say. 'The bottle of génépi was supposed to be an apology. For my inappropriateness in Le Bar.'

'A bottle of génépi? As an apology?'

'Well, there was another reason.' He tilted his head. 'I also thought we might get to enjoy it together. In the fantasy I'd constructed in my head, anyway.'

'In a hot tub, I imagine?' She was teasing, but he looked away, this time up at the star-studded sky.

'I'm such a moron.'

When he didn't say anything else, Tania said, 'I feel it's only fair to tell you that your line wasn't the worst one I've ever heard.'

'No?'

'Not even top five.'

'I'm not sure if I'm pleased about that or whether it leaves me feeling even more inadequate. Sad singleton eyes up super-sexy woman. Worst chat-up line ever ensues.'

She laughed softly. 'Have you ever had sex in a hot tub?'

He frowned. 'Oh, God. Stop punishing me. No, actually, I haven't. Why?'

'You've missed out. It's fun.' She watched his face, watched as his frown morphed into something bordering on surprise, then confusion. He looked at her, his face a hotbed of changing expressions. She liked the way he seemed incapable of hiding his emotions. 'I'm just saying don't discount it as an idea, but maybe keep the suggestion for a few dates in.' She smiled at him. 'Nothing wrong with your thought process, though.'

'Thanks for the tip.' He stared out at the sky again and they sat in silence. The unspoken questions hung heavy in the air. What were they doing, sat together on the edge of the world? Why were they both still here? What did they want from each other?

'Who made the snowman?' he asked, after a while.

'Madeleine did most of the work.' Tania smiled at the memory of Madeleine winding that ridiculous scarf around its neck, the satisfaction clear in her eyes as she pulled her woolly hat further over the curtains of her brown hair and stood back to admire her handiwork. Pressing a little of the snow into the palm of her glove, she bounced it until it fell off. 'She's lucky that the snow stuck together, sometimes it's too dry.'

From the corner of her eye she could tell he was watching her, the edges of his lips curling into the hint of a smile. He balled a soft fistful of snow from the roof.

'Yes,' he said. 'It definitely sticks together.' He launched it gently in her direction. It disintegrated against the arm of her jacket, partly sticking, partly shattering into shards of glitter in the moonlight.

'Oh, I see,' she said. 'Challenge accepted.' Her retaliation came in the form of a double handful of snow aimed at his face. It missed, hitting the roof behind him instead. She ducked down to grab more from the ground while he swiped snow from the roof and sent it arcing towards her. As she stood upright it hit her on the side of her neck, some of the snow melting instantly against her skin and sliding down the inside of her collar. The shiver was involuntarily. 'Bastard,' she squeaked, inhaling the word as the shock of the cold took effect.

'Oh, shit,' he said, laughing. 'I was aiming over your head, honestly.'

As he pulled off a glove, his gaze assessed the damage, the laugh gone with his concentration turning to the task in hand. An innocent enough action as he flicked the worst of the snow away, but every gentle touch of his fingertips was supercharged against Tania's skin. She hadn't been expecting such a strong reaction to his sudden proximity and she stood, stock-still, aware of everything and nothing all at the same time. She could smell pine needles, but wasn't sure if it came from the trees that surrounded them, or his skin. Breathing in again, the pine needles were joined this time by a note of cinnamon, or perhaps citrus.

She glanced up at his face, at the concentration written all over it, the ridiculously long eyelashes framing his serious nut-brown eyes, the beginnings of a shadow prickling his jawline. His lips, gently parted, breath escaping them in a puff of silver. Another shiver, but this time it had nothing to do with the last of the icy water trickling down her neck.

He continued to brush at her collar, even though the snow was long gone. It was as if he didn't want to relinquish his reason to be this close to her. The movement of his fingers slowed, became more lingering, more languid. He pushed at her hair, exposing more of her neck to the moonlight, giving his fingers more skin to trail their way across. The soft lines between his eyebrows creased as his hand stopped moving, resting lightly against the curve of her neck, tiny movements from his thumb caressing the skin beneath her jaw. Tania realised she was holding her breath, desperately hoping that he might replace his touch with his lips. She wanted the warmth from his breath against her neck, the feel of his lips against her skin.

Instead, he gently removed his fingers. He sighed and made to take a step back.

'No,' she said, prompted into action and folding her gloved hand around the collar of his jacket. She took hold of the material and pulled him closer again. 'You're not going anywhere.'

She'd planned to bring him up here and explain that, if all it was destined to be was a quick Christmas shag in the mountains, then she had more important people to concentrate on. That she had her friend to think about, that Clara needed her a hell of a lot more than Tania needed a time-sensitive fling with him. That she would be able to ignore the feeling in the base of her stomach; and the thoughts that had flitted through her mind all night would eventually subside.

That if they were just going to be wasting a little time together, then they were wasting one another's time.

But as her lips found his, and the arms he wrapped around her felt every bit as strong as she'd hoped they would, and she yielded to the pressure from his lips and his tongue and his heat, she knew it wasn't going to be that simple.

Chapter 21

'How long should we wait?' Clara said, checking her watch again. 'They left a good half an hour ago.' She glanced at Tom, busy as always in the kitchen, lowering her voice as she said, 'I don't think it's fair on Tom.'

The lift of Rose's eyebrows told her they were thinking along the same lines. If Tania did reappear any time soon, it was perfectly possible that food would be the last thing on her mind, anyway.

'I'll phone her, find out how long she's going to be,' Rose said, reaching for her mobile. A futile exercise, as it turned out, when Tania's phone lit up and began to vibrate its way across the coffee table. 'Great,' Rose said, cancelling the call.

'I hope she's OK.' Madeleine fiddled absently with a cuff. 'I just thought . . .'

'You just thought you'd play matchmaker,' Rose said. 'Which is cool. But rather surplus to requirements, where Tania is concerned.'

Clara got to her feet and headed towards Tom. In her opinion, a matchmaker was exactly what Tania *did* need. Her friend had never had trouble finding men, but the ones she found were, more often than not, trouble. She wondered if Gull fell into that category. And if he didn't, she wondered if Tania would allow him to get any closer to her than her statutory skin-deep approach to relationships.

'Tom, I think we should make a start on dinner. Can you keep some for Tania, and her guest if he stays?'

'Of course.' Flashing her an amiable smile, he wiped his

fingers on a tea towel as he checked the oven. 'Just give me five minutes to dish up and it'll be ready.'

Clara found herself smiling, too, reaching out a hand to rest on his arm. 'Thank you.'

His skin was warm under her touch, as were his eyes when he turned to look at her. 'Clara, it's my pleasure,' he said, the burr of his accent as soft as the words spoken.

An indeterminate amount of time passed for Tania, in Gull's arms. She lost all sense of time around the same moment she lost the ability to hold herself up. It was just as well his arms maintained their firm grip around her waist, her stumble simply prompting him to pull her against him even harder.

It wasn't that she'd never been kissed like this before. It wasn't anything as coy as that. It wasn't even how much he was turning her on, although that was at the high end on the scale of lukewarm to seismic. There was something else that was turning this into a kiss her knees seemed unprepared for.

The trouble was, she had no idea what that was. Her brain couldn't form the nebulous, fractured glimpses into a firm thought. And, at this moment, she decided it didn't really matter. She could try to pin that down at some other time. A time when she wasn't totally absorbed by the pressure from his firm body against hers, with the backs of her legs tight against the edge of the building and her concentration on his kiss blocking out the rest of the world. All she needed in this moment was his touch, her accompanying trembling told her that much. This moment was absolute.

Eventually, when he did pull back from her, checking his watch and swearing under his breath, she couldn't focus on anything properly.

'Tania,' he said, the words soft and warm in her ear. 'I've got to go.'

She frowned, unable to process his words. 'What do you mean?'

'It's gone eight, and I promised David I wouldn't be late.'

'Late? For what?' She was struggling with the lack of warmth, the cold air spiralling into the space where his body and his lips had been moments before.

'He's planned a whole elaborate engagement dinner for Niamh. It's supposed to be a surprise, although I'm sure she's already guessed what he's up to. And as the best man I need to be there. I said I'd be there.'

She frowned. Where had all these other people appeared from? A moment ago, it was just her and Gull, the only two people who existed, possibly on the entire surface of the planet. Suddenly there was a brother and his fiancée and a whole host of others crowding in on their moment.

'I'm sorry,' he said, taking one of her hands in his. 'I wasn't expecting to be here this evening. I wasn't expecting any of this.'

She shook her head. Nor was she. 'We'd better get back, then.'

He pulled her against him again, kissing her briefly, but with an intensity that had her reeling again. 'This week was supposed to be uncomplicated,' he said, more to himself than to her, then he smiled. One of his searing, bright smiles, which disappeared as quickly as it appeared. A bolt of lightning that blinded and then was gone. 'Can we agree that this needs to be filed in the "to be continued" category?'

All Tania could do was nod. As they headed towards civilisation, the starlight replaced gradually by the lights of Snow Pine Lodge and the rest of Près du Ciel, Tania trod into the ice her plans to tell him that flirting with him had been fun but was ultimately pointless. Because for the first time in her life she wasn't sure that it was pointless. It couldn't be if it made her feel like this, could it?

'Can we meet, tomorrow? Spend some time together on the slopes perhaps?' he said as they neared the lodge. His eyebrows furrowed together.

She wondered if the expression on her own face mirrored his. They knew next to nothing about one another and yet Tania had never felt so desperate to be in someone's company.

By the time they reached the driveway, Gull had messaged her phone, so they had one another's number, and a provisional plan was in place to meet the following afternoon.

As he checked his watch again, a pained expression settled on his features. Rather than speaking, he enveloped her in a hug and she reached her hands around his neck, tipping her head in the hope that he might kiss her again. Instead, he pulled a hand from a glove and ran a finger gently down the contours of her cheek.

'I'll see you tomorrow,' he said, the words phrased more as a question than a statement.

She nodded.

'In the meantime, have a think about what kind of dog we should get,' he said, disentangling himself from her. He grinned and headed across the drive.

'Dog?'

'For when we get a place together?' he said. 'I'd put money on you wanting a Pekinese,' he said, the grin broadening. 'Maybe one of those teacup dogs?'

Tania responded by gathering a handful of snow, balling it in her palms and launching it in his direction. Gratifyingly, it hit him squarely in the chest.

'No. Fair enough,' he said, brushing the snow from his jacket. 'My mistake. I've got it, now. A pug, right?'

She started to laugh as she scooped up more snow, but she didn't throw it, she just watched as he held up a hand in farewell and headed away from her, down the curving driveway and into the darkness.

Madeleine heard the main door click open from two floors up. It wasn't as if she were listening for it. Nothing like that. Of course not. She wasn't on tenterhooks waiting for Tania to return, she was completely relaxed about it . . .

Her fork paused midway to her mouth as she strained her ears to hear more. The rice she had balanced on the prongs jiggled and cascaded back onto her plate. Sliding the fork alongside them, she had to admit she couldn't hide her curiosity any further.

'Rose, did you hear the door?' she said.

'No. Is she back?'

'I think so, I definitely heard the door.'

There was no sound of voices. A single set of footsteps ascended, paused, ascended again. Tania bounced her hand on the top of the banister, her focus a million miles away.

'Irish wolfhound,' she said. 'Maybe a Dalmatian.'

'Excuse me?' Tom said. Closest to her and standing in the kitchen, he obviously thought she was talking to him.

'Oh, nothing. Sorry.' Tania threw him a distracted smile.

'You OK?' Rose said.

'Where's Gull?' Madeleine said. Might as well cut to the chase, she thought. Plus, she was disappointed. Disappointed that he hadn't come back into the lodge with Tania. Disappointed that, after everything, it looked as if her matchmaking had failed.

'He had to go. His brother's getting engaged. They've got some fancy dinner planned in Près du Ciel,' Tania said. She glanced at the plate Tom slid in front of her, frowning at it. 'I'm not really hungry,' she said.

'Try it,' Clara said. 'It's delicious.'

After forking up a couple of mouthfuls, she set the plate aside. 'It's very good,' she said. 'Thanks, Tom. But I'm really not hungry.'

Tom cleared the plates without further comment and started to cook pancakes for pudding. Madeleine watched him with fascination as he ladled the mixture into a frying pan and swirled it around before he lobbed them into the air with a precision which saw them not only landing back into the frying pan, but with the cooked side up. Something Madeleine had tried, in the privacy of her kitchen, but never managed to achieve. Peeling pancake from the wall, the floor and once the light fitting, was more her style. As was levering burned mixture from the frying pan with the same ferocity that she'd needed to remove wallpaper when she redecorated her flat.

'So, Gull's busy tonight,' she said to Tania. 'What about tomorrow?'

Tania glanced around the table. 'Do any of you mind if he skis with us tomorrow afternoon?'

'Why would we mind?' Madeleine said. Inside her head she gave herself a high-five, and did a couple of fist pumps for good measure. 'That sounds fun. Although, thinking about it, you might have to count me out, if that's OK? I thought I might take the bus to see what Près du Ciel has to offer. Kind of traditional for me to have a high-pressured Christmas Eve last-minute dash around the shops.' She grinned. 'Can't help myself. I thought I might avoid it this year, but even in the mountains I'm woefully unprepared for the big day.'

Tania smiled and nodded, albeit in a rather distracted way. Her attention had wandered across to the picture window, even though all that was visible in the darkness were a few lights from the piste bashers, crawling up the highest slopes.

'Has anyone checked the weather?' Clara said. 'That storm is supposed to be getting here soon, too. Isn't that right, Tom?'

'What's that?' he said, spinning the last pancake onto the stack and bringing them to the table.

'The storm. It'll be here soon, didn't you say?' Clara asked.

Tom collected a tray on which stood bowls of sugar, segmented lemon, and a glass pourer with maple syrup, putting that beside the pancakes. 'I'm not totally sure when it's due,' he said. 'It depends how quickly it tracks across the mountains.' He turned away from the table.

'Will you sit with us?' Clara said, patting the back bar of the chair beside her. 'You've done nothing but work since we arrived.'

Smiling broadly at Clara, he took a seat beside her. 'Thank you. I'd love to.'

As Tom passed the plate of pancakes, he said, 'I think you'll be fine to ski tomorrow. But when it does arrive, we'll be in for a rough couple of days.'

'Ooh,' Madeleine said, adding a layer of dramatic emphasis to her voice. 'We might all get stuck here, cut off from the rest of civilisation with the storm raging outside. That'll make it a Christmas to remember, won't it?'

Tom nodded. 'It's forecast to be pretty ferocious. Looks like Christmas Day could be wild and woolly this year.' He studied Tania for a moment and said, 'Will I be cooking for one extra tomorrow evening?'

'I don't know,' Tania said. 'Let's see how intense this storm turns out to be, shall we? And I'll let you know.'

Chapter 22

Madeleine pulled the duvet up until it covered her shoulders and scrunched herself down into the pillows. She adjusted the waistband on her pyjamas. It was conceivable that they were tighter tonight than they had felt at the beginning of the week, although that hardly seemed possible, with all the exercise she'd taken. Or fair.

All that skiing must have negated at least some of the cake she'd eaten, surely? She crossed her arms under the covers. But then, the exercise had a bigger mountain to climb than cake, didn't it? Three extremely square meals a day since she'd arrived in France. Alcohol. Hot chocolate on tap. The cake was nothing more than the foothills.

It would have been good to have been able to smile at the analogy. Instead, she sighed in annoyance, mixed with more than a little frustration. At herself, for being so weak-willed where food was concerned. At food itself, for being so appealing. At Tom, for being such a good cook. At the Cocoon, for making lunch so accessible. And yes, she might as well spread the blame as far as it would go, so she levelled some at the fresh mountain air, too. Guilty of making her feel so desperately hungry. All the time.

Tomorrow she wouldn't have bacon for breakfast. Nor would she succumb to the delights of a freshly baked croissant. Or any of the baguette, which she enjoyed topping with that awesome yellow butter. She'd been right when she thought there would be cereals and muesli available, she just hadn't appreciated that would be in addition to all the freshly prepared food. But tomorrow morning, she would have a small bowl of muesli. And nothing else.

With a promise made to herself, she felt a little better about the waistband situation. A little. It didn't stop her mind from wandering, though, and she couldn't stop herself teetering dangerously close to the edge of the pit of jealousy.

How was it that Rose, who also enjoyed a healthy appetite, had curves in all the right places, whereas her own curvy bits seemed determined to form in places that made her blocky, rather than bountiful? She couldn't even claim to be Rubenesque, that would be far too lofty a reach. Whereas the memory of Rose, wearing that red costume in the hot tub, would be seared into her brain for the rest of her life.

And after seeing the micro-bikini Tania was able to get away with? No, not get away with, that was the wrong phrase. Tania didn't 'get away' with anything. She wore that bikini as if it would owe her for the rest of its existence, just for having been allowed to grace the gentle curves of her milky skin. Madeleine would place money on Tania never having to worry about the tightness of her clothes. That woman was like a tall puff of fresh air. Mind you, to be fair, she hadn't seen Tania indulging in any cake, or the stray pieces of baguette laced with the bright yellow mountain butter Madeleine had discovered she loved, so perhaps it wasn't surprising.

'Willpower,' she muttered to herself. 'Or rather, a lack of it in my case.'

'Say again?' Rose said, appearing from the bathroom. 'Sorry, I didn't hear you.'

'Nothing,' she said, shuffling over to face Rose as she slotted herself neatly between the covers.

'I know you well enough to know it isn't nothing, Maddy. Your eyebrows are doing that thing.'

'What "thing"?' Madeleine wasn't aware her eyebrows did anything out of the ordinary.

'One of them kinks up when you're unhappy about something.'

'Does it?'

Rose tied a loose band around her curls, then nodded. She slid fully beneath the covers.

'I was just thinking that I've eaten too much this week. Thinking I should perhaps rein it in a little.' She patted her stomach under the covers. 'You know, to maintain the sculpted quality of my body.'

Rose grinned. 'That's the trouble with the mountain air. Makes everyone super-hungry.'

'Doesn't seem to make Tania overly hungry. Or Clara. Just me.'

'And me. Stop pouting, Maddy. It doesn't suit you.' Rose shuffled further, settling in. 'And anyway, Clara's far too preoccupied to notice anything much, let alone food. At least, that's what I thought. But I wanted to talk to you about that.'

'Clara's eating habits?'

'No, dimwit. Although it's not totally unrelated. No. Her and Tom.'

'I think it's nice that she's getting on so well with him. Don't you? I mean, surely it's a sign she's beginning to feel better about . . . things?'

'Do you really think so?'

Madeleine frowned. She didn't feel qualified to hold an opinion on how Clara was behaving. Or feeling. 'I don't know. I don't suppose it can be a smooth path, can it? Learning to live with the loss will take as long as it takes, don't you think? And I'm not sure how anyone ever learns to live with losing a child. Do you?'

Rose sighed. 'No. I don't.'

They lay quietly for a while, then Madeleine said, 'How long were Clara and Mike together?'

'Forever. I can't remember exactly, but she might even have met him before she met Tania. They got married the summer after she finished art school and got her first contract to illustrate children's books. He never came to the lodge, though.'

'Why not?'

'He didn't fancy learning to ski.'

Madeleine stretched out her legs. At least they were no longer full-on painful, but they were firmly lodged high up on the scale of aches. 'I don't blame him, it's not exactly a walk in the park.'

'You're doing brilliantly.'

'Hmm.' Closing her eyes, she allowed herself to enjoy the pocket of warm air forming around her. 'I think it has to be a good thing,' she said, her voice muffled by the pillow. 'Clara liking Tom, I mean.'

'Are you playing fairy godmother again?' Rose said, her voice equally muffled.

'Not really. I mean, just because they like one another, it doesn't mean anything's going to happen, does it?'

'No. I suppose not.' Rose sighed. 'It's just that . . . I hope Tom doesn't take advantage of her. I don't think she's really thinking straight, and I can't believe she's looking for someone new. So, I suppose what I'm saying is I hope he doesn't get the wrong idea.'

'Or maybe she's found someone to have an uncomplicated chat with. Someone who doesn't have the same closeness to her situation that you and Tania have. Maybe it's as simple as that.'

'Maybe.'

At some point, Rose clicked off the bedside light, plunging the room into almost complete darkness. She shuffled herself into Madeleine's warm air, running a cool arm around her neck as she drew in close. Smiling in the darkness, Madeleine allowed her fingers to track across the silky smoothness of Rose's camisole shorts. 'Will you tell me?'

'Tell you what?' Rose said, her voice soft and inches from her lips.

'I need to know this is what you really want.'

'Of course it is.' Rose slid her fingers into Madeleine's hair, trailing them through it as she inched closer.

'Are you sure? It's just, with Lysander being here, and

you wanting us to keep everything such a secret . . . I wasn't sure . . .'

'Maddy, I want this,' she said, with increasing conviction. 'I just have some things to work through for myself. And if you want me to, I promise to tell you every last gory detail of my life once I have. OK?'

'Perhaps not every gory detail,' Madeleine said. 'I'm retracting any line of questioning relating to the Donkey reference, for example. There is such a thing as too much information. But I don't want you to keep anything from me.'

Rose breathed a mint-laced laugh. 'Deal,' she whispered. 'On one condition.'

'What's that?'

'That you stop talking and start kissing me instead.'

Madeleine didn't need to be asked twice, she'd wanted more than the minty warmth from Rose's breath since the beginning of the conversation. She needed to taste her. She leaned in, Rose's lips unbelievably soft on hers. They parted as Rose let out a low moan, allowing her to deepen their kiss. Fingers tracked across fabric, buttons yielded to allow skin to touch skin and Madeleine sucked in a breath as the heat, which had begun to build in the hot tub, exploded back into her body like a tidal surge, flattening everything in its path. The memory of Rose in that tight swimming costume, knowing how hard the nipples under that red fabric could become, was enough to submerge her completely, the last strands of rational thought loosing and washing away.

Clara leaned back against the mixed fabrics of the cushions on the sofa. There were more sofa accessories than ever before, with a couple of the throws made from faux fur. At least, she presumed it was faux fur. Some of the cushions were covered in linens, or leathers, or a variety of velvets. The cushions were of varying designs and colours, but they all complemented one another. An interior designer had undoubtably had their fingers in this particularly lucrative pie, no doubt organised by Tania's stepmother. Brigitte liked to stamp her authority on the things she viewed as hers, a little like an animal marking its territory, with a casual nonchalance only a fool would think wasn't backed up by teeth and claws, if needed.

The interior of the lodge had been systematically upgraded every few years, and Clara hadn't visited in a while, but one of the most noticeable additions was the piece of art hanging on the wall between the picture window and the corner of the room. Mostly hidden by the Christmas tree, and luckily not in her line of fire when she'd launched her flute glass against the wall – was that only a couple of days ago? – the painting was undoubtably an original.

Clara levered herself from the sofa and took a closer look. She didn't recognise the artist, but the piece was classy. She had no trouble picking out its qualities, even though paint hadn't been her medium of choice at art school. But it had been Tania's. Clara hadn't seen any of Tania's work lately, she hadn't seen much of what anyone else was doing lately, but she had always held the opinion that Tania's talent with a paintbrush was another thing her friend was exceptionally good at dismissing with a shrug of a shoulder.

It didn't surprise Clara that a stranger's painting hung in this room, alongside the window that held the view Tania loved above any other. Just visible out of the corner of her eye, every time she looked through the window, was the reminder that her father hadn't asked for a piece of his daughter's work to hang on the lodge wall.

Clara sighed as she retook her seat. She wondered how much of that decision was Anthony's doing, and how much was a result of Brigitte's beautifully manicured iron fist.

Tom was still tidying the kitchen. A wash of guilt passed over her at having asked him to sit at the table while they had dessert. He had been polite and accepted, when he probably wanted to finish with his duties and get on with his evening. Maybe he wanted to head into Près du Ciel, have a few drinks in one of the many bars which were sprinkled throughout the underground complex. Maybe she shouldn't have asked him to join them, but she liked him. Liked talking to him. It felt normal.

Over the last couple of days she'd realised it was almost possible to feel peaceful for whole minutes at a time at Snow Pine Lodge. There were little pockets of time when, although the guilt remained sharp like a splinter under a fingernail, the grief didn't completely overwhelm her. There were fragments of time in which Mike and Poppy weren't spiralled into the black void, instead it was as if they were waving at her from a different room. Maybe it helped that they'd never visited Snow Pine Lodge together. Maybe it wasn't that at all.

'Can I get you anything else?' Tom's soft Scottish burr interrupted her thoughts.

She shook her head. 'No. Don't let me keep you. You've probably got somewhere you'd rather be.'

'Not really,' he said, switching off the kitchen lights. He hesitated as he looked at the twinkling fairy lights on the tree. All the bulbs were the same soft white, winding their way up the tree sparsely hung with nothing but delicate, handblown glass baubles holding miniature alpine scenes and a silver star at the very top. Elegant, if a little soulless, Clara thought.

'Our tree used to be covered in all sorts,' he said. 'Everything shoved everywhere. Nothing matching.' He huffed a laugh. 'Same God-awful fairy at the top. Always felt sorry for her, sat up there with the tree stuck up her backside for a month.'

Clara wondered which tree he was referring to. His childhood tree? Or a more recent one? Folding her arms, she did her best to banish the memory of the table-top tree Mike had bought when Poppy was crawling, keeping it out of her reach for fear of her pulling it over and being hurt. Or last year's one. The one Poppy helped decorate. Nothing but a few pieces of tinsel and some lights making it any higher up than Poppy could reach, baby fingers fumbling with every bauble but fierce determination in those blue eyes as she insisted on placing every single one on a branch. Several boughs ended up touching the floor with the weight of their festive load. Clara couldn't stop herself smiling at the memory, her eyes filling with emotion. She did her best to shake the tears away, blinking repeatedly to get herself back under control.

'I'll turn the lights off, shall I?'

She stood and rubbed at her eyes while he headed for the tree and flicked the power off.

'Well,' he said. 'I'll wish you a goodnight, then.'

'Yes. Goodnight, Tom.'

He made to walk away, then seemed to change his mind. 'I might be way off base here, but would a hug help?'

She frowned. How much of what she was feeling was written on her face, she wondered. She tried so hard to react as normally as she could to things, even when they were overwhelming.

'It's just, first Christmas after . . .' He squirmed away from saying the words, but she knew what he meant. 'It's got to be so tough for you right now. And, I don't know, I just thought . . .' His voice trailed away, his stance as awkward as his words.

'Yes please.' In a movement so swift it surprised them both, Clara bridged the gap between them and buried herself against his chest. After a few seconds, he wrapped his arms around her shoulders.

'I remember someone saying,' he said, his words buried in her hair, 'that every time they smiled, they felt themselves bleed a little more. The words have always stayed.'

She didn't reply, just burrowed her face into the soft fleece of his jumper, allowing him to tighten his hold. It wasn't so much bleeding, she thought, it was more of an arterial flow. After a while, she tilted her face to the side and took a deep breath, allowing it out slowly and deliberately. He took it as a signal, and perhaps that was what it had been. He loosened his hold and stepped away from her.

'What I mean is, I don't think anyone who cares about you wants you to do anything except be honest about how you feel. Don't smile if you feel like crying. Cry if you feel like crying,' he said.

'You're so kind, Tom. It's just that . . . Everyone is so concerned about the way *I* feel. And it's the wrong way around. I don't deserve it. The thing is, I still get to feel things. Mike doesn't. Poppy doesn't. They'll never feel anything ever again.' The words hitched in her throat again, but she wanted to finish. 'They're the ones people should care about, not me. Everyone's so concerned about me, and I don't deserve it.'

Tom stepped forward, attempting to envelop her again, but she edged away.

'Of course, you deserve their concern. You've been to hell. And you can't seriously expect the people who love you not to want to help, can you?'

'I suppose.' It was an inadequate response. She wanted to say that if they knew what really happened, they wouldn't. They'd understand why she didn't deserve their care. She wanted to tell him. She wanted to tell someone, to get it out in the open. To uncork the bottle which she'd been carrying ever since that day.

But her throat was too tight to say anything else, choked up by guilt. She left him standing beside the coffee table and went to her room. Kicking off her shoes and dumping her jumper on a chair, she climbed under the covers, pulling her mobile to her ear as she wrapped the duvet around herself.

Mike's words flooded her brain as she closed her eyes and listened.

Tell Mummy where we're going.

To buy ellie babies. Clara strained to hear Poppy's voice in the background, just as she did every time she listened.

That's right, Pops. Did you hear that, gorgeous lady? We're going to buy jelly babies for our favourite person. Which ones does Mummy like best?

Onge ones. Mumma loves onge ones.

And which ones does Poppy like the best?

Green. My like green ones.

Clara clutched the phone harder to her ear as Mike laughed. That warm, open, easy laugh that she had loved so much.

And do you think Mummy's going to enjoy her bit of peace and quiet without us?

Squeezing her eyes more tightly closed, she fought to stay quiet, fought to stop the scream which was forming somewhere beneath her solar plexus. Willing it to at least remain silent so she could listen to the rest of the conversation before the darkness overwhelmed her again.

Poppy misses Mumma a-ready.

We're going to have fun, though, aren't we?

Yes. My want ellie babies, Daddy.

Hope you're enjoying your lie-in, Clara. Have a great day and let me know if you want me to bring back some takeaway. The traffic is awful on the ring road, we've been stuck in it for a while. God only knows what the problem is, it looks clear on the other side, so we shouldn't be held up on the way back. See you soon. Love you. Bye.

Chapter 23

Christmas Eve dawned deceptively bright and clear. Tania stood at the picture window, thinking how impossible it was to believe that there was a massive storm heading their way. That, if it wasn't for the array of state-of-the-art equipment telling the meteorologists the weather system existed and was building up momentum even as she stood here taking in the perfect pink halo topping each mountain peak, there was no way anyone in Près du Ciel – or anywhere in the Alps – would believe it. After a while, she turned away and helped herself to some coffee.

Tom took a tray of glossy croissants from the oven, setting them onto the granite worktop, humming along to something Tania couldn't hear. The smell of freshly baked croissants and coffee was a winning combination, and she savoured a deep breath.

Pulling an earbud free, he looped it into the collar of his shirt. 'Did you hear they've named the storm?'

She shook her head. She hadn't forgotten her desire to disappear for the week. So far, she'd avoided social media, even though the pull to check her feeds had been verging on impossible to ignore. She hadn't checked any news providers, either.

Wondering what the media might be fixating on, whether it was anything to do with her or not, was an itch which took enormous amounts of willpower not to scratch. Had there been any further fallout from the situation with Rory, she wondered, or had everybody moved on to analyse another set of people and their inadequacies? With any luck the storm had taken centre stage instead.

Not for the first time, she considered what it must be like for someone like Tom, who checked the news in the same way as he checked his watch. Sometimes with an idle curiosity, sometimes with purpose or even fervour, but never with a feeling in the base of the stomach akin to having been intubated with liquid lead.

'Apparently, it's done quite a lot of damage in the UK, trees down, some damage to buildings, that kind of thing. They've named it Storm Clara.'

'Storm Clara?'

He nodded, pulled a packet of smoked salmon from the fridge and began peeling off the protective plastic. 'If you don't mind my asking, why is it that Clara thinks the car accident was her fault?'

Tania bristled. Her instinct was to close the conversation down. To tell him it was none of his business, and that he was talking rubbish to even suggest such a thing. A knee-jerk reaction, if she thought about it, but also standard protocol for a Harrington when dealing with outsiders wanting information.

'She doesn't,' she said.

Where had he got such a ridiculous idea from? How could Clara think that the accident could have been her fault? She hadn't even been in the car.

Thank God she hadn't been in the car.

Tania realised she'd never fully considered how she would feel if Clara had been in the car that day. If she'd died, too. She'd only ever looked at it from a single point of view, her point of view. A point of view through which she suffered Clara's grief, but through a filter. Tania had liked Mike very much, and Poppy had been perfection. A tiny replica of Clara. And although she felt their loss keenly, neither one of them had been *hers*. Not in the way Clara was. Clara was a part of who Tania was. The thought of losing her from her life was unthinkable.

Shoving her mug onto the table, she turned abruptly, taking herself back to the picture window. She hugged her arms around herself, staring at the view, the momentary blackness accompanying her thoughts almost too much to bear. Was this how Clara was feeling? Was this glimpse anywhere even close?

If it was, then it was no wonder her friend had to fight to survive every moment of every day.

Clara was surprised by the strength of Tania's hug when she entered the living area. It was unprompted, but not unwelcome. Tania wasn't usually one to be physically demonstrative with her emotions. She tended to keep them firmly in check, doing her best to watch what she said and what she did, especially in the public arena.

The invitation to Snow Pine Lodge itself was more indicative of Tania's style. The invitation to spend time in the space which Tania found more restorative than any other said everything. Clara knew what the mountains meant to her. Yes, the bars and the restaurants and the parties in Près du Ciel all had their place in the mix, especially when they were younger, but the draw was deeper than that for Tania. After all, someone like Tania could spend her time anywhere she liked. Invitations to gala evenings, red-carpet events and premieres littered her mantlepiece in the same way as fliers for the local dog walking service, or pizza delivery did most other people's. Lysander certainly spent more time crossing the Atlantic than he seemed to spend at the events he attended, and if that was what Tania wanted, she could do the same.

Instead, and especially this week, she'd chosen the quietness of the lodge setting for them to enjoy, and time spent in an outdoors that was hard to beat, however far you travelled. And Clara was under no illusion that she was the main reason for them all being here, this particular week, courtesy of Tania.

Today was Christmas Eve. Clara looked across at the tree, the lights already switched on and glittering through the polished clarity of the glass baubles, tiny drops of pine resin reflecting the light from the ends of the needles. No point trying to forget what the day was, although she wasn't sure how she'd made it this far. Was even more sure than before that she wouldn't have made it to this point if she had been at home. She closed her eyes and stopped seeing, concentrating instead on feeling the strength of Tania's hug.

'I want you to know how much I love you,' Tania said, the words barely more than a whisper. 'And I want you to know how much you mean to me.'

This was unfamiliar territory. Uncharted waters for them both, if the way they'd intensified their hold on one another was any indication. Tania never told people that she loved them. She just didn't.

'Clara, I really mean it. I need you to know.' The words were stronger, almost fierce, as Tania pulled back, her expression intense. She rubbed at an eye, as if worried there might be a tear in it, then hugged her a final time.

'I know you do,' Clara said, her face in Tania's hair. 'I know.'

As abruptly as it had begun, the hug ended. 'I just wasn't sure that I'd ever actually told you how much you mean to me. To all of us.' With that, Tania stepped away and headed for a mug already on the table.

Staring at the tree, Clara did her best to regain her composure, before the silence was broken by Madeleine tripping her way up the final few steps and Rose calling her a 'total klutz' from some point midway up the staircase.

Time for breakfast.

Tom was doing it on purpose, Madeleine decided. Just when she'd worked up enough willpower to forgo bacon in favour of muesli, he decided to make smoked salmon and scrambled eggs to accompany the freshly baked croissants. With little snips of chives topping the piles of fluffy egg.

The man was a monster. No two ways about it. There was no way he could possibly know it was one of her favourites. How on earth was she supposed to resist this latest temptation? The plan to have a small bowl of muesli went sailing across the room along with the crockery, in her mind's eye, the flakes of healthy, sustaining oats and nuggets of sultanas, the clusters of nuts arcing through the air and scattering across the enormous rug that covered the floor beneath the table. So much for willpower.

'Can I just have a small portion?' she said in desperation.

'No problem,' he said, flashing her a bright smile.

Madeleine studied the back of his head as he set about whisking more eggs, checking his hairline for previously unnoticed lumps, where the beginnings of horns might show up. Perhaps demons could completely submerge their horns within their skulls, she thought, to totally fool their human victims. Victims whose trousers were unmistakeably tight this morning. She leaned back far enough to see the whole of his back view. Looking for a forked tail, subtly hiding itself behind the folds of his black apron, perhaps.

'What are you doing?' Rose asked.

'Nothing,' she replied, pulling in her chair, and banishing thoughts of satanic forces at work in the pristine snow of the mountains. Pouring herself some tea, she did her best to ignore the slices of fresh baguette in a bowl in front of her and waited, with no small edge of impatience, for a plate holding culinary heaven with an aroma to match to arrive in front of her. She pushed negativity further away and picked up her fork.

'Is everyone happy to eat here tonight?' Tania said.

Madeleine nodded. Might as well give Tom another chance to weave his food spell even more thickly over them all. Perhaps by the time Christmas lunch rolled around, she wouldn't even notice the contract he would slip under her nose, wouldn't mind when he asked her to sign, using her own blood. Or, more likely, it would just be Madeleine rolling around. She wondered if he'd made mince pies. Perhaps there would be traditional Christmas cake, or a chocolate Yule-log, with a robin made entirely from sugar paste perching on one end. Would there be Christmas pudding, with thick custard? She hoped so.

'I think it would be sensible,' Rose said. 'In case the storm tracks in this evening. I love the bus ride back up the mountain, but not in a gale force wind.'

'The bus probably won't even run if the weather's that bad,' Tom chipped in, placing the final two plates on the table.

'Do you mind cooking for us again?' Clara said.

'It's what I'm here for,' he replied with a grin, heading back to the kitchen area.

Madeleine took a forkful of egg, marvelling at the way it all but dissolved in her mouth. The man could cook, there was no doubt about it, and she, for one, was glad that was what he was here for. Expanding waistline or no expanding waistline. But she wondered when he got to have time off. He'd been in the kitchen all week.

Maybe it was one of those *Downton Abbey* scenarios, where the Harringtons failed to consider such menial things. Madeleine imagined a scene, in which Tania's stepmother – dressed in a flowing emerald-green gown for some reason, the light shining through the golden halo of her Scandi-blonde hair – asked in a bemused tone for a definition of a weekend, because every day was a party in her world. Perhaps it was in his contract that he had to work every day, come hell or high water.

Perhaps her imagination was getting the better of her. Again.

'When does he get a day off?' she asked Rose, quietly enough for the others not to hear.

'I'm not sure,' Rose said. She batted the question across to Tania. 'Maddy wants to know when Tom gets a day off.' She grinned in Madeleine's direction. 'I think she's fed up with his cooking.'

'No, I'm not.' Madeleine's cheeks coloured instantly; she could feel the prickle of heat. 'Not in the slightest. I was just curious.'

'In March,' Tania said, her face ramrod straight.

Madeleine's cheeks notched up another step on the heat-ometer. She glanced around the table, then across at Tom, who was oblivious to the conversation, earbuds plugged in and head nodding to whatever he was listening to. She looked back to Tania. 'Are you serious?' she said. The arch to Tania's eyebrows looked serious, from where she was sitting.

Then, to her relief, Tania began to smile. 'No, I'm not serious. Of course I'm not. It varies a bit depending on who will use the lodge and how long they'll be here for, but he gets at least one full day off a week, plus he's free to do what he likes between serving breakfast and getting the evening meal ready.' The arch returned to her eyebrow. 'And when my father and Brigitte are here, there will be a whole host of other staff as well. We get the basics on my week. They get the deluxe treatment.'

Madeleine wondered what else those guests could possibly need. This week was registering highly on her deluxe scale as it was.

Tania pushed back her chair and stood. 'Right, let's get this show on the road, shall we?'

Chapter 24

'I think we should take the bubble to the very top,' Rose said. She knew Madeleine wouldn't be keen, but there was method in her madness.

True to form, Madeleine shook her head. 'I'll never be able to ski down from there. No way. I'll ski off the side of the mountain or something. I know I will.'

'But you need to see the view.' Rose wasn't backing down. 'Plus, we can come back down in the bubble, if you want to.'

'We can?' Madeleine's expression brightened.

'We can.' Rose nodded. 'And I'll treat you to a hot chocolate at the top, if you like.'

'When did I ever not like the idea of a hot chocolate?' Madeleine grinned, her features relaxing.

From the top of La Bergerie bubble it was possible to see clear across to the neighbouring resort, nestling in a completely different set of peaks. If Madeleine thought she'd already seen some amazing scenery, then she would need to hold on to her helmet this morning. And along from the bubble sat a restaurant which teetered on the edge of the world. It was named Roche Pure. Pure rock. Rather apt, but she wasn't going to tell Madeleine about the sheer drop of the cliff face situated behind the restaurant's decking and clear Perspex-screened seating area. The feeling that you were suspended over the edge of the very mountain top. She would wait for her to experience it for herself.

'Or we could come down the Vizelle run,' Tania said. 'It's a blue and the only steep bit is at the top.'

'Or you and Clara could do Vizelle, Maddy and I can go

down in the bubble and we'll meet up at the mid-station,' she said. If the storm made this their last day of skiing, Rose was determined Madeleine would enjoy as much of it as possible. The top section of Vizelle was steeper than Tania was letting on. Steep and uneven. Not a problem for a skier like Tania, but she was forgetting how little time Madeleine had spent on the slopes. She supposed it showed how well Madeleine was doing, in fact, that Tania thought she could cope with the viciousness of that top section.

Madeleine nodded. 'I like that idea the best. Hot chocolate and less risk of death by dangerous, out-of-control skiing? Win-win, if you ask me.'

Only minutes later, Madeleine wanted to swear, very loudly. She also wanted to take a large step away from the edge, but they wouldn't let her. Stood in a row, with Rose on one side and Clara on the other, she was perilously aware of the edge of the mountain ridge behind her. The sense of absolute nothingness, which felt no more than inches behind her.

Tania stood a little way back from them, nearer to the bubble station, her phone out as she shepherded them ever closer to the edge.

'That's close enough,' Madeleine hissed, through clenched teeth. 'For the love of God, that's close enough.'

Rose began to laugh, and Tania snapped a few more shots before she lowered her phone and walked towards them.

'Your turn,' Madeleine said, indicating for Tania to swap places with her.

Tania shook her head. 'That's kind, but I promised myself no media this week. Photos included.'

'Beautiful ladies, I take your photo.'

Tania was already shaking her head as the small man approached, a professional long-lens camera strung around his neck.

'I take you all together.' He pulled his camera to his face, gesturing for them to huddle up.

'No thank you.' Tania turned away. 'Not today.'

He shook his head, the woollen ear flaps from his bobble hat following his movement. 'Most beautiful ladies of the day, will you allow me the privilege? Photos available in Près du Ciel. Next to Ski World. Easy to find.' He held out a card, as if that might change the situation.

'The ladies said no.'

The voice came from behind the little man, the owner of the voice tall and broad and decidedly Gull-shaped.

'Hi, Gull,' Madeleine said, grinning at him.

The photographer retreated, the frown of annoyance on his face quickly replaced by a smile as he zeroed in on another group exiting the bubble station and greeted them with another well-practised compliment.

'We must stop running into one another like this,' Gull said. He looked at them all in turn, a smile tweaking at his face, but Madeleine couldn't help but notice the way the look in his eyes changed when he settled his gaze on Tania.

Madeleine was expecting Tania to smile at him. To greet him with warmth and possibly for the two of them to embrace. A kiss wasn't outside the realms of possibility, as she rolled the camera in her head. Maybe Gull would sweep Tania from her feet, twirl her around. That would make a fantastic shot, especially with the mountains in the background. Maybe they would wait until someone sent a drone out, to film them with a *Sound of Music*-style panoramic scene, and then go for it with the twirling and the kissing.

Except that Gull had his skis in one hand, making the whole twirling thing a little tricky, and Tania wasn't smiling. In fact, she looked annoyed.

'We didn't need any help from you,' Tania said.

Tania shouldn't feel annoyed, but if Gull thought she was incapable of dealing with one of the many mountain-top photographers, he was very much mistaken. They were like newborn kittens in comparison to most of the paparazzi she'd dealt with. It annoyed her that he didn't think she could cope by herself. That he felt they needed a man to back them up. That a woman couldn't say no for herself and mean it. If he even knew half of the things she'd dealt with over the years, he wouldn't have intervened.

But he didn't know, did he? Because he knew nothing about her. And that was how she wanted it to be, wasn't it? She couldn't have it both ways.

Gull's jawline tightened a little. He looked as if she'd slapped him. 'I suppose I should have expected that.'

'No need to be a bitch, Tania,' Rose said, under her breath but loud enough for everyone to hear. 'He was just trying to help.'

'I know we're supposed to be meeting later, but when I saw you here, I thought you might like to meet my brother, and Niamh. But I'm clearly overreaching again. I'll leave you to it.' He made to turn away.

Tania looked past him, to a small group standing a little way off. The photographer handing a card to a woman who zipped it into a pocket as she said something to the man standing next to her, making him laugh. Gull's brother – Tania recognised the green jacket and the frame. And the woman must be his fiancée, she supposed. A couple of others, their gaze shifting across to Gull every few seconds, looking impatient to get going.

'No,' she said, by way of an apology. 'I'd like that.'

'We'll head for the restaurant,' Clara said. 'See you there in a few minutes?'

Nodding, she allowed Gull to lead her across to the group.

'This is Tania,' he said, introducing each one of them in turn. She shook hands briefly and politely, each of them greeting her with open smiles and no hint of surprise. She had been mentioned, that much was clear.

'It's good to meet you,' Niamh said, holding her hand

a fraction longer than the others, her expression hard to read.

'I hope Gull wasn't late to your dinner. If he was, you can blame me,' Tania said.

'David was there on time, and he's the important one, so . . .' As she spoke, the Irish lilt to Niamh's voice grew stronger. She shifted her skis from one shoulder to the other and pulled off a glove, revealing a discreet diamond set into a gold band glittering almost as brightly as the snow in the sunshine. 'He took his time, but as usual with him, it was worth the wait.'

'It's beautiful,' Tania said. 'Congratulations.'

'It's the oddest thing, but I feel like you and I have already met,' Niamh said. 'I mean, Gull described you, but you know how useless men are at that kind of thing. The details were scant, let's put it that way.'

Tania wondered just how hard he'd been grilled. It was no surprise that the details were scant. Scant details were all he had.

Niamh studied her as she pulled the glove back on, then shook her head. 'Never mind me. Will you be taking Gull off our hands for the rest of the day?'

'If he likes.'

'Oh, I know he would like that very much.' Niamh laced her words with emphasis. 'Keep him for as long as you like.' Smiling, she dropped her skis to the ground and slotted her boots into them. 'Good to meet you, Tania. See you again, perhaps.'

The group slid away from them, Niamh turning and taking another long look at her before they disappeared over the lip at the top of the slope.

Gull watched them go, then took hold of her hand through its glove. He squeezed, then let her hand drop. She wished he'd held on for longer.

'Let's get a drink,' he said.

This time she didn't argue, didn't make things difficult. She didn't want to.

By the time they set their skis into a mound of snow beside the entrance to Roche Pure, and clunked their way onto the restaurant decking, the girls had already got their drinks and had colonised a table right beside the Perspex barrier. Much to Madeleine's horror, if her expression was anything to go by.

'No,' Madeleine said, shuffling out from the bench facing the breathtaking view. 'Rose, that's even worse, because I'm facing you and it looks like there's nothing at all behind you and if you lean backwards, you're just going to disappear off into the abyss.' Sidestepping to the end of the table, she perched on the edge of the chair heading the table, her eyes darting across to the chasm behind the decking. 'Fuckity-fuck,' she said, under her breath, twisting her head until the view was obscured behind the curtain of her rich chestnut hair.

'Are you OK?' Tania asked, even though it was clear Madeleine was anything but.

'Maddy's having an "adverse reaction" to the view,' Rose said, miming inverted commas around the words.

'Too right I am,' Madeleine said with a dramatic huff. 'There's a sheer bloody drop. Just there . . .' She waved frantically with the hand nearest the Perspex, keeping her eyes fixed on the table.

'Let's choose a different table, then,' Tania said. 'Grab that one, Gull.' She pointed to a free table behind him. He made a 180-degree swivel and set his gloves and helmet on the table. 'We can still admire the view from here.' She settled herself at one end of a bench.

Madeleine slid her hot chocolate onto the table and sighed as she sat down, her back to the view. 'Thank you.' She stuffed her gloves into her helmet and propped it beside her.

'No problem.' Tania glanced up at Gull. 'Will you get me a coffee?'

She said it without thinking, and his confused expression made her smile, then feel guilty. But he recovered more quickly than she did, checking the specifics before he headed into the restaurant. As if buying her a coffee was something he did every day of the week. As if letting him buy her a coffee was something she did with similar frequency. Tania sat in the sunshine at the top of the mountain allowing herself to enjoy the moment. To enjoy how easy that had been.

'He's really lovely,' Madeleine said, when Gull was well out of earshot.

'I think you might be right,' she replied, closing her eyes and tipping her face to the sun. Perhaps it could be this easy. Perhaps this was how it was supposed to be. Perhaps it was she who made everything in her life more of a battle than it needed to be.

Chapter 25

'You don't *look* terrified,' Rose said, peering at the tiny image of her, Clara and Madeleine on Tania's phone.

'Don't get me wrong,' Madeleine said as Gull emerged from the Roche Pure, a tray in one hand. Tania could see the concentrated furrow to his eyebrows as he negotiated the decking, weaving between tables rapidly filling up with thirsty customers. Madeleine continued, 'The view up here is quite something. But I don't need to be so very *close* to it to appreciate it.'

'I didn't realise you would be quite so worried,' Rose said, handing Tania back her phone. 'It's perfectly safe, otherwise they wouldn't be allowed to have tables there.'

'I'm sure you're right. But since when did logical thought get in the way of pure unadulterated terror?' Madeleine said.

Tania tapped her phone again as Gull set the tray down. He peered over her shoulder to look at the photos she'd taken of the other three. Leaning forward to swipe through them, he slid onto the bench beside her. She breathed in a waft of pine needles and cinnamon.

'They're great,' he said, pushing his thigh against hers as he passed her a coffee, then ripped the top from a sachet of sugar and poured it into his *vin chaud*.

Tania shifted on the bench to zip away her phone, then slid back against him.

'First time up here?' he said to Madeleine.

'How did you guess?' she said, pushing hair behind an ear. 'Was it my expression of utter terror that did it, or my uncharacteristic use of four-letter words which gave the game away?' Her grin was back.

'It's not as sheer as it looks,' he said.

'It bloody is over there,' Madeleine said, gesturing towards the wall of Perspex.

'Well, yes, OK. It is over there. Which is why there are nets set a little way down, just in case,' Gull replied.

Madeleine's expression took on a triumphant edge as she turned to Rose. 'See? Nets. Why would they need nets if it's so perfectly safe? Explain that to me.'

Rose rolled her eyes. 'That's just to stop morons high on something who decide they can defy gravity. Or fly. It doesn't apply to everyday people doing everyday things.'

Madeleine frowned. 'I am yet to be convinced. I just want you to know that.'

Tania smiled. 'Nothing wrong with a healthy sense of self-preservation,' she said.

Gull slid an arm around her waist, resting a hand on the small of her back. It made her shiver. She took a sip of coffee to cover the involuntary movement.

'I didn't notice much of a sense of self-preservation in your skiing,' he said to her.

'I'm always in control,' she said.

He slid a couple of fingers underneath the seam of the back of her jacket, tucking them inside the waistband of her ski trousers. Still layers away from her skin, but the effect was seismic. Turning until his lips brushed the air beside her ear, he said, 'Not always, surely.'

Goosebumps shot their way up her spine as he reversed his fingers' path until his touch was replaced by mountain air. She shifted, adjusting her jacket before she took another sip of coffee. Looking at him out of the corner of her eye, she was aware that the conversation about self-preservation was continuing. That they were discussing the way this resort marked the skiing areas with poles, not only denoting the colour of the run – green, blue, red or black, as well as mogul runs and the fun parks – but the fact that the poles to the left of the run were also marked with yellow bands, in case conditions were so bad that it became impossible to see where the piste was.

Tania had skied in those kinds of conditions, not through choice, but usually when a chairlift or a bubble took her up into the cloud cover, into a whiteout. Negotiating those kinds of conditions felt like skiing five minutes after downing a bottle of whisky. It became impossible to tell ground from sky, up from down, instantly creating a feeling of nausea and disorientation. It wasn't pleasant. If Madeleine ever needed to worry about falling off the edge of a mountain, those were the conditions in which it became a dangerous possibility.

Gull was telling them an anecdote about a similar experience with bad weather, but she didn't want to join in the conversation. Instead, she wanted to steal a look at him. This was the closest she'd been to him since their kiss the previous evening. As he chatted, he ran a hand around the line of his jaw, into his wild, mahogany curls and back out again. An unconscious action, but one that had her desperate to follow the same path, not with her eyes, but with her own fingers. Or better still, her lips. She wanted to know how his skin tasted, whether it felt soft under her lips in its relatively freshly shaven state. How that would change as the day progressed, as the shadow began to form. Would it be rough to the touch by the afternoon, or would she have to wait until the dark hours of the night to feel it like that?

She swallowed, trying to distract herself with what she'd forgotten was an empty coffee cup. It clinked back into its saucer.

'Can I get you another?' Gull said.

'No. Thank you.' She frowned.

'Are you OK?'

'I'm fine.'

'Do you mind my being here? I know we said we'd meet up later. Just tell me if I'm intruding on your plans.'

He couldn't have been further from the mark if he'd tried. It was as if there was nowhere else he could possibly have been, or her for that matter.

'Do you prefer Irish wolfhounds?' she said. 'Or Dalmatians?'

If he was confused by her sudden segue in the conversation's direction, the confusion was only momentary; the frown dissipating before it had time to form properly, replaced instead by one of his lightning smiles, bright and sudden, and gone again just as quickly.

'I like them both. I like pugs too, for the record,' he said, twisting towards her. 'Even if they are awkward little buggers.'

He traced a path down the side of her face with a fingertip, moving with infinite deliberateness until his fingers rested on her neck, his thumb caressing the skin below her chin with the tiniest of movements.

Clara cleared her throat. Tania was no longer on planet Earth, that much was obvious. Her attention had been on Gull, one way or another, since he'd appeared. And now he held her totally transfixed. But it wasn't that which surprised Clara. If anything, it pleased her. It took a lot to get, and maintain, Tania's attention.

What did surprise her, however, was that Tania was allowing him to touch her, in public. OK, so it wasn't anything more than the gentlest of touches. It wasn't an attention-grabbing PDA. It wasn't as if they were unzipping one another's clothing or kneading at each another like horny teenagers, all tongues and moaning. Somehow it was far more intimate than that. Or perhaps that was simply because she knew how out of character it was for her media-savvy friend to allow it.

Either way, she felt as if she were intruding just by looking at them.

She glanced across at Rose, deep in conversation about something with Madeleine, then fixed her line of sight out towards the Perspex screen and the drop away to infinity.

Her stomach lurched. Not because of the knowledge of the drop on the other side of the screen, she knew that was there. It was a known quantity, something to be admired from a safe distance. No, it wasn't that that made her stomach lurch. It was the realisation that she was alone.

It was a weird thing to say that she had just realised she was alone. She'd been alone for four months. She'd been alone since a sense of crashing exhaustion had pushed her into demanding a day to herself. Banning her husband and baby girl from the house so she could have a few hours to herself. A few hours. That's all she'd wanted. And Mike, being Mike, had complied without argument. He'd taken their baby girl and they'd gone to the shops to buy treats before they headed to the park. All so that she could have a lie-in, for fuck's sake. She'd got her wish, and then some. She'd had more than a few hours to herself. Because they never came home. She'd been alone ever since.

And, looking around the table today crystallised the feeling into an absolute. Even if it didn't end up being Gull, Tania would find someone she would be unable to hold at arm's length. It didn't matter what she said, someone would break down her defences, sooner or later. And there was a closeness between Rose and Madeleine that Clara wasn't sure she could interrupt. Wasn't sure she wanted to.

It didn't matter what they said about being there for her, they had their own lives to live. Lives they should feel free to get on with. Lives like the one she'd already had. And lost.

She'd had her time in the sun.

Clara watched a bird of prey making the most of the thermals created by the warm sunshine. Whether it was scanning the area for potential food sources, or simply enjoying a moment on the wing was impossible to tell. The feathers at the tips of its wings were stretched out, its tail jinking and tilting like the flaps on an aircraft the only sign of effort. Clara tilted back her head and closed her eyes, the morning sunlight bright against her eyelids. It wasn't anyone else's task to throw her ropes and pull her back up from the black hole she'd fallen into. That was for her to do. Somehow. If she wanted to.

Or she could just take a running leap as far out towards the bird of prey as she could and let gravity do the rest.

Chapter 26

In the end, only Gull and Tania skied down from the very top of the mountain. The other three took the bubble down to the mid-mountain station. Watching Tania and Gull at the restaurant, and then as they skied off together, had stirred up uncomfortable emotions for Rose. After what she'd said to Madeleine the previous evening, it didn't seem fair to her that they were sneaking around, hiding their relationship.

'What I don't understand,' Madeleine said, 'is how I felt so unnerved by that Perspex screen and its view at the summit, and yet here we are, in a metal and – oh my God I've just realised, Perspex – bubble held hundreds of feet up in the air by nothing more than some strands of twisted wire. And in here, I feel fine. I don't get it.'

Rose stared through the window, watching the brown sheets of sheer rock disappear beneath blankets of the purest white snow, the marginally less-sheer drops already criss-crossed by the scars of off-piste skiers' tracks.

'You're just weird. Nobody ever tell you that?' Rose cocked her head, then looked away.

'Are you annoyed with me? I know you took me up there specially to see that view.'

Rose didn't reply, just shuffled against the angled seating as she fought her feelings of frustration.

Clara leaned across. 'Sometimes it's hard to control our reactions to things, don't you think? Especially when they aren't what we were expecting them to be.'

'Too right. My reaction up there was properly extreme,' Madeleine said.

Rose stared resolutely through the scratched window as the snowy cliffs became populated by firs, sparsely at first and then with increasing density. Below their bubble she could see the rough stumps of trees unfortunate enough to have tried to grow in the path of the lift, the cleared area opening out as the mid-station came into view. Small groups of skiers twisted their way down through the tree-lined run, some stopping at the station to take a bubble back to the top, others continuing on their way, or heading for the café/restaurant situated beside the run.

Waiting outside the bubble mid-station were Tania and Gull. Rose spotted them without much trouble, Tania's distinctive jacket and matching helmet made her easy to pick out, but she found herself frowning, her breath steaming up the window as she craned her head. Not only were they standing face to face, skis slotted between each other's in an intimate jigsaw, but Gull had his arm locked around Tania's waist. They couldn't be closer together if they tried. Not actually kissing, she didn't think, but deep in conversation. The kind of conversation nobody would even attempt to interrupt.

The twist in Rose's gut wasn't entirely unexpected, she felt it every time Tania found a new man. It was about time she got used to it. She drew back from the window, glancing instead at Madeleine. There was absolutely no reason on earth why Tania shouldn't be stood with a man wrapped around her. And anyway, the issue wasn't anything to do with Tania, or the person she was with. The issue was with herself. Rose knew that well enough, too.

Seeing Tania and Gull brought things even more sharply into focus. People skied past the pair, with no more than a casual glance in their direction. It was something you saw every day, a man and a woman together. They blended into the facade of the commonplace.

Rose had done her best to fit into that mould, had tried for years to walk in shoes that just didn't fit. And now that she had finally found the place where she fitted best, she wondered if she was strong enough to stay there. It was one thing to tell Madeleine how right everything felt with her – and it did, in a way Rose hadn't ever expected to feel. It was another to work out how to tell everybody else. Her parents, who were expecting a conventional marriage and grandchildren at some point in the not-too-distant future. Mr Helsom at the accountancy firm where she'd just been made junior partner, with his openly homophobic attitude. Rose just wasn't sure she had the energy to fight the battles she'd been presented with. She hadn't asked for any of them.

Running a hand across her forehead, she turned to find Madeleine staring at her.

'You OK?' Madeleine said.

'Yeah. I'm just a bit tired.' She wondered how long Madeleine had been looking at her.

'Me too,' Madeleine said, offering her a small smile.

The bubble swung as it entered the station, the metal stabiliser clanking against the guide rails as it steadied the movement, the swing subsiding as the bubbles in front and behind concertinaed together and the doors swung open.

Heading out towards the piste, Madeleine said, 'I'm sorry I didn't fully appreciate the view.'

Rose shook her head. 'Forget about it. I should have warned you.'

'I want you to know something,' Madeleine said, stopping just shy of the snow, where the overhang of the building and the rubber matting opened out. Clara carried on walking, heading for Tania, who now stood outside hip to hip with Gull, waiting for them.

Madeleine lodged her skis on the ground. 'Putting my fear of precipice-like drops to one side,' she said, her irrepressible smile reasserting itself, 'I can safely say this is turning out to be the best week. Ever. So, thank you for wanting me to be here.'

'Do you know the strange thing?' Rose said, dropping the end of her skis onto the rubber matting.

'My obsession with snowmen?'

'No.'

'My inability to make a bed properly?'

'No, although now you come to mention it, how is it that you find that so hard?'

'Natural ineptitude,' Madeleine said with a grin. 'So, what is it? This strange thing?'

'I've been skiing with Tania, and Clara, for longer than I can remember, and I know you've only been here for five days, but it honestly feels like you've always been part of these trips.' She frowned, unsure if she'd vocalised her thoughts correctly.

Meeting Madeleine had been one of those random, chance encounters on – of all places – the steps outside Brockborough library, when the bottom fell out of the plastic bag Madeleine was using to transport her latest haul of thrillers and Rose stopped to help her pick them up. That chance meeting led to a coffee in the Brockborough Bean, the town's most artisan of cafés, where they discussed Baldacci versus Patterson. At the time, there was nothing more to it than that. They arranged to meet up again the following week, to continue the discussion. The discussion turned into a good-natured argument when Madeleine tried to insert King into the mix, but Rose would have none of it, determined that Stephen King would forever remain in the category of horror, not thriller. Before Rose knew it, she was looking forward to the weekly coffee; soon it was as if they'd been friends for years.

Seated at their favourite table in 'The Bean' as they'd nicknamed it, only a few months previously, talk turned to their choice of most fanciable classic fictional character. 'Let me guess,' Rose had said. 'I'm betting you're on Team Darcy. Am I right?'

Madeleine shook her head, the expression on her face still firmly embedded in Rose's memory when she said, 'No. I'm more into Elizabeth Bennet . . .'

The way the bottom of Rose's stomach twisted as Madeleine continued to hold her gaze, and she realised that she'd always far preferred the quiet strength and determination of Lizzie Bennet too – had always imagined her with the most amazing cheekbones – was without doubt a pivotal moment. And once she'd thought it, it was as if there had never been room for any alternative.

And the same thing had happened this week. Rose couldn't imagine skiing without her, couldn't seem to remember what it had been like, before.

'I know I'm hard work,' Madeleine said, 'but I didn't realise I'd been that much of a wormhole.' She grinned, then gathered up her skis, ready to head over to the others.

'Maddy? Wait a minute, would you?'

The tone of her voice must have given her inner turmoil away. Madeleine set her skis down again. 'What's the matter? You've been out of sorts all day.'

'I don't want to hide it any longer.'

'Hide what?'

'Us.'

'So, don't.'

'Yes, but . . .'

Madeleine had managed a casual-sounding set of replies and had applied one of her stock smiles to give herself time to assimilate what Rose was saying. It was what she had been desperate for, without question. But the expression on Rose's face was still guarded. As if she wanted to tell the others, but only if she could be sure it would all work out perfectly. Without any drama, or discomfort.

'But they're my friends,' Rose said. 'What they think matters.'

'What do you think they're going to think?' Madeleine crossed her arms. Which was no mean feat, with an armful of skis and poles. 'I'm fairly sure they're not going to turn us out into the snow and lock the door behind us. Or insist we pretend we're sisters. It's not the fifties any longer.'

It had been a while since Madeleine had come out. How she hated that expression. And why it was deemed necessary in the first place was beyond her. After all, straight people didn't have to confess their predilections, did they? They just got on with it. Like Tania and Gull, who'd known one another for little more than five minutes, but were stood in such proximity it must seem obvious to every passer-by that they couldn't wait to be closer to one another than jam and peanut butter in a sandwich.

To be fair to Rose, though, Madeleine knew how she was feeling.

In the end, the first outsider Madeleine had confided in – other than the girl she'd begun seeing, obviously – was a stranger, on a bus ride from Handleigh Parvill back into Brockborough.

To this day, Madeleine wasn't sure the old woman had heard her correctly; she'd seemed very enthusiastic about the news. Although Madeleine liked to think that she'd heard perfectly and that it was a sisterhood thing – perhaps the old lady was gay, too, and was celebrating Madeleine's seeming lack of inhibition, the progress of modern youth, the supposed openness of twenty-first century life. The old lady wished her luck, told her she felt sure it would all be 'marvellous'. All Madeleine felt was nausea. Once she'd told a complete stranger, there was no reason for her to stall any longer from telling her family. Her friends. And that proved immeasurably more difficult. But that was in the past, that was – as they say – ancient history. Her brother might still be ignoring her calls five years later, resolutely unable to accept his sister being gay, but she'd long since managed to convince herself that it was his loss.

'Why don't you kiss me?' she said, catching Rose unawares.
'What?'
'Kiss me, here and now. They'll see. Problem solved.'
Rose's features flexed into a frown. She shook her head.
'Why not?'

'I can't. Not like this.'

Madeleine sighed. She was being selfish. 'Fair enough. Sorry. I didn't mean to pressure you. I appreciate you saying you want to get it out in the open, and you'll know when it's the right moment, I'm sure. It's just that sometimes it's easier to rip the plaster off, you know?' The others looked completely confused about what the two of them could possibly have needed to stop to talk about beneath the bubble overhang, when there was so much snow waiting to be slid across. 'Come on,' she said. 'Let's ski.'

She wasn't sure if her boot hit a rock, or a lump of ice, but she hadn't got more than a metre across the snow before her foot was going in an unexpected direction and gravity decided to enter from stage left, again. She ended up face-planting in the snow, her skis falling one way, poles the other.

'Unbelievable.' Rolling onto her side, she held out a hand for Rose to help her.

It took a moment before any help was forthcoming, however, because Rose was too busy trying not to laugh. It was one way to defuse the tension, Madeleine supposed. She'd long suspected she was a comic genius. It was just that sometimes her timing was a bit off.

Chapter 27

'What are everyone's afternoon plans?' Clara asked.

'I'm not sure,' Tania said, stretching herself out against the leather of the banquette she occupied in the corner of L'Avalanche restaurant. 'There's no rush to move, is there?'

An unexpectedly chilled-out response, Clara thought. Tania tended to have a rigid idea of what she wanted to achieve in a day, often had things planned with something approaching military precision. And with the approaching storm, the skies already clouding over as they arrived at the restaurant, Clara thought Tania would be feeling the desire to get in some serious skiing even more intensely. Gull's presence seemed to be diluting her fervour – for the snow, at least. They sat opposite her, their thighs hard up against one another. The proximity hadn't gone unnoticed by her, even if it wasn't particularly obvious to anyone else in the packed restaurant.

Before Clara could comment on Tania's lack of focus, Rose beat her to it. 'Way too relaxed. I'm thinking alien body-swap. Who are you, and what have you done with the real Tania?'

'I like it,' Madeleine said. 'I think it suits you, Tania. Plus, relaxed is my idea of a holiday.'

Tania ignored them, looking at Clara instead. 'What do you want to do?'

In truth, Clara wasn't sure it mattered. She was prepared to go through the motions and join in with whatever the group decided. 'Honestly, I don't mind.'

'Well, like I said, I've got to head into the centre of Près du Ciel soon,' Madeleine said, checking her watch. 'Do you fancy joining me for a bit of retail therapy? Maybe a coffee and an inappropriate impulse buy or two?'

Clara nodded. 'Sounds good to me.'

'Rose is coming too, aren't you?' Madeleine tilted her head none too subtly towards Tania and Gull and raised her eyebrows. She looked a little like she was having a seizure, but Rose got the rather obvious message.

'Yes, Maddy, I'm coming too,' she said.

'Will you be all right without us?' Madeleine said to Tania, a grin forming on her face.

'Do you play poker?' Tania asked.

'No,' Madeleine said. 'Why?'

'Probably just as well.' Gull huffed a laugh. 'Yes, Madeleine. We'll be just fine,' Tania added.

'We won't be back at the lodge for quite a long time,' Madeleine said. 'And I'm pretty sure we won't need to use the—'

Rose elbowed Madeleine as she stood. 'You've made your point,' she said. 'No need to hammer it home.'

Madeleine began to smirk but didn't finish her sentence. Clara stood, too, shuffling out from the seating.

'Have a great afternoon,' she said, gathering her gloves and turning to follow the other two.

'Clara?' Tania leaned forward, stretching a hand in her direction. 'Are you sure you'll be OK?'

Clara smiled. 'Of course. Everything's going to work itself out, you'll see.' She headed after Madeleine and Rose, who were already halfway across the main bar area. At the top of the small flight of steps separating the two areas, she turned in time to see Gull lean towards Tania, his fingers brushing strands of her hair from her shoulder before he shifted and whispered something into her ear. Something amusing, judging by the uptick in Tania's expression.

Clara could have been a ghost, stood on those steps, watching but totally unseen. Remembering emotions, but sure in the knowledge that they would never be hers to enjoy again. She pulled in a deep breath and looked away.

Usually, lunch was nothing more than a pit stop. In fact, if Tania had her way, half the time she wouldn't bother to stop at all, would just grab a sandwich and eat it in the bubble lift.

Today was different, though. Tania couldn't remember the last time she would have willingly spent the whole afternoon in a mountain restaurant. But with Gull sandwiching her between his body and the corner of the bench seat, the last thing she wanted was to have to move. The combination of warmth and comfort laced with the undeniable frisson of excitement from his closeness was hypnotic. Plus, she told herself, Gull's knee was bound to be giving him cause for discomfort and he needed to rest it, even if he was pretending it was all fine.

'I get the feeling they know all about my hot tub comment,' he said, once the girls had left.

Tania toyed with the pot of condiments. 'You're a regular Sherlock Holmes, aren't you?' She grinned at him. 'They wheedled it out of me. I only met Madeleine this week. Let's just say she has a knack for getting to the bottom of things.'

'Is that proving to be a good or a bad thing?'

'Oh, I'm thinking it's a good thing.' After all, if it hadn't been for Madeleine, she wouldn't be sitting in L'Avalanche with him. And the longer she spent in his company, the more convinced she became that it wasn't a waste of their time.

'Do you want anything else to drink?' he said. 'Or should we think about making a move?'

Tania groaned. 'Can't we stay a bit longer?'

'I would happily stay put all day. But I'm a bit concerned about how the weather's turning. Plus, there's a hot tub with our names written all over it. I wouldn't want to disappoint Madeleine.'

'How selfless of you,' she said. It was true to say that the thought of Gull in the hot tub created a network of searing pathways of heat in her body. That just as she had enjoyed her illicit peek at him when he'd applied ice to his knee, she was sure that seeing some more of him, barely clothed and hazy through the steam rising from the water, wouldn't disappoint.

If they did go back to the lodge to take advantage of having the place to themselves, she wondered how it would play out. Whether it would live up to the fantasy he seemed to have created in his own head. Or her own one, which had been forming since they'd kissed in the light of the stars. Her cheeks flared with colour, the tip of her tongue running an unconscious path to moisten her lips.

'I do my best to think of the needs of others,' he said, his fingers touching and then tightening against the curve of her thigh.

She closed her eyes and drew in an extended breath. 'How are you making me feel like this?' she said, the words escaping almost silently as she breathed out.

'Sorry, what did you say?'

'Nothing. Perhaps you're right.'

'About what?' The lopsided smile was back.

'Not the hot tub. You're obsessed. No, we should probably make a move. Try to get a few more runs in. Especially if the weather is deteriorating.'

The bluebird skies from earlier that morning had started clouding over on their way to the restaurant, turning everything varying shades of dull grey. Choosing to sit indoors at L'Avalanche had seemed the sensible choice, and as they emerged from the windowless lower-level seating area and headed for the doors, it became clear just how much the weather had closed in.

Snow was falling in thick, fluffy lumps, blanketing everything, and soundproofing the world. It was impossible to tell one pair of skis from another, every set in the rack stood like a long-forgotten artefact coated in the dust and cobwebs of centuries. They brushed snow from skis situated in roughly the place where their pairs had stood, eventually locating their own and slotting them onto boots before they too became hidden by the rapidly accumulating powder.

Tania turned to Gull, snow already topping his shoulders. 'Shall we head straight to the lodge?'

Gull nodded. The weather had decided their fate. The tops of the mountains had disappeared into brown clouds, making the prospect of taking any lifts to higher runs unappealing.

The ski back to the lodge was slower than under usual circumstances and eerily silent. Through her goggles, the world looked yellow and lumpy, with even the most obvious of landmarks distorted by the sudden dump of snow. Fresh powder snow was what every seasoned skier loved – there was nothing better than making the first set of lines through pristine virgin snow – but in this instance the heavy, wet snow was being banked into unpredictable shapes by the sheer number of skiers heading off the hill.

Inexperienced skiers were finding conditions challenging, the sudden change of speed from the standard snow cover to a bank of newly laid snow taking many by surprise. Tania wondered how Madeleine had fared, hoping the others were safely back at base, or perhaps already in the subterranean complex of shops in Près du Ciel centre.

She stopped to help fallers, one of the unwritten codes of the mountain, and Gull did the same, making their own descent considerably more laborious. Even the wait for the final chairlift they needed to take to get into the correct valley to reach Snow Pine Lodge was muted. No shouts and grins, no excited skiers turning to see how far in their wake they'd left friends, no rapid discussion about where to go next. The focus was not unlike that she'd experienced waiting for the bubble to get onto the glacier, but for the opposite reason.

The queue was long, the wait cold and dull. The flipside of the excitement of the previous days. She shivered – this time with cold, and when Gull put his arm around her, looping his gloved hand beneath her shoulder blade to pull her close, she didn't object.

Eventually, they reached the front of the queue, taking the two spaces on the magic carpet closest to the lift operators. This afternoon their attention rested solely on tipping seats down for the next group of passengers, in between times shifting rapidly accumulating snow from the workings of the lift. No time for idle chatter or smoking Gauloises today.

Conditions worsened all the way back, the snow piling down so fast it became almost impossible to see the hand she held out in front of her face. Tania felt genuine relief when she located the post indicating the cut-through to the lodge. It was no more than a vertical resting place for yet more snow but, knowing this part of the resort so well, she had no trouble using the trees as a guide. Neither of them spoke until Gull lifted their skis into the locker and they'd brushed the worst of the snow from jackets and clonked their boots free of ice. Standing under the porch, Tania punched in the code and, once inside, pushed the door closed with a decisive click.

'Wow,' Gull said. 'That was extreme.'

Tania looked around. Three sets of boots already adorned the arms of the boot warmer; helmets and goggles lined the shelf above the coat pegs. Underneath the boots the flooring was wet, but they were no longer dripping. They'd been hanging there for a while. All credit to Madeleine, she thought, her shoulders relaxing a notch. She had been carrying an unconscious layer of worry, she recognised, that something untoward could have happened to her friends on their way back.

Another glance told her their snow boots were gone, a quick turnaround to get down to Près du Ciel centre by the look of things. Or, if her impression of Madeleine was on point, a quick exit to leave the lodge empty for her and Gull. The thought made her smile. She'd never been conscious of another woman actively supporting her where men were concerned – she'd never felt as if she needed support. After all, she'd never wanted anything more complicated than the obvious from a man, and they were usually more than happy to oblige in that respect. There hadn't been any need to delve much deeper.

'Will they close the lifts early, do you think?' Gull said.

She sat and unclipped her boots, easing her feet out and gesturing for him to do the same before she hung hers on empty arms on the rack. 'Probably,' she said. 'By the looks of things most people were heading down anyway. Do you want to let your brother know where you are?'

With boots and the rest of the paraphernalia dispatched, and a hurriedly typed text sent by Gull, Tania led the way up to the living area. The usually panoramic view from the picture window was obliterated by the falling snow, already easily a foot deep on the balcony and railings. Tania peered out, hands on hips. Madeleine's snowman had completely disappeared under a new mound; it resembled a snow hump, now, rather than an identifiable creation. She huffed a laugh, then asked Gull if he wanted a hot drink.

'I'd love a tea,' he said.

'If you want milk, it's in the fridge,' she said, pulling two mugs from a cupboard and dumping her mobile on the work surface.

He slid the carton of milk beside the mugs, then fixed his attention on the boiling water, watching it intently as it rolled and broiled in the clear kettle. Putting his elbows on the counter-top, he bent down to get a better look.

Tania viewed him out of the corner of her eye. 'What are you doing?'

'I just figured it's the closest I'm going to get to anything resembling a hot tub today,' he said, his focus on the kettle unwavering. 'I thought I'd make the most of it.'

She grinned and back-handed him on his shoulder. He wasn't wrong, the hot tub was buried under its own mound of snow.

'Ow.' He turned, rubbing at his arm.

'Big baby,' she said, reaching up to replace his fingers with her own, massaging at his shoulder through the stretchy fleece microfibre of his top. Aware his focus now rested on her, she concentrated on the sensation of the tautness of his frame beneath the mobile fabric, her fingers circling and teasing until they came to rest on the half-length zipper beneath his chin. Bringing up her other hand to hold the edge of the fabric, Tania eased the zip down, little by little. His Adam's apple bobbed up and down as he swallowed, the pulse from a blood vessel twitching the skin just above the edge of the collarbone she had uncovered. She allowed herself a glance up at his face, the arch in his eyebrows framing the heaviness of his eyelids. They must be weighed down by those incredible eyelashes, she assumed.

A million miles away, the kettle finished its boil and switched itself off.

Gull reached around her waist, slipping his fingers between the waistband of her ski trousers and the fabric of her thermal top and gilet. This time, he didn't stop there. He didn't stop until he'd separated the fabrics sufficiently to touch her skin, his fingers finding the dip where the muscles of her back sloped into her spine. His touch was as intense as an electric shock and she couldn't control a shiver.

'Are you cold?' he asked.

They both knew the answer, but she shook her head anyway. He spread his fingers out across the skin of her back and she shivered again, grinning as he pulled her close and his lips found hers.

Chapter 28

'For heaven's sake, just hurry up and choose, will you?' The frustration was clear in Rose's voice. It was fair enough; they'd already been in this shop for at least twenty minutes.

It was just that Madeleine couldn't decide between the silver and the purple key ring. Aware that she didn't know Tania well enough to make even an educated guess as to which she'd prefer, she was also determined to get her something for tomorrow. Items purchased for Rose and Clara already nestled in her rucksack.

Frankly, Madeleine hoped the biggest present Tania would be opening on Christmas Day would be Gull. Without being inappropriate, he was the kind of gift that you could unwrap time and again – the gift that keeps on giving, and all that.

She didn't want to be a fly on the wall in the lodge, she wasn't into that kind of voyeurism, but she wished she could be a fly on the wall in so far as she was desperate to know what was going on with the two of them. Only a fool wouldn't be able to see they were crazy about one another.

She might have joked about the hot tub in L'Avalanche at lunchtime, but with the weather as bad as it had become, she thought it unlikely to become Tania and Gull's destination of choice. A light dusting of snow was one thing, if anything it added to the whole experience. But a constant blanketing with the stuff wasn't likely to do anything much for either the heat of the water, or the heat between the two of them.

However, there was more than one way to skin a cat.

Fleetingly, she wondered where that expression had even come from. Why would anyone want to skin a cat? Madeleine didn't particularly like cats, in her opinion they were so busy being aloof that they missed out on all the fun, but she didn't feel the need to go and skin one.

It would make a good opening shot, though, for the scene now running through her head. Not the filming of anyone skinning a cat – it wasn't that kind of a flick – but having a cat wander elegantly along the wraparound porch outside Tania's room would be good. The camera could zoom inside, teasing the viewer with a peek at twisted sheets, a glimpse of skin, slick with sweat, a flick of perfectly blow-dried hair, a moan of ecstasy. Oh, yes, she had all the best Hollywood clichés at her fingertips.

'Madeleine, we're going to leave you here,' Rose said, the undertone of impatience cutting through the moment.

Frowning at the key rings in turn, she slid the purple one back onto the display. Paying for the silver one, she could sense Rose's continued impatience while the woman behind the till slowed her speech sufficiently for her to grasp that she was asking if it was a gift. *Un cadeau de Noël?* She nodded enthusiastically and, once it was wrapped in tissue paper, then sealed into a beautiful little gift bag, she left the shop.

'Why do people say, "there's more than one way to skin a cat"?' she said as they headed along another of Près du Ciel centre's labyrinthian corridors.

'I don't think they do, do they?' Rose said, dodging around a queue outside a pancake shop. Madeleine glanced inside. The place was tiny, barely more than a fridge and a frying pan, but the brisk trade and endless queue – and the mouth-watering aroma wafting in her direction – spoke volumes for the quality of its produce.

'It's definitely a saying,' Madeleine said. 'But I don't get why people want to skin cats. And why would they need different methods?'

'I don't think it's anything to do with cats,' Clara said. 'I think it's something to do with catfish, with how to prepare them for cooking.'

'Is it?' Madeleine wondered how Clara had that kind of odd information at her fingertips. 'OK, that makes sense, I suppose.'

'What doesn't make sense is why on earth we're talking about a random saying that I've never even heard of,' Rose said.

'It was just something I had running around in my head, that's all.'

Rose smiled. 'No surprise there, then.'

A familiar figure emerged from the delicatessen a way along from the pancake place. A small carrier bag swung from his hand. It was Tom.

'Hi,' he said, his smile warm and aimed at all of them, although Madeleine couldn't help but notice the way his gaze ended up on Clara. He waggled the bag. 'More cheese,' he said, wandering across to join them.

Clara laughed. She glanced at the others. 'Have we finished our shopping spree? Does anyone need to get anything else?'

'I'm all shopped out,' Madeleine said. 'We could always grab a drink down here? A hot chocolate or something?' She didn't want them to crash back into Snow Pine Lodge at an inopportune moment.

Rose shook her head, her spiral curls moving a fraction more slowly than she did. 'No more hot chocolate, Maddy. I'll turn into a cocoa bean. I wouldn't mind a glass of hot wine, though.'

'I'm on my way to the lodge now,' Tom said.

'Honestly, I think we should head back too,' Clara said. 'Even with the snowploughs out, the bus is going to struggle to get up the hill.'

'Fair enough,' Madeleine said. They reached a junction point in the corridors, the space opening out with more corridors spidering out from the area. In truth, she'd become completely disorientated in this subterranean world. She searched for clues, ideally a big sign with the symbol for the bus on it, accompanied by a large arrow. With no such obvious direction in evidence, Madeleine headed towards one of the passageways.

'Maddy, where are you going?'

She looked round to see Rose pointing in the opposite direction.

'It's this way,' Rose said.

As she began to undress Gull, Tania realised she wanted more than pure gratification from his body. She wanted to know who he was. She'd carefully skirted around all personal questions, determined to keep this nothing more than an anonymous encounter. Determined to keep herself anonymous. Or, at least, that was how it had started.

She pulled at the sleeves of his top, then gave up on that and felt for the hem running around his waist instead. She rucked the fabric up, shoving at it and exposing the pattern of dark hair running up from his navel and then spreading out to envelop his chest. He obliged with the rest of the removal, dropping the top onto the work surface behind him.

'Tell me who you are,' she said, running her fingers through the hair, seeking out the gentle undulations of muscles and ribs. It was his turn to shiver.

'What do you want to know?' he said, his breath hot in her ear.

'Everything. I don't even know your name.'

'Gulliver Richard Thornton,' he said, inching down the zip of her gilet, his words feeding directly into her brain, each sentence punctuated with a kiss. 'Born 9 June 1991. One brother. One sister. Grew up in Surrey. Boring childhood. We had Labradors. Joined the Foreign Legion for some adventure.'

'What?' She pulled away, frowning at the last comment.

He grinned, using her movement to complete the zip's journey. He slid the gilet from her shoulders and added it to form a pile of clothing behind him. 'That last one might have been more in my imagination. Your turn. I don't know anything about you, either.'

She shook her head. 'Don't change the subject. And your French isn't good enough for the Foreign Legion. What do you really do?'

'Is this another challenge?' he said, his fingers pushing at her fleece underlayer and then the tight-fitting elasticated base layer, finally finding and tracing their way across the skin of her stomach. 'One wrong answer and I'm out on my ear?'

'No. I just—' Tania lost track of her words as he traced a path around her waist, easing the layers of her clothing upwards to expose more and more skin to the cool air. His fingers moved confidently, circling and varying their pressure as he felt his way across her.

His head dipped to kiss her neck. His lips and teeth caressed and nipped at the skin just behind her ear as his fingers slid to the banding of her ski trousers. She sucked in a harsh breath as he felt his way around, teasing the zip fastening down a few notches, far enough to allow his fingers access to the edging of her underwear.

'Don't stop.' The words came on an exhale and she pushed herself against his hand. He edged a little further inside her clothing. She groaned. 'Oh, that feels so good.'

'Can we feel now and talk later?' His words were softly spoken, but Tania could hear the intensity behind them. She recognised it, because she felt it in the same way. 'I don't know about you, but I can't concentrate on both, and I know which one I'm more interested in, right now.'

She nodded, pulling his face towards hers as she lost herself in his touch. The questions could wait.

Rose usually enjoyed the bus ride through the resort, but so much snow had fallen since they'd entered the underground complex that she wasn't sure there would even be a bus. They huddled under the entrance to an underground car park, which doubled as one of the many stops for the *gratuit* resort bus. And when the bus did arrive, it was preceded by a snowplough.

The expression on the bus driver's face didn't lighten the atmosphere when they climbed aboard. These drivers usually flung their vehicles up and down the hill with as much abandon as the most reckless skier, but this afternoon, with the light fading fast, and the road through the resort reduced to a single track which required constant clearing, the journey up the hill was painstaking.

Sometimes Rose thought the drivers threw the buses around the corners a little too heavily in order to achieve a bit of wheel spinning, just to keep themselves amused, but today the wheels started spinning before the bus had gone fifty yards in a straight line. With infinite care, the driver coaxed the heavy vehicle up the hill, around the various and many corners, an oath escaping from his thin lips every now and again.

In truth, Rose didn't mind how long the journey took. Lysander was due to arrive back this evening, and the thought of it made her mouth go dry. Madeleine was right, she needed to get things out into the open. But somehow the imminent arrival of Lysander, and everything he embodied, was magnifying her sense of confusion, making everything crash back in on her.

Once the bus reached the summit of its route, still a few hundred yards short of the track to the lodge, the four of them stood and waited for the driver to open the doors.

'*Finis*,' he said, with a not insignificant amount of pathos. He waved flat hands backwards and forwards to emphasise his meaning. They moved in the same quick rhythm as the windscreen wipers. Clearly, he wasn't prepared to continue to drive in these conditions, and Rose didn't blame him.

'*Merci, monsieur*,' she said, heading after the others. Walking the short distance back to the lodge was surprisingly hard work. The snow came up above her boots, making each step an effort, and still more was falling, clogging her eyelashes every time she looked up to check she was heading in the right direction. She took her time, lagging behind the others.

'Tom, is there cake?' Madeleine asked, when they rounded the final stretch of track and the lights of Snow Pine Lodge came into view.

'Of course,' he said. 'It's a banana loaf today.'

'Yum. There won't be any cake at all when I get home. Probably not for the rest of my life,' Madeleine said, brushing snow from her face. 'So, I think I should make the most of it while it's on tap.'

'Logical,' Rose said. She couldn't help her grin.

'I thought so.' Madeleine returned the grin.

Clara punched the code into the door lock and the comparative warmth hit them like a wall.

'I'll make the tea, if you like,' Clara said.

'That would be amazing,' Madeleine said, her voice more of a shout. 'I'd love a cup of tea with my cake. I'll just grab a shower first.'

'Why are you shouting?' Rose said.

Madeleine dropped her snow boots onto the bench beneath the stairs with a loud clatter, and before anyone else had a chance to ascend she stamped her way up the first few steps. 'Just giving them fair warning,' she said as she continued to clump her way up the stairs, clearing her throat noisily on the first-floor landing. Nobody had ever managed to make more noise opening a bedroom door as Madeleine did, the noise fading away after she'd rammed the door closed.

Tom, his face laced with confusion, followed a few moments later.

Rose sat in the boot room, shaking her head, unable to shift the grin that had formed.

'She's an amazing person, isn't she?' Clara said, laying her gloves on the radiator to dry. 'You're lucky to have found her.'

Chapter 29

There was no sign of Tania and Gull, but Tom was busy unpacking the cheese he'd bought when Clara reached the top of the stairs. He looked up as she approached.

'Kettle's on,' he said.

'Great. Thanks.' She bounced fingers on the work surface, aware she should apologise for storming off the previous evening, aware that she should have done so at breakfast. Or on the bus ride back up the hill. Aware, also, that she couldn't bring herself to broach the subject. Instead, she plucked teabags from their container and shoved them into the teapot.

A pile of clothing lay at the far end of the countertop. Tania's mobile on top of her gilet, a rich plum colour with soft leather edging the collar, and beneath that an unfamiliar navy-blue fleece. It didn't take a genius to work out to whom the fleece must belong.

Clara remembered the first time she and Mike had removed items of one another's clothing. The clarity of the memory surprised her, her brain punishing her with a corresponding memory of later, her wearing nothing but his discarded shirt, the scent of him filling her conscious thought. Another memory superseded that one, a crisp winter's day, Poppy in her pushchair with Mike at the helm, breath spiralling away from all their mouths, Poppy unwinding her scarf for the umpteenth time and dumping it on the tarmac path.

She closed her eyes, wishing they weren't just memories, willing them all to stay, feeling tears rimming her eyes when they faded. Wishing she could jump in, be cushioned forever inside the memories, not remain stuck in this room – in this life – with its harsh lights and hard corners and other people's happiness.

She opened her eyes to see Tom watching her.

'Will it always be like this?' she said, doing her best to bite back the pain she could hear in her own words.

'Honestly?' he said. 'I don't know.'

She stepped away from the kettle, heading instead for the fridge. She pulled out a bottle of white wine and looked around for a glass. He placed a hand on the arm holding the bottle and shook his head.

'Don't,' he said. 'It won't solve anything.'

She smiled at him, a little too brightly. 'I don't want it to solve anything. I just want a glass of Chablis.'

'Please don't.'

She pulled away from his hold, a sense of calm enveloping her. 'If I want a glass of wine, I'll have one, Tom. I really don't need to ask for your permission.'

'Clara, let someone help you.'

She took a glass from a shelf. 'You don't understand. You can't . . .'

'I understand better than you think. But we can't help you if you won't allow us to. Clara, let someone in.'

She thought she would be able to, she'd really thought she'd be able to confide in him like she hadn't been able to with her friends. That the action would somehow open a magic fast-track back to a life she could see herself living. She'd been wrong. On two counts. She couldn't bring herself to confide in anyone, she realised that, now. But more than that, she decided, it no longer seemed to matter.

She shook her head. 'No, you don't understand. And anyway, I don't need anyone's help. Because I'm perfectly fine.'

Rose passed Clara on the stairs. Or, more accurately, Rose plastered herself against the wooden panelling as

Clara took the stairs at speed, a bottle and glass dangling from one hand.

'Clara, where are you going?'

With no response forthcoming, Rose continued up the staircase, the frown deep on her face by the time she saw Tom. 'What just happened with Clara?' she asked.

He shook his head. 'She was making tea. Then she started to cry and grabbed a bottle of wine instead. She said she's fine, but clearly . . .'

Rose believed she had been under no illusion about how difficult this week would be, for Clara, and by extension for all of them. But the last couple of days seemed to have shown a brighter Clara. Rose had almost begun to think that, as Tania had hoped, the mountain was working its magic. That it was somehow working its magic on all of them. It seemed that thought had been a little premature.

On her way to the kettle, Rose passed the pile of clothes. The mountain was working some kind of magic for Tania, that much was clear. But then, that was nothing new. The ease with which Tania seemed able to slip in and out of intimacy, her nonchalance where men were concerned had always been a trigger for Rose. Tania's ability to move on without seeming to break into a metaphorical sweat had always been astounding. How could she be so composed about that part of her life, when for Rose it was all so incredibly challenging? It had never felt fair. Rose knew it was an irrational response, that she hadn't experienced the same prickle of irritation when Clara had first introduced Mike, or married him, or told them she was pregnant.

Rose turned away from the clothes and flicked the kettle on, the water boiling almost immediately.

'Fastest shower ever,' Madeleine said, appearing at the top of the stairs, her hair still wet and hanging loose down her back.

Rose jumped. 'You've gone from noisiest person on the planet to stealth-Maddy,' she said. 'I didn't hear you coming.'

Madeleine smiled. She peered into the kitchen and greeted Tom before she said, 'It's part of my plan, Rose. Lull you into a false sense of security with my clumsiness, then shock you all when you discover I'm actually a highly paid international assassin.' She eyed the pile of clothes. 'Ooh, are those—'

'Before you say it, the answer is yes. At least, that gilet is definitely Tania's.'

'Oh goody,' she said.

Rose rolled her eyes.

'What?'

'You've forgotten our conversation about him being eaten for breakfast, then?'

Madeleine shook her head. 'I know you've been through a lot more with Tania, but I honestly think they're crazy about one another.'

'Or perhaps you just want them to be.'

'Perhaps I do. What's wrong with that?'

'Nothing.'

Madeleine picked up the pile of clothes, clamping the phone on top with one hand.

'Where are you going with those?' Rose said.

'Well, he's going to need something to wear later, isn't he? I'll put them outside her room.'

Rose nodded. 'Are you ever selfish?'

Madeleine smiled. 'All the time.' She turned for the stairs.

'Wait, I'll come with you. I think we need to knock on Clara's door.' She explained why as they headed down the stairs.

Clara let them into her room, grudgingly. The screw top from the bottle lay on the floor, a healthy measure of wine already missing from the bottle which stood on a bedside cabinet. She settled herself onto the bed, legs outstretched and crossed at her ankles, her back against the headboard.

'We thought we might share the bottle, if that's OK?' Madeleine said.

Clara waved a hand at it, holding firmly onto her glass in her other. 'Why not?' she said.

Rose took possession of the bottle; it was a moment or two before either of them realised they hadn't brought glasses.

'Spur of the moment decision,' Madeleine said, her cheeks flaming with enough colour to make Clara smile a little.

'Use the glasses in the bathroom,' she said.

Madeleine reappeared seconds later with two small tumblers and Rose poured.

'Bottoms up,' Madeleine said, taking a swig from her glass.

'I think that's across the corridor,' Rose said, her words laced with a layer of something Clara had heard before when talk turned to Tania and men, something with an unsettled edge to it. It wasn't judgement, exactly, nor was it jealousy, it seemed more deeply felt than either of those things. Rose took another large mouthful of wine and bent to refill her glass.

'I think it's great,' Madeleine said, pushing a swathe of chestnut hair and fixing it behind an ear.

Rose's expression darkened. 'You think it's great that she's over there, having sex with a complete stranger?'

'Yes. I mean, no – not when you say it like that. I didn't mean it like that. Because I don't think of Gull as being a complete stranger.'

'OK. Tell me something you know about him.'

'Um . . .'

'Surname?'

'Well . . .'

'Job? How about his hometown?'

'Nope. No idea.'

'Family?'

'A brother, who's just got engaged so is clearly not a total flake. And who gets on well enough with Gull to go on holiday with him and want to have him as his best man,' Madeleine said, with an edge of triumph in her voice. Her tone softened. 'Come on, Rose, you can't tell me you're jealous.'

Clara was surprised to see Rose empty her glass in a single mouthful, then reach for the bottle again. She was the one who was supposed to be sinking the Chablis, not Rose.

'I'm not bloody jealous, Maddy. You know I'm not. Far from it. She can have all the Gulls she likes. It's not that.'

'What's the problem, then?' Madeleine said. The way she said it gave Clara the feeling Madeleine already knew what the answer was.

'It's all so easy for her,' Rose said. 'Nothing ever seems to faze her.'

Clara frowned. She wasn't sure she agreed with that. Tania might have had it easy in a material sense perhaps. There was no shying away from the fact that monetarily Tania would never know the same struggles as most of the population. But, in Clara's eyes at least, Tania had paid in a different way for her financially easy ride. And she wasn't sure Tania was as unaffected by the circumstances she found herself in as Rose liked to think. 'Did I ever tell you what she said when I married Mike?'

Rose shook her head. 'What do you mean?'

'She said she was making the most of my ceremony because she wasn't ever going to have one of her own. I told her she was being ridiculous. I was so in love with Mike, I couldn't understand her insistence that she would never feel like that about anyone. But, Rose, you know better than most what her screwed-up family is like.'

Rose gave a sharp laugh, but she also nodded. 'I suppose.'

'That doesn't mean I think she's right, though,' Clara said.

'No?'

Clara shook her head. 'No.' She didn't elaborate. She didn't want to try to vocalise how, even though she had come to the realisation that she was alone in the world, she knew that the time she'd spent with Mike, the joy she'd felt at spending part of her life with Poppy was something she wouldn't swap for anything. And, whatever the consequences, love of that magnitude was something she wanted Tania to find. She wanted them all to find.

Nobody said anything for a few minutes. Rose emptied the bottle into her glass. Something was brewing, that much was clear, but Rose's expression remained buttoned up tight.

'We just thought we would check on you,' Madeleine said, her cheeks flashing with colour again as she broke the silence.

Clara nodded. She imagined the truth to be rather different, that they'd come to her room to stop her sinking into another alcohol-induced stupor. Not that she'd achieve that with a single bottle. Doubly so as Rose seemed determined to drink most of it, but that was beside the point.

'It wasn't supposed to be about Tania,' Madeleine continued.

'No,' Rose said, necking the rest of her glass. 'She always seems to end up as the centre of attention, though, doesn't she?'

'Whether she likes it or not,' Clara said, raising her eyebrows a little.

'I hope she stays the centre of Gull's attention,' Madeleine said, aiming a defiant look at Rose. 'Call me an old romantic if you like, but I think the two of them are perfect for one another.'

Rose scoffed a laugh. 'Based on what? We've already established we know next to nothing about the man. He really might be an international assassin.'

Madeleine grinned. So did Rose. Clara had no idea what was funny, but it seemed the two of them couldn't stay frosty with one another for long. Then Madeleine's grin slid away. 'No, Rose, I really mean it.'

Rose sighed. 'I know you do.' She finished her wine, setting the glass carefully next to the bottle. Her empty hands fidgeted, and she pulled at the edge of her sleeve. Then she picked up the bottle and tipped it against her glass before realising she'd only just emptied it. She slid it back onto the floor with a dull clunk.

Madeleine emptied her glass. 'I might get another bottle. Won't be a minute.' She touched Rose momentarily on her shoulder and smiled at Clara before she left the room.

Chapter 30

Tania did her best to ignore the noises in the corridor, the knocking on Clara's door, muffled voices, the door closing again. She didn't want to be dragged back into real life. Not yet.

Shifting a little, she ran her fingers along Gull's arm, but kept her eyes closed. Quietness descended, the sound of his calm breathing lulling her again. She trailed her fingers across his chest, creating a map in her mind.

'Exactly how long are you expecting me to lie here and take that?' he said, the resonant tone of his voice soft and low. 'It's only fair to warn you I'm going to have to retaliate.'

She smiled behind the darkness of closed eyelids, holding her breath as she waited for him to move, wondering where his touch would land first. He brushed at her outer thigh, his fingers feather light as they circled and travelled across already super-sensitised skin. Fingertips slid their way onto the softness of her inner thigh, following an invisible pattern, intricate like lace, on her skin. The effect on her was immediate. She opened her eyes and tried to wrap a leg around him, but he stopped her.

'Let's make it nice and slow this time,' he said.

It had been anything but slow the first time. Abandoning the clothes they'd peeled from one another in the kitchen, they'd headed for her room, Gull picking her up and shoving her against the bedroom door almost before she'd had a chance to close it. With her legs wrapped around his waist, he held her there as he stripped the rest of the upper half of her body. And stripped was the right term. There had been a desperation in his actions, mirrored in her own.

By the time he set her down and they'd ripped the rest of their clothes from one another, she was completely lost in the moment. So much for being in control. She couldn't explain why she'd spiralled so quickly, how it was that she'd climaxed moments after she felt him inside her. The only sense it made was how well it seemed to fit with much of the inexplicable nature of her time with him. For the first time in a long time the illogicality of the situation was the most logical thing in Tania's life. It was certainly the most pleasurable.

'I'm not sure I can do slow with you,' she said.

'Distraction techniques, then.' His fingers keeping up their twisting path on her skin. 'You could count backwards from a hundred. I've heard that works.' He grinned at her. Then he said, 'You wanted to know all about me, so how about you ask me a question.'

'What were the Labradors called?' She tried to picture dogs, a row of wagging tails, a Labrador of each colour stood side by side. Anything to dampen the fizzing of her nerve endings, anything to make it last longer.

'The earliest one I remember was Olive. She was black. I used to sit in her basket with her. Then Crusoe, also black. He got hit by a tractor and died. I cried for a week. After that we had two. Piper and King, they were yellows. Piper was a greedy sod and ate all the Easter eggs one year. Poisoned himself with them. Not fatally, luckily for him. Molly-May overlapped the boys, she was chocolate and smart as a whip. She had a litter with Piper, and my parents still have one of her descendants – Reggie.'

'What colour is Reggie?' Tania squirmed closer to him as he moved his attentions to her other thigh, his fingers alternating between the two. She ventured her own touch lower, the edge of his hipbone funnelling her fingertips even further.

'Chocolate.'

She felt for him, unable to stop herself from taking his

firmness in her fingers, rewarded by his description of the dog's colour ending in a sharp inhalation.

'Ask me another question,' he said, an edge of desperation creeping into his voice.

'How did the dog get hit by a tractor?' She wanted to hear the reply, but most of her conscious thought had already left the conversation, centred instead on her growing need to feel him inside her again. She was spiralling away, with the heat rising and pulsing in her own body and the scent of his sweat laced with their sex filling her senses.

'David had just learned to drive it and he didn't realise Crusoe was behind him.' The explanation was clipped, Gull's words becoming increasingly breathless as she gripped with her fingers. He groaned and took hold of a knee, encouraging her to widen her legs. She was rewarded in kind, her own breath coming as a gasp. She fought to keep the conversation at the front of her mind as she widened her legs further still.

'Why was he driving a tractor?'

'We're farmers,' he said. 'Arable crops.'

'Farmers?' Of all the jobs she'd thought he might have, this hadn't featured.

'Mmm. We grow stuff, you eat it. That sort of thing.'

Tania was barely holding onto the thread of the conversation, and it seemed Gull had totally lost interest. In one fluid movement, he moved on top of her and pulled her hips towards his.

From somewhere on the bedroom floor, Gull's phone buzzed. It could have played a fanfare, danced a jig, exploded in a volley of fireworks. It would still have been ignored.

'One more question.' She said it purely to tease him, fully aware her mind had lost its ability to form coherent thoughts.

He shook his head. 'No more questions.' He slipped his hands beneath her buttocks, lifting until her hips lay at the perfect angle.

'Do you need to start counting?' Her words were nothing

more than breath, spoken on a wave of need as his lips brushed at her neck, then settled millimetres from her own. 'One hundred, ninety-nine . . . ninety-eight . . .'

'Might need to start nearer to zero,' he said. His kiss was accompanied by an audible hitch as she guided him inside.

'Ten, nine, eight . . .' she breathed, his lightning grin the last thing she saw before she surrendered herself to sensations all over again.

Madeleine moved with deliberate slowness. She wandered up the stairs to the living area and asked Tom for more wine. It wouldn't hurt to give Rose a few minutes with one of her best friends, they might be able to help one another move forwards.

'Is everything OK?' he asked, handing her another chilled bottle of Chablis.

'Yes. No. Who knows?' she said. 'Jury's out at the moment.' She thanked him and headed back down to Clara's room. She knew he was asking about Clara, about her situation, but that wasn't what Madeleine was talking about.

It had been a while since Madeleine had last felt the need to discuss her sexuality with anyone, but she knew exactly how Rose must be feeling. Knew exactly why she was downing Chablis like it was the only liquid left on the planet. It was the fear of the unknown. The uncertainty of what was to come next.

In Madeleine's opinion, however, the fear of the unknown was often worse than the unknown itself. She was resolved to give Rose as long as she needed. They'd been an item barely a month and Madeleine already knew she wanted that month to turn into months, and with luck, years. And although Madeleine had never felt so right with anyone else, she recognised that the situation was a new one for Rose. It would take her time to work things out.

Having said that, Rose's reaction to the suggestion to kiss in the bubble mid-station had been quick and surprisingly resolute in its negativity. Madeleine frowned. Should she feel worried about that? It was one thing for Rose to begin to explore her sexuality in private. And eventually she would do more than broach the idea of being open about it, she would begin to test her wings, as it were. But what if her fledgling explorations and her final roosting spot ended up being in different nests?

It was one thing to enter a relationship with your best friend and to live happily ever after. It was quite another to end up being nothing more than a stepping stone on her path. The thought of the pain that would accompany loving and then losing Rose made Madeleine feel nauseous.

She filled her cheeks with air, and then puffed it out in a sudden exhalation. She needed to banish the negativity and trust Rose. She had to trust that it would all come good. She rearranged her features as she twisted the door handle, pushing into Clara's room with a grin and a wave of the bottle. 'Got it,' she said.

Chapter 31

Rose held her glass up, jiggling it impatiently as Madeleine twisted the top. Watching, hawk-like, as she poured. This was all going wrong. They'd come to Clara's room to check on *her*, not so that she could go off the deep end about Tania and Gull.

And the pointed end of the shard of icicle that seemed to have lodged itself inside Rose wasn't even about Tania. Or Gull. Up until this point she had managed to dance around the real issue. She'd hidden it, hidden from it. Madeleine was the only person who knew what it was truly about. Madeleine *was* what it was about.

She took another large mouthful, determined to hide from it for a little while longer.

'We just wanted you to know we're here for you, Clara,' she said. It sounded utterly inadequate.

Madeleine seemed to agree with the inadequacy of the words, she began to clarify. 'What Rose is trying to say, is that—'

Clara didn't allow her to finish her sentence. 'Don't think I'm not grateful,' she said, with a gravity to her voice, a firmness which took Rose by surprise. 'Everyone is so desperate to help me.' She frowned, her focus shimmering and disappearing from the here and now as it had done repeatedly throughout the week.

'Thing is,' Clara continued, her eyes refocusing as she took hold of her glass, 'I'm fine. I keep telling you all, I'm fine.' She frowned. 'Tom said something the other night, about letting the people who love me help me. And I get that. I know you

223

are absolutely trying to do that for me.' She looked at them, at Madeleine first and then her gaze settled on Rose. It was a direct gaze, one which didn't falter. 'And I never want you to think that I don't appreciate it. I wasn't expecting to enjoy being here, if I'm honest. I came because I knew being at home would be infinitely harder. But I've actually felt happy, there have been whole stretches of time here when I've been happy. And that's down to the three of you.'

'We just want to make it better for you, Clara.' Rose knew she sounded about thirteen, that the words were a plea, a wish to pull a wand from a back pocket and magic everything better. To make everything easy, for all of them.

Clara smiled, then set her glass down again. 'I know you do. That's why you will always be one of my most treasured friends, Rose. But it's never going to be better. He's always going to be gone. And I'm never going to be able to pick Poppy up and feel her winding her fingers through my hair. I just have to decide how I'm going to deal with that.'

'Oh, God. Clara.' Rose didn't know what to say. Even Madeleine, normally to be relied on for her chatter, was silent.

How could Clara be smiling? How was she not crying, like Rose was? She knew she was, because the tears were dripping down and hitting the back of the hand with which she still clasped her glass.

'It's fine,' Clara said again, more gently this time. 'It's all fine. I'll work it out. Can I ask something of you, though?'

Clara looked at Rose, doing her best to see past the tears, doing her best to concentrate on the dark eyes behind the soaked lashes as Rose nodded, then rubbed at the tears with the back of a hand.

She knew she was being a hypocrite, that what she was going to ask of them was hypocritical seeing as it was the one thing she hadn't managed to be, but it seemed more important to say it than it ever had before. 'Will you stop wasting time and be honest about your feelings?'

'What do you mean?' Rose said.

'You and Tania are more alike than you realise,' Clara said. She held a hand up as a frown threatened Rose's forehead. 'Hear me out. I know you think she has everything sorted. That she's the lucky one. That you are just muddling through life, that you make all the wrong choices, that your decisions are harder, and you can't face your reality. That people don't value the real you.' Rose's frown deepened, but her head inclined in something approaching a nod. Her corkscrew curls gave the movement away. 'The thing is,' Clara said. 'Tania feels all those things, too.'

'How can you know that?' Rose said.

Clara smiled. 'Because she told me.'

Rose shook her head.

'Yes, she did. She told me how much she wishes she were as self-assured as you are.'

Rose frowned. 'Tania's one of the most self-assured people I know. She's always as cool as a cucumber.'

'On the outside, maybe. But that's exactly what I mean. The face we show other people isn't always the full story, is it?' Clara was gratified to see the smile edge onto Madeleine's face. 'Madeleine knows what I mean,' she said.

'I know exactly what you mean,' Madeleine said, her gaze flicking repeatedly to Rose.

Clara warmed to her theme, edging her way towards what she really wanted to say. A partial truth, or at least as much of the truth as she could bear to reveal. 'It's probably because we do our best to protect ourselves, because we know that some of the choices we make will turn out to be the wrong ones. Or hindsight tells us as much. Sometimes we have no idea of their consequences, no control over the outcome.' She tried to swallow, but it felt like a ball of thorns had materialised in her throat. 'There are things that I wish with all my heart I could go back and change.' Refusing to allow tears to form, she blinked hard. 'But there are also choices I wouldn't change for anything on the planet. I nearly didn't go to the supermarket, the day I met Mike. I nearly stopped at the Potter Street corner shop instead.' She shook her head, as if that version of events, that parallel universe didn't even deserve airtime. 'And there are other decisions, other choices that become clear to us, that become the only logical route to take. The ones which, however hard they are to face up to, ultimately give us purpose. Or peace.'

She paused. The look was back in Rose's eyes, the one that had been there when talk first turned to Tania and Gull. 'But ultimately, it's all about *making* those decisions. Moving forward towards what is right for you. And maybe *who* is right for you, too. Regardless of what might come later down the line. Tania's hidden from her emotions for far too long, hidden from what would make her properly happy. And I think you have, too, Rose.' She glanced at Madeleine, whose gaze in turn was fixed on Rose. 'Although I get the feeling something might have changed for you lately?'

A beat passed, Rose hitched a breath as if she was about to say something, but instead she rubbed at her forehead and looked away.

Clara couldn't help but notice that Madeleine was biting at the edge of her lip, now, too. She was hanging on Rose's every move.

Rose pressed her lips together, her gaze flicking repeatedly towards Madeleine. Just say it, Clara thought. But Rose's brows flexed close together, and she gave an almost imperceptible shake of her head. She turned to the window and didn't reply.

Madeleine sighed. She looked disappointed.

Clara sipped at her wine, but it was warm, and so she slid the glass back onto the table. She nearly slipped away, through time, to a particularly persistent memory. A memorable hug with Mike, with Poppy wrapping her little arms around both of their necks. But this time she forced herself to remain in the here and now.

'Is it still snowing?' she asked. The view from this room was less panoramic than from some of the other bedrooms, not that it mattered in the almost complete darkness.

Rose nodded, shifting to one side as Clara padded across to join her. Snow was indeed still falling, but it was no longer falling straight down. The wind had picked up since their return and was whipping swirls of white past the glass. Silent swarms of ice-flies muffled by the double glazing.

'Doesn't look very friendly out there,' Clara said.

'Just as well we hadn't planned to go out for supper,' Madeleine said, joining them at the window. She peered out, then added, 'Not sure my snowman is going to survive this.'

A small pinprick of light, nothing more than a firefly among a swarm of ice-flies, arced its way up what remained of the lodge's driveway. Clara watched as the light danced about, flakes of swirling snow illuminating for an instant before they disappeared, replaced by another, then another. Someone was trudging through snow that was easily a couple of feet deeper than it had been when they arrived back from the centre of Près du Ciel a while earlier. The movement of light showed its owner was making slow progress and Clara realised that trudging wasn't an accurate description. Whoever it was, they were climbing through the snow with a dogged determination. They must be desperate to reach the lodge.

'Who is that?' she said, the answer hitting the front of her brain almost before Rose answered.

'It's Lysander,' she said, hugging her arms across her body.

Deliberately drawing the curtains closed, Clara turned to them. 'I might take a few minutes to myself, if that's all right with you two, then I think I'll go and see how Tom's getting on with the cooking.'

Madeleine nodded. 'Good idea. We'll get out of your way for a bit.'

Before Rose had turned the door handle, Clara said, 'Focus

on what's important to you, Rose. And if you know, then don't spend too long pretending otherwise, or worrying about keeping everyone else happy. Time is too precious.'

She watched them go, waited until they'd pushed her door closed, then she settled herself on the duvet, and pressing her phone to her ear, she played Mike's message again. It was easier to smile as she listened, this time.

We're going to have fun, though, aren't we?

Yes. My want ellie babies, Daddy.

Hope you're enjoying your lie-in, Clara. Have a great day and let me know if you want me to bring back some takeaway. The traffic is awful on the ring road, we've been stuck in it for a while. God only knows what the problem is, it looks clear on the other side, so we shouldn't be held up on the way back. See you soon. Love you. Bye.

'I love you, too,' Clara whispered. 'Even more than I ever realised.'

Chapter 32

Gull shifted himself up against the pillow. 'Your turn,' he said. 'You know everything of relevance about me, so it's time for you to answer a few questions, don't you think?'

Tania shuffled herself into the crook of his arm, her fingers playing across the lowest of his ribs. She'd known this moment was coming, that she couldn't maintain the pause in reality she'd created for much longer. That short of handing him his clothes and ordering him to leave, to avoid telling him, this was the next logical step. That she should be pleased he wanted to know all about her and there was absolutely no way she could bear the idea of him leaving, that she wanted to stay this close to him for ever.

But the moment he found out who she was, things would change. There was no escaping that, either. He would change, the way he viewed her would alter. She wondered how long it would take him to work out the connection between her surname being Harrington and Anthony Harrington. Maybe he wouldn't. Maybe he didn't have any interest in films, or the media, or current affairs.

Maybe he lived in a cave. Or under a rock.

There were people in the smallest communities in the centre of the Amazon rainforest who'd heard of Anthony Harrington. She knew this because her father had done one of those sycophantic documentaries in which he visited remote communities around the globe to find out more about their way of life. The production company maintained it had some tenuous link to the far-flung planets visited by Galactic Commander Robson and his crew in the films.

Tania maintained it was more to do with her father boosting his own ego than being of any direct benefit to those he was visiting. Regardless of the ethics, everywhere he went he was greeted as if he were a long-lost uncle. In one place someone had asked him to sign their flip-flops.

Everywhere he'd been, the residents had held contorted fingers aloft, making the sign every rank of crew member who encountered Galactic Commander Robson made in the films. The same sign Rory Flannagan had made, as a joke, the first time they'd slept together.

She wondered how Gull's expression would change. Because people's expressions always did. The eyes usually morphed first, became sharper, or more focused, or on occasion unadulteratedly calculating. The expression changed from one of boy meets girl, to boy meets meal ticket. Or from boy meets girl to boy meets route to fame; boy meets possible fast-track into acting in movies; boy meets way into Hollywood royalty; boy meets girl whose father is his all-time hero.

The eyes never said boy meets girl who just happens to be related to a famous actor.

Tania sighed. She allowed her fingers to continue their trail across his warm skin, trying to work out how to ignore reality for a bit longer. Because over the years, she'd learned that whatever thoughts she held of the latest man in her life, that man would eventually, without fail, be unable to see past the Harrington label.

'Tell me something about yourself,' he said. 'You decide what it is.' His hand closed around hers, holding it still. She glanced at him, tried to crystallise in her memory the look held in his eyes at that moment in time. The warm, genuine openness in those brown eyes, the intense desire she'd seen earlier softened into something more relaxed, but still incredibly sexy. He pulled at her hand, threading his fingers between hers. 'Shoe size?' He grinned.

'Six,' she said. 'And a half.'

'Favourite pizza topping?'

'Pineapple.'

'Really?' The disbelief in his voice was unmistakeable.

'No. I'm joking.' It was her turn to grin. 'I don't actually like pizza.'

'You don't like pizza?' His features darkened. 'That could be a deal-breaker . . .'

'Seriously?'

He laughed. 'No. No way. I was joking.'

'Oh, OK, yes. You did say you were good at bad jokes.'

'And I think I've just proved the point.' He pulled her closer. 'Where do you live?'

'Notting Hill.'

'In London?'

'Yes.'

'So, that's good, actually. That's only a couple of hours from me. I thought you might say you lived in Scotland, or Cambridge, or Cornwall. Somewhere a million miles away from Haslemere.'

It had occurred to her that his comments about favourite breeds of dog might just be flippancies, but he really was planning how to continue to see her when they got back to the UK. Tania pressed herself against him, wrapping a knee across his leg. God, how she wanted to hold onto this moment.

'You want us to see one another after we go home?' she said.

He shifted further up against the pillows, tilting his face to look at her better, a frown edging onto his face. 'You don't?'

She extracted her hand from his and ran her fingers across his forehead, feeling the wrinkles of concerned skin beneath her touch, then pushed across, moulding herself more firmly against the side of his body.

'What do you think?' she said.

'I honestly don't know,' he replied. 'I mean, I hope so, obviously. But I'm kind of waiting for someone to throw

231

open a door and yell, "Fooled you".'

Tania pulled away from him. 'You think this is just a joke?'

'No, no. I don't mean it like that.'

She could hear him huffing, he rubbed a hand across his forehead, then felt for the edge of her jaw, drawing her back towards him, before he spoke again.

'Put it this way, I've spent most of today pinching myself that this is real, especially after I made such a fool of myself in that bar.'

'And on that lift, and on the slopes, and . . .'

'But not in the hot tub. At least, not yet.'

She could feel him smiling, could hear it in his voice. She smiled, too. 'Plenty of time for that,' she said.

'You're insanely attractive, Tania.' The smile was gone, these words were serious. 'That's what I'm trying to say. You could have anyone, so why me?'

She didn't answer, instead she changed the focus away from conversation by leaning into him. She allowed her fingertips to trail their way across the lines of muscles on his chest and around the curve of his ribs, her fingers splaying out and inching down his back until she met the change in angle of his buttock. She pulled him against her, feeling him grow harder against her leg as she kissed him.

'Why me?' he breathed the words again, and again she ignored them. Because to answer with the words Tania wanted to use was completely outside of her frame of reference. Because the feelings she had been unable to pin down, that first evening when they kissed in the light of the stars, the nebulous thoughts and washer-drier stomach which kept her awake at night all pointed towards something she wasn't ready for. Wasn't sure she would ever be able to cope with. That somehow, even with her limited knowledge and understanding of this man, she already wanted him to be a part of her life with an intensity she hadn't realised was possible. Because it was just possible that she had already fallen in love with him.

She didn't say any of that, though. Instead, she said, 'Why not you?'

It was inadequate, but it would have to do, for now, because his fingers had found their way around her body, pulling her tightly against him again. She decided to allow her body to do the talking, to allow their new-found familiarity with one another to choreograph their movements. To hope that it would tell him everything he needed to know. Because in that moment, it was about as much truth as she was capable of giving.

Chapter 33

Clara unwrapped her bandage, peeling the final folds away with care. She turned her hand, ready to close her eyes if the cut was still oozy or otherwise difficult to view. It didn't look too bad, the slice seemed to have knitted together quite well, although it was far from healed. She would ask Tom for a plaster, there wouldn't be any need for another bandage.

If only her emotional existence was as easy to fix as her physical one.

She discarded the bandage, then checked her reflection, adding a little more lipstick. Clara was determined to make this evening count. Being at the lodge, being in the mountains in general, had given her the opportunity to gain a little clarity on her situation.

At the start of the week, she'd been looking for a way to hide. In a bottle, in her memories, in Mike's music. Looking for a way to put one foot in front of the other and work out what to do with the guilt she carried. She had felt as if she should be punished, that the kindness she'd been shown wasn't hers to claim, that the anger she had directed towards those people for their lack of understanding was unfair, even though she couldn't control it. She wanted them to see what she'd done, wanted them to know that she'd caused her own grief. If she hadn't been so selfish, none of it would have happened.

It seemed so trivial now, but the exhaustion had been all-consuming. The early mornings, the waking in the night. She loved Poppy more deeply than she could articulate, but there was never enough sleep. She was running on empty – and had been for a while – and then Mike began suggesting they try for another baby. She'd snapped, told him it wasn't the right time, demanded a little space for herself. A little time to be Clara, rather than Mummy. Just a few hours so she could read a book, perhaps sit in the garden and enjoy the warmth of the sun without constant interruption.

If she'd known what those few hours would cost her – no, not her, what they would cost Mike and Poppy . . . She would give anything to go back and change that day. To bite back her words and instead have a proper conversation with Mike about how she was feeling.

She had wanted to explain, to make her friends understand, even if it resulted in their disgust at her actions, or the uncomfortable shifting looks she was sure would accompany her revelation about that day. But she hadn't told anyone. She'd been unable to do that, she couldn't tell a best friend, or a stranger. And now, she wasn't sure it even mattered.

If things had been different, if she had become pregnant like Mike wanted, she wondered if that might have helped her through her grief. Whether having a piece of him still in her life would have absorbed some of the pain. Whether she would have been able to imagine how Poppy would have grown, whether it would have been possible to have caught glimpses of her daughter captured in the features and actions of a sibling. Perhaps the responsibility of another child would have forced her to be less introspective with her emotions. Perhaps she would have been able to soldier on. To put on a brave face. Having to put someone else's needs and feelings in front of her own might have helped her to make the best of it.

There was no way to know, though, because Clara wasn't pregnant. She was alone. In this room, her bedroom in Snow Pine Lodge, Clara was alone. When she went upstairs and joined the others, her closest friends, she would be alone. In the most crowded of spaces, Clara would be alone. Watching the bird of prey from the top of the mountain had crystallised the realisation. It had been her revelation, her moment of clarity.

She twisted the lipstick, watching the vibrant plum colour disappear into its silver housing. Slotting the top into place, she dropped the whole thing into the bin.

Upstairs in the main living area, Rose stared through the picture window, the swirling snow on the other side of the glass not dissimilar to the thoughts inside her mind. Clara had given her the perfect opportunity to tell her how she felt about Madeleine, had almost sounded as though she already knew. So why hadn't Rose just told her, got the whole thing out into the open?

The door opened and then slammed closed two flights down and Rose's shoulders tightened. Lysander was back, and that only made her swirl of emotions more complicated. Unmoving, she stared blankly out as she heard Madeleine sigh then take herself across to the hub of activity, where Tom had pulled a tray from the oven and was transferring its contents onto a serving dish with the shuffled scraping of a spatula.

Rose didn't acknowledge Clara, who appeared moments later and began to rifle through one of the lodge's cupboards, built into the space where the eaves dipped low enough in the dining area to make it impossible to stand upright.

She didn't react when Clara pulled a box from the cupboard and set it down on the table, then asked Tom if she could set an extra couple of places for dinner. For Lysander and Gull, Rose presumed.

She stayed put, eyes on the whirlwind of snow outside, brain elsewhere entirely. This was it. This evening was the evening when Rose needed to face up to things, to stop hiding from who she was. This was the evening when she had to find a way to tell everyone the truth. She owed Madeleine that much. She'd wasted so much time wondering, and

Madeleine had been so patient, so understanding. She'd repeatedly told Rose how it was her move to make when she was completely ready. But while Rose didn't feel like she'd ever be completely ready, she wondered for how long Madeleine really would be content to be a secret, their true emotions only expressed behind closed doors, or in the dark. Especially after some of the things Madeleine had said this week. And the possibility of losing Madeleine didn't bear thinking about.

It was as if Rose's mind was finally catching up with her body, which had never had any doubts. Her body had made its feelings known in no uncertain terms, left no room for discussion. She wanted Madeleine, with a fierceness that left her staring through this window, unsure she was capable of mastering the strength of that emotion.

Clara was right, she'd squandered enough time.

Once she'd gained back her breath, Tania slipped out of the bed. She was hot and sticky, and the after-effects of passion still roared through her. A glance back at Gull, the sheet pulled loosely across his frame as he steadied his own breathing, told her she wasn't completely satiated; that if there were a way to remain physically attached to him, then she would take it.

She also knew he was bound to ask more questions if she stayed in bed with him.

'I think I'll grab a shower,' she said, padding across the floor.

'Can I join you?' he said, the lightning grin flashing across his face, but this time it mellowed and stayed put.

'I'd be disappointed if you didn't.' A smile to match his settled on her own face as he threw back the sheet and crossed the room to join her.

Afterwards, Tania dressed quickly. She pulled on a pair of jeans and a loose-fitting jumper, then slipped her feet into a pair of pumps. Gull dressed with equal speed. Still naked from the waist up, and with an amused expression on his face, he ran a hand through his wet, tousled curls. Both stayed far enough apart to be unable to touch. It felt to Tania, as if now the genie of intimacy had been let out of the bottle, there would be no way to shove it back in. That it would be impossible for her to be physically close to him without wanting to touch him. Without being aroused by him.

'I don't know where my fleece is.' He glanced around the room.

Nor did she. She scanned the space, too. With a burst of heat in her cheeks she remembered they'd left some items of clothing in the kitchen.

She cleared her throat. 'I think it might still be upstairs.' The edges of her lips creased in amusement. 'I'll go and fetch it.' Chances were the others would be up there, in the living area. Chances were she might have to run the gauntlet of the others' curiosity when she fetched it. She didn't mind that, particularly. But she knew she was running out of time, running out of having Gull completely and purely to herself. And she did mind that. Because she was also running out of ways to avoid him discovering who she was.

'Thank you,' he said, bathing her in another of his lightning smiles, which she'd worked out were partly him expressing embarrassment, partly relief.

'No problem,' she said, opening her door. She didn't have to go far. A pile of clothes, including Gull's jersey and topped by her mobile, rested on the floorboards outside. If she had to make a bet, she'd put money on it having been Madeleine who'd delivered them. Picking them up, she retreated into the room, wondering if she would manage to control her grin as she thanked her; wondering how deeply her cheeks would colour with the embarrassment of having left clothes strewn about the place for others to find, then thinking how much she wanted to feel the heat of that moment with him, in the kitchen, all over again.

Gull pulled the soft jersey top over his head. 'Will I do?'

he said. He hadn't got clothes to change into, so wore the loose underlayers from his skiing outfit.

Tania slotted herself against him, breathing in deeply. 'You will do very nicely indeed, Mr Thornton,' she murmured.

'I haven't even got any shoes,' he said, the words reverberating through his chest and into the ear she rested against him.

'Part of my cunning plan,' she said.

'What is?'

'You can't run away, can you? If you've got no shoes.'

'Why would I want to run away?' he said.

'Scrabble,' Clara said, with an edge of triumph to her voice.

Madeleine looked at her sideways. 'You want to play Scrabble?'

'After dinner,' Clara said. 'Why not?'

'I don't think I even know how to play,' Madeleine said, still unsure as to whether she'd inadvertently strayed into the territory of an unforeseen social faux pas. Perhaps people really did still play board games on Christmas Eve. Perhaps stuffing yourself with a takeaway and watching *Die Hard* on the telly, maybe followed by a favourite Harry Potter – or even one of the First Galaxy franchise – didn't cut it for everyone.

She had heard that in Iceland people swapped books on Christmas Eve and then spent all night reading them. That had always been an idea she'd hankered after trying one year, when she had someone to swap a book with, someone to spend all night reading with. She'd hoped this might be the year, before Rose had suggested this trip. Having spent the last couple of nights together, though, she'd begun to wish she'd brought the books anyway.

She glanced at Rose. Wished she felt able to suggest it to her, right this moment. Madeleine wasn't usually stumped for conversation, but since they'd come up into the living area, it seemed as if Rose hadn't even looked in her direction.

It made their usual, casual, carefree inhabitation of one another's space difficult, to say the least.

It was as if things had become heavier, somehow. Weighted differently. Weighed down by an expectation about what should happen next. What needed to happen next.

Madeleine felt one of her eyebrows jack up. She'd never been conscious of her eyebrows' movements before Rose mentioned it, but she could feel it now.

'Or Monopoly, I suppose,' Clara said. 'I think there's a Monopoly set in the cupboard.'

'Clara, darling, I don't mean to be funny, but after the effort it took me to get here this evening, I'm going to need something more stimulating than Monopoly to keep me interested.' Lysander crested the stairs as he spoke, claiming their attention as if it were his unwritten right to have it. 'Mind you, if there's a pack of playing cards in there, I'm more than willing to take you girls on in a game of strip poker. Come to think of it, that's a far better idea, don't you think?' Gods-of-Olympus-made-mortal Lysander, complete with freshly showered and styled hair and clothes picked with a precise casualness which Madeleine now recognised, took up residence by the wood burner, hands outstretched towards the warmth emanating from the inferno of logs within.

'When did you get back?' Clara asked. 'Or, more to the point, how did you get back? It looks terrible out there.'

'Strangely cathartic, battling your way through snow,' he said. He taped his lazy grin to his face, but Madeleine thought he looked tired. More than tired, he looked exhausted. It showed in his eyes – even his precisely shaped 'get naked and swim in me' blue eyes couldn't totally disguise his weariness.

'The driver they organised to get me back here was totally useless,' he said. 'Wheels spinning in all directions, even with the chains on. Crappy Citroën van thing – a Land Rover HSE would have had much better traction, but the French will insist on buying in-house. We barely made it to the base of Près du Ciel. He stopped by the Les Amnetts apartments and flatly refused to drive any further up the hill. Said he was going to find a hotel room and that the agency would have to pay. Told me I should do the same. I told him he was a wanker, and he'd have more chance of freezing to death in his car than finding a vacant room. Then he rattled off a series of insults and we parted company.' He checked his watch. 'It's taken me hours to walk the rest of the way. Thank God I upgraded my climbing boots this winter. I've never seen the mountains like this – the whole resort is locked down.' He shivered, then hid it by spinning towards the kitchen counter and helping himself to one of the samosas Tom was arranging on a serving platter, before sinking onto the sofa nearest the log burner.

'Where's Tits, anyway?' he said.

'Tania's here, somewhere,' Madeleine said, a touch too brightly.

Nobody elaborated, and Lysander cocked his head a little as he looked at them in turn. His eyes narrowed a touch. 'I take it she's not alone, then?'

Nobody confirmed or denied. The corners of Lysander's mouth dipped down for the fraction of a second, before the half-smile reasserted itself. 'No surprise there,' he said. 'Can't help herself. Who's the "fresh kill" this time?'

Madeleine frowned. 'He's lovely, actually.'

Lysander laughed. 'Whatever,' he said. His attentions moved back to Clara. 'Poker later, then, my gorgeous Clara?'

Tom set the platter of Indian-inspired snacks on the low table in the centre of the living area, his attention flashing between Lysander and Clara. He reminded Madeleine, in that instant, of a guard dog, waiting to be given the 'attack' command. But Clara smiled. 'Don't be silly, Lysander,' she said. 'I want to play Scrabble.'

'You are a hard woman to please, Clara,' Lysander said, one side of his mouth teasing up into a smile for her. 'Scrabble it is, my darling.' He let out an enormous, unfettered, cat-like yawn, then looked around. 'Any chance of a drink? I'm dry as desert sand.'

Tania took a deep breath, then led Gull up the stairs to the living area. She scanned the room, noting Tom in the kitchen and Rose at the dining room table, fiddling with a green baize bag from the Scrabble box – the bag's contents chinking as she toyed with it. Madeleine and Clara stood between Rose and the person seated on the sofa which backed onto the stairs and faced the wood burner. It was Donkey, asking for a drink.

Tania had hoped he might have changed his flaky mind, forgotten about his decision to return to the lodge. Their late-night 'chat' had disintegrated into insult-hurling, as per every conversation they'd had over the last decade, and although Lysander's habits had worried her for just as long, she'd also known she wasn't on his list of people he took a blind bit of notice of. Even though Tania had seen a chink in his armour that evening, it had only been fleeting. Never before had it occurred to her that Lysander might turn to her for help. He'd always made it quite clear he had no need to sink *that* low. She'd wondered if the foul weather would persuade him to stay away, maybe even physically prevent him from returning. And yet, here he was, large as life and ready like a wrecking ball to demolish their carefully crafted evening.

She squeezed Gull's fingers a little more tightly, fighting the sinking feeling in the pit of her stomach, trying to ignore the buzzing in her ears at the thought that these might be the last few seconds of 'normal' in their relationship.

She wanted to remain the person who had attracted Gull in the first place. Some girl in a bar, nothing more, nothing less. She huffed at herself. Most people spent their whole lives trying to be something other than who they really were. It was human nature, to want what you didn't have; to view the city you'd never visited across the water with wistful longing while seeing nothing but litter and grime and broken windows in your own streets.

'You took your time, Tits,' Lysander said, head cocked in their direction. 'We're all dying of dehydration waiting for you.' Studying Gull, he eventually slid from the sofa, and squared up to him. 'Hello. I'm Lysander. Tania's brother. And you are?' He held out a hand, offered with just enough effort to look as if he meant it as a proper greeting.

'I'm Gull. It's good to meet you.'

Tania noted the twist in her brother's mouth as Gull extracted his hand from hers, to shake his.

'So, how long have you known my sister?'

An innocent enough question in the right hands, but Lysander's weren't the right hands. Gull must have sensed the undertones, colouring a little before he rallied. 'We met earlier this week, sort of bumped into one another.'

'It's a long story, Donkey. You'll get bored,' said Tania, knitting her fingers back into Gull's hand. 'Why don't we have that drink you're so desperate for, instead? Tom, will you open the champagne?'

With flutes of champagne handed round, Tania was grateful for a mouthful of bubbles. Lysander drained his glass in a couple of gulps, holding it out for an immediate refill. His attention remained on Gull.

'So, what do you do?' he asked.

'I'm an arable farmer,' Gull said. 'We grow wheat, barley, oilseed rape. That sort of thing.'

Lysander snorted a laugh. 'A bit random.' He shifted his gaze to Tania. 'I suppose that's another one to tick off your list, though, sister dearest. How many points for a farmer?'

Tania tried to tighten her grip on Gull's hand, but he eased his hand from hers. She thought he might move, break away from Lysander's intense focus. Instead, he wrapped his arm around her waist, pulling her closer.

'I think "farmer" scores top points, doesn't it?' Gull said. 'We've definitely got all the biggest equipment.'

Lysander's eyebrows hitched, then he tilted his head a little. 'Touché,' he said.

'How about you?' Gull asked. 'What do you do?'

Her brother laughed, but the laugh most definitely didn't reach his eyes. Tania wasn't sure whether he was amused that Gull didn't already know who he was, or whether he was annoyed at Gull for not immediately conceding to – as Lysander no doubt saw it – the most important player in the room.

The thing was, if she thought about it, there was no particular reason for Gull to recognise him. She'd feared an instant cognition, an immediate two-plus-two-makes-four moment in which Gull would look at Lysander and then her, with the inevitable, irreversible changes in his view of her taking place as she stood there, helpless to stop it. But there was no real reason for Gull to make the connection. Even if he had seen any of the multitude of adverts Lysander featured in, out of context like this, she supposed any recognition of Donkey was less likely.

'I'm into the mass marketing of clothing,' he said. The corner of his mouth hitched a little.

'You're a wholesaler?' Gull asked.

'More of a brand ambassador.' Lysander was playing with him, like a cat spiking at a mouse, trying to work out how to get a reaction. Or aiming to build a maximum detonation of embarrassment for Gull when he revealed his true profession.

'Oh, right. I don't think I know what that means, particularly,' Gull said.

'Must be something to do with living in the middle of nowhere,' Lysander said. 'Does a lack of sophistication go hand in hand with spending your days knee-deep in mud?'

'Lysander?' Clara broke into the conversation, slotting herself between the two men before Gull could retaliate. 'Come and help me with the wine, would you? Tom wants to serve dinner and you're holding up proceedings.'

With a final steely glance at Gull, and an indulgent smile for Clara, Lysander allowed himself to be led away.

Tania allowed a tight breath to ease its way through her lips. This evening wasn't going to be easy.

Chapter 34

With the wine in position on the table, Clara steered Lysander around the table and pulled out a chair.

'Sit by me, will you?' she said to him.

Clara had known Tania for a while before she met Lysander. He'd appeared one weekend, on the pretext of viewing one of Tania's paintings which had made it into a student showing, then proceeded to completely monopolise the situation. There was never any doubt about Lysander's ability to 'own a room', but the problem was he tended to own other people's rooms, as well as his. Especially when Tania was involved. Word had soon spread that day that Lysander Harrington was on campus. Clara wondered afterwards how many people had even noticed Tania's painting in the furore.

That kind of behaviour was nothing out of the ordinary, as Clara came to realise in the intervening years.

Clara raised her metaphorical hat at Madeleine, who slid into the chair on Lysander's left. Hemming him in. Rose settled herself opposite Madeleine, a tight expression on her face. Tania sat opposite Lysander, frowning at him and Gull took the final seat across from Clara. He grinned at her, a tell-tale sideways glance at Lysander hidden admirably with a quick rub of his fingers across his chin.

'Shall I pour some wine?' he said.

Tom's curry was delicious enough to render everyone almost silent as they ate. Or maybe nobody wanted to be the first one to break the quiet. Logs were added to the wood burner, sending sparks of orange heat spiralling up and outwards, hitting against the glass and disappearing. The wind continued to rage outside. From her seat, Clara could just make out the forms of some of the trees outside, bending and flexing and twisting like dancers in a silent disco.

Clara wanted to turn up the volume and hear what they were dancing to.

Eventually, Madeleine broke the quiet. 'If this storm keeps going,' she said, 'what happens about flying home? I've got to be back at work on Monday to help repair all the teeth people have managed to break on toffee and nuts. And nougat – you wouldn't believe the damage that stuff does.'

'Me too,' Rose said. 'Once Christmas is over there's always a general panic about sorting out tax returns – we're usually swamped. Not that we can do much about it if the planes aren't flying, I suppose. I'll have to do what I can via laptop.'

'We've got to get off the mountain first,' Gull said. 'We had a transfer service booked. Will that still run, do you suppose?'

'Jesus Christ,' Lysander said. 'Happy Christmas to you lot, too.'

'It's all right for you, Donkey. You don't have to worry. You just click your fingers, and someone will come running, isn't that how it works in your world?' Tania said.

Lysander laughed. 'Yours isn't that much different, Tits.'

Tania frowned, glancing at Gull. 'Anyway, let's not worry about that, now. The storm's bound to die down tomorrow, don't you think?'

Gull poured more wine and Tom cleared the plates, replacing the main course with a selection of authentic-looking Indian sweets and a pot of strong coffee.

'These look like fudge,' Clara said, picking up one of the slices, a delicate milky underneath with a chocolate-coloured top. 'What are they, Tom?'

'They're called *barfi*,' he said. 'They're made with milk.

The green ones are flavoured with pistachios and the plain ones are dipped in dark chocolate.'

'What did you call them?' Lysander said. 'Barf? Yum. Tuck in, everyone.' He chuckled at his own pre-teen joke.

'No,' Tom said, undented. '*Barfi*. You're partly right, though. The word does come from an old Persian word *barf*, but it actually means "snow". I thought that was apt.'

Clara smiled, then took a bite. They were good. 'And you made them?'

Tom nodded. For the first time, Clara saw some colour in his cheeks. He looked at her, at the half-eaten sweet still in her hand. 'Do you like it?'

'I love it,' she said, watching the smile spread across his face as she popped the rest of it into her mouth and let the milky sweetness dissolve on her tongue.

While she set out the Scrabble board, Lysander began to quiz Gull. He started with questions about the size of his farm – which was measured in something called hectares, a measurement with which Clara had a vague familiarity, even if she couldn't remember if they were larger or smaller per unit than an acre – and then he progressed onto a series of statements about how uncultured the countryside was, when you got right down to it, and how he couldn't understand how anyone could actually bear to *live* in the arse-end of nowhere.

Gull proved himself remarkably resilient. He answered Lysander's questions and explained – as if to a child – that Haslemere wasn't actually the arse-end of anywhere. And that he loved the fact that from the summit of one of the hills on the farm it was possible to see for more than ten miles in every direction.

'You can see forty miles from the Shard,' Lysander said.

'I suppose that might be true, but my view is filled with a lot more green, and a lot less grey,' Gull replied. 'I prefer my panorama, but each to their own.'

'Will you show me one day?' Tania said, almost under her breath.

'Of course I will.'

'Jesus wept,' Lysander said. 'Somebody bring me a sick bag. Never mind the *barfi*, I really am about to barf. Get a room, big sister . . . Or should that be get a room again?' He took a large swig of wine, then topped up his glass.

'Lysander, don't,' Rose said, her features tight and tense.

'Why not? Tits goes through men like she does shoes.' He raised his glass in Gull's direction. 'Forewarned is forearmed, one bloke to another and all that.'

Gull raised his glass in return. 'Thanks,' he said. 'Us uncultured country bumpkins need all the help we can get.'

Clara wondered if her game of Scrabble was going to work. Madeleine seemed relieved when she told them it wasn't going to be an ordinary game and the bickering ceased as she sorted the tiles into piles.

'I thought the whole point was that we picked the tiles at random,' Tania said, an amused frown on her face.

'Not this time,' Clara said as she finished her sorting. 'I'm in charge of this.'

Lysander topped up his glass again, offering the bottle around the table. 'My darling Clara can order me around any day of the week,' he said. 'Just tell me what we're doing, and I'll comply.'

Tania inhaled a strained laugh. 'First time for everything,' she said, under her breath.

'Right,' Clara said, decisively. 'Round one. You each need to pick a pile, and then make an animal name from the tiles you've chosen. Any questions?'

'Is this Scrabble for imbeciles, darling?' Lysander asked.

'Your words, not mine, Lysander,' Clara said.

Gull huffed a laugh, then took a pile of tiles. The others followed suit. Clara sat back and watched.

Tania was first to place 'elephant' on the board. 'Does it matter where we put them?' she asked.

Clara shook her head.

'Do we try to join the words together?' Madeleine asked.

'If you like,' Clara said.

Madeleine smiled, then slotted 'penguin' through Tania's word. 'What do we do with the extra tiles?' she asked. She held up the letter 'p' she'd saved.

'Nothing,' Clara said. 'Just put it with your others for now.'

Gull went next, slotting 'jaguar' through Madeleine's penguin and leaving his 'g' with his other discarded tiles.

Lysander frowned, shifting his tiles around. Rose looked across the table, then grinned.

'Maddy,' she said. 'Can I have your spare letter "p"?'

Madeleine passed it across, and Rose arranged that and some of her own letters to spell 'pangolin', meeting up with the 'n' of Madeleine's 'penguin'.

'What the fuck is a pangolin?' Lysander said. Uninterested in the answer, he pushed some of his tiles into place, adding 'ostrich' to the board, using the 't' from Tania's 'elephant'.

'You can't do that,' Tania said. 'Your ostrich is right up against Gull's jaguar.'

Madeleine began to giggle, and Rose joined in. Clara took the tiles from the board and concentrated on the next distribution. There was a serious point to this, but she wanted them to relax into the silliness of the game, first. To break down some of the barriers.

Clara had wondered how best to tell them all what she wanted to say. The message to each one of them was different. As she'd already witnessed, a conversation was too easily steered off-course or interrupted. She hoped that the use of single words would achieve her aims, maybe even without them realising what she had done.

This time the words were food based, Gull first to assemble his word and place it onto the board. Tania threaded her word through his, then did the same with their fingers, relaxing against him. Clara glanced at Lysander, willing him to keep any acerbic comment to himself. He was preoccupied, too busy shuffling his tiles around, perhaps determined not to be last to work out his anagram this time, his perfect features sharp with concentration.

Clara felt a pang of concern for him. He suddenly looked like a teenager, faced with something that genuinely piqued his interest. Lysander was all sorts of manipulative; there was no getting away from that. He'd made Tania's life more difficult than he had any right to. But it struck Clara that while the sibling rivalry was undoubtedly the product of a number of factors, his antagonism towards Tania was the only aspect of Lysander that appeared to have any real depth of emotion attached to it.

Clara hoped the final word she'd chosen for him would be helpful. While they finished sorting out their words – with Madeleine berating herself for her own stupidity when she finally placed 'chocolate' on the board – Clara found the bottle of génépi Gull had delivered for Tania, pushing it and a tower of shot glasses onto the table.

'I recognise that bottle,' Gull said, passing his arm around Tania and pulling her closer. 'Do we get to open it tonight?'

'So long as you don't mind missing out on the hot tub,' Tania said.

'I think we're past that, now, aren't we?' he said.

Tania twisted around to face him. 'God, I hope not.' She glanced at the window. 'Might be a challenge tonight, granted.'

'Here we go again,' Lysander said, his eyes narrowing as he looked at his sister. 'Do you ever think about anything but sex, Tits?'

'Why do you insist on calling her that?' Rose said. 'You realise it makes you sound about fifteen, Lysander. I think it's time you stopped it.'

'Do you?' He seemed amused by Rose's comment.

'Yes. In fact, there are a lot of things I think you should stop.'

'Like what?' He smiled at her and winked. 'You know I like it when you boss me around too.'

'Oh, for Christ's sake stop being a total dick, Donkey,' Tania said. 'Shut up so that we can get on with Clara's game.'

'Shall we have one last round?' Clara said. 'Then we can open the génépi and relax.'

'Sounds great,' Madeleine said, pushing the tiles together and shoving them into a pile in front of her.

Clara worked quickly to sort the tiles. This was the important round, the words that mattered. Her heart beat harder as she concentrated on getting the distribution correct. She wondered if it would work. Or whether this whole exercise would be viewed as a bit of nonsense. It had to work. She wouldn't get another chance to say what she wanted to say. She pulled in a large breath as she passed the piles out.

'We don't get to choose this time?' Rose said.

'No. This time the words are specific,' Clara said. 'I think they are particularly relevant to you.'

'How?' Tania said, leaning forward to gather her little pile. She set the letters out in front of her, brow furrowed. 'What kind of a word am I looking for?'

Clara hoped this wasn't going to fall horrendously flat. As parting gifts went, this one was obscure, to say the least. 'They are truths about each of you. Qualities you already have, even though some of you don't believe you do. Or something you know you need to do.'

'That narrows it down a bit, then,' Gull said, springing a grin in her direction.

Clara peeled the wax from the top of the bottle of génépi, then pulled the cork from the neck and poured measures into the shot glasses. She glanced across to where Tom was stacking the dishwasher. 'Would you like one, Tom?' she called.

He looked up, then shook his head. 'Not for me, thanks.'

'Clara, darling, you're going to have to give me a clue,' Lysander said, his tiles still a jumble.

She smiled and pulled the 'v' from his pile. 'Start here,' she said.

'I've got seven letters,' said Madeleine. 'Rose only has six. That's not fair. I need a clue, too.' She grinned in her direction.

Clara pointed to the 'g'. 'Your first letter.'

'Thanks,' Madeleine said, frowning at her pile of tiles. 'I think.'

Rose bit her lip as she settled her tiles into the correct order. *Honest.* She pushed the letters until they lay in an exact line, then looked at Clara.

'Time to be, don't you think?' Clara said.

Rose closed her eyes for a few seconds, then mixed her tiles up. Her gaze settled on Madeleine as she slid her tiles around.

'I've got it,' Madeleine said. *Genuine.* The tiles were spaced haphazardly, but she beamed as she poked at them and then looked around. 'Thanks,' she said.

'*Valued?*' Lysander looked surprised, pushing at his tiles with a finger.

'I wanted *cherished*, really, but there weren't enough letter h's. So, I had to settle for *valued*. You need to look after yourself, Lysander.' Clara wanted to spell out her reasons for giving him the word, worried he might manage to misinterpret. 'And the important people in your life, too.'

Clara turned her attention to the last two people, the last two words. Gull completed his. *Tenacity.* He laughed. 'I needed that to get through this game.'

Clara smiled, but she didn't think he'd totally understood. Hoped he'd work it out. Because he was going to need tenacity, to deal with being a part of Tania's life. So far, he seemed to be taking it all in his stride – even Lysander's jibes – but Clara knew there would be plenty of unforeseen challenges.

Tania shook her head. 'I can't get it,' she said. 'The only word I've come up with is *enough*, but that can't be right, can it?' She looked at Clara for clarification.

Clara stared at her. Waited for her to catch up. Hoped she

would. Because she was enough. She'd always been enough, even when she felt she fell woefully short.

Eventually, Tania's expression altered, softened. And Clara nodded. 'You always have been,' she said.

Chapter 35

'I get the feeling your brother is rather overprotective of you,' Gull said as Tania closed her bedroom door, and he closed his arms around her waist. After they'd downed another couple of rounds of génépi, the overwhelming desire to have Gull all to herself again became too strong for Tania to ignore.

She huffed a laugh. 'I wouldn't call him protective,' she said, wrapping her arms around his neck. 'Proprietorial, perhaps. He likes to be in control of situations, of people.' Shaking her head, she pressed herself against Gull, revelling in the way he tugged her closer in response. 'Anyway, let's not talk about him. Much more important things to do.'

Tilting her face to his, she paused. His gaze was on her, but his expression was quizzical.

'Why don't you think you're enough?' he said.

Tania hid her frown by burying her face in the soft jersey of his top. Up until this week, she would have pushed away from someone asking her such a personal question. She would have turned Clara's word game into a joke, become dismissive. She would have packed her feelings away, folded them up and shoved them into a dark corner. Like she'd done ever since she could remember.

She wasn't sure she had the energy to do that again. A few days in Gull's company had already unpacked more emotions than she realised she possessed, and there were others, queuing up in the background, waiting for their moment in the sun. She wanted nothing more than to tell him how she felt – how she really felt – about . . . Oh God, about so many things. But the first step on that road would be to tell him who she was. And at that moment, his attitude towards her would undoubtedly change anyway, and she would probably be packing those feelings away, all over again, whether she liked it or not.

'Does anyone ever think they're enough?' she said, hating the way she was still skating around the edges of what she really wanted to say.

Gull huffed a laugh, the sound reverberating through his chest. 'I think your brother is fairly well along that path. Talking of which, I got the feeling he wasn't being totally upfront with his job description. Am I right?' He shook his head. 'On second thoughts, I don't care. I know everything that's important, for right now. The rest of it?' He dipped and kissed her neck. 'I'm sure I'll find out in good time.' He tightened his hold on her waist. 'Unless, of course, I've seriously misjudged and you're actually a serial killer, stalking unsuspecting, gullible men and luring them to a luxurious, tinsel-wrapped end.'

'Do you look good in tinsel?' she asked, her lips tweaking into a smile.

'Have you got any? We could always find out.'

She shook her head. The Harringtons, or more precisely Brigitte, didn't 'do' tinsel.

'You'll just have to unwrap me as I am then, and make do,' he said.

Madeleine toyed with her shot glass, then set it down on the table. Rose, sitting at the opposing end of the sofa, sipped at a black coffee.

'Are you going to be able to sleep tonight?' Madeleine said. 'Caffeine after 9 p.m.? Recipe for disaster in my world. But then, you know that already.'

'It's Christmas Eve, I never sleep much.'

'Too worried about a random bearded man in a red suit making an unsolicited visit to your room?' It was possible Madeleine had downed a few too many shots of génépi. She felt foggy and warm, fluffy around the edges. Uninhibited.

Clara, drying the last of the pans for Tom while he packed away the crockery, laughed. It was a soft chuckle, rather than a guffaw, but Madeleine was happy that someone appreciated her sense of humour, because Rose looked unimpressed.

'What?' Madeleine kicked at Rose's foot with her own. 'It was just a joke.' She reassessed. Maybe now was the moment to mention the Icelandic book tradition. She was halfway through the explanation when Clara joined them, easing herself onto the other sofa.

'That sounds like fun,' she said.

'I've always wanted to try it. I've just never had someone to do it with. I've always wanted to share a bed with someone, you know, and spend all night reading together.'

'And now you can?'

Madeleine began to nod before she realised the implication of what Clara had said. She glanced at Rose, her cheeks spiking with colour.

'For what it's worth, I think that's the best news I've heard for quite a long time,' Clara said.

'Do you?' Rose's words were quiet, barely audible. But they were there, and Madeleine sat a little taller in her frame.

'All I want is for my best friends to be happy, Rose. I want you to be happy. That's all that matters.' Clara smiled. 'And I think you are. Am I wrong?'

A moment passed, a pause in which Madeleine held her breath. Then Rose clunked her coffee cup onto the table and returned Clara's smile. The tight lines evaporated from her face. 'No, Clara. You're right. I'm very happy. I just wasn't sure how to . . .'

'Explain?'

Rose nodded.

'There's nothing to explain.' Clara climbed to her feet.

'Continue to be happy, that's all that really counts for anything, in the end. I'm going now. I'll leave you two to it.'

'See you in the morning.'

Clara didn't reply. Instead, she thanked Tom for a great meal and wished him a good night, then scooped up the bag of Scrabble tiles from the table before she headed down the stairs. Rose slid across the sofa until Madeleine could loop an arm around her shoulders. It was a landmark moment for Madeleine, even if nobody was paying them any attention, and they stayed like that, body to body, while Tom continued in the kitchen, prepping food for Christmas Day.

'I'm sorry it took so long,' Rose whispered. 'Maddy, I think I love you.'

'Well, that's good, because I know I'm in love with you.' Madeleine had to spill the words quickly, unspooling them in a fervent whisper directly into Rose's ear. It felt good to have finally said them, even better when Rose took her free hand and squeezed. They sighed into one another, and she allowed her eyes to flutter closed.

Madeleine was jolted back to conscious thought – maybe she'd even fallen asleep – by loud footsteps on the staircase. Lysander's tousled blond hair bounced into view as he took the stairs two at a time. He appeared so rapidly that there was no way he hadn't seen the two of them lying arm in arm on the sofa, even if Rose did go to pull away a touch too quickly.

'Oh shit . . .' Lysander eyed the pair of them, his gaze settling on Rose. 'Now *that* I didn't expect . . . But I suppose it does explain a thing or two, doesn't it?'

Rose's frame tightened as she drew away from Madeleine, the pinch back in her features. 'Not that it's any of your business, Lysander.'

'Maybe not.' He frowned. 'But you always were the one I couldn't ever quite work out. Now I know why.'

Rose climbed to her feet, and Madeleine scrabbled up,

too, hoping what had become an evening to treasure wasn't about to be blown out of the water by Lysander.

'Well, Lysander, just for the record, I've never found you particularly entertaining, either.'

Madeleine had no idea what Rose was talking about, and Lysander looked equally confused, but Rose didn't get the chance to say anything else, because the sound of bare feet slapping their way up the stairs had Gull joining them. He paused at the top of the staircase, his expression melding excitement and confusion with a touch of embarrassment as he glanced down and tugged at the waistband of jogging bottoms which looked hastily pulled on. He snaked a hand across his naked torso before drawing a deep breath.

'Apologies. Ignore me. Just on the hunt for the bottle of génépi.'

Lysander plucked the bottle from the counter, checked how much liquid remained inside, and then held it out. Gull reached for it, uttering his thanks before he realised that Lysander wasn't letting go. With the bottle suspended between them, Madeleine could see the confusion on Gull's face, while Lysander narrowed his eyes. His perfect blue eyes no longer looked swimmable, in fact Madeleine considered their waters had frozen over as he fixed Gull with a sharp, calculated look. 'The last one was married. Did she tell you?'

'Pardon?' The muscles in Gull's arm flexed, but Lysander retained his hold, on the bottle and on Gull's attention.

'Lysander . . .' Rose's voice held a warning, but she was too late.

'Married,' continued Lysander. 'He's a film star. Rory Flannagan is his name – ask her yourself if you haven't heard of him. He has a baby on the way. Did she mention that?' Lysander shook his head. 'Her sheets have barely had time to cool down, and, hey presto. Here you are.'

Gull's features closed down. He let go of the bottle and glanced around as if seeing them all for the first time. His expression clouded with confusion. 'What?'

'No witty comeback for me this time?' Lysander said, waving the bottle. 'Don't want this after all?'

Gull squared his shoulders and reached for the bottle. This time Lysander let him take it, huffing a laugh as Gull turned and headed down the stairs.

'You really are a grade-A shit, aren't you?' Rose said.

'Well,' he said, winking at Madeleine. 'He is a bit of a wanker, don't you think?'

'I think the only wanker in this building is stood right in front of me,' Madeleine replied.

Gull had only been out of the room for a few minutes, but Tania was already missing him, missing the way his fingers had been tracing gently along the line of her jaw, then down the side of her neck as he suggested he go and grab the bottle of génépi. His fingers were featherlike, the sensation making her shiver. The absence of them made her sigh in frustration.

'Don't go,' she'd said. 'I don't need any more alcohol. Stay here.'

He was determined, though, pulling on his underwear and then his joggers and grinning at her as he cracked the door and slipped through it on silent bare feet. 'Won't be long.'

She'd resisted the ridiculous urge to tell him to stay forever. That she would be happy to inhabit that moment, that quiet moment in his arms, for the rest of her life. The way he'd batted back every one of Lysander's comments, the fact that he hadn't subsequently made any reference to her brother's slurs about her love life – there was an under-the-radar strength to Gull that she hadn't appreciated. Which only made him even more attractive.

But when he returned, his whole demeanour had changed. Dumping the bottle onto the bedside cabinet, he didn't acknowledge her, ignored her as he riffled through his belongings for his phone. With his back turned, he sat on the edge of her bed, the wide elastic band of his joggers bunched and folded in the small of his back. It looked uncomfortable. She wanted to reach out and set it smooth for him. Instead, she rested her fingers on his shoulder.

'Everything OK?' she said.

He turned at her words, or her touch, but this time, the expression on his face made Tania withdraw her hand. He didn't look like someone who was casually checking his texts. Turning the phone so she couldn't see the screen, his expression took on a sudden guarded edge, his jaw tight.

What had changed in the few minutes he had been away? What had caused a total transformation in his expression?

Oh, God. He knew. That had to be it. He'd worked out who she was. As she looked at the tautness in his face, another darker thought occurred to her – maybe he'd known who she was all along and this whole thing was a scam. Some nasty plan to gain access to the inside track of one of the Harringtons. He must have thought he'd struck it extra lucky to have Lysander here, too. Maybe he was busy texting a contact in the press and was annoyed that she'd interrupted him. Exclusive scoop incoming. What else could it be? Maybe she should make a grab for his phone and find out.

'What is it?' she said. A memory surfaced of Gull's phone buzzing earlier. She'd assumed it was his brother, returning his message. But perhaps it wasn't that at all.

'Please tell me what's happened.'

He let out a strange laugh. 'I should have known,' he said. 'I should have realised it was too good to be true.'

'What's too good to be true, Gull?'

He looked at her, the lines on his forehead more pronounced than she'd ever seen, the hard edge to his expression morphing into something else, something laced with disappointment, almost sadness. Looking around for the rest of his clothes, he gathered up what he could find in his arms and headed towards the bathroom, glancing at her a final time.

261

'Please tell me what's changed,' she said, sinking onto the edge of her bed.

He shook his head. 'I'm sorry, Tania. I need to leave. I can't do this.'

Chapter 36

Tania reached for her discarded clothes, pulling on an extra jumper when she shivered, unsure if the cause was cold air, or shock. Either way, the atmosphere in the room had nosedived.

She was desperate to know what had so upset Gull. Why he was intent on checking his phone. She wondered why finding out who she was related to would cause such a sudden desire for him to get away from her – if that was even the problem. Usually, it was the other way around. It tended to be Tania withdrawing from the situation when it became clear the other party no longer saw her as the main event.

It seemed unlikely that something had happened to one of the people Gull was in Près du Ciel with. He would have told her if that was what had upset him, surely?

Tania swallowed; her mouth had gone dry.

Had she just been played?

Perhaps this thing had nothing to do with any of the external factors buzzing around her head. Perhaps it had purely been about sex, despite all he'd said about wanting to continue to see her once they were back in the UK. Maybe that was why Lysander's comments hadn't bothered him. Perhaps that was how he operated. Played Mr Nice Guy, with enough of a hint of bad boy to pique a woman's interest. And once he'd got what he wanted, he was gone, like dry sand through your fingers.

Maybe he'd just texted his mates with word of his triumphant return.

She watched him as he emerged from the bathroom, tugging his top into place.

'I suppose you did say you just wanted sex,' she said. 'Right at the beginning. I should have realised you meant it.'

He frowned as he pulled on the edge of his fleece jersey.

'I hope I was up to scratch,' she said. 'Did you text your friends with all the details?'

'No. You don't understand.' She could see a muscle twitching in his jaw. He screwed his eyes closed, those amazing eyelashes pressed against the curve of his cheeks. 'You've put me in an impossible situation.'

She frowned. 'How? You're right, Gull. I don't understand.'

He stared at her. 'It's my fault, I suppose. You were so determined to stay anonymous. I would have played any game you wanted to get close to you, I didn't care about who you are. But perhaps I should have.'

'Why should it matter who I'm related to?' she said, the pitch of her voice rising to match her frustration. It seemed she'd come full circle. It was always the same. Why did being a Harrington always have to ruin everything?

'I am Tania Harrington, Titania Lisette Harrington if you want to be precise. Yes, my father is the sodding world-famous actor, Anthony Harrington. Galactic bloody Commander Robson. And, yes, my half-brother is that model everyone except you recognises from those adverts. So fucking what?' Her voice spiralled, the last sentence a shout.

To her surprise, he continued to shake his head. 'It's nothing to do with that,' he said. 'It's not about your name. Or your family. I already knew your name. I've known since the chalet manager came to collect me. He told me who Snow Pine Lodge belongs to. Told me all about the furore back in the day when the name was changed from Chalet Génépi. It wasn't difficult to put two and two together. And when Lysander took me for a dummy earlier, I played along. Because I couldn't care less about any of that. I've never been interested in celebrity stuff.'

That took Tania by surprise. 'But it's always about them,' she said, more quietly.

'This time, it isn't. It's about *you*.' Gull glanced at his phone, then shook his head. 'I saw Lysander, upstairs. He mentioned someone called Rory Flannagan. Said I should ask you about him.'

Tania continued to frown, her hands slipping from her hips as he flicked and scrolled some more, then held the phone up again. This time he showed her a piece from an online tabloid, the headline mentioning the words 'secret affair with a mystery woman'. The sub-heading going with 'Pregnant wife'. Tania didn't need to read any further. She knew exactly what it was about, the paparazzi shot heading the article, of an uncharacteristically chastened-looking Rory Flannagan on his way out of The Ivy, was enough of a clue.

'Is the mystery woman you, Tania?' Gull said, his gaze fixed on her.

'Is that what Lysander said?'

She supposed she should be grateful nobody in the press had been bold enough to name her.

The lawyers would have a field day with the journos and the Harrington machine would chew up and spit out anyone daring to name her. But in this instance, even if it happened that wasn't the point. Because while the Harrington machine would deny, and her father would refuse to acknowledge any questions on the subject, none of that would matter. In this moment, the only moment which mattered, Tania realised the only thing of importance was what Gull thought.

'Tell me it's not true,' he said.

She wanted to lie, to tell him it was nonsense. That Lysander was talking out of his backside. She wanted to ask him why it mattered so much.

She wanted to say that it was in the past, just a way to get at her father, nothing more. That it didn't mean anything. That she hadn't felt anything much when Rory had been on top of her, even though she'd made plenty of noise in the hope that her father had heard her. That the whole sordid thing was irrelevant and nothing to do with the here and now and the way she'd allowed herself to begin to feel about Gull. That he didn't understand how it worked, in the world she inhabited. And he didn't know anything about her family, about what her father had done to her mother, the way it had affected everything Tania felt about people, and relationships. About love.

And while she couldn't think of anything about her that was less important for him to focus on than her ill-judged fling with Rory, it clearly mattered to Gull. Although she couldn't quite work out why. Had she missed something?

'You and I are both single. Who cares what might or might not have happened in the past?'

'Damn it, Tania. Just tell me. Tell me it's a load of rubbish, that Lysander made it up.' He pocketed the phone, staring at her with a hunted look in his eyes. 'Please say it's not true.'

'Why does it matter so much? You're acting as if having a sex life should be punishable by being burned at the stake. Which, after what we've done today, is a rather hypocritical standpoint, don't you think? Anyway, it's the twenty-first century, Gull, in case you hadn't noticed. People can sleep with whoever they like. Or didn't you get that memo?'

He shook his head. 'Not when it destroys families,' he said, quietly.

Tania grabbed her own phone, scrolling newsfeeds to see if Rory and his wife had split. She felt hot, then cold, at the thought she might have wrecked the world of an as yet unborn child. Was that what he meant? She came across the same story Gull had already shown her but couldn't find anything more recent featuring Rory. The news from the last few days seemed dominated by Storm Clara, and the death of one of the original members of a seventies rock band.

Destroyed whose family? She looked at him for an explanation, then googled Rory's name to be sure. 'I haven't destroyed anybody's family,' she said. 'It was just a stupid fling. God knows Rory's had enough of them. It didn't mean anything. It was a way of annoying my father, if you really must know.' She eyed him for his reaction.

'That's what Ellie's husband said, too. That it was just a stupid fling. That it didn't mean anything.' Gull folded onto the edge of the bed, putting his head into his hands.

Ellie? Who was Ellie? And then realisation began to dawn on Tania, like the first tendrils of fear as they slid around her muscles when she lost control on sheet ice. Ellie was Gull's sister. Married. Pregnant. Cheated on.

Tania stared at her phone, as if Gull's sister's story might scroll into the screen and replace the last press photo of the paper-thin skeletal frame of Tony Finkle, recently deceased lead singer of The Panthers.

'I'm the first person to admit I'm no angel,' she said, setting her phone down on the bedside table. She took a seat on the tousled duvet, unable to ignore the way the pillows were still dented from where Gull had lain, only minutes before. 'But I don't go out of my way to hurt people, Gull.' She revised that statement in her head – she had gone out of her way to hurt her father. Or, at least, to try to.

Gull sighed. 'David and I tried to persuade Ellie to come with us on this trip, thought some time away might help her to think clearly. But she said she couldn't cope, it was all too much.' He drew in a ragged breath. 'She found out Harry was cheating on her quite by chance. None of us had any idea. What's worse is the woman is someone Ellie knows. She introduced them, for God's sake. She said she felt so stupid that she didn't realise.' He shook his head. 'He must have known Ellie was pregnant before he started the affair. They both must have. And they did it anyway. Bastards.' He spat the final word out with vitriol, his fists closing tightly enough to turn his knuckles white.

Tania closed her eyes. Wondered what it would be like for Rory Flannagan's wife if she believed her husband was cheating. Wondered if Rory and his wife had been planning to start a family before Tania began seeing him. Wondered, properly, what it would be like for Rory's wife to make that discovery. She tried to tell herself that it was different, somehow. That fidelity wore a different coloured coat in the kind of circles people like Rory Flannagan moved in, and his wife also knew that. She must have known what she signed up for when she married an A-list actor. Just as Tania's stepmother, Brigitte, had known all along that Anthony still visited Tania's mother, every now and again. And that the visits weren't to enjoy a cup of tea and a chat about the weather.

Tania knew she was clutching at straws, though. She could try to rationalise it any way she liked; the fact remained. She had slept with a married man. She had been in no doubt of his marital status, and she'd done it anyway. However hard she tried to dress it down, however much she'd tried to absolve herself, she couldn't wriggle away from the facts.

She tilted her chin. 'Yes, Gull, I'm the mystery woman. If I'm ever named, by the time my family's lawyers are finished, it will be as if I never even met Rory Flannagan,' she said. 'But I did sleep with him. I did it to punish my father for what he did to my mother. I'm not expecting you to understand that, and I'm not going to explain, there's no point if you've made your mind up to go. But you need to know that I'm not going to pretend to have an excuse. It happened. And when I found out that Barbara Flannagan's pregnant? I told Rory I wasn't going to see him again. I haven't seen him again.'

'Damn it, Tania. It's true, then?'

She nodded. There didn't seem to be much else she could do.

He swore quietly, over and over again, then drew in a deep breath. 'Just when I find someone who blows my mind.' He glanced at her. 'You blow my mind, Tania. I honestly feel like the whole of my life has been a rehearsal for this week, for meeting you. And now I don't know what the hell to do. Why didn't you tell me? Why didn't you tell me you don't care about things like marriage vows, commitment? Family. I would never have allowed things to go this far if I'd known.'

'But I do care. What do you mean?'

'The afternoon I damaged my knee, when I came here and told you about Ellie's husband – you agreed with me. You said you didn't know how anyone could do something like that. But you've done exactly the same to that man's wife.' He ran a hand through his hair. 'This is a nightmare. How can I give Ellie my hundred per cent support and be seeing someone who has done exactly the same thing as her so-called friend?' His head sank into his hands again.

'I don't know, Gull.'

Silence descended on the room. Tania pulled the sleeves of her jumper down until they engulfed her hands, then wrapped her arms around herself. She shivered again. It felt as if every heat source had been switched off, and the whole world was cooling down. That it might never warm up again. She could even hear the ticking of a cooling radiator, except that the radiators stayed on all night in the lodge. She listened more carefully, deciding it must be the wind outside, pulsing snow against the glass.

'I'm going to go back to my chalet,' he said, breaking the quiet. 'I need to think. My head is scrambled.'

'If that's what you want,' she said. She wrapped her arms against her body a little harder, aware her natural reaction to this kind of situation was reasserting itself. Her internal battalion of soldiers was hastily pulling on their uniform jackets and buttoning them up as they ran to form the line, to encircle and close her emotions down. To hold that line at all costs and shut him out, to minimise the pain. 'But nobody's perfect, Gull. I'm not perfect. And I don't know who you did think I was, but whoever that woman was, she was a million miles away from being perfect, too.'

'Will you let me call you tomorrow? Can we talk then?'

'Once you've had a chance to discuss me with your friends, your brother? Once you've passed judgement on me? No

269

thanks.' The words hitched in her throat, but this had started as nothing more than a prospective holiday fling. And she could shut it back down into being nothing more than that if she needed to.

'No one's passing judgement on you.'

'You already did.' She sighed. 'Everybody does. If you want to leave, that's fine. I'm not going to stop you. But don't call me tomorrow. Or ever.'

He frowned. 'Why not?'

'Why not?' Tania elbowed her battalion of internal soldiers out of the way. 'In the space of five days, you've gone from being a prat who made a clumsy drunken pass at me to someone I was genuinely beginning to think I could fall in love with. I'm sorry about your sister, but I won't be held to ransom by a situation I had nothing to do with.'

'Fall in love with?' Gull stared at her. He looked wrong-footed.

She shrugged. 'Yeah,' she said. A couple of the soldiers in her battalion lit up cigarettes and glanced at one another, unsure what they should do next. One of them kicked a roll of razor wire they'd carried out, as if it had just become redundant.

Gull frowned, then shook his head. 'I need to go. I need to think this whole thing through.'

'So, you go and think things through, Gull. But all the thinking in the world won't change who I am. I make crap decisions more frequently than good ones. I hardly ever get things right, even though my whole life is spent pretending I do. So, for this week, I thought I would just take some time out from being "me" and see what happened. And I met you.' She huffed a laugh. 'But real life always breaks back in, doesn't it? And one way or another, I'm always found wanting.' She shook her head. 'I'm sorry this didn't work, I really am.'

Gull pulled on his ski trousers, a troubled expression on his face. 'I need time to process all this. Surely you can appreciate that?'

'Phone me tomorrow, if you like.' Her eyebrows hitched, her internal battalion of soldiers hastily scuffing cigarettes out under boots and standing to attention. She wouldn't pick up his call, but if he wanted to believe she would, that was fine. Time to form the line.

She headed out along the corridor, flicking on light switches as she went. Gull passed her, the swish of his ski trousers sounded rough and harsh as he took the stairs. Tania paused outside Clara's room. The door was ajar, which was unusual, and Tania caught sight of a bedside light, illuminating the wooden panelling of the wall behind it with a warm glow. The light also reached over the top half of the bed, which was empty.

Tania frowned. Where was Clara?

Chapter 37

Tania pushed into the room. Clara's phone sat on the cabinet, bathed in the warm light from the lamp, alongside the baize bag of Scrabble tiles. Some of the tiles were laid on the table, spelling out a couple of words. Tania's frown deepened as she read them. She knocked on the en suite door. 'Clara, are you in there?'

She called out again, then twisted the bathroom door handle and pushed it open. The room lay in darkness. Tania held her breath as she pulled the light cord, but the room was empty. The rustle of fabric had her turning, but it wasn't Clara. Gull stood, framed by the doorway.

'I forgot I haven't got any snow boots,' he said, his face flexing with awkwardness. 'There's no way I can ski out of here in this weather.'

'There will be some in the storeroom, I expect.'

'What's wrong?' Gull said.

'Clara's not here.'

'Maybe she's upstairs?'

Tania glanced back at the words on her bedside table. Perhaps Gull was right, maybe Clara couldn't sleep, had headed back into the living space. That was a logical thought.

So, why had she spelled 'forgive me' with Scrabble tiles and left them by her phone?

At the end of the corridor Tania peered up the staircase. There was the faint flickering of firelight, logs burning out in the wood burner. She flicked the lights on and headed upstairs.

'Clara? Are you up here?' Tania scouted around the room, checking all the sofas and the tub chair in which Clara had sat to listen to Coldplay. She heard the rustling of Gull's ski trousers as he, too, climbed the stairs and looked around the space.

'She's not up here.'

'You sound worried,' Gull said. 'She's bound to be here somewhere.

'I suppose.' Tania wasn't convinced. The lodge was spacious, but there were only a few places Clara was likely to be – she checked her watch – at eleven at night. And there was absolutely no reason for her to be outside, in the storm which Gull seemed determined to face in order to get away from her. She should wake Rose, and Madeleine, perhaps they knew where Clara was. Maybe she was simply talking to Lysander. Or perhaps she was with Tom. There had been a frisson of an attraction of sorts between the two of them earlier in the week, a burgeoning friendship. Maybe it had become more than that.

Perhaps Tania should concentrate on her own situation, on finding Gull some snow boots and letting him go, rather than anything else.

But those words, spelled out in tiles?

By the time they'd established Clara was nowhere inside the building, all the lights were on and everyone was up. Tania watched as Rose pushed at the Scrabble tiles.

'*Forgive me*?' Rose said, glancing around. 'Forgive her for what? I don't understand.'

Tania shook her head. 'Nor do I.'

She heard the outside door slam closed. Tom headed up the stairs, snow cascading from his boots and the shoulders of his jacket as he entered the bedroom. He shook his head. 'No sign of her outside. But her jacket and boots are gone.'

Tania picked up Clara's phone. 'She would have taken this with her, surely, if she was going outside?' She depressed the home button, expecting to be faced with a request for a password. Instead, the phone sprang into life, with a photo she instantly recognised set as wallpaper. She'd taken that photo, the previous summer, when she went to visit Clara, Mike and Poppy at their cottage. A warm, sunny day, the three of them grinning wildly for the camera in the garden as Poppy yelled 'cheeses' at the top of her tiny lungs.

Tania blinked, her eyes closing around the memory of that idyllic day for a few seconds. Then she took a more careful look at the screen. All the icons usually positioned on the first screen had been moved, leaving a single video file in the centre, as if held in the palm of Clara's hand. Tania tapped on it.

It took her a few seconds to work out what she was watching. Clara had taken the video in this room, and by the looks of her clothes she'd filmed it this evening. She seemed insistent about an answerphone message she'd saved as a sound file, how she wanted it to be kept safe because it was Mike's last message.

She wanted Tania and Rose to know just how much she wished them to find the same kind of happiness she had enjoyed with Mike. That she thought they'd probably both already found it, if they would just open their eyes and see things clearly. And she wanted them to know just how much she treasured their friendship. But that it was all her fault Mike and Poppy had died and, as a result, she didn't want to try to find a place in the world. That she knew, now, how much she wanted to be wherever Mike and Poppy were. She wanted to find some peace. How she was sorry, how she couldn't cope with the idea of any more days without her family and how she hoped they could forgive her, because she knew this was the best decision.

Tania looked around at the frozen horror on Rose's face, the disbelief on Madeleine's.

'We've got to find her,' she said.

* * *

'Shit,' said Rose, as she fumbled the laces on her snow boots. She took a breath and tried again. How hard could it be to tie a sodding bow? Eventually, the laces complied, she jerked tight an extra loop on each boot to make sure they stayed tied, then looked around. Everyone was ready, hastily dressed in ski trousers and with jackets tightly zipped, snoods and fleece hats covering heads, gloved hands clutching torches raided from the storeroom.

She didn't vocalise the questions occupying most of her immediate thoughts. How on earth were they going to find Clara? She didn't have an avalanche transceiver built into her jacket like Lysander and Tania did, so where would they begin the search? Conditions outside were awful. Tom had phoned the emergency services, members of the PGHM – the Peloton de Gendarmerie de Haute Montagne – were on their way, and although he'd relayed the message from them that everyone was to remain in the lodge, there was no way they could sit around and twiddle their thumbs. However hopeless their searching might feel, it had to be better than doing nothing. Even if they would all be floundering around in the dark.

Tania and Lysander knew the area best, with Rose the next most familiar with their surroundings. However, with the wind raging outside, snow being whipped in every direction and snowbanks pushed up according to the whim of the storm, Rose looked out at the unfamiliar scene with no more confidence in the geography than someone visiting the place for the first time. They split into teams of two, the idea being to have someone who knew the area better with someone who didn't. There was a brief argument about also pairing one of the men with each of the women, but when that meant Madeleine would have to pair with Lysander, Rose shook her head.

'No, Maddy and I will stick together.' She shot a worried look at Lysander but he simply nodded.

'Tom,' he said, 'You're with me.' He flicked the switch on

his torch, checking it was working. 'We'll head out towards Rhodos and search that side of the wood.'

Gull had laced himself into some snow boots Tania had unearthed in the storeroom. It occurred to Rose that he'd already been wearing his ski trousers when Tania woke them. She frowned as Gull glanced at Tania and she said they would check to the left of the property, work their way out towards the old cattle sheds and the piste – Grande Pillar – which ran along that side of the property. After seeming to be so comfortable in one another's company, they now looked awkward, as if they'd been arguing. Regardless, Tania hauled open the door and clambered out onto the bank of snow, and Gull followed.

'Keep your phones on,' Tania said. 'And if we haven't found any sign of Clara in an hour's time, we'll regroup, OK?'

Everyone nodded. Tom and Lysander headed out, followed by Madeleine. Rose slammed the door behind her and led Madeleine around to the back of the property. They half walked, half climbed over the banks of snow which had formed. The cold wind had crusted the top of the swathes, and some of the time the crusted surface held their weight, but Rose's feet kept dropping into the drifts, sometimes just a few inches deep, sometimes up to her knees. It was exhausting, and they were making frustratingly slow progress, with Madeleine having the same problem, squeaking with surprise every time she disappeared up to her knee, or hip, in the snow.

Eventually, they made it into the tree-line. Rose leaned against one of the trunks to grab a breath.

'How the hell are we ever going to find her in this?' It was the first time she had vocalised her thoughts. She didn't want to give off negativity, but the wind whipped the words from her mouth; the trunks of the firs all looking identical and the lights from their torches dancing in the darkness revealed precious little in the way of detail.

Perhaps they should have stayed put and left it to the professionals.

'No sign of any footprints,' Madeleine yelled. 'Or perhaps that should be foot holes.' Beneath her hood and the scarf that she had wrapped around her chin, Rose could still see the glimmer of irrepressibility on Madeleine's face. Rose allowed herself a quick laugh, which was promptly stolen by a gust of wind.

'Let's head into the trees,' she shouted, gesticulating at the lines of conifers. Madeleine nodded. Once they were amongst the trees, perhaps they would be more sheltered from the worst of the storm.

The path, which usually led out over the little bridge crossing the mountain stream and towards the cowshed at the very edge of the piste, was gone. Once the lights from Snow Pine Lodge had faded and all they had were their torches, Tania struggled to identify any of the landmarks she usually used to guide herself. It was bizarrely disorientating, to know an area so well and yet suddenly not to know it at all.

Not a million miles away from how her entire life felt, at this moment.

Gull was making slower progress than her, he kept sinking into unexpectedly deep patches of snow. She waited for him. She was partly grateful that he was still here, that he hadn't mentioned returning to his chalet once they realised Clara was missing; had resolutely said he would help when they realised why she was gone. But he was slowing her up. She looked around, willing him to hurry.

Tania knew the PGHM were unable to use a helicopter in these conditions, and that would mean they were at least an hour away, an hour that Clara might not have. If she were serious about her intentions, it wouldn't take long to freeze to death in these conditions. It was one thing to endure subzero conditions, to dig yourself into a snow cave and conserve what little body heat you might have, to hang in there and cling to life while you waited for help to arrive.

It was quite another to use the conditions to achieve the opposite effect.

'Hurry, Gull.' She couldn't keep the frustration from her voice, even though it was clear he was moving as quickly as he could.

'Keep going,' he called, waving her on. 'I'll follow.'

She headed in what she thought was the right direction for the mountain stream, her feet juddering on and sinking into the snow to differing depths with every step. There seemed no sign of any other prints in the snow, no clue that Clara had come this way, but there hadn't been any sign leading in any direction – and they had to look somewhere.

Eventually, her familiarity with what few landmarks remained told her they were nearing the stream. She couldn't see it, nor the little footbridge which she'd crossed with Gull only a few evenings previously. Stopping to take a breath, she half turned to check on Gull's progress. As she did so, the bank of snow she was standing on gave way, and what had been solid under her foot became quicksilver. As one foot and then the other slid away from her, the suddenness of the movement threw her off balance and she pitched forwards into what had been snow, but which now was rapidly turning into snow-filled air.

As she fell, Tania flailed her arms, desperately trying to keep some idea of which way was up, with the powdery snow obliterating her vision. She hit something solid with a knee – a rock, she assumed – the burst of pain like a bright explosion in her confusion, another shooting pain joining the first as her hip collided with something else. She slid further, the pain intensifying as she slithered to a halt on the bruised side of her body. She pulled in a breath, trying to work out where she was and how badly she was damaged. In the couple of seconds it took to register that nothing else screamed with pain, and she wasn't buried under snow, a new sensation seeped in, weaselled its way alongside her other thoughts and then overwhelmed them. She was getting really cold, really quickly. And this cold was right against her skin, it had somehow trickled inside her clothing and was everywhere. And then her brain reasserted itself.

It was ice-cold water. She was in the stream.

Chapter 38

'This is hopeless,' Madeleine muttered as she shone the beam from her torch behind another of the endless fir trunks. She shone the beam around in an arc, catching the reflective strips on the back of Rose's jacket in the light, thinking for a second that she'd found something other than snow, and trees, and more snow. 'Clara, where the hell are you?' She didn't expect a reply. The stark facts were that if Clara was determined in her intentions, they were never going to find her. Not in time, anyway.

And, in the meantime, Clara's closest friends were out in terrible conditions, risking their own lives to try to save hers.

Madeleine couldn't help the wave of anger crashing through her thoughts, as Rose moved to another tree, then another. The desperate exhaustion in her movements wrenched Madeleine's heart into her throat. What had Clara been thinking? How dare she put her friends through this? Didn't she know they would risk everything for her? And how were Rose and Tania ever going to enjoy Christmas again – or even a trip to the mountains for that matter – if all they managed to find was her body?

At least there was a modicum of shelter under the trees. Firs evolved their instantly recognisable shape specifically to prevent a build-up of too much snow in their canopies; so snow was still falling, sometimes in large lumps which Madeleine had managed to avoid, but they were far more protected from the wind while they were between the trunks. Madeleine looked up, trying to see an end to the tree-line. Then she turned around, looking down the slope this time, back towards where she imagined the lodge stood, if they hadn't wandered totally off-course. All she could see were trees, and snow, and more trees. And as she looked, she realised that although they had been searching for the best part of forty minutes, they had checked a fraction of the places where Clara could be. And that was if she had even walked this way. She might just as easily have headed out along the track Tom and Lysander were searching, taken herself off across the piste to God only knew where.

She shook her head and turned again, pushing off from the trunk beneath her hand as she took another step, then another, towards the next tree.

'Wherever you are, Clara,' she said to the snow behind the next tree, 'you'd better be alive, so that I can bloody well kill you myself.'

Ignoring the searing pain from her knee and hip, Tania righted herself and pushed up clear of the water, as far as she could. The water wasn't deep, but it flowed quickly and was bone-achingly cold.

She could hear Gull calling her name, the light from his torch flashing in her eyes as he searched the hole through which she had fallen.

'Stay back,' she called. 'Don't fall.' It had become difficult to speak. Without warning, her jaw chattered her teeth together in a rhythm over which she had very little control. The light from the torch disappeared, instead lumps of snow fell around her, crystals of ice clinging to her face as she looked up. The hole grew larger as Gull raked armfuls of snow out of the way.

'Are you all right?' he shouted. 'Are you hurt?'

'I'm OK. But I'm in the water.' She'd lost her grip on her torch in the fall. Without Gull's light she was in almost complete darkness, the echoing sound of the rapidly moving stream filling her senses as she scanned around but failed to find her torch.

More snow cascaded onto her head and the light re-established its beam in her direction. She looked up.

'Reach up towards me,' Gull shouted, he sounded as if he were in an echo chamber. He shoved the hand not holding the torch as far down as he could, gesturing for her to stretch up. She shuffled until she was underneath him, then reached up as far as she could, the tips of her gloved fingers brushing his. 'Hang on,' he said, retracting his hand and the light from the torch, both replaced by more falling snow as he dug again.

Tania realised she couldn't feel her feet any longer, that the pain in her knee and hip had become foggy, as if she were no longer sure whether they hurt at all. She looked up at Gull; he lowered himself as far over the edge of the unstable snow as he dared, arm outstretched again. He gestured for her to reach up and she did so, this time his hand closed firmly around her wrist. He pulled her arm tight, tucking the torch away as he leaned down and took hold with both hands. Tania grabbed at him with her free hand and somehow, with Gull pulling, she managed to scrabble partway up the craggy rocks edging the stream. Gull changed his grip, taking an unceremonious hold of whatever piece of clothing or part of her body he could until she was free of the hole.

He rolled onto his back, breathing hard and swearing under his breath. She wanted to curl into a ball but couldn't seem to muster up the energy to move at all.

They didn't stay still for many seconds, Gull pulling her roughly to her feet and shining the torch in her face. Then the beam of yellow light made its way over the rest of her.

'I'm OK, Gull,' she said, through chattering teeth.

'No, you bloody well aren't. Christ, Tania, one second you were there, the next you were gone.' He wrapped her up in a hug, squeezing her until she was fighting for breath. He pressed a cheek to hers. 'I thought you were . . .' He didn't finish the sentence, instead he released his grip, studying her in more detail. 'You're soaking wet,' he said.

'I fell into water,' she said, attempting a grin and a shrug of her shoulders. The grin morphed into more teeth chattering, the shrug into a shiver. 'The stream.'

'I'm taking you back to the lodge.'

'No, I'll be fine once we get moving again. We've got to find Clara.'

'I'll come back out and carry on searching,' he said.

'But you don't know where to look,' she said.

'Not sure you're doing a whole lot better, if I'm honest,' he said, gesticulating towards the edge of the hole, the edges of his lips curling up in a grin, which was gone just as quickly, replaced by a look of fierce intensity. He grabbed her again. 'I can't lose you,' he said, the words hot and fast in her ear.

'And I can't lose Clara,' she said. She took a step away from him, bounced around on feet she couldn't feel, ignored the pain in her knee and hip which she very much could feel again, and reached for his torch. She needed to find the footbridge over the gully. It must be roughly in this area, but she hadn't appreciated how difficult it would be to find. She'd mistakenly thought the planks would be easy to spot, even by torchlight.

'We should leave the search to the experts,' Gull said. 'You're going to get frostbite.'

'Half an hour ago you couldn't wait to get the hell away from me,' she said, scanning the area with the torch. 'Now you want to tell me what to do? Good or bad decision, I've already made it. I'm carrying on. You can do what you like.'

He took hold of her arm, demanding her attention. 'Christ, Tania – I'm not telling you what to do. I'm showing concern. There's a difference. And, just for the record, the last thing I wanted was to "get the hell away from you" as you put it.'

Tania made to pull away, to carry on the search for the bridge, but he held her firm.

'You were desperate to leave,' she said, frowning as he shook his head. 'And this isn't the moment. Clara's the priority. Not us, or me, or whatever the hell this is.' She waved a sodden gloved hand between them, to emphasise her point.

He ran his free hand across what little of his face showed between the woolly hat pulled down over the crown of his head, and the zipper of his ski jacket, toggled right up to cover his chin. 'No. You're right.'

He let her go, and the weak yellow glow of the torch picked up something sticking upright, only about twenty feet to their left. Without replying, Tania forced her feet into action, wiggling what she thought were toes as she shuffled across. With the back of a sodden glove, she pushed at the snow and uncovered the edge of the footbridge.

'Here. It's here,' she said, but Gull was already there with her, pushing at the snow and kicking a path across the chicken-wire-covered boards that formed the walkway. Before she could take a step onto the wooden planks, Gull caught her arm.

'Are you *sure* you're fit to go on?'

She nodded, flashing the torchlight in his face, and catching the flicker of concern crossing it. 'Honestly, I'm fine,' she said.

'I'm just not sure I can carry both of you,' he said as they crossed the stream and headed on towards the cattle sheds.

Desperate as she was to look everywhere, Tania realised it wasn't only Clara who was running out of time. The pain in her knee and hip, although intense, wasn't the problem, nor were the fires raging in the nerve endings of her wet fingers. The lack of feeling in her feet was a problem, though. As the cattle sheds at the edge of the piste loomed into view, Tania considered that Gull might have been right, that perhaps she should have headed back to the lodge instead of pushing on.

She continued to wriggle her toes. There was a sensation of movement, a shadow of it, which she hoped was a good thing. Once Gull had said the word 'frostbite', she couldn't fully get it out of her head. Online videos of amputees talking about 'ghost pain' in limbs they no longer had scrolled through her head like a rolling news banner. Plus, they'd been out for getting on for an hour and hadn't even found a sign that Clara had travelled in the same direction.

The determination to keep on looking remained uppermost, though. Tania headed past the sloping roof against which Gull had pressed her to kiss her only a little over twenty-four hours previously. She navigated the drifts of snow against the side of the building, sliding her way to the fronts of the buildings, to the heavy wooden doors, protected from the worst of the weather by their orientation towards the trees.

'Clara?' she shouted. 'Are you here?'

Even though they were relatively sheltered, snow was still banked up against the doors. She tried to peer through a crack in the shuttered window, holding the torch below her chin to get a little light into the space. Gull passed her, heading for the second shed, the second set of heavy doors.

'Tania, over here.'

There was no mistaking the urgency in his voice. She moved in his direction and immediately saw why. The snow in front of this set of doors was much shallower than everywhere else. She twitched the torchlight around the entrance area and saw a wedge of snow to one side of the door. Glancing at Gull, she wondered if he'd seen it, but he was ahead of her, already feeling along the edge of the doors, trying to find the catch.

'I need some light,' he said.

She pointed the torch at the door for him and yelled Clara's name, telling Gull to hurry, then stood glued to the spot as he yanked the door open far enough for them to get inside.

'Is she in there?' she said, unable to bring herself to look. 'I can't . . .'

Gull gently took the torch from her and stepped inside.

Chapter 39

Tania didn't realise lips could actually turn blue. She'd always thought it was one of those sayings, exaggerating for effect. But Clara's lips were blue, her skin translucent. She was slumped against the corner of the shed, on a pile of old hessian sacks, to all intents and purposes lifeless.

Gull pressed shaky fingers against Clara's wrist, dipped his head and tried again, this time pressing against the side of her neck. He shook his head, unzipping her jacket far enough to shove a hand inside, resting it over her heart in search of its beat.

'Christ Almighty, I can't tell. I think there's a pulse, but my fingers are so cold. I can't really feel anything.' He shot a wild look at her. 'Call the others, tell them we've found her. Get the medics to go straight to the lodge. I'll carry her there.'

'OK.' Tania felt helpless. She watched Gull lift Clara, as if she were a feather, folding her carefully into his arms. Her own fingers flapped uselessly against the screen of her mobile, eventually managing to find and dial Lysander's phone.

She stumbled her way after Gull, watching her every step, trying not to notice the way Clara's head bumped lifelessly against Gull's shoulder. She wanted to reach for him every time she saw him stagger and regain his balance and carry on, all the while moving as quickly as he could, retracing the steps they made on the outward journey. The snow had stopped falling, and although the wind was still strong, the moon had finally put in an appearance alongside the stars, layering an eerie silver hue onto everything.

Tania could have cried when they got close enough to see the lodge's lights. She did cry when she saw Lysander and Tom, waiting with the lodge door wide open. Tom took Clara, lifting her straight up the stairs. Gull followed, giving Tom whatever details he could.

Lysander knelt in front of Tania and pulled at the frozen laces of her snow boots. He yanked until they came free and then levered her feet out.

'Fuck's sake, Tania, your feet are like ice blocks. You're all wet. What the hell happened?'

It was the first time in years he'd called her Tania through choice.

'I fell into the mountain stream, Sander. If Gull hadn't been there . . .'

It was as if he hadn't heard her, instead he took her in a bear-like hug. 'I need you, Tania. That's why I'm here, why I came back. I need you to help me – I can't do it alone. You've always been the strong one, and I've been such a shit to you. But I love you. Will you help me?' She started to shiver, her teeth chattering again as her brother held her tighter still and she edged her arms around him until she was hugging him back.

'Where is she?' Rose barrelled up the stairs and burst into Clara's room, Madeleine close behind her.

'How is she?' Madeleine said.

Clara looked deathly pale. They'd put her into her bed, with the covers tucked tightly around her shoulders. She still had her ski jacket on, Rose could see its collar zip sticking into her neck, and someone had pulled a fleece-lined bobble hat onto her head.

She reached to straighten the collar. Clara must be alive, the logical side of her brain told her that much, but she looked so still. She didn't look as if she were even breathing.

Rose turned to the others, taking in their expressions. Tom's concentration didn't stray from Clara, the concern in his expression clear. He sat on a chair on the far side of the bed, his phone in one hand. 'The medic team is on the way. I've been speaking to them ever since Gull found her. They're going to phone when they're a couple of minutes out.' With his free hand he tipped back the corner of the bedclothes, shuffled a hot water bottle to one side and reached for Clara's wrist. He pressed his fingers against it, fell silent for a while, then nodded. He replaced the covers. 'Her pulse is stronger now.'

'Is she going to be all right?' Rose asked.

Tom raised his eyebrows. 'I don't know. I think so. I think they found her in time.' He glanced at Gull, then fixed his attentions back on Clara.

Gull stood with his back against the wall. He, too, was still in his ski trousers, although he had abandoned his jacket somewhere. He looked exhausted.

'Where was she?' Madeleine asked. 'I couldn't find the end of my own nose out there; it was so awful. Thank God you found her.'

'She was in one of the cattle sheds,' Gull said, his voice as weary as his appearance. He ran a hand across his forehead.

'Cattle sheds?' Madeleine sounded mystified.

'They're out by the Grande Pillar piste, Tania and I used to hang out there when we were kids.' Rose frowned. 'Where is Tania?'

'She fell into the stream, I wanted to bring her straight back, but she insisted we went on looking.' He shifted his weight from one foot to the other. 'I should have made her come back . . .'

'What's happened?' Rose said, his expression making her nervous. 'Where is she? Is she OK?'

Gull never did answer, instead Clara began to move under the covers, a sighing moan accompanying the rustle of the sheets. 'Mike? Where are you?' she said, in little more than a whisper. 'Where's Poppy?'

Tom found her hand under the covers and held it as her

eyelids fluttered open and she blinked, repeatedly and slowly. 'Mike?' She sounded confused.

'No, it's Tom,' he said. 'You're safe, Clara. In Snow Pine Lodge. Rose and Madeleine are here, and so is Gull.'

'No,' Clara said, her head twisting from side to side, the fleece hat working its way up and away from the crown of her head. 'No, Mike's supposed to be here, and Poppy. Where are they?'

Rose glanced at Madeleine, who shook her head. Nobody replied to Clara's question, the silence broken by Tom's phone, chirruping with an indecent cheerfulness. Rose perched on the side of Clara's bed, as Tom rose from his chair, and took hold of Clara's other hand.

'Keep her talking,' Tom said as he left the room, heading downstairs to let the medic in.

About what? Rose thought. Her dead husband and child? The fact that she's not dead, as she thought she would be? As she hoped she would be . . .

'I'll be back in a second. I'm going to make her a hot drink,' Madeleine said, her path crossing with Lysander in the doorway. He ignored her, his gaze settling on Gull.

'Tania's asking for you,' he said.

'Really?' Gull pushed off from the wall.

'Don't sound so surprised,' Lysander said. He frowned, then said, 'It's possible I owe you an apology.'

Gull shook his head. 'Not necessary.'

'Thing is, she genuinely likes you. Our relationship might be dysfunctional, but she's still my sister. I've cocked up in so many ways, but I do try to look out for her, whatever she thinks to the contrary. And we don't take to strangers on our patch too easily. I was a bit of a shit to you, earlier.' He shrugged. 'It tends to be a Harrington trait.'

Unlike earlier, Rose couldn't help noticing how – for once – Lysander wasn't competing for the higher ground.

'Cuts both ways. I knew exactly who you were. Even country bumpkins wear Ralph Lauren.'

Lysander cocked an eyebrow. 'Fair play. And for the record you should probably get the full story on her relationships from Tania, not me. I'm not exactly what you'd call a "reliable witness".' He mimed quotation marks.

'I already have.' Gull paused. 'Shall we start again?'

Lysander extended a hand for Gull to shake, but Gull kept his hands in his pockets.

Once bitten, Rose thought.

'I don't think we're there yet,' Gull said.

Lysander drew in a breath, then nodded. 'Let's see how things pan out with you and my sister, shall we?' He tracked Gull as he left the room.

Once the door closed behind Gull, Lysander switched his focus onto Clara.

'Hey there,' he said, the tone of his voice softer than Rose had ever heard from him. He rounded the bed and settled in the chair Tom had just left.

'Lysander?' Clara blinked repeatedly as she looked at him. 'What are you doing here?'

'Darling Clara, why didn't you tell anyone how you were feeling?' He took her hand, clasping it in his and bending down to kiss it. 'If Tania hadn't found you in time . . .' He shook his head. 'The thought of it is unconscionable.'

'That's a big word, Lysander,' Clara said, her voice little more than a croak.

He huffed a gentle laugh. 'Talk to me, you crazy minx. Tell me what you were thinking.'

Rose slipped from the edge of the bed and came to rest beside him. She put a hand on his shoulder. 'I'll leave you two to talk,' she said. 'I'll be back in a bit.'

Tania had almost stopped shivering by the time there was a gentle knock on her door.

'Come in,' she said, holding her breath as best she could between shivers as she waited to see who would enter her room.

'You're still here,' she said.

'I'm still here,' Gull said. 'I wanted to wait until I knew Clara was OK. She just woke up.'

'Oh, thank God.' The shivers were back, but she pulled the covers from her body and swung her legs over the edge of the bed.

'Where are you going?' he said.

She frowned. 'To see Clara, of course.' She stood, inhaling a sharp breath at the piercing pain in her hip and knee. Sinking back onto the edge of the bed, she clutched at the fabric with her fingers as the pain edged away.

'How are you feeling?' he said.

'I'm fine.' She had to force the words out from between gritted teeth.

An eyebrow arched. 'How are you really feeling?'

Did Gull really want to know how she was feeling? Tania wasn't sure she fully knew herself.

Frustrated was the first word that fluttered into focus in her brain. The conversation she'd just had with Lysander, after his sudden outpouring in the boot room had left her head swimming. On top of everything that was happening with Clara, Lysander had chosen this moment to decide his life was out of control. Ironic, really – Tania had known it for the last few years. Not that Lysander had wanted to hear her. Not that she'd tried all that hard to tell him either, truth be told. Watching the way Lysander lived his life was a little like watching a train derailing, but in slow motion. Everyone knew it was all going to go horribly wrong, but there was absolutely nothing anyone could do to stop it. And now the carriages had finished piling into the soft earth and he was finally ready to lay bare the full extent of his problems and turn to her for help, was just when Tania already had more than enough on her plate with Clara.

Did Gull really want to know how she was feeling?

Because she was also confused, and more than a little angry. She'd come fingertip-close to a meaningful relationship with a man – with him. Something had unlocked deep inside her, like a flower finally deciding to come into bloom. She'd begun to imagine a different kind of a life, only to have the rug pulled out from underneath her. Maybe that was unfair, maybe she'd tugged at the rug herself without even realising when she allowed Rory to seduce her all those months ago. And after everything, after being uncomfortably honest – more honest than she'd ever been before, especially with a man – that man had decided he couldn't continue, couldn't countenance remaining close to her. Wanted nothing more than to get away from her. And yet here he was, still able to act with such civility.

She wanted to shout at him, throw things. Beg him to reconsider. She'd begun to feel as though he might be the person with whom she could properly explore her feelings. But now they were both behaving like polite strangers again, and she was battling to pack those feelings away. The box in which they'd previously fitted now seemed far too small.

If Gull really wanted to know how she was feeling, then, despite everything else, the only emotion Tania was aware of which was worth a damn, right at this moment, was sadness. Clara had tried to take her own life. Clara was so unhappy that she'd actually tried to end it all. And Tania had allowed it to happen. Sadness muffled everything else, pushed every other emotion and sensation aside as it settled like a heavy blanket.

Tania decided to misinterpret Gull's question. Or perhaps it wasn't a misinterpretation. Perhaps he really was asking after nothing more than her physical well-being. Either way, it was a far easier question to answer.

'My hip's sore. Plus, it feels like someone is jabbing my toes with needles, but apparently that's a good thing. It's also an irrelevance. How is she?'

'She's asking for Mike and Poppy.'

'I suppose she is.' Tania fiddled with the edge of the padded throw, unable to stop the slump in her shoulders. 'I thought it would help her, to come to the mountains. Not make things worse.'

'Why do you think it made things worse?' Gull edged onto the bed, reaching across to take one of her hands in his.

'Because she just tried to kill herself,' she said, an incredulous tone slipping into her voice.

'And you don't think that might have happened wherever she was?' He checked the watch on his wrist, his eyebrows arching. 'Christmas Day, without the people she loves the most? Without her child? It doesn't get much worse.'

'I suppose not.' Tania shivered again, and Gull pulled the throw up and around her shoulders. 'I had no idea she was feeling *this* low. But maybe subconsciously I feared it. Perhaps that was why we brought her here in the first place, so that she wasn't at home, alone. Rose and I both knew she was struggling. But maybe it was childish to think being in the mountains would make any real difference.'

'It's never the place, though, is it? It's the people that matter.' He pushed a strand of hair out of her face, the skin between his eyebrows wrinkling as he studied her.

She managed a thin smile. 'We didn't do a very good job of being the people that mattered, then, did we?' Another wave of sadness crashed over her. After everything they had tried to do, it still hadn't been enough.

'I think you're selling yourself short. She's still here. And that's down to you. There's everything still to play for.' He pulled the throw more tightly around her shoulders. 'Listen, I'm no expert in this sort of thing. She needs some professional help, that much is clear. And she needs her friends. If she wants to find her way back from this, she's going to need you more than ever before.'

'I wanted to thank you before you go.'

'For what?'

'For saving Clara,' she said. 'It wasn't me, it was you. If you hadn't been there, I don't think I could have got her back in time.' She didn't mention her own rescue from the icy stream, she hoped her gratitude about that went unsaid.

She stood, ignoring the pain as she shuffled her feet into some fleece-lined boots and reached for an extra jumper.

'Can I come with you?' he asked. 'Just to check on her before I go.'

She didn't reply, instead she took his hand and led him from the room.

Chapter 40

They decided to take it in turns to stay with Clara for the rest of the night. The medic wanted to get her to a hospital. He spoke in fluent English about the treatment she should receive, the complications that could arise from exposure, the long-term effects. But Clara refused to go. The fact that she was coherent enough to argue the point had the medic frustrated, but with a flourish of arms and Gallic raising of eyebrows, he conceded. Told them to keep her warm and hydrated, that he would be back to check on her in the morning. Told them that they were all idiots for going outside to look for her. Told Tania she was lucky and would keep all her toes. Wished them a *Joyeux Noël* without even a hint of irony and then left.

When it was Madeleine's turn, she shuffled along the corridor and settled herself into the chair beside Clara's bed, the lamp on the bedside table dimly illuminating the room. She listened to Clara's rhythmical breathing for a while, studied the knots and grain in the wooden panels of the wall. She should allow Clara to rest, she supposed. They were all hanging with exhaustion, after all. But she wanted some answers.

'Why did you do it?' Madeleine said.

Clara's eyelids fluttered open. She glanced in Madeleine's direction, then stared at some point in the middle distance. 'You heard Mike's message. That's why.'

Madeleine frowned. In the post-Clara-video panic to get

outside and look for her, nobody had considered Mike's voicemail to be of importance. 'We didn't listen to it, we were a bit busy having a full-on panic about you. Why? What's in his message?'

'Listen to it. Then you'll understand.'

Madeleine frowned, reached for the phone, which lay on the table between them, and swiped the screen into life. 'Are you sure you want me to?' Nobody but Clara had listened to this message. Up until this point the contents of this message had been a private communication between husband and wife. Madeleine wasn't sure she should be the first outsider to hear it. 'Perhaps I should get Rose. Or Tania?'

Clara shook her head slowly. 'I'd rather it was you, to be honest.'

She wanted to ask why, but the expression on Clara's face dried the word up before she could say it. Whatever was in this message, it was clearly of enormous importance to Clara, and not just because it was a recording of Mike's voice. There was more to it than that. She pressed the phone to her ear and listened.

Tell Mummy where we're going.

To buy ellie babies.

Madeleine glanced at Clara, wondering how many times she'd listened to these voices since the accident. She could feel involuntary tears prick the back of her eyes at the sound of Poppy's voice.

That's right, Pops. Did you hear that, gorgeous lady? We're going to buy jelly babies for our favourite person. Which ones does Mummy like best?

Onge ones. Mumma loves onge ones.

And which ones does Poppy like the best?

Green. My like green ones.

And do you think Mummy's going to enjoy her bit of peace and quiet without us?

Madeleine glanced at Clara. Had Mike taken Poppy out because of something she'd said?

Poppy misses Mumma a-ready.
We're going to have fun though, aren't we?
Yes. My want ellie babies, Daddy.
Madeleine wondered how deeply listening to this message
wounded Clara every time she heard their voices.

Hope you're enjoying your lie-in, Clara. Have a great
day and let me know if you want me to bring back some
takeaway. The traffic is awful on the ring road, we've been
stuck in it for a while. God only knows what the problem
is, it looks clear on the other side, so we shouldn't be held
up on the way back. See you soon. Love you. Bye.

With deliberate care, Madeleine checked the recording
was finished and then placed the phone back on the bedside
table. She pulled in a long breath.

'What happened that day, Clara?'

Clara cupped her hands over her face, hiding behind them as
Madeleine repeated the question. At one stage, not so long
ago, she had been desperate to reach this point, to reach a
place where she could unburden herself to someone. And
now that moment was at hand. She drew her hands away
from her face and sighed, tipping her head so she could see
Madeleine.

'Mike wanted another baby, that was the problem.'

Madeleine looked confused. 'You didn't want another
child?'

'No!' Clara levered herself up against the pillows. 'It wasn't
that. It was just . . . I was so tired. Poppy used to wake a
lot at night, and it was always down to me to deal with her
because Mike had to get up for work the next day. I was
exhausted. And then Mike started suggesting we try for
another baby. I couldn't think straight, and I needed a bit
of time to myself, that was all I wanted. Just a few hours
alone.' She tried to stop the quivering in her lips.

'So, you argued?'

Madeleine clearly didn't understand. Clara shook her

head. 'Mike didn't argue, he wasn't that kind of a man. He was more than happy to take Poppy out, said it was about time they spent the day together. Daddy–daughter time, he called it. But that's what makes it even worse.'

'What do you mean?'

'He willingly took her. He was talking about taking her to the park, maybe visiting a toy store to buy her a game, or some building bricks. Getting some lunch somewhere. He was insisting I should have a lie-in; told me he would get Poppy some breakfast and they would fend for themselves while I relaxed at home.' A sharp laugh punctuated her words. 'He must have decided to take Poppy to the supermarket to buy me some sweets. And that's when they had the accident.'

'Oh, I see,' Madeleine said.

'Do you? They only went because I wanted a lie-in, a bit of time to myself. They only went because of my selfishness. They only died because of me.' Pulling in a sharp breath, she shook her head and fixed her eyes on the ceiling again.

'Because you wanted a bit of time to yourself?'

Clara nodded.

'You think it's your fault, because you wanted a bit of time to yourself? What's wrong with wanting a few hours on your own? Survival 101 if you ask me. I'm amazed it took you that long.'

'But they would have been at home, they would have been safe, if I hadn't forced the issue.'

'Forced?' Madeleine shook her head. 'No, Clara. No. You said he was happy to spend some time with Poppy. You said he wanted to.'

Clara closed her eyes, the skin pinched tight together between them.

Madeleine changed tack. 'Did you ask for the sweets?'

'No. But Mike was always doing things like that.'

'So, you didn't tell him to go to the supermarket?'

Clara shook her head.

'And you had no idea what time they would be on that road?'

'No. What difference does that make?'

'Did you know what time the lorry would be travelling along that stretch of road? Or that its tyre was faulty? Or that the traffic would open out and the lorry driver would decide to overtake, rather than staying in the inside lane?'

'How could I know any of those things?' Clara frowned.

'Exactly. How could anybody know those things?' Madeleine shuffled forward on her seat. 'That's what I'm trying to say. Nobody could know those things were going to happen, in exactly that way, at exactly that time, could they? Not you. Not Mike. Not anyone. Because it was an accident. An *accident*, Clara.'

Clara shook her head. 'No, he wouldn't have gone if I hadn't insisted. It's my fault.'

Madeleine raised an eyebrow. 'What if he'd chosen a different route to the supermarket, been quicker, or slower getting Poppy ready? What if he'd stopped for fuel, or been ahead of the lorry in the fast lane, or stopped in a lay-by because Poppy needed something? What if there had been roadworks and the road had been single lane that morning rather than just busy?'

'But none of those things happened. And it doesn't change the fact that they were there because of me. Please stop it, Madeleine. I will always feel it was my fault.'

Madeleine nodded. 'I understand that. I don't want you to feel that I don't get what you're saying. You will always feel a sense of responsibility, I get that. But it wasn't your fault. It wasn't anyone's fault. And that will always be the case, too.'

Clara sank back against the pillow, her eyes tracing a path back to the ceiling, to the spider's web crack in the grain above the doorway, allowing Madeleine's words to percolate. She'd always imagined how the expressions on people's faces would alter when she told them, the hooded look of disgust descending as they realised the part she'd played in that morning's events. How they would confirm her guilt. Her selfishness. Had she got that wrong?

'I'm sorry I was never lucky enough to meet Mike, or Poppy,' Madeleine said. She reached out and took hold of Clara's hand, an action that surprised her, until she saw the tears building in the corners of Madeleine's eyes. 'And I can't express how awful it is that they're gone. But, Clara, there's no way he would have wanted you to have succeeded tonight. You must know that.'

'I just want them with me, Madeleine. I want them back.' Clara kept her eyes on the crack in the ceiling, watching as it blurred and then refocused as tears formed and fled from her eyes.

'Of course, you do.'

'And I can't have them back, so the next best thing is to go to them.'

'No, it isn't. The next best thing is to keep them alive through you. Nobody knew them like you did. It's your job to explain to us just how great they were. Was Poppy blonde, like you?'

Clara nodded, unable to stop the hint of a smile raising the corners of her mouth.

'Was she as sassy as I imagine her to be?'

'When she didn't think anyone was looking, she used to drag a kitchen chair to the worktop and climb on it so she could get herself a biscuit. I could hear her huffing and puffing with the effort of moving it, the chair legs scraping on the floor.'

'Did she put the chair back afterwards? I always did.'

Clara laughed. 'No. And she would point blank deny she'd moved it. "My not move the chair, Momma. A ghostie did it."' The smile stayed put on her face at the memory of Poppy, flecks of chocolate around her lips, a look of absolute sincerity on her face.

'A girl after my own heart,' Madeleine said. 'I'll do almost anything for a biscuit, too.'

A knock at the door took both of their attention. Rose pushed through the door, a couple of mugs in one hand.

'Is she awake?' she whispered. 'I brought hot chocolate.' She drew closer to Madeleine and said, 'I couldn't sleep without you.' She sank onto the second chair which had been placed beside Clara's bed at some point that evening. Clara stayed quiet and still as Rose leaned forward and kissed Madeleine softly on the lips.

'About time,' Clara said.

'You're right,' Rose said. 'None of us are allowed to waste any more time.'

The smile that lingered on Madeleine's lips buoyed Clara and she shuffled herself up until she was sitting, accepting one of the mugs from Rose.

'Clara was about to tell me all about Poppy and Mike,' Madeleine said, turning in her direction again. 'Weren't you? I want to know everything. Tell me all about them, Clara.'

So, she did.

Chapter 41

The storm had lost most of its intensity by sunrise. It must have, Tania thought, because she could no longer hear the force of the gusts of wind striking at the window. Traces of weak light extended their way past the edges of the heavy curtains, like slithers of the future pushing their way into existence. Undaunted and undiminished by the night's events.

She sighed and shuffled under the covers. Even though her eyes were grainy and sore, and her body ached and complained with every movement, she supposed that she must have slept, for a while at least.

Slipping out from the covers, she abandoned the layers of warm fleeces and thick socks she'd worn throughout the night. She gave a cursory glance over the beginnings of the bruising on her hip and knee, was relieved to see that her feet looked normal, then pulled on some different clothes and headed along the corridor. She poked her head around Clara's door. Lysander sat in the chair, his head lolling to one side as he dozed. Clara was curled up in a ball, her breathing rhythmical, sleeping deeply. Tania eased the door closed again and headed upstairs.

Tom was already busy in the kitchen, the aroma of freshly baking pastries filling the space.

'Morning,' he said. 'How are you feeling?'

'I'm fine, thank you.' She smiled at him. Such an ordinary exchange, but this morning it couldn't mean more. 'How are you?'

He nodded. 'Yeah. Good. Coffee?'

'Yes, please.'

She headed for the picture window. She'd never seen Près du Ciel looking like this. The storm had died right down – or moved on – and it was no longer snowing. Instead, the wind had carved itself into almost everything she could see. Snow was banked up like static Atlantic waves glittering in the morning light. The track up to Snow Pine Lodge looked all but impassable. She frowned as she found herself wondering how long it must have taken Gull to get back to his chalet. After they'd spent some time with Clara the previous night, he insisted she should get some rest. She remembered how she was struggling to keep her eyes open, even though she knew this was probably the end with him. He seemed immovable in his desire to leave, and she supposed she had no right to expect him to do anything other than that which he felt he needed to do. Her relationships with her friends were the most important things in her life, and she supposed it must be the same for him with his siblings. It would have been unfair of her to expect him to ignore everything his sister was going through just because that would have been more convenient.

She fixed her gaze on the winter-season lights lower in the valley; the ones which hadn't been blown away were still twinkling. If he did phone her today, and if she answered his call, she wondered what he might say. Whether a fresh new day and some time away from her might deepen his resolve. But his resolve to do what?

She turned, noticing the little Christmas tree, with its own set of twinkling white lights, a discreet pile of presents stacked underneath. She reached down, looking at the labels. One each, for Clara, Rose and her – all from Madeleine. She huffed a laugh. Trust Madeleine to manage, amongst everything else that had happened, to remember presents.

She heard the outside door open, then slam shut, footsteps on the stairs. Lysander was with Clara in her room. The footsteps were heavy. They didn't sound like Rose's, or

Madeleine's. Tom didn't react. Perhaps it was the doctor, coming to check on Clara, perhaps Tom had given him the door code to save time.

She was about to ask when Gull appeared at the top of the stairs, carrying an armful of logs.

'Thanks, mate,' Tom said. 'Stick them in the corner, would you?'

'You're still here?' she said, the confusion clear in her voice.

He set the logs down, adjusting something on the log burner on his way across to her. The flames intensified, then settled again. 'Yes. I'm still here.'

'Where were you, where did you sleep?' She frowned. 'I thought you'd gone.'

He paused as Tom passed them both mugs of coffee, before retreating to the kitchen. Then Gull said, 'I was almost at the door when Lysander poked his head out from his room. Told me I was a fucking idiot if I planned to go out in that weather again, when there were two perfectly comfortable sofas up here I could sleep on.' He reached a hand to the small of his back, rubbing at it. 'He's a liar, by the way. Your sofas are seriously uncomfortable. I know, because I tried them both.' He lit up the room with one of his lightning grins, then it was gone again. 'Anyway, you needed to rest. We all needed to rest for a while.'

'But I thought you were determined to go.'

'I was.' He frowned. 'Then I realised I could think just as easily on a sofa up here as anywhere. I should have told you where I was, I'm sorry.'

Tom removed a tray of pastries from the oven, setting them onto a cooling rack. He headed for the stairs with more filled mugs. 'I'll take some coffee down for Lysander and Clara. Be back in a few minutes.'

Once he'd made his tactical retreat, Tania and Gull stared at each other. Gull's eyebrows flexed and arched, his face working through a myriad of emotions before he said, 'Lysander said something else.'

'Oh, God. What?' Tania wondered if the Donkey had gained an upper hand, if the glimpse of the brother she'd seen the previous evening had disappeared again just as quickly.

'He said that if I walked away from you, I might just regret it for the rest of my life.'

'He said that?' She'd half-expected Lysander to have come out with some sarcastic put-down, something about not letting the door hit Gull on his way out. She hadn't expected that.

'Yes. And, all things considered, I think I agree with him. No, I *know* I agree with him.'

Tania studied his face. His eyes held the same soft openness as they had the day they'd sparred over lunch at the Cocoon.

'But what about Ellie?'

'You were right, last night. It's not fair to lay something my brother-in-law did at your door. I'll work it out with her, somehow.'

She nodded.

'Plus, I think you and Ellie would really like one another. And she could use a decent friend.'

'You've got it all worked out,' she said.

'Let me be your sledgehammer,' he said, burying his quick grin under a heavy frown. 'Sorry, another terrible joke. Appalling timing. And I'm fully aware I might have cocked it all up anyway, with you. If you want me to go, just say the word.'

Tania lifted the mug from his hand and set it down alongside her own. She moved closer to him, reaching up to slip her hand across his shoulder and around the back of his neck. His hands closed around her waist and he pulled her tight.

'I've only just found you,' she said. 'Why would I want you to go?'

The kiss was so gentle that Tania wasn't sure it happened, Gull's head dipping to touch his lips against hers with an imperceptible softness. 'Thank God,' he whispered into her ear, as he wrapped his arms even more tightly around her.

If this was Tom's version of a pared down Christmas lunch, Madeleine thought, as she carried the dish of roast potatoes to the table, then she wanted very much to be around when he cooked a full-blown one. The potatoes smelled divine, the tops of each one like a golden halo of crispiness.

'How do you get them to be so perfect?' she asked.

Tom followed her over, a plate of sliced turkey in one hand, a bowl of vegetables in the other. 'Parboil them, then sprinkle them with semolina before they go in the oven, it's my top roast potato hack.'

Clara nodded. 'That's how Mike used to do them, too.'

'How come I don't know any of these things?' Madeleine said, plonking the potatoes in the centre of the table. She shrugged. 'Too busy enjoying the fruits of other people's labour, I suppose. I'm going to have to take a cooking course.'

She took a seat next to Rose, pushing the cracker to the side of her place setting and taking the napkin onto her lap.

'That's a great idea,' Rose said, a grin on her face. 'Because I can't cook, either.'

She felt Rose reaching for her hand under the table, taking hold of it and squeezing. This was easily her most memorable Christmas Day to date. In Madeleine's opinion, it cruised effortlessly ahead of the year when her parents' next-door neighbour dressed up as Santa, then got monumentally drunk and spent the afternoon dismembering the gnomes in his garden; shouting about how they hadn't packed the presents properly in his sleigh, and that they were worse than useless and could all expect their P45s in the New Year.

She glanced across to where Lysander sat. The chiselled perfection of his jawline was pointedly turned away from her, the focus of his deep-water blue eyes resting entirely on Clara, as he offered her some vegetables. He still hadn't acknowledged her existence since she'd called him a wanker the previous evening – which now felt about a million years ago – and Madeleine wondered if he ever would. Her gut told her probably not, and in all honesty, she could live with that.

As she looked around at the others it struck Madeleine that to a casual observer, this table might look like millions of others. The scenario of a group of friends and family enjoying Christmas lunch together copied and pasted into a large proportion of the homes across the western world. And the calmness that had enveloped the lodge this afternoon was most welcome, in her opinion. After the excesses of the previous week, she was very much hoping the only excess that would occur today would come in the form of one too many roasties.

She noticed Tania's gaze had come to rest on her. No, not on her alone, it was on Rose too, her eyeline flitted between the pair of them. Rose was asking Tom about his taste in fiction, her fingers still entwined with Madeleine's under the table. Had Tania noticed Rose's comment about cooking? Or the stretch in Rose's arm, across onto her lap? On impulse, she lifted their hands into view and dipped her head down to kiss the back of Rose's, before sliding them back out of sight. Rose glanced her way and smiled, her corkscrew curls springing across her shoulders, then carried on with a comparison between which actors Tom felt were best suited to play his favourite fictional character on the big screen. It felt so natural, but Madeleine had done it on purpose. She looked at Tania again, watched as Tania flexed her eyebrows into a momentary frown before an expression of enlightenment settled onto her face, alongside an almost imperceptible nod. Madeleine allowed herself a small grin, and Tania smiled too, before her attention was distracted by Gull offering her some wine. Madeleine felt the last tension held by her shoulders melt away as she sighed contentedly, at last untangling her fingers from Rose's and helping herself to some potatoes.

Chapter 42

As Christmas Day relaxed its way into evening, Clara sank back against the multitude of cushions banked in the corner of the sofa. The flames in the wood burner rose and fell, hypnotic swirls of orange and yellow, every now and again the sinking of a log was accompanied by a hiss and a firework of intense sparks. Someone had put the TV on, a film playing in the background which nobody was watching. On the other sofa, Tania leaned against Gull, the little key ring Madeleine had agonised over purchasing the previous afternoon dangling from her fingers, the silver Près du Ciel pendant glinting in reflected light as she twisted it one way, then the other. The pair of them looked so comfortable together. Gull's hand rested casually across her collarbone, Tania's legs were folded up on the sofa, her feet hidden from view under another cushion as her body moulded into his.

At the dining table, Tom and Rose were teaching Madeleine how to play poker. If the amount of laughter was anything to go by, Clara presumed Madeleine wasn't even close to perfecting her 'poker face'. Or perhaps it was something to do with the amount of génépi liqueur both girls had downed.

She smiled as another peal of laughter rang out. Something had shifted inside her since she'd opened up to Madeleine the previous evening. When Madeleine started to laugh at the mention of Poppy's biscuit escapades, it seemed so natural to tell her more. And once the memories began to tumble from her lips, all about her baby girl and then about Mike, it seemed as if she had been selfish to keep them all to herself for so long. The pull to be with them was still strong, it was still gnawing away at her, but it seemed there might also be legitimate alternatives to consider.

Footsteps heralded the return of Lysander, bouncing up the steps from a self-confessed 'comfort break', his eyes a little too bright as he slotted himself onto the sofa beside her. She frowned. Lysander's reliance on chemical stimulus wasn't a secret, at least, not between Tania's closest friends.

'Clara, Clara, Clara. Have I ever told you just how damn beautiful you are?' He sniffed, then wiped at the side of his nose. Clara glanced across at Tania, in time to see her grip the key ring in the palm of her hand, a crease between her eyes forming as she watched her brother.

'Yes, Lysander, you have,' Clara said. 'About a hundred times. You know something?'

'Not much, nope. What you got for me?'

'You don't need that stuff. You should stop taking it.'

He tilted his head at her, in mock confusion, but she knew he knew exactly what she was talking about. He dropped the expression, visibly sagging before he said, 'Easier said than done.'

'I don't doubt it,' she said.

He paused for a long moment, his expression serious, then said, 'OK. I'll cut you a deal, my gorgeous Clara.'

'Will you?'

He sniffed again, decisively this time. 'Yes. I will. I'll get some help for my little problem if you agree for me to organise some professional help for you, too.' He wrapped an arm around her shoulders. 'What do you say?'

She shrugged. 'Sounds good to me.'

'There is one condition,' he said, a lazy smile seeping back onto his face.

'What's that?'

'I'm never saying, "My name is Lysander and I'm an addict." I just want to put that out there right now.'

'Deal.'

He squeezed her shoulders and climbed to his feet. 'Right. Time to mix a cocktail or two, I think.'

Madeleine's poker lesson had come to an end, and Tom crossed the living area and perched on the other end of the sofa.

'How are you doing?' he asked.

'I'm OK.' She frowned, shuffling against the pile of cushions to better face him.

'How's the pain?'

Clara had tried in vain to stop herself from screaming when her hands and feet had regained their feeling the night before. Luckily, Tom had been with her when it had happened. He had been there to tell her not to worry, that the intensity of the pain was normal. He'd held her as she sobbed, rocked her while it felt as if someone were degloving the skin from her hands and feet. 'It's nearly gone. Did I thank you?'

He settled back against the folds of the piece of furniture. 'Nothing to thank me for, Clara.' The burr in his voice rolled over the words. Then he frowned. 'I should have said something earlier . . .'

'About what?'

'I wanted to say something when I found out about your family, but there's nothing worse than someone saying they understand exactly what you're going through, is there? Because it feels like nobody could even get close to what it's like.'

'What do you mean?'

'I lost my girlfriend.' He ran a hand up the tattoos on his other arm, the fingers lingering on some lettering Clara hadn't paid any attention to. 'Just over two years ago, now.' As he retracted his hand, she looked more closely. 'Heather' was inscribed on his skin, the word surrounded by an intricate web of foliage and flowers. 'Stomach cancer. The doctors didn't pick up on it because she was so young. "Atypical" was the word they used.' His lips compressed as he drew in a slow breath. 'I'm not saying it's the same, not at all. I can't imagine what it feels like to lose your baby. But I should have told you you're not alone. That's what I wanted to say, I just didn't know how to.'

'Oh, Tom, I'm so sorry.'

'Thanks.' He studied her for a few seconds, as if weighing up what to say next. 'Thing is, I went heavy on the booze for a while afterwards. Nearly lost myself to it. I think I would have disappeared completely if I hadn't gone cold turkey. It's why I'm here, too, doing the season. It helps to keep moving onto new things. I was a chef in a hotel in Edinburgh; we both worked there. But I couldn't stay afterwards. Too many memories. Anyway, it's not about me, I don't want you to think I'm making it about me.' His fingers felt their way back to the patch of skin with the name tattooed on it. He rubbed his thumb absently over it. 'I just want you to know there are people who want to help.'

'You still miss her as badly?' Clara asked. She recognised the look in his eye, wondered why she hadn't seen it earlier in the week.

He drew in a deep breath. 'It's not as simple as that. Yes, I do. Some of the time. Then, sometimes I go for whole stretches of time when I don't think about her at all. And then I feel guilty. That's what I meant yesterday, when you asked if it would always feel so intense, and I said I didn't know.'

Clara nodded. 'I really enjoyed myself, the other day. And then I couldn't contain how bad that made me feel.' She sighed. 'I just don't know if I can do this.'

'You can.' Tom shuffled closer, taking one of her hands in his. 'I'm the proof. Two years, three months, and a handful of days later, I'm still doing it. I won't pretend there's a miraculous cure. But it changes, it eases. And it will for you, too.' He glanced around the room, and she looked up, too. Tania and Gull were no longer on the other sofa, they were standing with Lysander, whose blond hair she could just see behind Gull's broad frame, ducking and flicking as he waved a cocktail shaker around with vigour. Rose and

Madeleine were still at the dining table, playing cards. 'And you've got your friends. Don't underestimate them.'

'I don't. Only a fool would.' She grinned at him, then the expression slid from her face. 'Can we talk some more?'

'Anytime.' He reached into a pocket and pulled out his mobile. 'We could swap numbers if you want.'

'I'd like that. And maybe I could come back to the mountains. We could all come again. After all, you're going to be here until the spring, aren't you?'

'Aye, and I could source a whole range of weird and wonderful cheeses ready for your next cheeseboard adventure, if you like.'

'I would.' She smiled. 'That's settled, then.'

'Right, gather around everybody.' Lysander's voice cut through the room. 'Christmas margarita time.'

Clara climbed to her feet, following Tom as they headed across the room. With a glass in everyone's hand, Lysander held a hand up to gain their attention.

'Unaccustomed as I am to making speeches,' he said, pausing just long enough for Clara to recognise he was waiting for them to laugh, a tic in his eyebrow when she obliged him. 'Thank you, Clara, my darling. As I was saying, unaccustomed as I am, certain events of the last few days have meant I feel the need to say something on this visit.'

'Since when did you need an excuse to monopolise attention?' Tania's words could have been barbed. At the beginning of the week, Clara would have expected them to have been laced with venom. Instead, they were spoken with a level of indulgence she'd rarely heard before. Hard to miss the concern held in Tania's glance, though. Lysander was high, and everyone in the room knew it.

'Thanks for that, Tania,' he said. 'Never expect her to back down, Gull. Because she won't.'

Gull tightened his hold on Tania's waist. 'I wouldn't want her to.'

Lysander laughed, cocking an eyebrow at the pair of them.

'You might have nailed it this time, then, my sister dearest. Let's watch this space, see how it all shapes up. It would be good to finally get her off the street.' He threw her a theatrical kiss, making his margarita slop over the edge of the glass and run down his hand. 'Damn. Anyway, that wasn't what this was meant to be about. Although I suppose, in a way, it's all linked. You know, how fate or circumstance or whatever means that chance meetings can lead to so much, while in turn we struggle so much with the people we're destined to be with forever.'

Clara drew in and held a breath as Lysander's gaze slipped to Tania, his chin dipped, his expression momentarily one of a little boy needing a hug. Tania mouthed something that looked like *It's OK*. Then she nodded and his concentration shifted again, this time to the star-studded night sky outside the picture window. 'I love this place,' he said. 'Always have.' Without warning, he strode between them, heading for the window, leaving the semicircle of his audience turning in his wake.

'Are you done?' Tania said, her face a hotchpotch of bemused surprise, still with its back note of concern. 'He never normally walks away from a captive audience.'

'Maybe I've changed,' he said. 'Maybe we're all changing. Growing up. Getting to grips with the hand life's willing to deal us. I'm not trying to bring the mood down . . .'

'So, shut up and drink the bloody cocktail instead, Sander.'

'In a second. Thing is, what I really wanted to say was that although I've met more than my fair share of A-listers and celebrities, even royalty – so many stars – I've reached the conclusion that this little group of people right here – you – are the brightest stars in my life. You're also the strongest people I know, and . . .' He crossed the room again and took Clara's hand. 'I also know that we're all going to be just fine, because we're going to stick together. We're going to help one another make it to tomorrow, and the next day and the day after that. That's all I wanted to say.'

'Took you long enough,' Tania said, but she was smiling.

He raised his glass. 'A toast – to Snow Pine Lodge and the mountains; to the people we treasure, however near to us or far away they might be; and to squeezing every last drop of happiness out of our todays and our tomorrows.'

As she sipped her margarita and felt Lysander's fingers squeeze hard around her own, Clara wasn't at all sure he'd remember his toast tomorrow, or his promise, judging by the bright pinpricks of heat in his cheeks and his current level of agitation as he jiggled and spilled more of his drink. And she knew that for her, happiness would be hard won, certainly in the near future. But as she glanced around the group, at Madeleine and Rose clinking glasses, their focus totally on one another; at Gull bending to kiss the trace of cocktail from Tania's lips; at Tom's gentle open smile as he slipped his juice onto the table and passed Lysander a napkin to mop his hand, she could at least imagine that there would be days to come. And, for the first time in a long time she wanted to find out what tomorrow would bring.

Acknowledgements

Writing a novel begins as a solitary pursuit, but it ends up being such a team event – and I think mine might just be the dream team.

Firstly, I want to thank my wonderful agent Anne Williams from KHLA. She's utterly calm and always reassuringly positive. Her guidance and support are unparalleled.

The entire team at Embla Books are amazing – I'm so lucky to be working with you all – and special thanks go to the editing team, for your invaluable input and attention to detail.

A huge thank you to Tanya Gibbins, Hanne Bonczoszek and Clare White for being the best friends anyone could ask for – and for doubling up as cracking beta readers. Fossilers Four Forever!

And even though they are as annoying as they are lovable, I couldn't have done any of this without my family. Support comes in many forms, from unconditional through to the 'boot up the backside' kind, and I'm thankful for all of it.

These acknowledgements wouldn't be complete without a heartfelt thank you to the readers – every single one of you is treasured more than you will ever know. Thank you for choosing to pick up my book.

Turn the page for an exclusive extract from the wonderfully feel-good and escapist novel, *A Summer on the Riviera. . .*

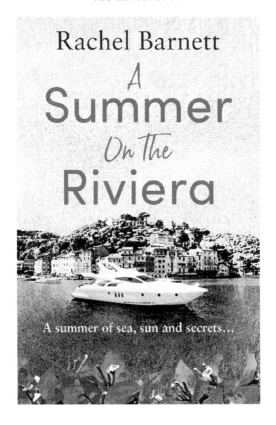

Rachel Barnett

A
Summer
On The
Riviera

A summer of sea, sun and secrets...

Available to buy now!

Chapter One

Bella glanced around the cabin – it was smaller than she'd imagined, cramped, and she wondered why she hadn't realised she would be sharing with another member of the crew. At least there was a porthole in the room, a tiny oval of blue light. Dumping her rucksack on the lower bunk she sank down beside it and took a deep breath. This was really happening. A new job, a new challenge. Maybe even a new life.

Life begins at the end of your comfort zone – one of her brother's favourite phrases chose that moment to pop into her head. If Jay had said it once, he'd said it a thousand times, and she wondered how much of her decision to change direction had been to do with him and his encouragement.

Several years' worth of covering every aspect of hotel work – working silver service dinners and fine dining occasions at The Magnolia, then for the last couple of seasons, managing the entire waitstaff and catering department – hadn't exactly felt like living outside anybody's comfort zone. Not to Bella, anyway. Unless you counted an early brush with disaster when she was almost fired for speaking to a guest as she served their potatoes.

While she had spent years folding napkins and arranging petits fours, dealing with last-minute staff illness and guest tantrums, her brother – they weren't biologically related, but had been adopted together – had nearly finished medical school. Although his route into the medical profession hadn't been easy, and finances were tight, he had brains to spare and was loving life at London's King's College. Their parents were puffed up with pride at his achievements, and she could understand why. Jay's star was set very firmly in its ascendancy – more than that, he was working towards something he'd always dreamed of achieving.

Meanwhile, Bella had become very proficient at keeping her mouth shut while serving potatoes. To her credit, she could manage even the tiny baby new ones, covered in melted butter and sprinkled with the most delicate strands of chopped chives, despicably keen to roll away from her spoon and fork combo. Catching them up into groups of five was harder than it appeared – it took skill, as did placing the treacherous little marbles on each plate in exactly the same spot without dripping melted butter onto anyone's Jimmy Choos.

But was knowing a terrine fork from a cake fork, and having an intricate knowledge of the difference between the shapes of red, white and dessert wine glasses really something to write home about? The thought that being able to head off a staffing disaster due to an outbreak of flu, accommodating last-minute menu changes from demanding diners, and sitting behind a desk ordering cavolo nero and new tablecloths might be the sum total of her worth had become unsettling. Continuing at The Magnolia while the years spooled away into the future couldn't truly be the way she wanted to spend her life.

It was ironic, really, that while her parents had done everything they could to help Jay fly the nest, Bella had been left with little choice but to stick around, ignoring a deeply embedded yearning to travel. To see the world, not just the view from The Magnolia's sun terrace. Burying it deep, because there was no way she would ever manage to earn that kind of money on her hotel salary. And fully understanding there was no way she could ask her parents to help support her, when every spare penny was already winging its way to help with Jay's living costs. Which was why landing this job had been such a dream opportunity.

Was it possible today was the start of more than a new job? Could she unpack more than her belongings, and begin to believe she had discovered a way to earn her way around the world? Or, at least, the parts of the world that butted up against the sea?

A plink from her mobile had Bella checking her messages.

This one was from Jay, suggesting she was going to "kill" this new job, and he wasn't the slightest bit jealous of her. He took great pains to explain how little he cared that she was sailing around the Med for the summer getting – as he put it – "an epic tan", while he would be spending every waking hour in scrubs, bathed in artificial strip lighting.

She began to type a reply.

'You can't leave your stuff there – that's my bunk.'

The unexpected voice made Bella start, her finger slipping across the screen as she looked up to see a lean blonde woman, hands on hips and standing firmly in the doorway, a proprietorial expression on her face.

'Yours is the upper one.' The woman advanced into the cramped space, pulling open some tiny doors to reveal a couple of miniature cupboards. 'Your stuff can go in here.'

Sliding her bag onto the floor, Bella held out a hand and did her best to ignore the line of frost advancing in her direction.

'Hi, it's nice to meet you. I'm Bella.'

'I know who you are.' The handshake was terse. 'Jean-Philippe said you'd arrived. I'm Mel. Second stewardess. You know we have less than twenty-four hours until the guests arrive, right? There's still plenty to do and you're the one in charge.'

The one in charge . . .

'The captain's waiting for you – he's got the manifest for the charter guests.'

'OK. Thank you so much.'

The frost retreated from the cabin as Mel left. Bella sank back onto the lower bunk, considering for the first time since she'd left home the full extent of the role she'd taken on when she accepted this job.

Chief stewardess. Although the charter yachting industry didn't seem to have caught up with the rest of the world where equity in job titles was concerned, Bella was more focused on what the job itself would entail. Like a cross between being a hostess, silver service waitperson and ultimate facilitator for whatever the yacht's charter guests – or owner – required. Hospitality at its very finest. This yacht was referred to as having seven-star service, with every whim catered for, and Bella was now in charge of everything that happened inside it, while witnessing first-hand the beautiful scenery of the Mediterranean Sea. It had all seemed very doable, in theory. Most of the work she'd been doing for years on dry land – how different could it be to achieve it on a yacht? If this worked out, and the tips were as good as everybody told her they were, she would then be able to fund some winter travel, maybe find work on other boats, in other parts of the globe. The start of a new life.

It also sounded like it could be fun.

She supposed the wobble of nerves was only natural – this was the furthest away from home she'd ever been, and she knew nobody aboard *Blue Sky*. The interview with the captain had taken place over the internet and she had no idea what to expect from any of the guests – or the rest of the crew for that matter. After her brief and rather chilly chat with Mel, it looked likely Bella was going to have her work cut out with at least one staff member.

She just needed to take a breath, remember the calm poise she'd cultivated to keep musket balls of potato on a shallow spoon, and smile. With a serene, balanced approach, the rest of it would surely fall into place. That was going to be her theory, anyway.

After shoving her luggage onto the upper bunk, Bella slipped her mobile into a pocket and untied her hair, running fingers through its length in place of a brush – which was still buried deep somewhere inside her bag. Hooking some of the dark strands behind her ears, she took a quick peek at her reflection in the tiny mirror on the wall. Satisfied she hadn't smeared what little mascara she was wearing all over her cheeks and didn't look a total disaster, she headed out to locate the captain.

The entire crew had assembled in *Blue Sky*'s formal salon. Bella perched on the edge of one of three chesterfield leather sofas dwarfed by the dimensions of the room. After the confines of the crew area, the difference in the guest space was stark. The contrast between upstairs versus downstairs was evident in every polished chrome light fitting and highly glossed oak-panelled wall, in the enormous Persian rug adorning the teak hardwood floor, and the recessed ceiling with Michelangelo-esque paintings of gods and goddesses handing one another fruit. This room screamed opulence, without the slightest pretence at an apology.

To be fair, it wasn't all that different to working in a five-star hotel. Everything front of house was designed to impress the guest, while the chipped flooring and peeling paint backstage were at the bottom of everybody's list.

Clutched on Bella's lap was the earpiece and two-way radio which from here on in would be worn by every crew member, ensuring communication was consistent – and immediate. "I'll do it in a minute" or "I didn't realise I needed to . . ." didn't cut it on a superyacht any more than they did in a top-flight hotel. The only appropriate response to a request for a crew member to jump was to ask, "How high?"

The captain – Jean-Philippe Kirque – was in full swing. He had already introduced all crew members, new and old. Bella tried to take in all the names on this first pass and was gratified to note she wasn't the only newbie. This was also the third stewardess's first day aboard.

'As you know, our first charter guests arrive tomorrow, and we have much to prepare. Food delivery arrives in . . .' the captain checked his watch '. . . less than an hour, so at least one stewardess must be on hand to assist Tobias with provisioning the kitchen.'

As the briefing continued with specific tasks to be undertaken by the deck crew, Bella took the opportunity to take stock of the people with whom she would be spending – in extremely close proximity – the next three months.

If she had to hazard a guess, she'd put the captain in his early fifties. Short in stature, chunky and intense, deeply ingrained crow's feet spreading out from the corners of his eyes. He carried a rich tan that went some way towards balancing out the salt and pepper of his no-nonsense closely cropped hair and beard. She already knew he'd captained yachts for over twenty years; he'd told her as much in her interview. Before that he had served time in the navy. A lifetime spent at sea. Hopefully that meant *Blue Sky* was in the best hands.

Other members of the deck crew stood against the walls, including an engineer and bosun; there would be far more staff on board than guests.

Everyone, including the pair of well-built Greek deckhands – Yannis and Dimitri – had excellent English, the captain announced, his own accent richly continental.

Directly in Bella's eyeline, at the opposite end of the chesterfield, Mel was sitting bolt upright. Listening intently to the captain, she had positioned herself in such a way as to make absolutely sure she couldn't so much as glance in Bella's direction. Or was Bella imagining the frostiness was reserved solely for her? Maybe Mel was a naturally reserved person. Perhaps Bella should wait a while before she jumped to conclusions and not allow the insecurities she felt about the newness of everything to overshadow her perceptions. Nestled between her and Mel was the final stewardess, Jessica. Also overshadowed by the stress of the day, if the flashes of a nervous smile were anything to go by.

Jean-Philippe handed around sheaves of A4 paper, stapled at the top-left corner and covered in photos.

'Our first charter group are due on board at midday tomorrow. I think you will recognise the principal guest?'

The shuffle of papers made it over to Bella. She took a copy and passed the rest on, scanning the photos on the top sheet and nodding as she read the accompanying details. A smile crept onto her lips. She'd seen this face a hundred times – probably more – in one of her all-time favourite TV programmes. She'd avidly watched every episode of the female detective duo series, starting when she was about eleven.

'Felicia Kennedy,' the captain continued. 'The British actor who starred in many Hollywood films, and is currently playing the lead role in the television drama *Murder in Mayfair*. Please notice she doesn't drink red wine and needs all fresh flowers to be removed from her stateroom at least two hours before she retires for the night.'

He continued with his brief, but all the information was typed on the pages. She could memorise the details later. Right now, Bella couldn't stop herself from checking who else would be on board. Below Felicia's PR shot was a photograph of her husband, Nikolai. Not often seen in the press, and notorious for being private, he was a strikingly handsome older man. With a chiselled jawline and no trace of grey in a head of Scandi-blond hair, he had a faraway look in his eye, as if something of much greater import than the taking of his photograph had occurred just out of shot.

Turning the page, Bella's face lit up even further. Patti Prior, the actor who played sidekick to Felicia's character in *Murder in Mayfair*, would also be on the cruise. Patti portrayed with aplomb the role of a displaced Yank, thousands of miles from home and endlessly baffled by the British. Plus, she was the constant butt of Felicia's character's sarcasm. Undeservedly so, Bella thought, as it was habitually Patti's character who was the one to solve the weekly murder, even if she didn't get the credit for it. Patti's trademark red lipstick and even brighter auburn hair shone from the page almost as vividly as her smile.

Beneath that was a photo of someone Bella didn't recognise. Patti's daughter, Hannah. Same red hair as her mother, but no smile. A self-conscious pose. Not a pout for the camera, but definitely a calculated expression.

Bella flicked to the next page and her breath caught in her throat. She scanned the words quickly before settling her gaze back onto the photo and allowing it to rest there. Leo Kennedy-Edge. Felicia's nephew. Bella did her best to swallow, but her throat wouldn't comply with the request. Because staring at her from the page was one of the most attractive men she'd ever seen. Melting almond eyes set below eyebrows quirked in a half-question, a mop of hair as dark as her own, cut short at the sides and layered over the crown of his head. A jawline softened slightly by a beard, which appeared to require minimal maintenance, but probably took endless tweaking to make it look *that* good.

Doing her best to drag her gaze away, she turned to the final page, to see a photo of a middle-aged man with thinning mousy-brown hair and a thickening jawline. Felicia's lawyer, joining the yacht part-way through the trip, and staying for the remainder.

Bella flicked back to the front page. What a way to start her yachting career – with the first set of guests including two actresses she'd adored for years. Not to mention the glorious Leo Kennedy-Edge. This was going to be a proper adventure. She risked a glance along the chesterfield at the other stewardesses, and then across at the rest of the crew. Nobody seemed as excited as she felt, and she did her best to tamp her grin down to a manageable level, to control her levels of anticipation.

Because it was time to focus – time to remember the rules. Her rules. The rules that had enabled Bella to be successful in the roles she'd held until this point. And up near the summit of the list – even higher in the pecking order than not dropping potatoes onto designer footwear – was remembering that the guests, whether they were in a hotel, or on a boat, were an utterly different animal to people like her. That, even if they seemed nice, they weren't ever going to be her friends. The important thing was to make them happy, keep their glasses brimming, and hope for a healthy tip at the end of their trip.

Mel slid a glance around the salon. J-P was working his way through the list of guests for the first charter of the season. A beard suited him. Her molars clamped together, top set tighter and tighter against the bottom set until she felt the muscles in her jaw ache. God damn him. It grated at her to have to admit it, but he looked good.

Perhaps she should have applied for a job on a different boat, made a fresh start somewhere else. Somewhere without the history and baggage she'd built up over five years on *Blue Sky*. It would be easy enough to get second stewardess roles on any of the yachts doing the circuit; she knew the job like the back of her hand. And what had happened the previous summer – it hadn't been her fault. None of it was her fault.

Her work record was impeccable, or at least that was the way it would appear. J-P had guaranteed her that much – had gone as far as to say he'd support her applications for chief stewardess roles on other superyachts if that was what she wanted. But something deep inside Mel told her that wasn't good enough. That to metaphorically jump ship – or to be pushed overboard by J-P – weren't options she was prepared to explore. It was all too easy, too simple for him.

Yes, things would be awkward for a while, but she could cope with awkward. Forcing her jaws apart far enough to be able to wiggle at her cheek muscles with her fingers, she risked a sideways glance at Bella Mason. Brand-new chief stew. No previous yachting experience, but with an impeccable shoreside record in five-star hotels, latterly on the Cornish coast. Had J-P done it on purpose? Employed someone like Bella over Mel's head in an attempt to give her the final push she needed to leave?

Looking away before Bella noticed her stare, Mel arched defiant eyebrows and settled her gaze on their oh so illustrious captain. Held his eye when he glanced her way, allowing herself the tiniest hit of satisfaction as he momentarily stumbled over his words, and continuing to focus her attention on him while he composed himself and ran through his familiar spiel about standards, service, charter guests expecting the highest possible level of attention, nothing's too much trouble, blah blah blah. Mel crossed her arms and hoped J-P would notice the huff of her irritated sigh. She knew this bit off by heart.

Two things were crystal clear in Mel's mind. Firstly, this season was going to be anything but smooth sailing for the newbie, Bella Mason. She was all bubbly right now, with her barely suppressed puppy-dog excitement over the first set of charter guests – she was practically panting with enthusiasm. But it wouldn't be long before the reality of life on board a superyacht began to bite; it always did. And if Bella didn't crumble of her own accord, Mel might have to think up a few tricks to aid the disintegration.

Secondly, if Jean-Philippe Kirque thought he was going to sail through this season as if nothing had happened, then she was going to have to use this *Blue Sky* summer to remind their captain that she hadn't forgotten. Any of it.

About the Author

Rachel Barnett lives in the beauty of rural Wiltshire, almost within touching distance of Stonehenge. After a career as a primary school teacher (yes, it is as exhausting as everyone says), and then creating a little monster of her own, a chink of spare time saw her taking as many creative writing courses as she could get her hands on. Suitably equipped, she has finally managed to hide away from everyone for long enough to achieve her lifelong ambition of writing novels.

About Embla Books

Embla Books is a digital-first publisher of standout commercial adult fiction. Passionate about storytelling, the team at Embla publish books that will make you 'laugh, love, look over your shoulder and lose sleep'. Launched by Bonnier Books UK in 2021, the imprint is named after the first woman from the creation myth in Norse mythology, who was carved by the gods from a tree trunk found on the seashore – an image of the kind of creative work and crafting that writers do, and a symbol of how stories shape our lives.

Find out about some of our other books and stay in touch:

Twitter, Facebook, Instagram: @emblabooks
Newsletter: https://bit.ly/emblanewsletter

Printed in Great Britain
by Amazon

29337951R00191